A Difference of Opinion

Nancy Dane

Tate Publishing & *Enterprises*

This novel is a work of fiction. However, several names, descriptions, entities, and incidents included in the story are based on the lives of real people.

The opinions expressed by the author are not necessarily those of Tate Publishing, LLC.

Published by Tate Publishing & Enterprises, LLC
127 E. Trade Center Terrace | Mustang, Oklahoma 73064 USA
1.888.361.9473 | www.tatepublishing.com

Tate Publishing is committed to excellence in the publishing industry. The company reflects the philosophy established by the founders, based on Psalm 68:11,
"The Lord gave the word and great was the company of those who published it."

Cover and Interior design by Nathan Harmony

Published in the United States of America

ISBN: 978-1-60696-958-8
1. Fiction: Historical
2. Fiction: War and Military
09.07.09

Other Books by Nancy Dane

Tattered Glory

Where the Road Begins

Dedication

To my husband,
the love of my life and my best friend

A Word from the Author

A Difference of Opinion, book two in the *Tattered Glory* series, is not in reality a sequel, but a novel of parallel timeframe. This is Nelda Horton's story, a young woman with Union sympathies in a staunchly Confederate town. Although it is fiction, many events are based upon real experiences of Union sympathizers as documented in the Southern Claims Commission Files and in *Tattered Glory*, a history book of Civil War Arkansas. The source documents relate how women spies in Arkansas on both sides of the conflict delivered secret information, which in some cases had great bearing on military decisions.

The military action is factual. However, except for known historical figures, the characters are fictional and meant to portray no one. Brief mention is made of a few real people: Colonel John Hill, whose company was charged with the responsibility of stopping bushwhacking in Johnson County; Major Hall McConnell, who was killed while leading a Rebel charge at the White River; and Ruben and Berilla Markham, who owned and operated the Markham Inn in Lewisburg.

I owe thanks to many for assistance with this book, first and foremost to my wonderful husband, my best critic and invaluable collaborator who keeps me apprised of the male point of view. And for all who read and edited the manuscript—Nancy Cook, Jackie Guccione, and Sheree Niece—a big thank you!

And once again thank you, Chris Kennedy, for another beautiful cover shot.

Special thanks to two busy men, Dusty Richards and Dr. Rick Niece, for sharing their valuable time and gracious endorsements.

To all who read *Where The Road Begins* and waited patiently for a sequel, be assured that I am already hard at work on it.

January 4, 1863

From the *History of the Twenty-Seventh Arkansas Confederate Infantry*

"A march of four miles from Spadra on Sunday morning brought us to Clarksville on Spadra Creek. Just before reaching the outskirts of town we were halted and formed in regular order and marched through in military style. Our regiment went through the town to the tune of "The Homespun Dress," played on the fifes and drums...

Oh Yes, I am a Southern girl,
And glory in the name,
And boast of it with far greater pride
Than glittering wealth or fame.
We envy not the Northern girl,
Her robes of beauty rare.
Though diamonds grace her snowy neck
And pearls bedeck her hair.
Hurrah, hurrah, for the sunny South so dear.
Three cheers for the homespun dress that Southern ladies wear."

By Silas C. Turnbo
Edited by Desmond Walls Allen

Prologue

Nelda Horton held out her hand to her father. Her foot had barely touched the ground when a young black boy took the mare's bridle and led the buggy away with her shawl still lying on the seat. The night was balmy. She knew with such a crowd the house was sure to be stuffy. In the long queue still waiting to alight, women smoothed hair, straightened gloves, and rearranged silk over stiff hoops. She didn't bother with the knot of dark hair on the nape of her neck. She wore no gloves. And she barely flicked the dust from her narrow skirt.

She had feared they were late, but the musicians were still tuning up. The notes hung strident and grating on the honeysuckle breeze. "Who's playing?" she asked while holding her skirt to climb the high steps bordered by ornate lanterns.

Through foyer windows, light spilled onto the porch from a chandelier boasting one hundred and twenty four tapers. She knew the exact amount, for years ago, along with the Morrison children, she had hung over the third story banister to count them.

"The Matthers clan," said Phillip. "They're a rowdy lot, but they know how to make music."

They nodded to several cigar-smokers on the porch. Once inside they joined the crowd pressing into the drawing room where the musicians stood, six brothers, all young giants, with identical flashing smiles, varying shades of red hair, and vivid blue eyes. The eldest raised a fiddle and the room stilled. As the bow gently caressed strings, Nelda held her breath. Notes flowed, unhurried and sweet in a melody as gentle as birdsong. Abruptly, the bow halted. In the silence, puzzled eyes fixed on

Allen. Then, with an impish grin, he plunged into a boisterous reel that was soon taken up by guitars, mandolin, and banjo. Laughing couples began to dance.

Mary Beth Morrison whirled past and waved. The auburn-haired beauty wore a yellow gown low on satin shoulders and draped over the widest hoops in the room.

Then Nelda's eyes found what they sought and her smile softened. At the far end of the room, near the wide marble fireplace, stood Fred Reynolds conversing with a knot of men. His black hair curled slightly above a starched white collar and his broad shoulders stretched a finely tailored suit.

She glanced toward the musicians and hoped the Matthers would play a slow waltz.

Allen, sawing away on the fiddle tucked under his chin, caught her eye and winked. She looked away, but a tiny grin played the corners of her mouth.

That Allen is a rascal, she thought. Immediately the grin faded. Just then, in the hallway came whoops and whistles that suddenly erupted into shrieks and laughter. The music stopped. Every eye turned toward the door. Bo Morrison and his brother Drew rode horses into the mansion and down the long, polished hall. The paints' hooves thundered on the shiny hardwood. Bo reeled drunkenly in the saddle while holding aloft a blood-red banner that had white crisscrossed bands spangled with blue stars. This Confederate flag had made its first appearance earlier that day at the April muster of Johnson County militia.

Tabbatha Morrison whirled to her husband. "Robert, stop laughing! Make your sons get those fool horses out of the house. They'll scar the floor!"

When she took a step forward, he stopped her with a hand on her arm. "No harm done. They're already leaving."

With a frown, Nelda turned to Phillip. "Papa, can you believe—"

She stopped short when a loud accusation filled the room.

"Reynolds! I call that treason!"

Fred Reynolds gave a slow, deprecating smile. He set a glass of punch on the mantle before replying. "But Gill, Arkansas is still part of the *United* States."

Gill bristled. "By gawd! Not for long! And then the likes of you will be wearing tar and feathers."

"Gentlemen, gentlemen," Robert Morrison intervened. "We're disturbing the ladies. Let's continue our discussion in the library."

"Thank you, Robert, but I'll take my leave. I apologize for the disturbance." Fred bowed to Tabbatha who stood nearby looking vexed, her eyes as black and hard as the jet earbobs dangling in her ears. "Mrs. Morrison, thank you for your hospitality. It's always an honor to be your guest."

Nelda watched him leave and then with troubled eyes she turned to survey the room. Judging by the gaiety, the flag had upset few here besides her and Papa and Fred.

Chapter 1

August 1861

Nelda sat bolt upright. She waited, listening. Through the open window came nothing but the usual chorus of rasping katydids until Sirius growled again, low and menacing. These days the old hound rarely stirred himself enough to growl. The front gate creaked and his deep-throated barks rang out. As a strange glow sent shadows dancing on the bedroom wall, Nelda sprang from the bed and ran to the window. Two hooded men crossed the yard, holding flaming torches high. Near the gate on horseback milled a dozen more. All wore hoods and brandished torches.

Fear stabbed her heart. She knew what mobs were capable of—and no doubt this mob was zealous, fired with patriotism. In Arkansas the word rebel was now synonymous with patriot.

"Hey, Yankee lovers! Head north if you don't wanna roast."

She turned when her mother rushed into the room, her gown ghostly in moonlight.

"Hurry!" urged Louise. "They're going to burn the house!"

Nelda's jaw hardened. "No! I'm not running from that rabble. Where's Papa's shotgun?"

A rock thudded and shards of breaking glass crashed across the floor. In an instant a torch arched the black sky and flames burst, lighting the dark room. Louise gave a startled cry. As her nightgown caught the blaze like a wick, she ripped at the gown, sending buttons flying. Nelda grabbed the counterpane from the bed and used it to smother her mother's flaming gown. Then she quickly seized the torch and flung it into the empty fireplace.

"Della!" she screamed for the servant.

Louise tore off the gown. It smoldered at her feet. She stepped back, and with a moan, she clutched her leg while the nauseating smell of singed flesh mingled with acrid smoke.

"Mama, where's the shotgun?"

"Don't! They'll kill you!"

Nelda had already run from the room. She winced as pain from broken glass shot through her feet. On the landing, she paused, shaking.

"Della," she shouted again and then coughed from sucking in smoke-filled air. Downstairs came the sound of smashing glass. For an instant a ghastly flicker lit the hall. Then an explosion of light and a loud crackling came from the dining room. Frantic, she held the rail and hobbled to the bottom of the stairs.

The front door flew open, kicked in by heavy boots. Like a rabid animal, Nelda sprang at the invader. Her fists pounded a broad chest. But an iron grip forced her aside as a man rushed inside. He ran into the dining room and began jerking down flaming drapes.

Limp with relief, she sagged against the wall and watched as he stomped out the blaze. As the flickering light from the fire abruptly dimmed, she felt her way to the hall table and lit the lamp. Every step was torture. Thick smoke stung her watering eyes. Using the gown sleeve, she wiped them and then shuddered to see the smoke-filled hall and her bloody tracks. She rolled her foot to the side and hobbled to the stairs.

Louise appeared at the railing, her face as white as the counterpane draped around her. The hand holding the blanket shook. "Who's in there?"

"I'm not sure." As the stomping in the next room ceased, Nelda coughed hard before adding, "But he put out the fire."

Louise gathered the counterpane tighter at her throat and turned abruptly. "Oh, I must get dressed."

Nelda stifled a hysterical laugh. Only Mama would worry about propriety at a time like this. Sinking to the floor, she moaned and felt the bottom of her feet. Her teeth gritted as she pulled out a big shard of glass. She grimaced, realizing she would need a needle to probe for more.

As a man came into the hall, she stood gingerly on one foot while holding to the wall for support.

"Are you hurt?" It was Allen Matthers. Sweat plastered his red hair and trickled down his face, and there was a black smudge on one broad cheek.

He looked out the front door.

"That damned Bo," he muttered, but stopped when he saw Nelda's wide-eyed stare.

Her lips went white as she too looked toward the door. "That was Bo Morrison, wasn't it? And Drew?" She recalled seeing two skittish paint horses in the torchlight. She felt faint. "*How could they?*" she whispered. She stared at Allen with stricken eyes. "The Morrisons are our best friends. I've always treated Bo and Drew as if they were my younger brothers—and Mary Beth is like a sister. Why would they want to burn us out?"

"They're liquored up and crazy with war fever," he said. "Ever since John Hill's men got back from that victory in Missouri, these boys have been scared the war will end before they get a foot in. By tomorrow they'll be sorry about this."

"You weren't with them?" she asked, still dazed.

His face grew hard. "I do my share of hell raisin'," he said, "but I don't pick on women or burn down houses."

She flushed. She had not meant to insult. Although Allen was older than Bo and Drew, he was often with their rowdy crowd.

As she floundered to apologize, he interrupted. "Where's your pa?"

"He left yesterday for Little Rock."

"I'd feel better if he was here." His eyes were blue ice. "But don't worry. That gang won't be back."

She caught her lip in her teeth. Allen had been gallant and kind; she had repaid with insult. She tried again to apologize.

"I said sit down, Nelda." He pushed her into the tall-backed entryway chair and then, after wiping his hands carefully on a handkerchief, he knelt in front of her. "Give me your foot. You're bleedin' like a stuck pig."

She flinched as he probed the tender flesh with calloused fingers. But his huge hands were surprisingly gentle as he took a pocketknife from his pocket, and using the point, carefully lifted the end of a long, thin sliver and pulled it out.

"Ouch!"

"I'm sorry," he said but kept probing for more, "I'm trying not to hurt you, but it's got to come out." He talked while he probed. "You won't be dancing for a while," he said. "And I know you like to dance."

She was too heartsick to make small talk. Her mind still analyzed the betrayal. Of course everyone knew she and Papa had opposed secession. They had written numerous articles against it in the newspaper. And Papa had long suspected Robert Morrison of wanting a high place in the new Confederate government. But for Bo and Drew to burn them out! Lifelong friends. It was beyond comprehension.

Wincing at the pain she asked, "How did you happen to see the fire?"

He rocked back on heels and looked up. "I was on my way out of town, when all of a sudden, that bunch rode past. Still had on gunnysack hoods. Then I saw the flames." He stood and wiped blood from his knife onto the side of his trousers before putting it back into his pocket. "I think I got it all. Wash your feet good and put salve and bandages on 'em." He glanced outside. "Old Tom still work for you?"

She nodded.

"Have him give them a look tomorrow. He's good at doctorin' horses, and I figure he'll know what to do if you have any trouble."

Louise came haltingly down the stairs. Shoes had replaced her house slippers. Her trim figure was fully clothed and her fair hair neatly pinned up. Except for the limp she looked as graceful as usual. She carried Nelda's shoes and robe.

"Young man, was it you who put out the fire?"

"Yes, Mama," Nelda answered for him. "Allen Matthers."

"Thank you so much!" She came forward, and after handing Nelda her robe and slippers, she took his hand. "If you hadn't come along, I fear the house would have burned completely down," she looked toward the door and added, "and who knows what else might have happened."

"Glad to help," he said, "but I wish I'd been sooner. That room is a mess. Sorry about all your pretty things."

"I'm just glad we're alive," said Louise. Nonetheless, it was with a drawn face that she got the lamp and started into the dining room.

Nelda slipped on the robe. With a grimace she tried easing the shoes onto throbbing feet but changed her mind.

"Where's Tom?" asked Allen.

"He sleeps in the tack room. Since he's so deaf, I doubt the commotion even woke him."

She nodded when Allen said, "I'll go wake him and send him in to board up the broken windows and keep an eye on things." He looked toward the dining room. "Do you have a gun?"

"Yes," she said.

"Know how to use it?"

"Yes."

"Get it and keep it close."

Her eyes followed his toward the scarred, smoky room. "I intend to," she said.

"Then I'll be goin.'" He turned away.

Nelda—feet bare, thin body in a soot-covered gown, and long chestnut hair a tousled mess— watched his broad back disappear. She wished she had not offended.

"Will I ever learn to keep my mouth shut!" she muttered.

Then with jaws clenched against the pain, she limped into the dining room. Her eyes widened at the damage done in so short a time. The beautiful drapes were blackened tatters. Smoke stained the walls and the ceiling, and a layer of soot covered the brass candlesticks and the red velvet upholstery. The smoky air tasted bitter and rough on her tongue. It was a grim ending to a dismal day, her twenty-fifth birthday. Mama was not ten feet away and yet she felt alone, so very alone.

In spite of that, when she gazed at the smashed windows, the chill tracing her spine suddenly became laced with anger. How dare Bo and Drew do such a thing!

Louise, statue still, held the lamp in one hand while surveying the wreckage. Bewildered, she faced Nelda.

"You're so like your father, I don't suppose this will even shake you—but I'll never feel safe here again."

Mama was wrong. She felt totally devastated.

Days later the acrid odor still saturated the stifling room. With little success Nelda tried to purge the smell by fanning the front door. Louise refused to have the broken glass replaced. She said the boards made her feel safer. Nelda hated the barricades, a reminder that she and Mama were barred like lepers from former friends and neighbors.

She tucked her hair tighter into the severe bun and used the corner of a white apron to blot August dampness from her brow as she gazed past the neatly trimmed yard and the gate trellis covered with spice vine. Her mare, Lily, cropped grass in the pasture just beyond a big weathered barn. Then her eyes turned north. Just out of sight down the lane, the buildings of Clarksville baked in noonday sun, but only the steeple of the new Methodist church was visible through the tall black walnut trees shading the yard.

Town might as well be miles away, she thought. Although there had been dozens of hurry-up war weddings, it had been months since she had been invited to any function. With a sigh, she looked north toward the hills where Aunt Becky lived. When the weather cooled she would love to go for a visit. Mama would object. Even after all these years, she had not forgiven Aunt Becky for marrying beneath her social class. *Come to think of it,* she pondered, *Mama rarely forgives anyone who opposes her.*

Just then a barefoot youth came into sight running down the dirt road. He carried a cane pole in one hand, but he did not head for the creek. Instead he opened the gate of the white picket fence and hurried down the walk toward her where she stood on the wide wrap-around porch of the tall white house. Her heart skipped a beat. It was the Hadley boy—the one who delivered telegrams. Telegrams usually meant bad news.

"Hello," she greeted, not taking her eyes from the paper he pulled from the pocket of ragged trousers.

He barely nodded. "Mr. Reynolds said to bring you this."

Fred! She took the missive with unsteady hands. Instead of a telegram, however, it was a letter. And a quick glance proved the handwriting belonged to Papa. She exhaled a disappointed breath and then quickly scolded herself. In spite of all resolve, the mere thought of Fred had turned her knees weak. She realized with chagrin that her heart had begun pounding at the mention of his name.

"Thank you. Wait just a minute and I'll get some money."

The sun-browned face briefly wore the trace of struggle. "Naw. Mr. Reynolds done paid me."

She wanted to be generous. The boy had a hard life, an orphan being raised by his elderly grandfather. And he was the subject of many whispered conversations, for his father had stabbed his mother to death, and then been hung for the crime.

"I think a bit more would be in order," she said. "I see the job hindered your fishing trip."

He scowled. "I done been paid," he growled and turned away.

She hardly noticed the rude behavior. It was becoming normal these days.

"Mama," she said stepping through the parlor doorway where Louise sat drinking coffee, "the Hadley boy brought a letter from Papa."

"Oh, wonderful!" Louise reached for it. When Nelda remained standing, she frowned. "Nelda, do sit down."

She sank onto the sofa where a bed sheet now hid the soot-covered velvet. Her nose wrinkled. Although she had scrubbed and scrubbed, a stale odor still permeated the room.

"I do hope Mr. Danley has returned from Richmond and no longer needs Phillip at the *Gazette*," said Louise. Then she sighed. "Of course when he gets home, he'll be a lost sheep without the *Star* to get out. Owning that newspaper was his lifelong dream. I never saw him more heartbroken than the day he locked the doors."

Nelda sorely missed Papa. He claimed she was his right arm. And she supposed she was since he had lost his own at the battle of Buena Vista in the Mexican War. She missed his dry wit and stimulating conversation and the camaraderie of working with him at the office. And how she missed getting out the paper—the smell of ink, the flutter of meeting a deadline, the challenge of wording an editorial just right. Since she had first worn long skirts and pinned up her hair, the newspaper had been her true love. That is until Fred. At least now she was spared seeing him every day! The sight of him caused such raw pain, it was almost physical. She wondered if the hurt would ever fade.

Louise interrupted her reverie as she squinted and held the missive near the lamp. Her refined voice was a soft drawl.

"I am hale, hearty, and doing fine, except for missing you both. I have taken a boardinghouse room near my job. It is plain but comfortable. The proprietor, Mrs. Ellis, is of a fine old southern family, still a bit haughty in spite of having fallen on hard times. She is, however, as fastidious as you, Louise. She insists the maids keep the rooms immaculate. The only real discomfort here, the cook lacks versatility. Daily, we are served fried meat, beans laced with fatback, and hot cornbread.

"When time allows I will relate some humorous anecdotes about my fellow boarders, or better yet, share them in person when I get home. I regret that can't be anytime soon. But I am glad things are going well for you."

Louise looked up. "I didn't write about what happened. There's nothing he can do, and I don't want him to worry.

"I agree," said Nelda, "but he'll be upset when he sees this room and finds out we didn't tell him." As lamplight lay across Louise's glum face, she thought, *He'll be more upset to see Mama failing.*

Louise's face was drawn and yet she still hid her years well with the trim figure, rigid carriage, and no hint of gray in the finely coiffed blonde hair. Although her features were well proportioned and finely molded, beauty was lacking due to a suggestion of haughtiness that arched her brows too high and narrowed her lips.

"We'll cross that bridge when we come to it," she said, stopping long enough to take a sip of coffee from delicate china. The cup gave a pleasant tinkle as it met the saucer.

Nelda thought it ridiculous to use the translucent Spode china in the grimy parlor. But Mama had always used the best china, even for everyday.

"There'll be time enough to tell him what snakes the Morrisons turned out to be," Louise added bitterly. "I'm not overly surprised at Bo. He always was an unruly child and a worse adult. But Tabbatha! Why, she won't even speak to me!"

"With Robert's political aspirations, I'm sure he warned his family to be wary of any Union taint," said Nelda.

"Political office is a poor substitute for friendship!" scoffed Louise.

Nelda cocked an eyebrow. "Apparently not to Robert."

"Well, I expected better from Tabbatha."

After clearing her throat, Louise read on.

"I suppose you heard about the recent Confederate victory at Wilson's Creek. That, coupled with last month's victory at Manassas, has our citizens declaring the war won't last another month and won't even come to Arkansas. I wish it were gospel; but validation of prophecy lies in fulfillment—there I fear our optimistic seers will fall short.

The New York Tribune first reported a great victory for the Union at Manassas (or Bull Run as the Union calls it). As the facts came in, the paper had to print a retraction. It said all was lost to the American army, even its honor."

The letter went on, *"When the northern line finally broke, the fleeing troops ran pell-mell into a group of Washington's fine ladies and gentlemen who had come to watch the battle from a hill outside the city, bringing along picnic lunches!"*

Louise shook her head in disbelief. "Yankee women must be different. I can't imagine wanting to see men get maimed and killed."

Nelda's lips curled. "Especially not while nibbling a chicken leg and biscuit. But last year when I went with Papa to Little Rock there were southern ladies at the state convention shouting as loudly as the men to hang Isaac Murphy when he wouldn't vote secession. I think given the chance they'd have pulled the rope!"

Louise sighed. "I suppose you're right." Her eyes traced the smoky room. "War does bring out the worst in people." She shook her head again. "I hope Phillip's hard-headed determination won't get him killed."

Nelda knew Mama was thinking of the Methodist preacher from Oil Trough who was hung at Searcy last week for plotting insurrection.

Louise shook her head. "All this killing over who controls the purse strings—"

"It's more complex than that," Nelda objected. She studied Louise's tense face. She knew Mama was not politically minded. Even when Papa had paced the library and railed against secession, she had never voiced an opinion. And yet Nelda suspected her heart leaned toward the Southern cause.

"Humph! You needn't tell me this is about states' rights or freedom for the Negro. It's about money—money and power. No politician is going to war over slaves—to keep them or to free them—unless there's money involved." She sighed. "Of course money never mattered to Phillip. He's always been an idealist. And an outspoken one." Her eyes swept the darkened room. "More's the pity."

Nelda huffed an aggravated breath. "Oh Mama, just read the letter."

Louise shot a displeased look but complied.

"Here in Arkansas, there are grave problems with the appointed Confederate generals. Bradley's men have refused to serve under him, declaring him incompetent and ousting him. Although Pearce is still in command, he is not faring much better. The authorities at Richmond finally became concerned enough to do something. They sent Brigadier General Ben McCulloch.

Does the name ring a bell, Louise? He is the fellow Tap served with in the Texas Rangers, the one Tap was always praising. McCulloch does have a sterling record as a ranger and an Indian fighter. I saw the general yesterday and introduced myself. He asked about Tap. He seems as impressed with Tap, as Tap is with him."

Nelda interrupted, "I barely remember Uncle Tap. I was very young when he visited."

Louise caught her lip in her teeth. Her eyes grew sad. "It's been years since he wrote. I used to send letters. But after he joined the Rangers, he rarely replied. He was a good boy, but always wild for adventure." A frown puckered her brow as she dropped her eyes and read on,

"McCulloch found things in a sorry state here. There is great lack of arms, ammunition, and supplies. And there are reliable reports that a large Union force in Missouri is planning a push against us. Please God that it not be so!"

Louise lowered the page and looked up. "Before Phillip left, he told me that he could never write as anything other than a loyal Confederate—in case the correspondence was intercepted."

Nelda nodded. Her eyes traced the room. In the South speaking out against secession had been dangerous, and writing about it in the newspaper even worse. She remembered that in the beginning even Papa had doubts. While editorializing about the Lincoln-Douglas debates, he had confessed agreement with Douglas on some points. According to the Constitution each state did have the right to sovereignty in all things local and not national. And when the Constitution was framed, twelve of the thirteen states were slaveholding. But eventually Papa had sided with Lincoln. The Negro was created equal and constitutionally entitled to life, liberty, and the pursuit of happiness. "*Otherwise*," he had written with passion, "*we're total hypocrites and the Constitution isn't worth the paper it's written on!*" With the penning of that article, sales of the *Star* had abruptly ceased.

Nelda's thoughts returned to the present as Louise continued reading.

Now, I must close and get to work. I pray you are both well and comfortable—I would add happy, but who can be happy in these difficult times? I love you both and pray for you constantly and am assured that you do the same for me. Your loving husband and father, Phillip T. Horton.

She read the hastily scribbled postscript.

"Dear Wife,

Upon further reflection, I agree with your decision to remain in Clarksville.

If there is an invasion, Little Rock will be a certain goal, whereas, I imagine Clarksville will be of little significance. It is good to know you are safe and surrounded by good neighbors.

Nelda's brows rose in disdain—if he only knew! Her eyes traveled the room again and then narrowed. She hoped the vandals got what they deserved! If it were ever in her power, she would make certain they did.

Louise picked up a small silver bell from the lamp table. Almost instantly Della appeared. The ebony-skinned woman was the color of strong coffee with a hint of cream. She stood tall and straight and without deference in her bold black eyes. Nelda could imagine her in African dress, the haughty princess of some heathen tribe.

"Della, I'd like more coffee, please."

Without speaking, Della turned away and soon returned, coffee pot in hand, to pour steaming liquid into the china cup. As the fragrant aroma filled the room, she quickly left. She had maintained a hostile silence begun the day after the fire when she arrived home in gray dawn to endure one of Louise's tongue-lashing about the evils of loose morals. Nonetheless every Saturday night she still slipped away, Nelda suspected, to be with Gill Harris' handsome black named Gideon.

Nelda's pen stilled as she sat at the desk in fading light and pondered what next to write. It was difficult. Papa was keen. If she were not extremely careful, he would know something was amiss. She glanced out the library window.

In the back yard Della stood on one side of the fence and Gideon—slender, tall, and arrow straight—on the other. They seemed to be arguing. He shook his head as she grabbed his arm. Then he gathered her into his arms, and with the fence between, kissed her, long and hard. He picked up a bundle lying on the ground and ran across the field. When Della turned, tears poured down her face.

Nelda sighed. So Gideon was running away. It was a wonder he had not done it sooner. Gill Harris was known to be a harsh master

The next morning she was not surprised when Della did not appear. Her bed had not been slept in and her clothes were gone along with some food from the pantry.

Inconsolable, Tom cried openly and often. When a week passed, he gave up hope of his daughter's return.

"Any word from Della?" Nelda asked the lanky man as he shuffled into the kitchen with a bucket full of water.

He stepped around the wet area where she knelt with scrub brush in hand and set the bucket down beside her. Sweat glistened on skin so black it looked blue. He shook his grizzled head sadly. "No, missy, not a word from that no 'count chile," he said.

"Maybe she'll come back soon," she tried to reassure.

"Ain't no tellin' where she at—runnin' off like that with that no account Gideon. That gal don't know she got it good right here."

"I feel sorry for Gideon if Mr. Harris ever catches him," she said. "He'll flay him good."

"He sure ain't like your pappy. Your pappy's a good man. Years ago Marse Phillip done give me and Rose our freedom. And when Rose died birthing Della, your pappy paid fer a black woman to nurse my poor motherless chile. Now that no 'count Della done run off. I plum hates to face Marse Phillip when he come."

Nelda looked at her swollen, red hands immersed in the lye soapsuds. She had no idea how hard Della's life was now, but her own had altered drastically since the girl disappeared. Something always needed washing and dusting and scrubbing. In the past it had never occurred to her just how much work was required to run the big house. She had enjoyed a gracious life, taking it for granted. Now, it required hours of work to even have decent gowns to wear now. She detested the mountains of ironing! Standing over a hot stove to heat the flat irons was torture in the August heat, and ironing for hours at the table made her back and legs ache. It made matters worse that Mama insisted almost everything be starched stiff enough to stand.

She sat back on her heels and pushed sweat-dampened hair from her forehead. While holding the dripping brush in one hand, she reached the other to her aching back. Her eyes fell on the big calendar hanging near the window. August twenty-first.

"Mary Beth's birthday," she whispered. She had never before missed her party. For an instant the pain of Bo's betrayal was a fresh, raw wound. On the heels of that memory came a more painful one.

Last year she had danced with Fred. It seemed a lifetime ago. He had danced with others, but at the time she had felt singled out and special—even beautiful. They had been good friends, able to talk for hours. Since his lumber mill was just down the street, he had often popped into the newspaper office.

Now, for the thousandth time, she groaned in humiliation. She supposed there was no fool like a starry-eyed spinster. With her plain face and too large hazel eyes and definite lack of buxomness, how could she have thought he would find her attractive!

Her face flamed remembering their last encounter. He had reached for a paper lying on the chair beside her. She thought he reached for her hand. With heart-leaping joy, she had grasped his hand. Red faced and bewildered, he drew back and began stammering about a wife in Indian Territory. Her dreams suddenly turned to ash. At the time she had been too embarrassed to ask why he had never mentioned a wife. Since that day they had never spoken of it again. And Fred, as usual, had been circumspect.

It still seemed impossible that refined Fred could have an Indian wife tucked away somewhere. Of course all she had really known about him was that he came to Clarksville to settle his dead brother's affairs. And as soon as the lumber mill sold he planned to return home. When the mill did not sell right away, she had hoped that he would decide to stay permanently.

"Missy, you got company waiting on the front porch," Tom reported.

She swept off the damp, wrinkled apron and tossed it aside. While hurrying down the hall, she smoothed back her hair and peeked out the curtain. She sucked in a shocked breath. As if her thoughts had materialized, Fred Reynolds stood on the porch!

With back turned, he looked toward the road. A pang swept her seeing his black hair hanging far below the white collar. Usually it was shorter, the way she used to cut it. When she cut Papa's it was no trouble to cut his, she had assured him. She had not told him how much she enjoyed standing near, breathing his scent, and running her fingers through the thick waves as the scissors snipped…

Now she nervously tucked her hair again, and steeling herself, willed the tremor from her voice. She opened the door and invited him inside.

As he turned, she gasped. "Fred! What happened?"

An angry red gash on one cheek oozed blood. His face was battered and dirty. One brown eye was swollen shut. His beard, always neatly trimmed, was matted with dried blood and his bottom lip was split. When he spoke, she saw a front tooth was now a broken, jagged mess. Nelda imagined it had taken more than one man to give him such a beating. Fred was not tall but his arms were as muscled as a blacksmith. With difficulty she stopped her hand from going to his face. Instead she stepped back to let him enter.

"Where's Louise?"

"In there." She nodded toward the parlor.

"Come in, Fred," called Louise. "Forgive my appearance, I…" she sucked in a horrified breath. "Who did that?"

"Zealous patriots," he said, "or thugs—depending on one's perspective." He lowered himself carefully into Phillip's chair while gingerly holding his right elbow. "No, Nelda, I'm fine," he said as Louise sent her after a wet cloth and some salve. "I'll doctor up a bit when I get home." He turned his head sideways to focus the good eye on Louise. "I came here first because I was afraid they might pay you a visit. But just now as I came up the walk, they rode by, rushing to dole out justice elsewhere, I suppose," he said bitterly. "I'm relieved you're both safe. I'll come back later, after I've cleaned up." He stood. "Nelda, see me out," he said. After motioning her to follow outside onto the porch, he shut the battered, patched door behind him. With a frown he gripped his elbow again. She wondered if the arm was broken.

"Louise looks bad."

"It's her leg," said Nelda, "It is bad. It hasn't healed from the burn and her head is getting worse. Our Doctor Mitchell left with the troops."

He nodded. "There's not a doctor left in town."

"Uncle Ned's granny is some sort of herb doctor. He claims she can cure all sorts of ills. I've been toying with the idea of going—"

"Don't go to the mountains by yourself," he cautioned. "It's too dangerous. Lots of riffraff are hiding out up there to stay out of the army."

She nodded. "I guess I could send Tom. Of course Mama will have a conniption." She gave a wan smile. "Wouldn't it be ironic if Uncle Ned's kin saved Mama's life."

He started to grin but grimaced from pain. He licked the puffy lip. Then he frowned. "I'd go, but I'm in no shape. I think this arm is busted." He went on, "Seeing the shape Louise is in, I decided not to worry her, but I think you should know—that gang mentioned Phillip. You need to be very careful."

"I suppose they attacked you for speaking out against secession," she guessed.

"I never was one for keeping quiet, so now they think Phillip and I belong to a secret organization plotting against the Confederacy."

"How ridiculous!" She spat out. His expression brought her up short. *Was Fred part of such a group?* Her mind whirled. *Was Papa?*

Her eyes narrowed. "Did Bo and Drew actually leave with Captain McConnell?" she asked with suspicion.

"You're shrewd, Nelda, just like your pa," he said. "They left but they're back on army business."

"They were your attackers?"

"There were several."

Her jaw hardened. "Bo and Drew need killing." When Fred's good eye widened at her vehemence, she added, "If Mama dies, they killed her—them and all that bunch."

"Maybe so," he agreed, "but they're not all bad. Mostly just young and full of fight. Since there's no Yankee soldiers around, we're the next best thing." He looked down the road and then at her. "But I'm afraid this isn't over yet."

"They better not show up here again," she said. Hard eyes said the threat was not idle. But her eyes softened and grew worried as she watched him limp away. Frowning, she scolded herself and drew a ragged breath. She had too much moral fiber to romance a married man, even in daydreams.

Somewhere nearby a woodpecker hammered. The old hound, Sirius, lay in the shade of the wide oak tree, wagging his tail but not bothering to rise as Fred passed.

Nelda reentered the house and saw Tom standing at the far end of the hall at the open back door. Grizzled head bare, he held a straw hat and his eyes were troubled.

"Missy, we got to do som'pin bout Lily and them hogs in that pen yonder."

"What are you talking about?"

He cut his eyes to the woods behind the house and shuffled from one foot to the other. "We needs to hide them animals."

Although they purchased most of their meat elsewhere, Phillip insisted on butchering the pork, smoking the hams and shoulders with a recipe handed down in his family for generations. Nelda was already wondering how they would manage at butchering time. Now she looked toward the woods. "Tom, are there runaway slaves in the woods?"

He hung his head. "Yes 'um. And iffen they don' steal them shoats, someone will. Folks is takin' anything ain't nailed down these days. And that Lily she's a fine mare."

She bit her lip. He was right. "Where would you hide them?"

"They's a hog trap down in the woods. I can toll the shoats there and pen 'em. Folks might still find 'em but least ways they'll be hid a little bit. But Lily"—he screwed up his face— "law, missy, I don' know whats to do with her."

"For now, I guess, just put her in the back pasture. At least that way fewer people will see her."

"All right, but that pasture fence ain't gonna stop no thieves."

She took a deep breath. "We'll just do the best we can." With furrowed brow, she went into the parlor.

"Mama, do we have much money here in the house?"

Louise stopped rubbing her head and looked up from the sofa where her leg was propped.

"We'd have as much as Robert Morrison if your father were a better businessman. He gives it away almost as fast as he makes it," she complained. "Why? Do you need something?"

"No. Tom just started me thinking. There's lots of robbery going on now. Women left alone can be easy prey. I wonder if we should hide what we have."

Louise tilted her head as her brow knit. "I suppose it would be wise. Yes, go upstairs and look far back in my wardrobe. Under my camisoles is a cash box."

Nelda hurried up the stairs and found the box. It was heavy. There must be a large amount of cash or possibly some gold inside. She took the box to Louise.

Louise pointed toward the library. "Put this inside Phillip's type case. Surely no one would think to look there."

"I don't think that's a good idea—the case looks valuable. Someone might take it." Nelda bit a fingernail. "Perhaps we should bury this or at least hide it in the barn."

"No. The barn could burn. Bury it. Tonight after dark."

The next afternoon Nelda went to the barn to find Tom. On the way her eyes strayed toward the flowerbeds where rainbows of zinnias were beginning to dim and the leaves to curl and brown, but the yellow and orange marigolds still remained as bright as spring. She paused to study the spot where the night before she had buried the moneybox by moonlight near the backdoor. A flagstone concealed the disturbed earth quite well. She did not think anyone would notice.

In a shaft of mote-filled dust, Tom sat on an upturned keg shelling dried corn into a bucket. He stood when she entered.

"You needs something? I ain't doing nothin' but shelling this corn to take to them shoats hid out yonder in the pen."

"I need you to go to the mountain, to Ned's granny to fetch some medicine for Mama. Her leg is festering and she's burning up with fever. If we don't do something right away, I'm afraid she'll die."

Eyes wide with fear and black face gone ashen, he shook his head and took two backward steps. "Law no, missy! I ain't gw'in up there. They'd shoot old Tom and take Lily."

He had a point. It was likely someone would take the mare from him.

"All right, Tom. I'll go. I'll leave early in the morning. You'll have to watch after Mama until I get back."

"Yes, missy, I do that." His black eyes alight, he bobbed his head, almost giddy with relief. "I do that. I go get Lily fer you, and I take good 'ker of Miz Louise."

Chapter 2

A red sun was peeping over the horizon when Tom led Lily from the barn. Nelda threw a pack of supplies across the back of the saddle and climbed up. For the journey she wore a riding skirt and blouse, and although the heat had been oppressive, she tucked a slicker into the pack in case of a storm.

"By riding hard I hope to make the trip in a day. If not I'll spend the night at Aunt Becky's."

Tom shook his head. "Don't think you kin make it in a day. Round trip be more than forty miles. Likely you'll have to stop the night at Miss Becky's. Tell her old Tom says hello."

"I will. And I'll get back as quickly as I can. Tom, you take good care of Mama."

He ducked his grizzled head. "I will, missy. I take good ker of her. You be careful, missy. Lots of devilment gw'in on these days." His lips drew into a displeased frown when she mounted. "I still say Miz Louise gwan'a be mad at me for lettin' you ride astraddle."

"Tom, my back would break riding sidesaddle on this trip."

"Keep that pistol handy—but don't shoot yourself," he cautioned.

"I'll be careful. And you take care with Papa's old shotgun. I loaded it for you."

As she rode from the barnyard, she cast worried eyes at the house. Mama had looked worse than ever this morning, hardly speaking. Nelda wished for some neighbor lady to check on her throughout the day, but there was none. She would have to trust Tom. Hopefully, Fred had recovered enough to help if need be. Her shoulders sagged. How quickly old friends and neighbors had deserted them!

She cut across the pasture of short grass, brittle and brown, and then through a small patch of scrubby woods where the big timber had been harvested and the wide stumps remained. She took to the road and rounded the bend. Ahead she spied the unfinished construction of the new Methodist Church. Before the war a few brick buildings had gone up near the two-story white frame courthouse with its high cupola, but most of Clarksville's small wooden buildings still hugged the dirt road grandly known as Main Street.

There were few people stirring. Nonetheless she kept her eyes straight ahead to avoid possible hostile stares. She rode through town and across the long covered bridge spanning sluggish Spadra Creek. It was almost dry now. Brassy skies had withheld rain for weeks.

After leaving the dim shadows, she blinked coming into bright sun. When she topped East Hill and looked toward the Morrison mansion, her jaw hardened. How many times she had ridden down the tree-lined lane and entered the red brick house. Would Tabbatha Morrison feel the least bit guilty if Mama died?

When the mare began turning, Nelda pulled rein. "No, girl, not today," she said bitterly. "Not ever again," she whispered. Stiffening her back, she spurred Lily to a cantor. With a round trip of forty miles ahead, she should put all else out of mind and concentrate on getting help for Mama.

Miles melted away under Lily's brisk hooves. For a ways the trail climbed and then leveled into flat country with tillable land lying fallow, for this year the farmers gripped rifles instead of plow handles. A few modest farm houses stood near the weedy, overgrown fields and in the distance overlapping blue peaks rose, still miles away.

She passed both wagons and riders. In the past folks would stop to chat, to inquire who you were, where you were headed—just being neighborly. Now there were no friendly greetings, at most a few subdued nods from grim-faced old men and cold stares from pinched-faced women. But Nelda was too harried to care. Along with concern for Louise, thoughts of Fred worried her mind like persistent gnats. She tried to dispel them. That proved as successful as swatting gnats. She drew a deep breath and patted Lily's neck.

In the morning freshness, cardinals, wrens, and mockingbirds sang and darted about in the trees. But as the sun climbed higher, the birds stilled. Shafts of sun filtered through tall oaks, dappling the road with leafy patterns. Heat beat down on dust-covered goldenrod and Queen Ann's lace growing alongside the road; the heads bent low begging for rain. She hoped there would be none today, and the way the sun beat down without a cloud, rain appeared unlikely. Sweat soon wet the mare's back. Nelda's own brow grew damp. She crossed Minnow Creek and passed through the little settlement of Hagarville, which consisted of a few houses, a small church, and a blacksmith shop. According to local gossip there were several pro-union families here. She wondered if they had experienced retaliation.

She passed the Garrison farm. She remembered the day that George had come, with desperate eyes, asking for a job at the newspaper. He was a nice boy and a hard worker, supporting himself and his mother with nothing more than odd jobs. Until the newspaper had shut down, softhearted Papa had paid him twice what others in town had paid. After that George had joined the Confederate Army. She wondered how his mother was faring now that she had returned to the farm and her drunken husband.

Where the foothills ended the trail narrowed and grew steeper. She pulled Lily to a slower pace. The air grew heavy. The afternoon would be stifling. At least the mountain would be somewhat cooler. According to Uncle Ned it was usually ten degrees cooler in both winter and summer.

It was a relief to climb down at a creek crossing to stretch her legs and get a drink. While Lily plunged her muzzle into the crystal water, Nelda held the reins and looked toward the mountains. At first they had appeared so far away, but now they loomed near. Would the old woman be home?

Would she have a cure? Would it be in time to save Mama? That thought made her climb back into the saddle and hurry on her way.

Midmorning she passed a ramshackle cabin near the trail. A slatternly woman with a baby on her hip hailed her from the front door, but after seeing the rumpled dress and uncombed hair, Nelda waved but rode on and stopped to eat a piece of ham and a cold biscuit in the shade of a giant oak tree near a stream. She afforded herself the luxury of a few minutes rest, sitting on the ground with her back propped against the tree trunk while Lily cropped grass nearby. A sudden breeze lifted damp curls from her forehead. It was the first time in ages she had gone riding. If the circumstances were not so dire, she would enjoy the outing.

Soon the trail grew steeper and rougher. Unlike the fertile valley—prosperous in rich bottom land that grew fine cotton—the mountains were dotted with poor hardscrabble farms and crude log dwellings. Next door to the Indian Nation, western Arkansas was in many ways a frontier. But Nelda thought the pine covered hills and hollows and the majestic views from the rugged mountaintops were unequaled in beauty.

Although she had met no other travelers for several miles, game was plentiful. White-tailed deer bounded away between dense trees. Occasionally a doe would stand until she rode near enough to see the soft velvet eyes. Squirrels scampered from the trail. Then standing on hind legs, they turned to watch as she rode past.

Lily began to lag. Nelda's back ached; worse still was the stabbing pain in her left side. She had to climb down and walk a while to ease it. It had been too long since she had ridden. Both she and the horse were out of shape. She looked at the deep wooded hollow alongside the trail and realized it was still a few miles to Aunt Becky's cabin. Although she had never been to old Mrs. Tanner's cabin, if she remembered correctly, Uncle Ned said it was on the left fork of the trail about a mile before reaching his house. She hesitated, wondering if she should give Lily a breather. She decided to press on. She wanted to arrive at Granny Tanner's as soon as possible. Lily could rest then.

On the tall ridge ahead a flock of wild turkeys suddenly scattered in a flash of bronze, black, and white, running across the trail and into the hollow. As Lily shied, Nelda patted her neck to calm her. Then she urged her forward toward the place where the trail shouldered the ridge and narrowed before dropping into the hollow.

Just as she reached the narrow gap, she abruptly pulled rein. A few paces ahead a group of horsemen blocked the trail. Her heart raced. It might be crazy to point the gun. She was unprovoked. But she sensed danger. Papa had always warned to never ignore instinct. Drawing the pistol, she cocked it.

"Well, looky there, Jess. That little gal's got that there cap-'n-ball revolver leveled right between yer big blue eyes." The fat man who spoke and then haw-hawed was both unkempt and menacing. But the young man he addressed as Jess gallantly swept off a hat and bowed. He had black hair and blue eyes and was exceptionally handsome. She dared not take her eyes from either. Jess was in front. If they decided to charge, she would shoot him first.

He looked at the leveled barrel. "We appear to be blocking yer path. Beggin' yer pardon, ma'am. We'll just pass on by." His horse took a step.

"No!" She gripped the gun with both hands. She would not let them pass. They could surround her. This was no ordinary group. There were five men leading several more horses loaded with packs. They looked hard-bitten, tough—and in spite of Jess's good looks—sinister. From the lather on the horses, she surmised they were fleeing.

Jess glanced back down the trail. Perhaps they would hurry on and leave her alone. Then again, perhaps she should hold them for whoever chased. Jess did not wait for her decision. He spurred his horse forward, and with a leap, lunged it against Lily's chest.

Nelda was knocked sideways. The pistol fired but the shot went harmlessly into the sky. Barely slowing, Jess grabbed the gun and then her, dragging her from Lily's back. He pulled her face down across the saddle like a sack of grain onto his lap, kicking and yelling.

"Get the horse," he yelled back over his shoulder and went pounding on.

Blood rushed to her head and dust flew in her face. What should she do? Where would he take her? She had no weapon now, only her brain. *She must think!* But it was hard with the air jolting from her lungs with every leap of the horse. All she could see through watery eyes was the heaving side and the churning feet of the animal as Jess slowed and turned off the trail, heading downhill into the woods.

The fat man rode alongside. "I'll tote her, Jess."

"Just shut-up and ride, Heavy."

Another man spoke, "Why you takin' her Jess? She'll just slow us down!"

"If whoever's chasing us, catches up," Jess replied, "we'll use her as a bargaining chip."

"Let me up," she puffed. "I can't breath!" When she began to struggle he gave her a rough shake.

"Lay still or I'll clot you one!"

He sounded mean, but unless she got up soon, she would pass out. Fred had warned her to be careful. Tom had warned her, and so had Mama. She had been careful. And yet here she was, her life in mortal danger. Of that she had no doubt. These were vicious, unprincipled men. She must find a way to escape!

She raised her head enough to see his pistol scabbard. She might jerk it free. No, he was bound to grab it before she could. As her head jolted down again, his pants leg chaffed her face. Her eyes widened. She still had a weapon. She opened her mouth and bit down hard, locking her jaws into his leg with all her might.

He yelled and then jerked her up by the collar. "You little devil!" He struck her hard with an opened hand. As her head jerked back, pain shot across her jaw and neck. Black spots danced before her eyes. Jess started to shove her back down, but hesitated. He pulled her back up. "Sit here and behave yerself, or I'll shoot ya." He shook her hard. "You hear?"

"Yes," she whispered, holding her jaw.

In spite of Jess's arms being tight around her, he ignored her, intent only on getting away. At a breakneck pace he threaded his way through heavy timber up hill and down. In places she held her breath, certain they would slide off the steep bluffs into the ravine below. Her head and side throbbed but she hardly noticed. Each mile took her farther from hope of rescue. Fear made her hands clammy.

Eventually he left the high ground and worked his way down into the bottoms. The valley was narrow here, hemmed in by high rocky bluffs and steep hills. There was no trail, but Jess, for the most part, had followed the creek. After several miles, he pulled rein.

"Sam, climb that hill yonder and watch our back trail. If they're still trailing, see if you can pick 'em off from the rocks. We got to give these horses a breather."

Sam nodded and rode off at a fast trot. After pulling Nelda from the horse, Jess dismounted and held the reins while his horse drank.

Her trembling legs would hardly hold her. She quickly sank onto a nearby rock and looked back up the hill where Sam had disappeared. How she prayed someone still followed—and she prayed Sam was not a good shot!

The horse raised its head and blew sending a spray of water flying.

Then a shadow fell and Nelda looked around. Revulsion knotted her stomach and turned her blood to ice. The big-bellied man leered at her. Although he was younger than forty, a skin condition had reddened and creased his face and dirt was embedded in each weathered wrinkle. His lips and nose were thick and his curly black hair hung limp with grease. The bushy beard was tangled and matted.

"Jess, you keeping her for yerself?"

"Hell, Heavy, wasn't that woman this morning enough to last you for a while?"

"Aw, she was old," he said with a wave of his hand. "And at that last place you hurried us off so fast I never even got a smell of that one. This 'uns young. And she's got purty hair." He reached to touch a strand of her hair that had worked loose.

She slapped his hand and jumped up. "Don't you dare touch me!"

Jess laughed. "Seems she ain't interested, Heavy."

Heavy chuckled. "They never are. But that don't worry me none." He turned to Jess. "I'll trade fer her. What ya want?"

Jess rubbed his jaw. "I'll have to think on that for a bit. Like you said she is young—and she ain't bad looking. I might just keep her."

"Aw, Jess." He looked back at Nelda. "I got forty dollars hard cash money."

Jess looked interested but he said, "I've paid more than that for a horse."

"Yo're lying. You ain't never *paid* for a horse in yer life!"

Jess grinned. "She is a might thinner than I like 'em. Tell you what, give me the forty and throw in that rifle I been wantin' and you can have her."

Blood drained from Nelda's face. She wanted to run and run and run. But her knees buckled. Heart pounding, she sank down hard onto the rock.

"Please, no," she whispered.

That tickled Heavy. He laughed as he tossed the rifle to Jess. Just then Sam returned, the horse's sides heaving as he pulled to a stop.

"Didn't see anyone," he said. "But a buck went running past like something had spooked it."

Jess looked back up the creek and frowned. He glanced at the sun standing at about four o'clock. "We'll push on. We'll ride in the creek for a ways and lose 'em. Sun will be down in a few hours. Gets dark early under these hills."

Heavy pulled her from the rock. "You're riding with me now, darling."

She cringed and struggled, but to no avail. He kept hold of her wrist and dragged her onto the horse behind him.

"You give me trouble," he growled, "I'll tie you up and drag ya."

She swallowed. He would. And enjoy doing it. Avoiding contact with his sweaty back, she leaned back as far as possible. Without even Jess as a buffer, she was now this beast's possession. Waves of terror accompanied each new thought. She had heard of women in such circumstances doing away with themselves. And surely death would be better. She wondered—if it came right down to it—would she have the courage? But she would not give up—not yet.

There was a tall, rocky cliff on one side. Jess edged his horse into the stream flowing at its base while the others followed single file. At first the creek was swift but shallow. Soon, however, it fanned out into deeper holes where water splashed onto Nelda's boots and skirt. When Jess urged his horse ahead, they followed, not daring to gallop on the slick rocky creek bed. Thick brush and trees crowded the bank where white water foamed around protruding rocks. Just ahead the stream narrowed and large boulders jutted. There the creek curved out of sight. Nelda heard the roar of a waterfall. She surmised Jess must know the country, for without slowing, he plunged around the bend and Heavy followed. But suddenly, pulling rein hard, Jess almost sat the horse on its haunches.

On a big sorrel in the middle of the stream sat Allen Matthers. A few feet beyond water plunged over a short but rugged falls. Allen's shotgun pointed at Jess's chest. He motioned Jess aside, keeping both him and then each man covered, as one by one, they splashed round the bend, and stopped in surprise.

"Throw 'em down." At Allen's command they threw the weapons gingerly into the creek and raised both hands.

Here were five against one, and yet they were afraid. Jess sounded calm but Nelda saw his body tense.

"Allen, I never knowed that was you after us or I'd have stopped to palaver."

"Sure you would, Jess."

"I swear I never knowed this was yer neck of the woods—"

"Well it is," Allen bit out, "and you got something there belongs to me."

Jess spoke fast, "I never knowed she was yer woman or I'd not have hit her, but she throwed a gun on me, Allen, and then she bit me, so—"

"Hell," snapped Allen, "I don't mean the woman! She ain't mine. I mean the liquor," he pointed the gun toward the pack horses, "and the corn and the house provender. That was my pa's place you raided. That was my ma you scared half to death."

"I swear I never knowed, Allen!" Now Jess was desperate. "We never hurt her, never touched her."

"Yeah, I know," said Allen slowly. "That's why you're still breathin.'"

Relieved, Jess sagged back into the saddle. "I swear we won't never come near yer place again." He spun toward the men. "Hey, boys, unload them packs and put 'em on the bank."

"No. You boys just mosey on back to Jasper, but leave the guns and the packhorses. Leave the white mare too. I'll tell Ma you sent her a present for scaring her half to death."

"*All the packhorses*? Come on, Allen, I need my horses," entreated Jess, leaning forward and spreading his hands beseechingly.

Allen's blue eyes grew steel hard. "Dead bushwhackers don't need horses."

Jess tensed and drew back in the saddle. "You'll let us keep our riding stock?"

Allen hesitated. "I reckon—so you'll clear out of here."

"I keep the woman," said Heavy.

Nelda's heart stopped.

"I reckon not," said Allen, his eyes narrowed.

Jess turned to Heavy. "Don't be a damned fool!"

With a murderous scowl, Heavy hoisted her off the horse and dropped her. She landed hard on her back and went under the swift current. Floundering, she fought for footing and emerged strangled and coughing. As she clawed her way to the bank, Allen gestured downstream just a bit with the shotgun.

His voice was brittle. "Don't ever let me catch any of you around here again."

As they spurred their horses, Jess and his sullen-faced gang shot Allen dark looks. Nelda stood on the bank and watched them go. Then unaided she floundered back through the water and caught Lily's bridle while Allen, keenly alert, fished the guns from the creek and stuffed them into his saddle bags. He lashed the rifles onto the packhorses, and after gathering all the lead ropes, he remounted.

Mute and pale, she also mounted, but clumsily, hindered by the clinging, wet skirt and sloshing boots. Hairpins had come loose, letting her tight bun go limp. She mechanically twisted the knot and re-pinned it with the few remaining hairpins.

"Hurry up," he barked. "Follow me. No telling when they'll circle back."

She cast terrified eyes downstream. "You think they'll try to jump us even without their guns?" When he did not answer, she kicked Lily's flank and splashed after him. Over and over, she glanced back.

After a while he left the creek, and then rather than circling the last steep ridge as Jess had done, he climbed it. Soon he stopped and dismounted. Along with the pack animals, he led his sorrel up the hill. She did the same, scrambling fast to keep Lily from stepping on her heels. Rocks and pebbles rolled beneath her feet and briars scratched her face and tore through the thin blouse to cut her arms. There was no trail here. It appeared to her that Allen had picked the roughest possible ascent. The wet boots chaffed her feet, and by the time they finally reached the top, blisters had begun to burn her heels. She stopped to get her breath. But he mounted, and without looking back, trotted along the lip of the ridge and then turned and headed into the woods.

Sucking in a deep breath, she also mounted and followed; although she doubted he cared if she did or not. She wanted to go straight to Granny's. However, she was unsure of the direction. Besides she might run into those men again. It was better to follow Allen.

They hurried through the woods at a brisk trot whenever possible. When Allen reached a wagon road, he began to gallop. Nelda spurred Lily. They rode for miles without stopping. She grew numb from exhaustion. But anything was worth the effort of putting distance between herself and Heavy. She shuddered just thinking of him.

The sun dropped below the horizon when, finally, they reached a farm right alongside the trail. She followed Allen into the barnyard.

Chickens squawked and pigs scattered in front of the milling horses. Although the farm animals looked fat and healthy, the barn, the outbuildings, and the cabin were rundown; roofs sagged, porches leaned, and the fences were in disrepair. Her nose flared at the odor drifting from the un-mucked barn,

If this is the Matthers home, she thought, *they must spend more time fiddling than working.*

Allen chewed his lip a minute and looked back down the trail. "I should have killed them."

"Yes, you should have," she agreed. "Why didn't you?"

He looked disgusted. "Just what in the hell do you think would have happened to you if they had bested me."

She dropped her eyes. Her flesh goose bumped. *She knew what would have happened!* Then she looked up. "But they'll come for these horses and shoot you in the back to get them."

His brows drew together. "I figure that's about what they'll try," he said slowly.

She was suddenly jarred by a thought—if she hadn't been there he would have killed them ... or died trying. Now he would be in constant danger. She owed a greater debt than she had realized.

Suddenly he looked at her and grinned. "So you bit Jess, did you?"

A stout woman rushed from the cabin and into the barnyard. Gray-streaked brown hair sagged from a loose knot at the back of her neck and her calico dress was limp and grease-spotted. "Saints be praised, Allen!" she cried. "You got our stuff back!" She clapped her hands in glee. She reached for a tall churn and embraced it as though it were a long lost loved one. "They took everything on the place could be hauled horseback. The blackguards would have taken the kettle off me fire, but it was too hot." And then she gave Nelda a sharp look. "And glory-be, who might this be?"

"Nelda Horton—Becky Loring's niece." Allen dismounted and began jerking packs from the horses, "Pa and the boys not back yet?"

"Naw. They're late." She added, "I hope they've not had trouble."

"Here, you two help me get these horses unloaded. Ma, sort out what needs putting back in the house. I'll put the rest in the barn. Hurry up. I need to get these animals hid."

Nelda collected the guns while Mrs. Matthers piled the packs of household goods onto the ground. Allen unloaded a dozen jugs and several sacks of corn and toted them into the barn. With a groan, Nelda picked up her pistol. It had followed the others into the creek and would need a good cleaning before it could be used again. She looked down the trail and stiffened. "There's riders coming!"

"Don't fret, dearie," said the woman. "It's just Pa and the boys."

A gang of hounds rushed forward, tongues out and tails wagging, to sniff Nelda's skirts and to mill between the half-dozen horses that soon filled the yard.

"Hey, Son, where'd you get them animals?" called a mountain of a fellow, an older version of Allen with a booming voice.

"Who cares about that," added another. "Where'd you get the gal?" Hoots of laughter follow the sally.

"Hey, that looks like our stuff on them critters," observed the older man, pulling rein on a huge dun horse.

"It is," said Allen, dragging a pack off the back of a lathered horse.

"Red, a bunch of bushwhackers hit here right after you left," the woman put in. "They must 'a been watchin' and seen you leave. Took everything tweren't nailed down!"

"Well, I'll be damned!" The big man's eyes glittered. "Son, you hunted 'em down?"

"Stop your jawin' and help me," ordered Allen.

Nelda observed that all the Matthers jumped when Allen gave orders, even his pa. They were a rough looking lot —all big, brawny, and unkempt—but handsome in a rugged sort of way. Allen was the only one decently dressed and clean-shaven.

When the horses were unloaded, he turned to the youngest, a boy about seventeen.

"Dillon, haul this plunder back inside. Seamus, get these animals to the cave. Make sure the gate is good and tight, you hear?" He looked at another boy, a bit older than Dillon. "You better go with him, Shawn. He might need help."

As they rushed to do Allen's bidding, Nelda sat on a fence rail and wiped her face with the tail of her skirt. She looked around, trying to imagine beautiful, pampered Mary Beth here. Mary Beth was sweet on Allen. But if Allen ever brought her home to meet the folks, he'd get a surprise. Nelda knew Mary Beth. One look at this place and these people and she would be gone forever. Nelda, herself, could hardly wait to leave.

She frowned. It was getting late. She must get to Granny's. She dreaded riding in the dark. She stood and led Lily through the gate. As she mounted and placed her feet in the stirrups, Allen came near.

"Which way to Granny Tanner's," she asked. When he stared at her, she became keenly aware of her tousled hair and wet, bedraggled clothes.

"It's too far. You need to stay here tonight. You're exhausted and you need some food."

She opened her mouth to argue. A sudden vision of Heavy grabbing her in darkness dissuaded her. She slowly dismounted but eyed the cabin with dread. Would this horrible day never end?

He took the pack from her horse. "Ma, Nelda is spending the night. Make her comfortable."

Kate beamed. "And welcome you are, dearie. You look worn to a frazzle. Come inside and rest yourself." She turned to Red. "Hurry along now. Supper is waiting. I'd like to get off me feet me self."

Nelda followed her through the door into a large dim room that was as wide as it was long and filled with clutter. As Kate lighted a lamp, Nelda noticed with relief there was no filth. The floor was swept and the hearth clean. The piles of plunder lay strewn about; hats, coats, shirts and britches; boots and chaps and bedrolls; bowls, plates, tin cups and utensils; musical instrument cases alongside bullet molds and nippers. The bushwhackers had indeed taken everything a horse could haul.

In the center of the room mismatched chairs surrounded a mammoth table of rough oak. In the far corner was the only decent piece of furniture, a high-posted bed with tall layers of mattress. The bed was neatly made with two pillows and a faded quilt. A few things—unwanted by the bushwhackers—old hats, a worn sunbonnet and a shawl hung from pegs on the wall. In another corner a black and tan hound rested on the floor with half-dozen squirming pups clamoring over her.

Near the gigantic rock fireplace Kate had retrieved a stack of pots and pans. A delicious smell wafted from pots sitting on iron racks over coals glowing in the deep cavern.

"Sit yourself down, love. I'll have your plate filled in two shakes of a dead-dog's tail." She ladled stew from a huge kettle into a pewter bowl and sat it in front of Nelda. With a folded rag she quickly slid aside the lid of a dutch oven and drew forth a golden-crusted biscuit, split it open and slathered it with butter from a crock on the table. "Them thieves helped themselves to the stew—wolfed down the whole pot full! I had to make more. Funny thing—they took no notice of the other foodstuff except for what they ate. I reckon they only wanted stuff to sell."

Nelda inhaled the aroma of lean meat and potatoes in thick brown gravy and suddenly felt light-headed. If Kate didn't hand her a spoon soon, she would turn the bowl up and drink!

"Go ahead, dearie, eat up. We don't stand on manners here. Oh, of course you'll be needin' a spoon," she noticed and fetched one from the pile on one end of the table.

Nelda had never tasted anything as wonderful as the rich, hearty stew. And the biscuit was as light and flaky as any she had ever had.

Kate sat down with anxious eyes. "I ain't a fancy cook—lord knows keeping those big bellies full don't give me time to do much of that. But I hope you like the stew."

"Mrs. Matthers, I can honestly say, I've never had better."

Kate beamed and jumped up. "Well, then," she said, "I'll just get you some more before those big oafs come in and devour it all." While she dipped, she cut her eyes sideways and asked. "And how did you happen to meet up with Allen this fine evening?"

Nelda gave a short version of what had transpired and her reason for traveling.

"Tis God's mercy Allen found you!" She shuddered. "They was a vile bunch, especially that fat one. Old woman that I am, he undressed me with his eyes—and would have done worse had the other one not been in such a hurry." She looked up. "Saints be praised we neither one came to harm."

Nelda gave a silent amen.

"Too bad about your ma. But Granny can do wonders. She's got the gift, you know." Kate set down the full bowl. "I know your Aunt Becky. But we ain't what you would call friends … she sort of keeps to herself," Kate finished lamely as if she wished she hadn't spoken. "Ned is just the nicest man and that Elijah is a fine one."

The room was soon filled with broad shoulders and loud talk. Each man stepped to the shelf holding a washbasin and washed and dried hands before straddling a chair at the table. As they quickly fell to eating what Kate had dished up, Nelda looked chagrined at her own grimy hands. Nonetheless she kept eating until the bowl was again empty and the last crumb of the second biscuit gone.

The boys cast glances her way; but deep in conversation, the men ignored her.

"You know they'll come fer them horses, son."

"I know, but I figure it'll take them a few days to get up enough guns and guts. Just in case we'll post a guard tonight." He spoke to the brothers nearest his own age. "Seamus, you take first watch and Patrick can spell you at midnight. Mack, you're on at three."

Without missing a bite, each brother gave tacit agreement while—as Kate had prophesied—the full pot was soon emptied.

Allen stood. "Where's your gun, Nelda? I'll clean and reload it."

She thanked him, and he carried it outside.

"That was good, Ma." One by one, they went outside to sit on the porch in the gloam. A couple of them kissed Kate's forehead as they filed past. She smiled, and then she reached to cuff Shawn on the ear as he leaned his chair onto the back legs.

"Get them dirty boots off the table!"

He complied. His boots, along with the front chair legs came down with a bang. "Ma, did you make any sweets?"

She snorted. "I stood over the washboard and put out a washing big enough to break me back, and then swept out this pigsty the best I could with all your trappings underfoot, and cooked your supper. Then I got set upon by thieves—scared out of me wits—and had to cook more supper because the blackguards ate the other. And still you're wanting pies and cakes! Outside with ya before I bash your skull in," she quarreled. But her smile was soft as he also kissed the top of her head before rambling out the door.

She signed. "Fine boys they are. But I always wanted a daughter…" She glanced at Nelda. "You're mother's lucky, that she is. A loving daughter is a thing to treasure." She began stacking bowls into a dishpan and filled it with water steaming in a teakettle. "Not that I'd take the world for me sons. And I hope someday to have daughters-in-law and a house full of grandchildren. But those big lugs out there don't seem in no hurry—Allen's twenty and eight and Mack not two years behind. Dillon's me youngest, and he's more than sixteen already. How fast they grow!" Her face grew sad. "How many brothers and sisters do ye have?" she asked.

"I'm an only child."

"Gracious me!"

Kate sounded as scandalized as if she had admitted to some indecency.

"How sad—oh, how much you've missed, lassie." Her eyes were sympathetic.

Allen had his mother's eyes, Nelda noted. Red's were the gray of a thunderstorm, but Kate's were the blue of an October sky and crinkled at the corners from smiling.

"Here I am talking your ear off and tis plain to see you're dead on your feet. Go sit on the porch while I tidy up and then we'll soon be off to bed."

Nelda longed to simply lie down and shut her eyes. Just now even the hard floor would be acceptable. However, she did as bidden and walked outside onto the porch where the men lounged, now replete and silent.

The road fronted the house. Just beyond it the creek shouldered a tall bluff, over which a full moon had just risen to shed silver light on the rippling water and fill the porch with light and shadows. Up the creek an owl hooted and nearby came the mournful goodnight of a whippoorwill. Fireflies twinkled like stars under the pines. As she watched them flicker, she wondered, for the thousandth time, how Mama was faring.

Red stood to offer a chair.

"No, no, keep your seat," she said. "I'll just sit here on the top step." She sat down and leaned against a post. Although she could see outlines, Allen's was not among them. She closed her eyes and must have dozed. Her eyes fluttered open as he climbed the steps. He sat in the chair nearest his pa.

"Horses are fine. Didn't see anyone stirring." He picked up her gun and took out the cylinder. He drew an oily rag from his hip pocket.

Kate stepped through the door. "Poor dear, she's gone to sleep."

But Nelda watched through half-closed lids as Kate fanned herself with her apron.

"Nice out here, but hot as blazes inside. Patrick Shawnesey Matthers, I've been waiting thirty years for that kitchen out back you promised me.

Red stretched and yawned. "And you'll have it, my pet. Just as soon as I can get to it." He reached to pull her onto his lap.

She sat for a moment, playfully tugged his beard, and then gave him a quick peck on the cheek and stood. "Seamus, give your ma a chair. I'm dead on me feet." When he stood, she dropped down and tucked her hair tighter into the sagging knot.

Red picked up a jug and drank freely. He passed it to Allen, but with a shake of the head, he declined. Kate reached under her chair for a tin cup and held it while Red sloshed in a generous amount.

She swallowed and licked her lips. "Ummm," she said. "I'd run you off, Red Matthers—heathen protestant that you are—but no one else can make whiskey to suit me."

"Now, Ma, I never said I was turning protestant. I just said Simon's preaching at that funeral made sense. And even you agreed."

Yawls came from the yard where Dillon and Shawn wrestled. Dillon was youngest but apparently strongest for Shawn's protest rang out.

"I said 'nuf! Why didn't ya quit!"

Dillon laughed. "You're such a liar, I didn't think you meant it." He gave Shawn's head another squeeze before turning him loose. He came to the porch and sat down. "Pa, you remember last year when that wildcat jumped on old man Millsap's cow?"

Red grunted, struck a match, and lit a pipe.

"Well, Vernon said just last week that same cow took the blind staggers and commenced foaming at the mouth. Old man Millsap said she had the hydrophobia and shot her. You reckon it could take that long for it to get you?"

"I've no idea. But it might, I reckon." A swirl of fragrant smoke wreathed his head. "Cats and skunks is bad to have rabies. We need to kill 'em out. There's getting to be way too many varmints."

"Rabies scares me to death," said Kate. She shuddered and then she suggested, "How about a little music to rest me weary soul?"

Seamus went inside and returned lugging several cases.

"We'll wake her," worried Allen.

"No," said Nelda, "I'm awake. I'd like to hear."

He took the fiddle from the case and started playing softly. She sat straighter. It was the melody he had begun one night at the Morrison's, the night Bo and Drew had raced through the halls on horseback with a Confederate flag. This time Allen's bow continued caressing the strings softly. The strains echoed off the far bluff in exquisite sweetness. Her eyes stayed closed but she heard every haunting note.

A hush descended. Then Kate spoke.

"Law, and ain't that lovely," she said. "Brings tears to me eyes. What's the name of that tune, son? I don't recall hearing it before."

He laid the fiddle on his knee and shrugged. "Haven't named it yet."

"You made it up?" ask Nelda, her eyes now open.

"Yep," he said and lowered the fiddle.

Her eyes rounded in appreciation.

While Patrick tuned his banjo, Seamus took a French harp from his pocket and blew a few test notes. Soon they played in rollicking style. As soon as one song ended someone suggested another and they were off again. Captivated, Nelda pulled her skirts over her knees, hugged them to her chin, and studied the group. In the midst of the conversation, banter, and laughter, she felt lonely.

In a lull, Red cleared his throat, and in a deep bass, began singing a ballad about an emigrant, a dying girl who left Ireland on a ship but never reached the new shores.

"Ach, that was fine, me love," said Kate. "And how often it proved true," she said sadly as if recalling a perilous trip herself. "Seamus, let's have *The Young Man's Dream*."

He dried the harmonica on his pants leg and put it back into his pocket. He leaned back against the log wall and then began singing, his tenor voice, clear, strong, and true, each note lingering in the summer night.

Kate dried her eyes on her apron. "Makes me homesick. Even after all these years," she said softly. "We'll never see it again, will we love?—heather on the moors."

Red reached to pat her leg. "We got a fine home right here. The mists over Piney are every bit as nice as them in Ireland. And don't be forgettin' the bad—the reasons we came away. A man is free here to work his land and be his own man. You wouldn't be wanting our boys back there, now would you?"

She sighed. "No—no, of course not." She shook her head and took another drink. Then she lifted the cup in mock toast. "Allen—*Drink to Me the Parting Glass*—and then we're off to bed."

He tucked the fiddle under his chin. Nelda thought he winked at her, but in the dim light, she could not be certain. He fiddled a while and then stopped to sing. She had heard him play on several occasions, but never before had she heard him sing. He had a fine baritone.

Of all the money e'er I had,
I spent it in good company.
And all the harm that ever I've done,
Alas! it was to none but me.
And all I've done for want of wit
To mem'ry now I can't recall
So fill to me the parting glass
Good night and joy be to you all

He played a refrain and then began to sing again.

Oh, all companions e'er I had,
They're sorry for my going away,
And all the sweethearts e'er I had,
They'd wish me one more day to stay,
But since it falls unto my lot,
That I should rise and you should not,
I gently rise and softly call,
Good night and joy be to you all.

The fiddle refrain rose in unison with the harmonica.

If I had money enough to spend,
And leisure time to sit awhile,
There is a fair maid in this town,
Who sorely has my heart beguiled.
Her rosy cheeks and ruby lips,
I trow she has my heart in thrall,

So fill to me the parting glass,
Good night and joy be to you all.

"Old as the hills of Ireland—but still one of my favorites," said Red. "The very tune Uncle Seamus sang the night he died," he avowed.

"The first time he died or the second?" asked young Seamus with a grin.

Nelda looked around and Red chuckled. "Uncle Seamus had a right famous burial," he explained. "It was a grand wake. Lasted three days. And I, me self, helped carry him to the cemetery. He was a big man and the coffin wide. We was just passing through the gate when Uncle Seamus commenced knocking. In haste we set him down and pried the lid open. And sure enough, he sat up, eyes open wide. In great amaze we toted him back to the wake and went inside for a few more pints. When we come back out, there he was, sitting stiff in the coffin and stone cold dead again." Red's eyes began to twinkle. "While passing through the gate this time we was careful not to bang the sides on the post."

Along with all the rest, Nelda laughed aloud. Then Allen stood. "Once Pa starts telling tall tales, he doesn't know when to quit. Nelda needs sleep. She has to be off early."

Kate stood. "Miss, you'll sleep with me. Pa will bunk out here with the boys. In hot weather they just throw bedrolls on the porch."

"Oh, Mr. Matthers! I hate taking your bed."

His eyes twinkled. "Well, I'm sure the boys wouldn't object to you bedding down out here. But their ma ain't likely to approve. Not to mention yours." He laughed as her face reddened.

She tried to stand and faltered. Allen reached a hand. "No wonder you're stiff. You've had quite a day."

She thanked him and followed Kate inside. Her face reddened again as she heard Allen praising her spunk to his father. In reality all she had done was be stupid enough to get kidnapped by bushwhackers. He was the hero.

In the dim room Kate pulled off her apron and slipped off her dress. Then wearing her chemise, she crawled into the tall bed.

"Thunder-pot is on the back porch, love. And don't worry; the boys never go back there. They go to the woods."

Nelda felt her way to the back porch and found the necessity sitting under a bench just where Kate had directed. By the time she returned, Kate was already snoring softly. She felt inside the satchel and found her nightgown. Before slipping off her outer clothes, she pulled it over her head and then quickly stuffed her arms into the gown and pulled it on. It was the first time she had ever gone to bed dirty. Mama would be aghast. But as tired as she was, it didn't seem to matter.

The corn shucks rustled as she climbed into bed, but Kate's breathing continued uninterrupted. Nelda hugged the outside of the mattress and turned her back to the faint whiskey scented breath. In spite of weariness, the events of the day raced before her eyes. She thought with a shudder how differently this evening could have been. She could still smell the vile sourness of Heavy's body and feel his handprints burning her skin. She would be forever in Allen's debt!

His family intrigued her. She had a feeling that Kate was right. She had missed much. She wanted to think about the Matthers but her eyelids rested heavy on her cheeks.

It was still dark outside when Nelda smelled the unmistakable aroma of fried ham. She rubbed her eyes and tried to sit up. With a groan she lay back again.

Kate rose from bending over the fireplace.

"The coffee's hot and breakfast is almost done. Allen said you'd want an early start."

She forced her feet over the side and sat up. It took all her willpower to pull on clothes and boots. Every joint and muscle screamed from the effort. She wondered how she could possibly ride today. And yet, she must!

She hated wearing dirty clothes but she had no others.

"I brushed the dust off your skirts," said Kate, "And got the worst mud off your boots."

"Thank you. You've been so kind."

"Oh, it's been a pure pleasure, dearie."

After Kate had stuffed her with ham, crisp fried potatoes, and more fluffy biscuits she felt better. The hot coffee helped most of all. She got the satchel and stood.

"Mrs. Matthers, there is no way I can thank you enough for your hospitality. I don't know when I've enjoyed myself more. And under the circumstances, that is a miracle. If it weren't for worrying about Mama, you'd have a hard time getting rid of me."

"Oh, now!" Kate beamed. "Listen at you now! It's glad I was to have you. What a lovely lass you are. And I'll warrant my Allen has noticed."

Nelda reddened.

"Come back anytime. Oh, please do. We'll be that glad to have you!"

She gave Nelda a big hug and a kiss on the cheek.

Surprised, Nelda timidly hugged her back. She was unused to such displays of affection. Papa often patted her head. But Mama rarely hugged and never kissed her.

"Goodbye," she said and glanced once more around the homey room.

She stepped softly past the sleeping forms on the porch. It seemed most of the Matthers were not early risers.

In the pink sunrise mists rose over the creek and hugged the rock ledges rising just beyond. Puffy clouds, crimson-edged, rimmed the bluffs where dark shadows were being driven before the rising sun. She stood for a moment drinking in the beauty. The earth was still, silent, and peaceful. Then a rooster crowed. She recalled her errand and hurried down the steps.

Allen waited at the barn lot gate. Lily was already saddled and bridled.

"Must have rested well," he said. "You look better this morning."

"I don't think I even turned over. But I must say, I have muscles I never knew existed … and they're all sore."

He grinned. "Need help mounting?" His eyes were bright in the morning light. They crinkled just like Kate's when he smiled.

"No, thank you. I'll manage."

"Keep your gun handy."

"I will." She hesitated, searching for words. "Allen … If I hadn't been there, you'd have finished them back at the creek. Now I've put you—and your family in danger. I'm truly sorry. I can't thank you enough for—"

He stopped her. "Never mind all that. You're burning daylight. By the way, did you come up through Hagarville?"

"Yes."

"There's a shorter way. Not as good a wagon road but on horseback it's not bad." He told her where the trail branched off the main road on the far side of the mountain. "Stay on that. It runs right alongside Bear Branch and comes into town west of Spadra."

She nodded and climbed into the saddle. "You have a wonderful family," she said.

He looked pleasantly surprised.

"How do I get to Granny's?"

He pointed west. "About a mile that way the trail forks. Take the left one. You'll come to her place before long."

"Thank you," she said and rode out of the yard.

"Hey, Nelda!"

When he called out, she pulled rein and looked back.

"More than likely Jess is rabid. Since you bit him, you'd better ask Granny for a cure." He grinned and waved.

It was disappointing to be so close and yet not pay Aunt Becky and Elijah a visit. It had been months since they had been to town, long before Uncle

Ned left for the army. Nelda had been disappointed when he joined the Confederacy; but, no matter what Mama said, he was a good man.

She kept on the trail and found the Tanner cabin without difficulty. It was off the road, fronted by a field where stumps still dotted the rough ground. A bit of smoke drifted lazily from a stone chimney. Compared to the Matthers' homestead, Nelda considered this place prosperous. The cabin was small but well built, the logs tightly chinked and the chimney straight. Both barn and fences were in good repair. There was no clutter lying about and the vegetable garden was weed free and the woodpile neatly stacked.

When a hound came from under a porch held up by rock pilings and bayed a greeting, Granny stepped through the door, drying her hands on an apron covering a long brown calico dress. Then she smoothed her gray hair back into its neat bun. "Kin I help you?" She was a tiny woman with deeply wrinkled skin and bright black eyes.

"Mrs. Tanner, I'm so glad you're home!" Nelda slid from the saddle, almost too stiff to walk. She looped the reins over the near porch rail but decided to move Lily to the other side beyond the steps to avoid the mare browsing on a rose bush growing near the steps. "You don't know me, but I'm Becky's niece, Nelda Horton."

When the old woman's face tensed Nelda remember that Ned's kin had been no more pleased about the match than had Mama.

"Uncle Ned said you are good at doctoring. My mother is in bad shape," she quickly said.

The old woman's black eyes snapped to attention. "What's her trouble?"

"A bad burn that won't heal."

"What color is hit? Does hit have a bad smell?"

As Nelda answered each question, Granny, head cocked and brow knit, was intent as the best physician. Nelda felt relief with the telling. Granny emanated competence.

"Come and rest a spell." She led Nelda inside and pointed to a rocking chair sitting near the door while she muttered under her breath, "Yeller spine thistle ..."

The cabin was crude, but neat. A colorful spread on a four-posted bed brightened the drab room, as did the braided rugs scattered on the puncheon floor. A spinning wheel sat in the corner, and a loom, with partially finished cloth, crowded against one wall in front of a window.

Granny looked around. "Viola, where a'ir ye?" she called.

A door opened and rail-thin Viola, with gray hair drawn tightly back into a knot, came into the room. "Ma! You know my head's a'throbbin' and I'm a layin' down. What you hollerin' for?" She stopped short. "Oh, company! I had no idee.'" She smoothed her dress and looked shamefaced at the sharp tone she had just used on her mother-in-law.

"This here is Becky's kin," said Granny. "Keep her company while I get some yarbs together." She leaned her cane against the wall, and then the old woman, nimble as a girl, climbed a ladder leading to the loft.

"Land sakes! Ain't it hot this morning."

Nelda barely listened as Viola chattered away. It was all about her aches and pains and the misery she had to endure because of ill health.

Granny was gone only a few minutes before coming back down the ladder with a cloth bag in her hand. "This here"—she came close and pulled the bag open, sending forth a pungent, spicy odor—"is thistle blossoms. Brew 'em to make a strong tea to wash the burn with." She handed over another bag. "And this here is wild black cherry root and the inside bark off a dogwood tree. Make a tea fer yer ma to drink. Hit will he'p her sleep and sooth a fever." She reached into her big apron pocket and drew out a small bottle. "This here is salve—ginseng, pennyroyal, willer bark, lots of stuff. Put this on the burn after you use the thistle water." She screwed up her face and thought a minute. "Yep, I reckon that'll do the trick... along with prayin.'" She smiled.

Her teeth were still strong and even, a rare thing in a woman her age, noted Nelda. Perhaps her herbs were responsible.

Granny went on, "I give the good Lord credit fer my cures. I reckon he give me the gift of knowin' what yarbs to use, but hit's the praying does the most good."

Nelda rose and took the medicine. "Thank you so much, Mrs. Tanner! I was at my wit's end. I'll get right on home and begin using these."

The wrinkled face had softened until Nelda said, "Please tell Aunt Becky about Mama."

"I don't see Becky much," the old woman said, her mouth downturned. "But if you wait just a few minutes, you kin tell Elijah. He's coming over. You're here awful early," she observed.

Nelda related in sketchy details her experiences of the day before.

"Cutthroat no-accounts. Hope Allen kills every last one of 'em. I been scart something like this would happen. With the men away to war, the thieves move right in and do as they please. Lucky fer you that Allen had more sense than to run off to the army." She waved a hand toward a chair. "You may as well sit a spell. Elijah will be here any minute."

Indecisive, Nelda glanced outside. She would like to see Elijah. And according to Allen, the shortcut would save miles. She decided to wait a few minutes longer.

"Company's a treat. Gives my poor ears something to hear besides Viola's miseries. Caleb is gone to Dover, so Viola's got no one to complain to but me."

With anxious eyes, Nelda sat at the kitchen table, sipping a cup of mint tea.

"I hope Elijah hurries. I'm so concerned about Mama—"

"Life and death is in the hands of the Lord," affirmed Granny. "She won't get took before her time." She sat down beside a large floor loom and picked up a ball of yarn and began to wind it on her shuttle, a long thin piece of wood with two half circles carefully cut and smoothed in each end. She noticed Nelda's interest.

"Guess you ain't seen too much of this done, have ye?" she asked while pressing down on one of the foot treadles. The warp threads separated, leaving a space between them through which she easily slipped the shuttle, now, freshly wound with yarn. She tamped down the thread with a beater, lightly, then after using the treadle again, she tamped firmly to set the new thread in place. "This here loom was the first piece of furniture my man made after he built the cabin. We slept on the floor till this was built."

The loom was an ingenious design made from sturdy timber. Small branches had been cut from limbs and smoothed to make the uprights and cross pieces. It seemed to have grown here, an organic part of the house. The way Granny caressed the wood, Nelda could tell the old woman loved it.

"This here piece, where all the warp threads go through, is called a reed. Hit's made from river cane splits, every single one carved by hand. Many a night my man sat by the fire, a carvin' those little pieces—couldn't be no longer than the space between the cane joints. And this piece the weaving is rolled on is called a breast beam." The shuttle passed back and forth and then Granny tamped the wool into place.

Nelda left the chair for a closer look. "What happens when you don't have any space left to weave in?"

"Loosen these here little ratchets." She reached over and undid a small block on the front beam of the loom and one on the back. "And ya roll the whole weaving toward you till there's more space to work in." She reset the blocks and resumed her weaving.

"If you made that beautiful blue coverlet on the bed, you're certainly an expert," said Nelda.

"Oh, I made that years ago." Granny waved her hand, dismissing the compliment. Then, simpering, she added, "but I have to say, that dye has held up right good—'specially after all the washings."

"I've never seen anyone weave before. It's fascinating."

"Ain't much hard—if you got a knack fer it," said Granny in false modesty. "This here nut brown ain't colorful but hit'll make a good stout coat fer Ned—three ply wool." She cut her eyes sideways and her lip curled. "Becky ain't no hand to make cloth. She buys that shoddy stuff at the mercantile. Ned will need better now that he's a'marching with that army in all kinds of weather." Abruptly she sobered. "I shore wish he hadn't jined up ... liable to get hisself kilt," she muttered.

Viola looked up from plying a needle in course cloth. "Not if it ain't his time," she said with a smirk.

When Granny shot her a sour look, Nelda hid a smile. She suspected this roof was hardly large enough for both women.

She sat the cup back onto the table. "I'd love to see Elijah, but I must be going. Please tell him I'm sorry I missed him. And I'll try to send word about Mama."

Granny rose and followed her out the door. "I hope you got a slicker. My bones says it's gonna storm before sundown. Hit's bad getting caught in these mountains in a storm. Lots of lightning and lots of tall trees fer it to strike. Won't help your ma any if you get yerself kilt."

Nelda looked up. The sky was cloudless and blue. She would not, however, gainsay anyone as wise as Granny.

"I have a slicker in the saddlebag. Thank you so much for the herbs, Mrs. Tanner. I hope to see you again."

"Be kerful," the old woman called. "Keep yer eyes open fer bushwhackers!"

Nelda waved.

She followed the road over the mountain, as Allen had instructed, and where the trail took off at a steep incline, she followed. Where the terrain allowed, she loped the mare, but she had to slow on the steep rocky downgrades. She thought about Allen. She wondered if the bushwhackers would return soon, or if they would wait to catch him off guard. Allen was canny but anyone could get a bullet in the back. She fervently hoped he did not. She was grateful for the risk he had taken to protect her.

She found the turnoff just as he had described and turned Lily onto it. For a short way the trail penciled the top of the mountain where the view stretched for miles. It appeared to be a vast uninhabited wilderness. Heavily timbered hills of hardwood and pine converged into a deep gorge where rocky bluffs towered over a dry streambed strewn with rocks and boulders. A hawk, giving a shrill call, circled high over the trail that led down into the hollow and disappeared under tall pines.

She took a deep breath and paused. Indecisive, she looked back the way she had come. It would take hours to go back. And Allen would not have directed her this way if he had thought she would get lost.

She patted Lily's side "Well, girl, it appears we have some rough traveling ahead."

Without hesitation the mare started forward. Pebbles rolled down the hill under her hooves as she began the decent. Nelda, every nerve taut, leaned back in the saddle and hung on as the trail wound down into the creek bottoms. Occasionally it grew dim and overrun by cattle tracks. With a little searching it was still perceptible. She had followed the creek barely two miles when Lily began to snort and sidestep. Since the mare was usually tractable, Nelda knew something was wrong.

"What is it, girl?" she whispered and felt the hair standing on her own neck. How she wished she had not come this way! With fearful eyes, she searched the woods but saw nothing. "Do you smell a bear?" she asked the mare.

A sudden snarl sent Lily plunging forward. She broke into a run. Nelda gripped the saddle horn and stared back with wide, terrified eyes to see right behind her a sleek black cat jump from one oak into another. It was the size of a large dog and had bright tawny eyes. Nelda had heard of the mountain panther but had never before seen one. Instantly she had visions of the rabid cow slobbering and dying. Lily needed no urging, and yet she urged her.

The cat, however, sat still and watched them flee.

Not until they were far down the trail did Nelda pull rein. Her heart finally began to slow and she let out a deep breath. Her mouth was parched and her tongue felt like leather. Although there were a few pools left in the creek, she took a canteen from the saddle instead of drinking from the bug-covered, stagnant water full of darting minnows.

"Lily, I'm gong to give Allen Matthers a piece of my mind. To send me this way he must think I'm some kind of tough mountain woman!"

However, she passed the morning without further mishap. Her thoughts whirled ahead. How was Mama? Would the herbs help? She finally faced the thing that had hovered like a buzzard preying on the edges of her mind. *What would she do if Mama died?* Could she stay alone with only old Tom as help? She supposed she could go live with Aunt Becky or she could join Papa unless he thought Little Rock too dangerous.

At noon, while Lily browsed tall grass along the creek bank, she rested in the shade and ate the biscuit and ham that Kate had sent along. She enjoyed the tasty meal and thought about Kate. She liked her. Allen's mother was in many ways coarse and unrefined. And yet she had goodness—as did all the Matthers clan. Salt of the earth, Papa would call them. It was plain to see that Allen had grown up surrounded by love and gaiety. It seemed strange that, even with all her advantages, she envied him. Oh, not that she didn't love Mama and Papa! And she practically worshipped Papa. But hers had been a staid upbringing, and in many ways, cheerless.

She sighed. It was hard to imagine having music all the time. She loved music. She had always regretted no one in her family played. Music was available to her only at social gatherings. Yes, in many ways she envied the Matthers!

She stood and stretched and untied Lily from the bush. "We've made it this far, old girl. With any luck we might just live to get home."

The trail was clear here and she relaxed and let Lily have her head. The mare seemed in no mood to lag. Nelda suspected the horse was as anxious to get home as she was. By mid-afternoon, she grew drowsy. Stifling a yawn, she looked up. With dread she saw tall purple thunderheads roiled in the west. Soon lightning danced behind the clouds and the tops of pines swayed in a rising wind sharp with the smell of rain. In the distance a wild turkey gobbled.

Large drops soon pattered the dusty road and wet her arms and head. She groaned. Rain would delay her more. She stopped again, long enough to don the slicker and then rode on, dreading the long wet ride ahead.

The storm grew fierce. After each brilliant flash, thunder pounded the rocky ledges above. She could barely see through the deluge. Ahead jutted a bluff with an overhanging rock. She dismounted, pulled Lily into the lee, and with her back to the wind, hunkered down and waited.

As crashing thunder shook the ground, she cringed in awe. The roar was deafening. Although she had watched fierce storms from the window and been wetted by numerous rains, never had she been exposed to such elements. Any moment she expected to perish from a lightning bolt. Nothing had ever made her feel so small and insignificant.

Finally, the darkest clouds blew over the mountain and the thunder lessened. Water coursed down the creek bed and swirled around the rocks and boulders. The noise of the rushing creek almost equaled thunder.

When the worst had passed, Nelda mounted and rode on. The storm had wasted valuable time. She fretted over Lily's slow plod, but with the rain pouring down, the wet red clay was too slick for the horse to do otherwise. Hunkering in the slicker, Nelda rode on, dreading what waited at home.

The downpour eventually turned into a drizzle that stopped soon after sundown. Night fell long before she reached town, but Lily went on through the darkness with sure-footed certainty. Nelda's head sagged. Her heavy lids finally fell shut. She wasn't worried about dozing. Now it was just a matter of staying in the saddle and letting Lily have her head.

She was not sure how long she dozed. The clip-clop of Lily's hooves wakened her. They must be near the creek for toad frogs called in deafening numbers. Lily sensed barn and feed ahead and her pace quickened. Nelda's heart also quickened. What waited at home?

Chapter 3

The house loomed dark as Nelda rode in. Her mouth went dry with dread. She was somewhat relieved upon seeing a small shaft of lamplight peeking between the boards at the windows.

"Tom," she called.

He heard and shuffled from the barn.

"Praise de Lord! We been mighty worried. I tole Miz Louise you must a' stayed on de mountain again tonight 'cause the storm catched you."

"How is she?"

He shrugged. "I don' know. She jest lay there."

He took the reins as she almost fell from the saddle. How stiff and sore she was! It was a minute before she could walk. She got the herbs and the pistol from the saddlebag and hobbled toward the house. "Give Lily plenty of grain, Tom. She's earned it."

Pale and drawn, Louise lay on the settee in the parlor. She managed a glad cry when Nelda came in.

"You're home! I'm so relieved!" She sighed and eased back onto the pillows. "This has been the longest two days of my life. I could imagine all sorts of things … especially after those men came today."

"What men?"

"A gang of them banged on the door but I wouldn't let Tom open it. I told him they were up to no good. They finally went away."

Nelda frowned. She decided not to relate her own adventure. Mama would never want her to leave the house again.

"You look feverish."

"My head is splitting. I need a cup of coffee."

"First I want you to try some herb tea." Nelda held out the pouch. "Mrs. Tanner sent lots of different herbs—some for burns and pain and fever. She says they'll fix you right up. I'll go brew some right away." Before leaving the room she turned and looked back. "Mama, you're going to be fine."

Oh, how she wanted it to be so! Even though they failed to see eye-to-eye on many things, she had a growing realization that—as Papa was fond of saying—blood was thicker than water. Close friends and neighbors had disappeared. Yes, she needed Mama.

For the next two weeks, Nelda faithfully bathed Louise's burns with strong thistle tea. The ugly swelling began to recede.

"I will have to thank Mrs. Tanner," Louise said as Nelda examined the burns and pronounced them almost well. "I declare I think her herbs saved my life. I do believe I'll be able to go to church on Sunday."

Nelda grew still. "Mama, we can't go to church."

"Nonsense. I'm much better."

"Don't you realize we're not welcome? We've had no invitations to anything—and not just the flag making, but the weddings and dinners."

Both women jerked at a knock on the front door. Caution was becoming second nature. These days Nelda never opened the door without looking from a window in the entry.

She peeked out. Then she sucked in a shaky breath, stepped back, and smoothed her hair. She drew in a deeper breath. It did not slow her racing pulse. As she opened the door a warm breeze invaded the long hallway in a sultry draft.

Fred's face had healed, the only remaining signs of the beating, a few faint bruises and a crook in his nose where it had been broken and his arm in a sling.

"Come in," she invited. "I'm glad to see you've almost recovered."

"Thanks," he said, "But I'm in a rush. I have business to attend. I just came by to give you this letter. I saw Phillip in Little Rock. He hopes to come home soon."

"That's wonderful," she said while reaching for the letter. "I didn't know you were going to Little Rock," she added. "We would have sent him a letter. The mail is so uncertain these days."

His eyes darted around avoiding her face. "Uh, I hadn't planned to go. The trip came up unexpectedly."

"Oh, I see ..." she said. But she didn't see at all. It was unthinkable for him to go and not tell them. He would surely know they wanted to send Papa a letter. Perhaps Fred wanted to avoid her as much as she did him.

Now he shuffled, looking uncomfortable. "Nelda, I would appreciate it if you didn't mention to anyone that I've been traveling."

"Certainly," she said, instantly suspicious. What was Fred up to? "Thank you for bringing the letter," she said as he hurried down the walk. Eyebrows narrowed, she chewed her jaw. *What was Fred's pressing business and why had he gone to Little Rock without telling them?* She thumped the letter against the palm of her hand and looked after him. She would ask Papa when he came.

She brightened. It would be wonderful having him home. She hurried to the parlor to give Louise the letter.

Phillip wrote, "*I am well and the job goes along with only a few bumps and jolts. I must say, working for C.C. is never boring. I am not sure how much news you get these days. I am not even sure if you received my last letter. I have not heard from you lately. I hope you are both safe and well.*"

Louise looked up. "I'm so glad he didn't know about my leg. It would have worried him to death."

She read on, "*I miss our talks, Nelda, so I will do the next best thing and write a few details of recent happenings here. After the Wilson Creek battle, without Rector's approval, Pearce dismissed his men. The governor is furious. The state army in the northwest now numbers only eighteen. (I would not write of this so freely were it not common knowledge.) I suppose many of the men are back in Johnson County now, at least for a while. The troops were outraged because of no pay, but most of all they had no intention of leaving Arkansas, as rumor suggested they might be ordered to do.*

"C.C. claims Rector is working hard to see the men do not re-enlist in the Confederate Army. He wants them in his state force. Rector is using General Burgevin to plot to that end. Neither side is getting many volunteers. As the governor himself said, a man once in camp rarely takes service again. But General Burgevin keeps trying. Burgevin and C.C. have become such bitter enemies, if I even mention the man's name, C.C. almost bites his cigar in two. His last two editorials have not been complimentary to the general.

"Everyone is gearing up for the coming November election. Under the Confederate constitution we will be allowed four congressmen to replace the delegates selected by the convention. Felix Batson is running for our district and I think he has a good chance against Thomason. If you see him, tell him I said, Hello.

"Enough about all of this for I fear this is boring my dear Louise. I miss you so much, my dear. I plan a trip home as soon as C.C. can spare me for a few days. Until then keep me in your prayers. C.C. has hinted about having me go east to cover the war, but I will certainly come home first. All my love, Phillip."

"Oh! I hope he can come soon," said Nelda. "It seems he's been gone a year already."

Louise drew a shaky breath. "More than a year," she said and her lips trembled.

Sometimes Nelda forgot how lonely Mama must be. Of course Mama missed Papa more than she did—if that were possible.

The next day Nelda was in the barn currying Lily when Tom hurried inside.

"Miz Louise say to come. You all got a guest—the preacher man."

Nelda pulled off the soiled apron and began smoothing her hair. It would be good seeing Brother Wheeling again. Since Papa left they had not been to service.

She frowned to find him seated in the ruined parlor. Of course Mama would never consider receiving guests in any other room.

"Please forgive the disarray and stuffiness in here," apologized Louise. She looked up. "Oh, Nelda, there you are. Would you please bring coffee."

"No, thank you," the pastor declined. As he glanced around at the boarded up room a keen look of shame crossed his face. He dropped his head and stared at his hands. After a bit he looked up. "It appears you've had some bad times. I've neglected you terribly, failed you as a shepherd."

"You could have done nothing." Louise looked at the destruction. "It was a mob of drunken men."

"I meant since then…" his voice trailed away and he stared at the floor. As his gray hair fell forward lamplight shone on a bald spot. He twirled the hat in his hands and drew a deep breath. "Last night Mabell and I had a midnight visit, too."

"Oh no! Did they wreck your house?" Nelda quickly asked.

"No, just broke a few windows. But that was enough." His jaw grew rigid. "You know Mabell's heart is weak. It almost killed her. I won't stand by and let it happen again. That is why I've come—to tell you we're leaving, going to Iowa to Mabell's people. Louise," he entreated, "you should leave too. You and Nelda are welcome to come with us."

"No," Louise shook her head, but stopped abruptly to rub her temples, "but thank you so much for offering. We'll be fine. Phillip should be home soon. I don't think anyone still believes that silly rumor that he's an officer in the Union Army."

"People have a way of picking and choosing what to believe," he cautioned, "and you and I both know Phillip and I made many enemies over being outspoken against slavery." His mouth drew into a thin line. "When I think of all the people Phillip Horton has helped in this town!" He shook his head. "But in spite of that, his politics, like mine, are unpopular just now.

"Nelda," he said with a wan smile, "that book you loaned me was my undoing."

She nodded. She knew that Harriet Beecher Stowe's novel, *Uncle Tom's Cabin,* had created a nationwide stir. Some were stirred to anger. But others had become staunch abolitionists. Nelda had not personally witnessed atrocities such as Mrs. Stowe's novel described, but she had heard of beatings and there had been a scandal involving Bo Morrison and a young slave girl.

"Do you want to leave?" Louise asked, her eyes worried.

Nelda sat with hands folded in her lap. Where could they go? Iowa was out of the question. They would only be a burden to the Wheelings. And Papa said Little Rock was a mess. People had already fled in droves, a third of the population going north and many others heading south. If the state were invaded it was no place to be. Besides, Papa might not remain there. He thought Mr. Danley might send him somewhere else soon to cover the war. If he thought they should leave they would discuss it when he came home for a visit. For now their chances were as good here as anywhere. This was the only home she had ever known. She had been born in an upstairs bedroom. No one had the right to force them out! Anyway, Mama was not well enough to travel.

"No," her voice was calm and decisive. "I think we should stay."

"So do I," said Louise with finality. "But thank you again, Edward. When this mess is all over, I hope you and Mabell will return."

"Perhaps we will," he said. He fished a pocket watch with a gold chain from a deep vest pocket and clicked open the case to check the time.

Every Sunday service in memory Nelda had watched him consult the heavy gold timepiece to see if his sermon was becoming too long-winded. As a child she had joyfully anticipated that checking of the watch. It meant service was almost over—it was almost time for the closing prayer, almost time to be free of the hard bench and Mama's command not to wiggle. Now as he snapped the watch shut she sensed finality of a different sort. They would never see him again.

"I'll be going. I promised Mabell I'd be right back. She's afraid to be alone." He stood and took Louise's hands. "God Bless you, Louise. Goodbye."

Nelda escorted him down the hall to the front door. He stooped and kissed her forehead.

"I'll miss your sunny smile, Nelda Jean. God bless you." He clamped on the black hat and went down the shaded rock walkway into bright sunshine.

She sighed and shook her head. The hotheaded rebels were wreaking havoc with everyone who opposed them.

As weeks passed isolation took a toll on Nelda's spirits. The newspaper had been the hub of local activity with her and Papa being two very prominent spokes. Now she was not even privy to friendly gossip. She wondered if the shunning bothered Fred. He must also be experiencing it. In opposing secession he had been as outspoken as Papa.

The last week in September Bo Morrison came home on recruiting business. Nelda supposed Mr. Morrison had killed the fatted calf. Buggies and wagons passed by all afternoon headed for the picnic and dance.

That very afternoon Louise insisted Nelda go to the store to purchase more yarn for the winter socks and muffler she was knitting for Phillip. It was a warm, cloudy day with a stiff wind stirring the oaks on the courthouse square and whipping dust from horse hooves and passing wagons. She noticed subtle changes since her last trip. Both black gum and sumac had reddened. Her heart sank at this omen of fall. Usually she embraced it, loving the riot of color and the crisp, cool days; but now any portent of winter made a hard knot in her stomach. It meant more hardship, more isolation. Her steps lagged. The store would be crowded today. In spite of vowing not to care she still dreaded the snubs. One consolation—she assumed Mary Beth would surely be at home primping, so there was little chance of running into her.

The bell above the door tinkled as she stepped inside. Inside were several men and a few women.

"How do, Miss Nelda." Old Enos Hadley hugged the stove as if it were December. He was a tall gangling old gentleman with a long bushy white beard, and one of the few people who still greeted her cordially. "How's yer ma?" he asked.

"Fairly well, thank you, Mr. Hadley."

"Tell her I send my consillitations."

Nelda hid a smile. Enos was a courteous old man and a fine moral gentleman. But She and Papa had shared many private laughs over his butchery of the English language.

A dusty-booted farmer leaned on the counter while choosing a set of harness and talking with Emmitt. "I'm glad they made James Fagan a colonel," he declared. "Back in forty-six we left Clarksville together to help settle that dust-up with the Mexicans. We were just kids. Even so, Jim was a fighter—and smart to boot. Before this war is over, he'll make a name for himself. I just wish he wasn't in Virginia. He ought to be in charge of things around here. He knows the country."

Enos perked up his ears. "Well Fagan or no, I tell ya," he inserted, "Lee's got to cross the Shenander River, make a raid through the North and order his men to commit suicide as they go, or the Southern Confederacy's busted."

"Aw Enos, suicide means to kill yerself," protested the farmer.

Emmitt Gossett had turned his attention from the men to glare at Nelda.

She glared back and walked with head held high on past the bonneted, full-skirted women at the fabric table. She met every eye as she made her way toward the yarn table and then pretended intense interest in just the right weight and shade of gray yarn. To her annoyance Mary Beth stood on the far side of the table looking lovely, as usual, in a yellow gown and matching bonnet. She refused to lift her eyes. Nelda, growing irritated, forced her to look up.

"Well, Mary Beth, I presumed you'd dropped off the face of the earth. I can't remember the last time we spoke…oh, yes. It was last April the night of your party, wasn't it?"

"I suppose so." She looked around nervously.

"I heard you're having a dance tonight to celebrate Bo's visit."

"Yes," she stammered. "And I have to go." She put down some ribbons and quickly took her leave.

With resentful eyes Nelda watched her scurry from the store. Just then a woman spoke from behind.

"Yo're Phillip Horton's daughter, ain't ya?"

She turned to see a careworn woman dressed in neat but worn calico peeping from under a broad-brimmed slatted sunbonnet. It was Aunt Becky's sister-in-law, Opal Loring.

"Yes, ma'am."

"I remember when ya used to come play in our yard while yer pa got his horses shod." The woman lowered her voice. "I heared . . ." She hesitated, glanced around, and whispered again, "We heared about yer fire. Reckon you could say we're in the same fix." She stopped speaking as another woman drew near and she kept quiet until the lady made a selection of yarn and passed on. She looked around again. "You knowed our boy James is with the Union Army?"

Nelda nodded. She had heard disgruntled mutterings about that.

"After he left to join up we had our winders smashed. And someone took a shot at the mister. Barely missed him—hit buried up in the barn door. I wisht we could leave here and head fer the mountains, but he says no. Hit's our place, and we got jist as much right to stay as the Rebels, he says. I says, yes, Jim—the right to stay and get shot! I told him that him and Fred Reynolds is gonna get us all kilt!" Abruptly she put a hand to her mouth as if she regretted those hasty words.

Fred! What did Fred have to do with these people? Nelda longed to ask, but she had no desire to stand whispering to Opal Loring. Already Emmitt, with elbows on the counter, stared their way, a scowl on his wide face. The farmer had gone and for the moment he was alone.

"Mama will be worrying if I don't hurry." Nelda eased away, hoping to avoid any more confidences. Somehow she sensed danger in learning more. But how strange to learn Fred Reynolds and Jim Loring were somehow yoked! Fred was an educated, prosperous businessman, Jim Loring an illiterate farmer barely scratching enough from his land to feed his big family. They had nothing in common—nothing apparently except a devotion to the Union.

Emmitt took the money she held out for the yarn. He looked down the aisle and spoke loudly to impress the other customers. "I'm surprised you're still here, Nelda Horton. I figured you and your ma would have scurried away north by now to join your pa."

"Papa has *not* gone north. He's in Little Rock. And Mama and I are scurrying nowhere." She hoped her voice carried to the far end of the store. "You have a short memory, Emmitt! Not three years ago, you came hat-in-hand to beg a loan from Papa and he gave it. And without interest!"

As old Mr. Hadley chuckled, Emmitt had the good graces to flush.

"I paid back every penny," he mumbled.

With blood boiling, she stormed from the store and ran headlong into a broad chest. Allen Matthers caught her shoulder to keep her from falling.

"Whoa!" His face lit with a smile to match the one in his dancing blue eyes.

"Sorry," she apologized. The wind blew a tress of her hair into his face. She grabbed it and stuffed it back into the knot on the back of her head.

His eyes twinkled. "Been biting any bandits lately?"

She relaxed a bit and smiled. "Only three or four."

"Hey," he added impulsively, "I know you ain't going to the shindig at Morrison's. But there's a dance tonight over at Cabin Creek. How about coming with me. I have to fiddle a few sets at Mary Beth's; but then I could come by for you."

"No, thank you, Allen."

"A little fun would do you good."

As she shook her head and took a step backwards, tears sprang to her eyes. "But I appreciate the invitation. Have fun tonight." She whirled and began walking fast. She seldom cried but suddenly there was no stopping the tears.

"Nelda, wait up!"

His heavy boots thumped the ground. She groaned. Her face was a red-eyed mess.

He caught her shoulder gently and turned her around. He lowered his voice. "You don't have to worry about these folks. They ain't political. They don't care a tinker's damn about who's in what army. They just like to dance."

His grin was infectious. And his words had her considering. She had been cooped up for an eternity, but would she dare go with Allen? There was, of course, a social barrier. She would never consider becoming closely associated with him. But one little dance hardly signified....

She pinched her lips between her fingers. The more she considered, the more she was tempted. She had no fear of wagging tongues. No one was speaking to her these days anyway. Although she was a grown woman and could do as she pleased, a scene with Mama would be unpleasant. Mama had such rigid notions about mingling socially with people whom she considered beneath her.

"Yes," she decided, *"I'll go. But I'll just slip away and not upset her."*

Just as the hall clock struck nine, Nelda, carrying slippers tucked under a light shawl, tiptoed on bare feet out the back door. Now that fall was approaching the night air had a bite, especially on a clear, cloudless night like tonight. All the stars hung near enough to touch, like bangles on a bracelet, she thought, looking up. She knew it was silly but she felt like a young girl tonight shivering with anticipation. By the time Allen arrived Lily was saddled and waiting in the barnyard. Nelda had worked quietly. Old Tom, asleep in the tack room, had not heard a thing.

"Glad you decided—"

"Shush!" she stilled his booming voice.

He glanced at the house and the dark windows. "It's like that, is it," he said with a chuckle.

She led Lily through the gate and mounted. As the horses walked side-by-side, Allen's big sorrel dwarfed Lily. The horse just suited Allen. Everything about him seemed bigger than life.

"How's your pa liking Little Rock?" he asked.

"Oh, he loves writing for the newspaper—any newspaper—but he misses home."

He nodded. "I ain't much on Little Rock, myself. I been there but I was glad to get back to the mountains."

"Allen, I noticed on muster day last April that you didn't seem any more enthused with the new flag than I was."

He cut his eyes toward her. "Why, Nelda, how flatterin.' A thousand people there and you noticed me."

She laughed. "You stand head and shoulders taller than everyone. And with that coppery hair you're a bit hard to miss."

He grinned. His even teeth gleamed in starlight. "Pretty night. Ain't it?"

"It certainly is," she agreed.

He had avoided her question. Of course she did not blame him. Personal politics had become a guarded thing, especially if one was pro-union. And she suspected he was. On muster day most people had cheered and thrown hats into the air at the first sight of the new Rebel flag, and then they had given three rousing cheers for Jeff Davis. Allen had stood silent with big arms crossed on his chest and a slight frown on his face. But tonight he was certainly jovial. He rode along with a jaunty air as if he hadn't a care in the world.

"I want to thank you again for saving me that day at the creek."

"Aw, in a couple more hours you'd have been bossin' the whole bunch—including ol' Jess."

When she pulled rein he stopped alongside. "Allen, I know what would have happened to me if you hadn't come along."

His lips thinned. "Then Jess is the one who should be thanking me. He'd be dead now if any harm had come to you."

For a moment she was taken aback. She meant nothing to him.

Then she realized no decent man would tolerate such a thing. It was a comforting thought. She nudged Lily's side and rode on.

The way to the cabin was a well-traveled trail running parallel with Cabin Creek, a silver ribbon in the night. After a few miles they turned onto a narrow trail where treetops arched overhead obscuring the sky. A screech owl swooped and landed in a tree on the creek bank. It's plaintive call made Nelda shiver. She laughed silently at herself. She must be feeling guilty to have such goose bumps over a silly old owl.

They had gone almost a mile, passing no dwellings, when light loomed ahead. Lanterns swung on the porch of a sizable cabin. She was surprised at the large number of horses hitched all around. Abruptly she had misgivings. In a crowd of this size there would be plenty of Confederates. She had been foolish to come!

After Allen got his fiddle from a pack on the horse's back, he held out a hand to help her dismount. The bearded, solemn-faced group on the porch stared. A few said, "Howdy," to Allen but ignored her. She wanted to turn right around; but his firm hand on her elbow steered her inside.

When they walked through the door, every eye turned. From the wide-eyed gapes of the youngsters, it was obvious strangers were rare at their parties. The room was full of bearded men, homespun-clad women, and scores of children with bare feet. Although Nelda's green watered-silk had no frills, it was finer than any here.

The main room was large for a cabin. A huge fireplace took up one wall and tall rafters overhead held a string of dangling lanterns. There was little furniture, a few straight-backed chairs and a long pine table shoved against a log wall. Her eyebrows rose seeing a dozen corked jugs sitting alongside platters piled high with molasses cookies. There was usually liquor at town parties. But it was always nicely hidden in a cut-glass punch bowl or in jugs that stayed outside and discretely out of view—imbibed in, nonetheless, by almost every man present.

"Hey Allen, get that fiddle tuned up. We come to dance!"

"Howdy, all," he called. "So yo're ready to dance."

"We shore air." The scrawny man who spoke was unsavory-looking, bearded, ragged and dirty. When he grinned and stepped near, Nelda noticed one eye was crossed making his head tilt as he stared at her.

"Since Allen's gonna be busy, I'll ask you fer the first dance."

"Sorry, Harlow, Dillon already has dibs on the lady."

Harlow glowered as Allen took Nelda's arm and propelled her forward. She expelled a relieved breath as he steered her away and toward the young giant.

Tonight Allen's brother was clean-shaven and neatly dressed in clean clothes. Allen spoke low to him and he nodded.

When the first sweet notes of the fiddle filled the room, she began to relax and put her hand into the huge paw of the young Matthers. The last time she had danced, she had been in Fred's arms. The remembrance was an arrow to her heart. No, she would not remember—not tonight. She would pretend, at least for the evening, that all was right in her world. Allen was right. It had been far too long since she had any fun.

My! Allen could fiddle! And these people loved to dance. The style was faster, more abandoned, than she was used to, but she liked it. It was all she could do to keep up with the racing feet and twirling steps. Dillon was a good dancer and light on his feet for such a big young man. After two more sets, he handed her off to another Matthers brother, the one named Shawn. He was not quite as good a dancer, however, he stayed off her toes. Nelda laughed as she whirled. She saw Patrick and Mack twirling pretty girls. One was a Taylor girl from Clarksville whom she vaguely knew.

When the dance ended she sobered. On the far side of the room Harlow hunkered near the wall. He stared like a hungry dog eyeing a chicken. She gave an involuntary shiver. He stood and walked toward her. She tensed. But he stopped near a skinny woman with jet-black hair.

"Now yo're gonna see some real dancing" said Shawn. "Harlow can out-jig anyone"—he pointed to the dark-haired woman—"except Salvicy Lucas!"

Harlow began to jig. Everyone stopped to watch. The crowd clapped the beat as his feet flew, stamping time to Allen's fiddle and Seamus' harmonica. But the woman's flew even faster. Her bones seemed disjointed as she flailed to the beat. Nelda was mesmerized. Never had she seen such dancing!

When the jig ended Harlow shot her a triumphant look out of his narrow eyes. Chilled, she quickly turned away, thankful that Dillon once again claimed her for the next reel. After two more sets, Allen declared it was time for a break. He soon joined her.

"You must be having fun." He grinned. "Your eyes are sparklin.'"

She smiled. "Dillon is an excellent dancer. Shawn is not half bad either."

"Hmmm," he said. "Reckon, I'd better let those two play the music before they steal my girl away. Thirsty?" he asked.

"Yes, I am. This kind of dancing is work!"

When he led her toward the table her brow wrinkled. He laughed. "Don't worry," he said, bypassing the jugs and taking a dip of water from the wooden bucket, "I won't get you any moonshine." He handed her the dipper. "But it is the best around." His blue eyes twinkled. "I know for a fact."

Nelda assumed he had made it. The Matthers clan was known to make the best whiskey in the county. Even Papa occasionally bought a jug to lace with honey and use for a bad cough; she hated the fiery stuff, but it worked. Now the water slid down her dry throat, wet and cool.

When Dillon and Shawn took up guitar and banjo, Allen danced with her. She felt dainty in his strong arms. He was—she realized with surprise—an excellent dancer, the best she had ever danced with; and she realized, with flushed face, that she was enjoying herself. It would be something to mull over. For now she surrendered to enjoyment.

After midnight the party was still going strong. With regret Nelda told Allen she must leave. When he turned the job of music making over to his brothers, the gaiety went on without missing a beat. She glanced back as they rode from the yard. A thin man stood on the porch in the shadows. She could not be certain, but he looked like Harlow.

As they rode through the starry night Allen was unusually quiet.

At first Nelda made polite small talk, but finally, swaying to Lily's easy gait, she quieted and almost nodded off to sleep. Except for the sound of night peepers and the occasional croak of a bullfrog, they passed the miles in silence. Near the barn he pulled the sorrel to a stop. Nelda yawned when Lily also stopped.

"Gracious, I'm tired."

He smiled. "You cut quite a rug, little lady."

"I had a wonderful time." She hesitated and then added. "I have to admit, though, that fellow named Harlow made me uncomfortable when he kept staring."

"Can't hardly blame him for staring at a pretty gal," he said. "I stared myself."

She hooted. "Allen Matthers, I know I'm as plain as an old boot."

For an instant his brows drew together. "No you're not. Oh, maybe you're not a real looker like Mary Beth. But you have a way about you," he said soberly. "You've got brains and spunk. I'd say that was worth a heap more." For a long moment he was quiet. He looked down while toying with the reins held loosely in his big hands. The he looked at her. "You've seen where I live," he finally said. "We don't have much in common."

He had spoken without a hint of drawl. And she thought it odd that he had used perfect grammar.

"No, we don't," she answered.

He let out a deep breath and shifted in the saddle. His solemn mood seemed to vanish. "Well, I'm glad you had a good time. You deserve some fun."

"I may pay for it tomorrow." She groaned. "I'll be lucky if I can even get out of bed."

His drawl returned. "There's a dance in the mountains tomorrow night. Wanna come?"

She looked away. She would not let this get out of hand. "I imagine I'll be staying home for a while. Mama isn't well."

He nodded. "Need help unsaddling?"

"No. I can manage."

As he turned away he said. “Good night, pretty lady.”

She chuckled and then softly called, “Allen.”

He looked back.

“Thanks for taking me.”

He tipped his hat and rode away.

In the barn doorway, she stood and watched his broad back disappear. She stroked Lily’s face. “Old girl, I’m beginning to suspect there’s more to Allen Matthers than meets the eye.”

Chapter 4

There had been no letter from Papa in weeks. Nelda was worried; but she tried not to alarm Mama. She waited until Louise had lain down for her afternoon nap before heading for town. If there was no letter she hoped to send Papa a telegram. Because military matters took priority over civilian needs, it was doubtful she would be allowed to send one.

The wind was rising. It looked like rain. She wrapped her shawl tight and hoped she would not get caught in a downpour. With hardly a glance she hurried past the coral brilliance of sugar maples growing near the road and the trees and bushes resplendent in orange, red, and gold. Upon reaching the Methodist Church, she slowed. A lady never appeared to hurry. Mama had drilled that into her since childhood.

Nearing the courthouse she slowed even more. A group of cavalry had gathered there, preparing to mount. She wished she could avoid them, but both the post office and the telegraph office were inside the courthouse. Just then skinny, blond-haired Drew Morrison exited the building. Nelda's eyes narrowed.

She wondered if Robert had paid for the sergeant's stripes on his son's sleeve. It was being done in the Confederate army. He had bought Bo the rank of lieutenant.

Drew stepped back, waiting, as a soldier shoved a man out the door. Abruptly, Nelda gasped. *Fred! And he was hurt!* His hands were tied and his face was a bloody pulp. Drew held a gun pointed at his chest. In a belligerent tone he ordered him to mount up.

Angry tears stung her eyes as she ran forward. "What's going on here?"

"Army business."

"Let him go, Drew."

He hooted in derision. "What's you're interest in the squaw man?" Then his eyes suddenly stilled. "I hope your pa's not in on this."

Nelda's face blanched. Her stomach knotted and her mouth went ash dry. "Papa hasn't done anything wrong."

"Well Fred has." His eyes were hard. "He's been trying to convince the Indians to join the wrong army."

Her mind whirled. Fred's wife was Chickasaw. His recent travels must have included a visit with his family—and perhaps some recruiting for the Union.

"After a trial in Little Rock, he'll hang." He turned away.

She grabbed his arm. "Drew, don't—"

He lowered his voice, "Nelda, if you know what's good for you, you'll stay out of this."

Taking advantage of the distraction, Fred spurred the horse. It leaped. He tumbled, but somehow managed to stay in the saddle. The startled soldiers charged after him.

"Hurry, Fred!" she whispered. Her fists clinched. If only she had a gun!

Drew raised the pistol. Nelda hurled herself forward. Grabbing his arm, she clawed at his face and eyes and hair. When he shoved her back she sprang again. He knocked her to the ground. She did not see when he fired. But she jerked from the explosion.

He should have missed. There were soldiers in the way. The horse was running and Fred was weaving. But Drew did not miss. Fred jerked and then flopped from the saddle. A foot hung in the stirrup as he hit the dirt. Dragged by the bolting animal, his body flopped and twisted. Blood wet the handsome wavy hair and dripped onto the ground.

Nelda started to rise. Then she sank back down, her eyes wide with horror. *"Fred… oh, Fred!"* She was uncertain if she spoke aloud or if her heart screamed in silence.

The horse did not get far. A mounted soldier grabbed the dangling reins. Another piled off and lifted Fred's foot from the stirrup. Drew's face paled and his hand shook when he lowered it. In spite of squeezing shut her eyes, she could still see the limp, blood-soaked body on the ground. For the first time in her life she felt scalding, red-hot hatred. She felt no better when Drew turned away and retched, throwing up and splattering on his shiny new boots.

After wiping his mouth on a handkerchief, and without raising his eyes, he mumbled,

"Peters, take this lady home. She lives right down the road, beyond the church."

The young private took her elbow and raised her from the ground. She followed where he steered, but as long as possible, her grief-stricken eyes stayed on the crumpled heap on the ground.

Fred Reynolds was buried without ceremony, simply tossed into a hole at Oakland Cemetery like so much refuse and covered with dirt, the only dirge a mournful wind twisting brown leaves clinging to tall oaks near the grave. Nelda stood beside the grave, dry-eyed but bereft. He would never know how passionately she had loved him. It passed through her tortured thoughts to feel sorry for his wife. The woman did not even know her husband was dead.

She returned from the burial and hurried to the sanctity of her bedroom and sat tiredly on the bed. A beautiful leather-bound Bible lay on the dressing table. She had been pleased when Papa gave it last Christmas. Now she stared at the book with cold eyes.

Day after dreary day passed. Her eyes became dark caverns for she slept little. Although she had telegraphed the sad news to Papa, there had been no reply. She tried to believe he was hurrying homeward. But as the days became a week, she had to admit otherwise. Something was wrong.

Louise grew thin and nervous. Restless as butterflies, her hands were always plucking at something. She avowed that Fred had been the last friend they had in town and now that he was gone there was no one to turn to, no one to ask for help.

Nelda agonized. But she could not pray. Finally she decided to send Papa another telegram.

The day was crisp and pungent with fall. She was too anxious to enjoy the mild weather. The streets were empty, the courthouse quiet. Once inside she encountered no one except the telegrapher in the dim office.

"No, Miss Nelda, the troops all left, pulled out last week." John Gallaher, a short, balding old man studied her with quizzical eyes. "Like I told you last time, I have to get permission from the army before sending telegrams for civilians."

She spread her hands beseechingly. "Mr. Gallaher, you fought alongside Papa in Mexico. You know he's a good man." She waited and let the remembrance sink in. "Something is wrong. We haven't heard from him in ages."

He pursed his lips and then shrugged. "I reckon what the army don't know won't hurt 'em."

"Oh, thank you." She breathed a relieved sigh as he tapped out the message to Mr. Danley in care of the *Gazette*. Palms sweaty, she paid the fee and thanked him again.

Not anxious to return to the dreary house, she walked slowly. The sun momentarily peeped through gray clouds and turned foliage into blazing glory. But with her heart as dead as winter, the brightness seemed a mockery.

It was three long, anxious days of waiting before the reply came. Her hands trembled as she took the envelope from the Hadley boy. Barefooted and bareheaded, he stood on the front porch in no hurry to leave.

He's smirking, she thought. *He knows what's inside*. She paid him and shut the door. For a moment she closed her eyes and held the telegram to her breast. Then she went in search of Louise. She was in her bedroom staring out the window.

"Mama, it's a telegram."

Louise paled. She dropped into the chair at the dressing table. After a long moment, she reached a thin, blue-veined hand to take the missive. Nelda stood and looked over her shoulder as she opened it.

The black words jumped off the paper.

"Just returned town. Phillip jailed. Treason. Hope to aid release. C.C."

Louise moaned and sank into a crumpled heap. Blood drained from Nelda's head and spots danced before her eyes. Determined not to faint, she grabbed the back of the chair. Someone had to help Mama.

They made hasty preparation to rush to Little Rock. Tom was readying the buggy to take them to the dock to catch the next steamer when a letter from Phillip arrived.

"Dear Ones," he wrote, *"I hope you have not been overly worried by my failure to write. I am hale and hearty and optimistic that I shall soon be released. I am charged (without proof) of being involved in a secret union known as the Peace Society, an organization that poses a threat to the present government. Rector fears the group worse than he fears Yankee bullets. He has issued orders for all suspects across the state to be brought to Little Rock and tried for treason. Although there are many awaiting trial, I feel the charges against me will soon be dropped."*

Nelda realized he had not received her telegram about Fred. Under the circumstances it was probably just as well.

The letter went on. "*C.C. has just returned from Richmond and he was furious to find me jailed. He considers my arrest a personal vendetta against him. He and the governor do not get on, and he has made bold comments in the paper. In spite of his trouble with the governor, be assured that C.C. is a powerful man with good political connections.*

"I am certain I will be released soon and hope to come to you shortly. Please do not try to come here and do not worry.

"I must make this short as C. C. is here waiting to take this letter. I love you both and pray you are safe and well. Love Phillip"

Nelda was ecstatic. "He'll be fine now that Mr. Danley is back in Little Rock."

"I hope so," said Louise, doubt coloring her words. "Phillip always tries to put a good face on things to keep me from worrying—"

"Rector is too smart to try Papa without proof." Nelda's confidence wavered. Was there proof? Was he involved? Her stomach knotted.

Sleepless nights followed anxious days. When she did sleep her dreams were nightmares, filled with scenes of Fred, hands tied behind him, his lifeless foot dragging from a stirrup—or she saw Papa hanged, dangling from a noose. She had never seen a man hanged, but she had once seen Tom hang a hound for chasing chickens. It had gasped and flopped and struggled until he finally let it down. In her dreams Drew held the rope, laughing all the while, as Papa struggled like the hound. She awakened trembling, and in spite of the cold bedroom, soaked with sweat.

One morning in early November Tom stood at the back door. "Missy." His breath made a frosty cloud around his bare head. He twisted his hat in gnarled hands and looked shamefaced at the ground. "Lily's gone. So's the cow…and Marse Phillip's shotgun. I was asleep and never heared a thing. They never took nothing else. They never found the shoats in the pen. I done checked. It appears something spooked 'em off real quick. I found this here glove on the ground."

Nelda's heart had plunged to her knees. Lily! She had raised her from a colt and she loved the mare. If only she had awakened! She would have stopped them! Now she had no way to travel. And how would they manage without the cow? Now there would be no milk or butter.

"Don't fret, Tom. It wasn't your fault. If you had wakened they might have killed you."

He looked relieved and backed away. "I mighty sorry, missy. I know you done loved that mare."

She let out a deep breath. Yes, she would miss Lily dreadfully. She hoped the thieves would not abuse her.

A week later she still glanced toward the barnyard unconsciously searching for the mare. She felt the loss keenly. Today while drawing water from the well in the back yard her eyes roamed the pasture. Nothing but crows dotted the landscape.

"Lily, I hope you're all right," she whispered.

The pulley creaked as the bucket descended. When it splashed she pulled the chain, hand over hand, and raised it from the well and then tipped it into a pail.

She returned from the well, set down the brim-full pail of icy water, and for a moment warmed her hands at the stove. She added short sticks of oak to the small fire and carried more wood into the library. Since it took too much wood to keep the entire house warm, she had urged Louise to move into the small room at the back of the house, the winter kitchen. Louise had refused. She insisted they must maintain some semblance of dignity. Nelda compromised. While a small blaze burned in the library, the bedroom fireplaces remained cold. At night they climbed the stairs, shivering until hot bricks wrapped in thick cloths warmed the cold beds. Nelda dreaded December and the colder months ahead. And yet she had no longing for spring. There was nothing to look forward to.

Hearing a knock on the front door, she brushed bark from her skirt, picked up the revolver, and walked down the hall. She peeked out and laid the pistol on the hall table before throwing open the battered door.

"Uncle Ned!" She quickly hugged him.

When he smiled Nelda understood how cultured Aunt Becky had fallen in love with this dark-eyed mountain man.

Then Nelda hugged her cousin. Elijah, their grown son, was equally handsome. And he was smart as well as handsome. She gave him a radiant smile.

"Elijah, how you've grown!"

She turned back to Ned. "I thought you were away with the army."

"My company is home for the winter," he explained. He touched the busted door. "What in the world happened here?" When Louise appeared in the hall his eyes widened.

Nelda could imagine how awful she and Mama must look. Mama was tired and worn and had huge bags under her eyes. She knew she looked just as bad.

Elijah whispered, "I never saw your ma in a work apron."

"How do, Louise," greeted Ned.

Louise's greeting was cool, and yet Nelda was relieved. This time Mama did not cut Ned with angry eyes and a lashing tongue. Instead she ushered him down the long hall past portraits of stuffy-looking ancestors in wide gowns, tight britches, and high collars. She led on past the closed parlor door and into the dim, chill library where, in spite of the frigid air, only a gnat-smoke fire burned. The room smelled of old books and musty leather and the lingering odor of pipe tobacco held fast in long brocade drapes. While Elijah hunkered on the hearth, Louise pointed Ned to Phillip's chair.

She began to apologize, "We no longer use the parlor … " Her voice trailed away. But she still sat as stiff and formal as if she were on the velvet-covered parlor chairs.

"I suppose you heard that Phillip has been jailed?" she asked.

"What!" Ned was astonished. "Whatever for?"

"Treason. Of course it's ridiculous," said Louise. "Phillip went to Little Rock to do a favor for an old comrade from the Mexican War days. Mr. Danley is now editor of the *Gazett*e. When he was appointed to the new military board, he asked Phillip to fill in for him at the paper while he went to Richmond on business for the Confederacy." Louise continued, "But Phillip had barely arrived when he was accused of being part of an underground group trying to sabotage the new government. Governor Rector ordered arrests made all over the state." As she explained she drew forth Phillip's latest letter from her apron pocket. "No one who spoke out against secession is safe. Some of our *neighbors*," her voice grew snide, "even tried to burn us out. We're afraid to even answer the door these days."

"So that's what happened to the house," he said. "Well, where's the home guard? They're supposed to keep it safe around here."

"I have no idea," said Louise. "They certainly weren't in evidence the night we were vandalized."

His eyes thinned as he scanned the letter and then passed it to Elijah, who quickly read while the others talked.

Nelda had read the letter so many times she could quote it. "Since the governor and Mr. Danley are feuding," she explained, "Papa can't count on Mr. Danley for help."

Ned struck a balled fist into his palm. "Jailin' a good man like Phillip. The governor must be crazy."

"Papa says he is power crazy," she agreed, "but he's the one in the governor's chair and Papa's the one in jail. Uncle Ned, do you have any idea how we could get him out?"

He drew a deep breath. "Can't say as I do," he shook his head sadly. "I don't know about these kinds of things. But I'll think on it. In the mean time what needs doing around here?"

Louise sat even straighter. "We're managing very well, thank you."

"Oh Mama!" Nelda shot out. *"You know we very well are not!"* She turned to Ned. "Our girl Della ran off. And the army killed the only friend we had left in town. Shot him right at the courthouse." For a moment she put a hand over her trembling mouth and swallowed tears before going on. "Tom is too old to do anything except feed the chickens. He used to milk the cow but a few nights ago some men came and stole her." She bit her lip. "And they rode off with my mare. Tom didn't stop them—even though I had given him Papa's shotgun. They took that, too." She sat up straighter, swallowed, and wiped her eyes with the back of her hand. "Thankfully they didn't get the hogs. Tom hid them down in the woods by the river."

"Damned bushwhackers!" he muttered, shaking his head. Then he stood. "Are them hogs big enough to butcher?" he asked.

"Yes," said Nelda, "and we need help with that."

"No time like the present," he said. "I reckon it's cold enough to fly in and do it right now. Louise, is that all right by you?"

She gave a stiff, curt nod.

"I don't suppose you know how to handle pork?" he asked, "Make sausage, lard, and such?"

Her eyes flashed. "In spite of what you think of me, Ned Loring, I do know how to work," she spit out. "I can do all of those things."

He took a step back. "No offence intended, Louise. I just knowed you was used to servants and such—"

Louise rose and came forward. Nelda's eyes widened when she took Ned's hand. "Forgive me. I had no right to snap. It is very kind of you to offer help. We do need it." With an unsteady hand she rubbed her head. "Confession is good for the soul, Ned." She glanced at Nelda. "I fear my pride is being laid in the dust. And I richly deserve it."

Wind moaned around the house. A tree limb swayed, tapping the window like nervous fingers.

Louise pursed her lips. She breathed deeply before adding, "When Phillip met me I was visiting Ma's wealthy kin in Forth Worth." She looked at Ned. "But when we married Phillip took me away from a one-room soddy on the banks of the Red River. My pa was a drunk. He never owned a pot to piss in or a window to throw it out."

Nelda stared transfixed. What was Mama talking about? Why, she was from a wealthy family who had given her two slaves on her wedding day—old Tom and his wife, Rose… Nelda pulled her shocked mind back to hear what Mama was saying.

"My mother died a year later when Becky was born. Tap had run off from home when he was fourteen. He only came home occasionally. There was no one to care for the baby. I took her… heaven knows Pa didn't care. And Phillip loved Becky like our own." With face paled, she went on, "Phillip came from a wealthy family." She faced Nelda. "The portraits in the hall are your papa's family—not mine like I always claimed." She bit her lip and her eyes filled. "I'm sorry, Nelda."

Louise lifted a dainty handkerchief with trembling hands. She dabbed her eyes and then looked at Ned. "They disapproved of our marriage, but I've been far more unkind to you than they ever were to me. Will you forgive me?"

Ned nodded. He worried the hat in his hands. "We've all got our faults, Louise. I don't reckon yours is any worse than mine."

Looking relieved, she said, "Becky has no idea. I created a make believe past for her. When Phillip got the opportunity to move here, I was overjoyed. Publishing a newspaper had always been his dream. And I wanted a new start far away from anyone who knew my past." She gave a dry laugh. "Pride goeth before a fall. And God is certainly punishing me now." She closed her eyes. "Sweet Phillip. He sympathized and let me go on in my folly."

She suddenly rubbed her head. "Yes, it is a good day for butchering."

Ned cleared his throat, looking uncomfortable. Then he nodded. "We'll get the hams and such salted down today. I'll come back in a few days to help Tom start the smoking. By then the meat will have took on enough salt and be ready to hang." He smiled at Nelda. "Get the knives ready. Won't be long before we'll have sausage to grind."

She gave a wooden nod and sank down into Phillip's big chair. Dazed thoughts chased through her mind. All her life she had been tutored in the behavior of an aristocrat. Her very character had been molded by the ghosts of Mama's regal ancestors peering down from the Copley portraits, disapproving of every flaw, every slip in decorum. It was inconceivable that Mama's family had been little better than white trash!

Nelda and Louise were busy gathering up knives and cutting boards when Elijah came inside.

"Pa told me to fetch some coals so we can get a fire going under the wash pot."

"There's also a large kettle of water heating on the stove," said Nelda. "After you get the fire going outside, I'll bring it out to add to the pot."

As soon as the kettle boiled she carried it outside and through the back gate. The air was bitter with the hint of snow in low gray clouds. Bare trees edging the pasture were black and stark against the sky. Beyond the back fence the short-legged wash pot sat over a blaze. Her eyes squinted against smoke. With care, she held her skirt back and poured in the steaming water. The fire gave off welcome heat.

Elijah fed sticks into the flames. "Getting this lye water right is the tricky part," he said. "Too hot will set the hair. Then it's might nigh impossible to scrape. But if it's not hot enough the hair won't slip a'tall. Pa is a good hand at butchering. He knows exactly the right temperature."

A shot rang out, soon followed by another.

"Pa's already killed both hogs. I wish there were some more pine knots to hurry this fire along," worried Elijah. "Nothing burns hot quicker. I hope you have plenty of gunnysacks."

"There should be plenty in the barn," she said.

Just then a wagon rounded the barn. Ned drove and Tom walked alongside. He whoa-ed the mules and stopped the wagon near the fire. Two large white hogs lay on the bed, heads lolling with a bloody gash in each throat.

Elijah looked at her. "Reckon you better go inside?" He grew uncomfortable. "I mean, Ma never helps with this part and I just figured you'd rather not."

As she got a whiff of hog and hot blood, her brows rose. "You're probably right. But I'd like to watch. I've never seen it done, and I'm curious."

Elijah ran to the barn and came back with an armful of burlap sacks. Ned placed some on both hogs.

"I'll scrape this one," he said. "Tom, you and Elijah can work on that one." As he talked he quickly raked a finger into the hot water. Satisfied with the temperature he dipped a pan full and poured it over a section of one hog. Then he wet an equal portion of the other animal. The wet sack held in the heat until the hair loosened. Ned tested the spot by giving the hair a jerk. When it began to slip, he removed the sacks and went quickly to work. He held the knife at each end and used the blade as a scraper. Without cutting the skin it rolled the hair off. Elijah and Tom did the same.

Each man worked on a different area, again and again, scraping a knife across the steaming flesh. As hair peeled off they occasionally stopped to wipe the gore onto a gunnysack. When one portion was done, Ned repeated the process in a new spot.

Nelda was fascinated. Papa was right. There was a skill required to do anything well. Obviously Uncle Ned was proficient at butchering.

"Looks like I'm just in time!"

She whirled. It was Allen. This time he drove a wagon pulled by two red mules.

He whoa-ed them and stepped down. "I can smell fresh sausage a mile away."

"Howdy Matthers," called Ned. "You're a sight for sore eyes. Sausage ain't quite ready yet, but more hands make the work light. What you up to?"

"Making a little delivery to the camp for Pa."

Ned grinned. "Red doing a little business with the army, is he?"

"Not the entire army. But there's a few gents with discriminating taste." Allen tipped his hat. "Howdy, Nelda."

She nodded. She had not seen him since the dance. It seemed a lifetime ago. The memory made her self-conscious.

Allen climbed down and approached the men. "Here let me help." He held the hog's hind legs steady while Ned forced a strong stick through the gambrels.

"Nelda Jean!" Louise called from the doorway. She frowned and shook her head when Nelda came inside. "You ought not be out there," she scolded.

Nelda shrugged and continued watching from the window. Allen had thrown back his head in a hearty laugh. She wondered what had tickled him.

When Ned threw a rope over a strong limb in the nearby oak tree,

Allen stepped over and tied it to the gambrel stick. As Ned started to hitch the other end to the mule, Allen shook his head. His loud voice carried even through the closed window.

"Hell, Ned. It'll take ten times longer hitching that mule. I'll hoist the thing."

She saw Ned smile but could not hear the reply. Soon, however, both he and Allen pulled the rope and the hog dangled in the air.

"Nelda, come look in the bottom cabinet for my big enamel bowl. It kills my knees to squat down. And then fetch some coffee beans. We need to have a big pot of coffee for the men."

"Yes, Mama."

The next time Nelda looked out, Ned was splitting the hog down the belly. As gray entrails spilled into the washtub, she turned away, glad to have heeded Elijah's suggestion.

The butchering progressed rapidly. Before long Elijah was bringing in firm white slabs of leaf lard to be cut for rendering and scrap meat and fat to be ground into sausage. As Louise cut scraps of fat and lean into a long strips, Nelda fed them into the hopper and turned the crank on the large mill clamped to the table.

With the back of one greasy hand, she pushed a stray lock of hair from her forehead. When the pile of ground pork grew tall in the bowl, she dumped it into a large gray crock sitting on the floor. "I wonder where Della is. I wish she were here."

Louise snorted. "She probably wishes that more than you. She won't find anyone else who'll treat her so well." She suddenly stopped mixing and faced Nelda. "I guess you think I'm awful—or crazy—for carrying on such a deception all these years." Her lips trembled. "You can never know the shame I felt—the longing. Oh, not to be rich. The poverty wasn't pleasant; but it was the degradation, the humiliation." She paused. "Pa was a loud drunk. I was the drunkard's daughter, the one people wouldn't let their children play with." She bit her lip. "I swore that would never, never happen to Becky—or to you." She gave a hollow laugh. "Isn't it ironic how I changed from persecuted to persecutor. It's a wonder Ned will even speak to me."

Nelda stopped turning the crank. "I don't think you're awful—"

Before she could say more Louise interrupted.

"Enough said. Thank God I grew plenty of sage and red pepper last year. I doubt Emmitt has a bit left in the store," she said as she bent over the crock and added sage and then used her hands to kneed it into the ground meat.

Nelda regretted the moment of intimacy had passed so quickly. Mama rarely let her inside the high walls.

Louise scooped meat into a ball and began to flatten it in her palm. "I'll fry a patty of this and test the flavor. I usually don't add enough salt."

She fried one and soon the succulent aroma of fried pork filled the kitchen, almost overpowering the hearty smell of strong coffee and baking bread. Satisfied with the taste, she made more patties. She had just removed a pan of biscuits from the oven when the back door opened.

Elijah poked in his head. "Sausage and biscuits. Nothing on earth smells better."

"Tell the others to come inside and warm a bit and have some food and a cup of coffee," Louise ordered.

"Yes 'um." He grinned. "And I doubt I'll have to tell them twice."

The men filed in, letting in a blast of cold air and expressing loud appreciation for the wonderful smells. They washed in a basin and dried hands and faces on the towel hanging nearby. Filled with broad shoulders, the kitchen seemed to shrink.

Tom remained outside until Louise insisted he come inside. "We won't stand on ceremony today, Tom. We'll all sit in here."

Even then, he refused to sit, but hunkered near the stove looking uncomfortable to be eating in their presence.

Nelda handed Allen his coffee. As their eyes met, she was startled anew at the color, deep blue as bright as the sky. He smelled of cold air and wood smoke and the faintest hint of whiskey.

The food quickly disappeared. When the last drop of coffee was drained from his cup, Ned looked at his pocket watch, frowned, and stood.

"We better get back to work. It's getting late. Becky will worry."

Allen stood.

"Why don't you and Lige get on home? I was planning to stay the night in town anyway. Tom and I will finish up salting everything down and cleaning up."

"You sure?" Ned looked relieved at Allen's nod. "I really appreciate it. Even if we hurry along, we won't get home before dark." He put on his hat. "Tom, I'll be back in a few days to help start the smoking." He shook Allen's hand and then stopped near Louise.

She stood. Her eyes filled. "Ned, there's no words—"

"There now. You'd have done the same for me."

"You're a good man. My sister is a fortunate woman."

When Louise gave him a quick hug, Nelda's mouth dropped open.

She quickly shut it after noticing that Allen studied her over the rim of his cup. As he took a sip of coffee his eyes were smiling.

For the rest of the afternoon she barely had time to glance out the window. Occasionally, when she did, she saw him still busy at the task.

Mid-afternoon Louise dropped into a chair and gripped her forehead. Her face was ash gray. "I'm sorry but I have to lie down."

Nelda looked up from a steaming skillet of sausage. "Of course. I should have noticed you were overdoing. Don't worry. I'll finish this."

"Be sure to double fry each piece in two different pans before you put it into the crock. Then make sure it all gets covered with grease from the last pan. Grease from the first pan always has too much moisture and that spoils the sausage. But don't try to finish everything today. It's too much. Have Tom set anything left in the cellar. It will be cold enough there to keep for a week. We'll render the lard later."

She had just left the room when Allen came inside carrying a large bowl of meat scraps. He set it on the table and then washed his hands.

"That's the last of it. We finished trimming up the bacon, hams, and shoulders and got everything in the salt."

"Thank you so much." Nelda stood and stretched to ease the crimp between her shoulders.

"Looks as if you could use some help." He hung his coat on a chair back and grabbed the crank.

"Gracious. You don't have to do that. What doesn't get done today will keep until tomorrow."

"Maybe I enjoy the company."

She turned back to the stove and smiled. "In that case, if you'll stay for supper, I'll fry tenderloin."

"Ummm," he said. "If the good Lord made anything better, he kept it for himself."

The mill creaked as the handle turned. "Are you going to render outside?" he asked. "I know most folks do to keep from smelling up the house. But ma says almost as many women have died from catching their skirts afire as have died from having babies. It's a heap safer to use the stove."

"I probably will. It would certainly be better than standing outside in the cold."

She wished he wouldn't stare. She knew she looked a fright in the greasy, bloody apron. And her hands were too greasy to tuck the hair straggles back into the drooping knot.

Then he looked down and began cranking again. He chuckled. "Mary Beth would starve before she'd get her hands greasy."

Her brows rose. He was right. She supposed if Allen ever did win Mary Beth, he would have to do the butchering all by himself.

Two weeks later, on the third of December, the first snow fell. Nelda, sipping a cup of steaming coffee, stood at the kitchen window and watched it swirl down, soft and white and pure, changing the ragged ground into a thing of beauty. Pastor Wheeling had often preached about salvation making black hearts whiter than snow. So far she had seen little evidence of it. Brother killing brother. Neighbor hating neighbor.

She glanced overhead and sighed when Louise rang a bell. Today she had not even bothered getting up, and it was long past noon. The headaches seemed to consume her. Even Granny's herbs were no help.

"Nelda Jean," the querulous call drifted down. "Brew some fresh coffee—and make it strong. This is cold and tasteless."

"Coming Mama," she called, trying not to resent the intrusion. She would have to climb the stairs to get more coffee beans. Ever since the thieves had struck, Mama had insisted they hide the precious beans under her bed. And lately there had been looting over on Piney Creek. Mama was more fearful of losing the coffee than the meat in the smokehouse. Just then a knock on the front door stopped her halfway up the stairs. No one had come since Ned's last visit. That had been days ago. Before traversing the long, cold hall Nelda got the pistol.

Opal Loring stood on the doorstep, holding a tattered cloak tightly closed at the throat. She wore men's heavy brogans on her feet, the kind Tom wore. Nelda opened the door and drew Opal inside while hoping no one had seen her.

"Mrs. Loring, what's wrong?"

The woman was white and shaking. "They got Jim," she panted. "He's locked up at the courthouse. I'm afeared they're gonna hang him or shoot him like they done Fred. They say he's a traitor."

"Oh, I'm so sorry," said Nelda. And she was. But why had Opal come here? Didn't she realize it would only bring suspicion on this house?

Louise, dressed in a woolen wrapper and slippers, came haltingly down the steps. "What's wrong?" she called.

Nelda looked back to see her gripping the banister with one hand, and in the other, the heavy metal poker from the bedroom fireplace. *That's good*, she thought. "*Mama is learning to be on guard every minute.*"

Opal stepped forward. "You got to help, Miz Horton." Her plea rushed through thin white lips. "Soldiers got my Jim. Now he's locked up at the courthouse."

Louise blinked. "What could I possibly—"

"Yore man, he could do something."

"Phillip is in jail himself, at Little Rock," said Louise, indignant.

Opal's face fell. "Jim said to get him word..." She floundered. As hope dimmed, her eyes grew more desperate. "Maybe he could get word to someone or something—I don't know. Jim said to tell him. I'm awful scared," she finished lamely.

Louise came forward, her chin lifted. "Your husband is mistaken. Phillip could do nothing. Nor would he. If your husband is innocent, then surely the authorities will let him go."

Nelda's eyebrows rose. That was not true. Not in these times. Her thoughts were a whirlwind. First Fred and now Jim. *Why had Jim sent word to Papa*? What possible connection could there be between Jim Loring and Papa? Her knees felt weak.

Opal twisted the cape tighter. "Won't you please jest get him word... a telegram. I kin pay." She drew a folded bill from a pocket and tried to press it into Louise's hand.

Louise drew back. "Please leave. And don't come back. We can't help you." Then she wheeled and returned to the stairs.

Nelda's eyes followed her. This was not disdain—Mama was afraid. Did she know more about this? Nelda bit her lip and then turned to deal with the tearful woman.

"Mrs. Loring, I'm sorry. But Mama is right. I don't think Papa can help at all. He can't even get himself out of jail." Then she asked, "Did Mr. Loring say anything else? About Papa, I mean?"

Opal's eyes hardened. "Jest that he was a friend."

Nelda felt faint. Proof of treason against Papa—that was what the Rebels wanted. Could Jim Loring supply that proof? Would he?

"Mrs. Loring," she quickly said, "I'll do all I can to get word to Papa. If he can, I know he'll help. But as Mama said, his political connections are at odds with the governor just now, so I don't think he can do much for Mr. Loring."

Opal put the money forward again, but the way her gaze hung on the bill, Nelda suspected it was the proverbial widow's mite. "No, you keep it," she said, folding the woman's work-worn hand over the money. When Opal's jaw tightened she quickly added, "Use it for the children."

Opal withdrew the trembling hand. "Well, I thank ya. And thank ya fer trying to help. You ain't cut from the same bolt of cloth as yer ma," she said and turned on her heel and left.

A shiver traced Nelda's spine. She searched the street. There was no one else in sight. Why did she feel as if someone were staring? She quickly closed the door and once again peeped through the window. Heart pounding, she leaned against the closed door. *Papa! Oh Papa! What have you done?*

She dreaded going to the courthouse. But it must be done. Papa needed warning. If only Mr. Gallaher would break the rules again! Without a word to Louise she scurried from the house, and hastened toward town through a cold drizzle mixed with sleet and an occasional snowflake. As the wind picked up, sleet pelted harder. Icy wind cut through the cape and whipped sleet into her face. She avoided the worst puddles, trying to keep her boots dry, while she formulated what to put in the wire. It would have to go through Mr. Danley, so it must not arouse suspicion.

"Jim in court. Advise action." Yes, she decided, that would do.

Except for a few horses tied at the courthouse, the streets were empty. Before the war Clarksville had been a thriving town. Now, it was a strange haunting place, a dead town. Most of the merchants had closed shops to join the army. Others had run out of merchandise, much of it confiscated by the Confederacy. As she passed the empty store windows they stared like enemy eyes. The fanciful thought made her shiver.

She was relieved to arrive at the courthouse and scurry inside out of the gale. She turned a corner and almost collided with Drew Morrison.

Rage filled her, red-hot and consuming. Blood pounded in her head, burning her ears.

Three day's growth of blond beard roughened his face. The fine uniform was mud-spattered and wrinkled. His eyes narrowed in suspicion.

"Are you here to see Jim Loring?"

"No," she quickly denied.

"I don't trust you—"

"How dare you speak to me about trust, Drew Morrison. After trying to burn us out, I can't believe you have the gall to even speak to me," she shot out.

"I think your pa is involved in this," he said. "Some enemies of the South aren't carrying guns but they need shooting just the same." After walking away, he turned back. "I'm on my way to Little Rock. Care to send him a message?"

Fear drained the anger from her face. How she hated him! How she hated the whole rebel Confederacy! She hurried away but his threat haunted.

Mr. Gallaher hesitantly agreed, and frowning, he tapped out the message. Nelda paid him extra to deliver any return message as soon as it arrived, day or night, and then she hurried home through the storm to wait.

That evening in fading twilight Opal Loring stood on the front porch. Snow coated the steps, marred only by her brogans. Nelda opened the door, foreboding strong upon her.

"Mrs. Loring, won't you come—"

"No. I know yer ma said fer me not to come no more. But Jim said to warn you," Opal interrupted. "They're tryin' to get him to name your pa, to say he was part of some secret bunch that they say Jim and Fred belonged to." This time neither fear nor beseeching colored her flat voice. "When no one else was around, Drew Morrison told Jim it would go easier on him if he'd name other traitors—including your pa. Otherwise he says he'll hang for sure."

"Oh, no!" cried Nelda.

"Jim is already hurt bad. When he wouldn't talk, they beat him." She went on, "One of my boys was hid in the bushes a'trying to talk to his pa through the winder. He seen the whole thing."

"Oh, please come inside out of the wet," urged Nelda.

Opal shook her head. "I got to get home to the young'uns. I got six of 'em at home to raise by myself." She did not acknowledge that Louise had joined Nelda in the frigid hallway. For a moment she gazed into the gathering night and bit her lip before going on. "I don't know if Jim belonged to no such group..." She drew her mind back from where it had gone wandering. "He don't aim to talk. But they could hang yer pa."

Louise, groaning, sank into the entryway chair and buried her face in her hands. Opal's face was stone. Nelda put a hand on her arm as she turned away.

"Mrs. Loring, I am so sorry. I truly am." She bit her lip. Is there anything we can do for you? Please, I mean it. Is there anything?"

"Ain't nothing to be done," said Opal, "unless you know a way to get Jim away 'fore they kill him."

"Nelda give her some money," said Louise.

"I don't take handouts," she said, drawing up tall.

When Opal's face hardened, Nelda rushed on, "With your husband in jail you must have expenses, things you need—"

"We'll manage without no charity."

"You're being ridiculous, Mrs. Loring," insisted Louise. "Pride won't fill an empty stomach or put decent shoes on your feet."

Nelda cringed at the brusque, offensive tone and hastened to add, "It wouldn't be charity, Mrs. Loring. Mama and I want to—in some small way—repay Jim for his loyalty to Papa."

But Opal's jaw hardened even more, and with spine stiff, she turned away.

"Thank you for the warning," Nelda called after her. "We appreciate it so much."

She watched her trudge into the darkness, the oversized boots slapping up and down on her thin feet until snow and night swallowed her.

"I have to do something. Those Rebels won't stop—not until Papa is dead."

Louise's head jerked up. "Nelda Jean, don't you dare do anything foolish!"

Nelda silently argued, *"It is not foolish to help Jim Loring. Perhaps I can even save Papa's life in the process."*

The pistol was heavy—she had never noticed before just how heavy. Now the weight pulled against her waist where it was tucked into a belt under the long blue cloak. She had not slept. It would be a miracle this morning if her shaking hand could hold a steady aim. During the long night she had faced the fact that, if caught, she might hang.

Snow still fell thick and fast, obscuring bare trees and buildings. Except for her floundering steps, it lay deep and undisturbed until she neared the courthouse. There, wagon and horse tracks had churned the whiteness, sullying it down into muddy ruts.

Nothing stirred now. A deathly silence hung over the town. She stopped, facing the tall snow-coated courthouse. It stood cold and accusing before her, this symbol of law. She shrank, remembering how Papa had taught her respect for due process. But there was no true law now—only a mob of hotheaded rebels! If it became necessary to use the gun, would it be a sin to pray, to ask God to make her aim true?

Her mouth was dry. She wanted a drink of water. Then her stomach knotted. No, water would make her vomit. She felt for the pistol and found comfort in the awkward bulk of it as she started forward.

"Hey, Nelda."

She whirled. Allen Matthers rode up. And trailing on a rope wrapped around his saddle pommel was Lily! The mare saw Nelda and threw up her head and nickered.

"Lily! Where did you get Lily?"

He dismounted. "I was just on my way to your house. I found your horse when I was tracking some of my own stock that was stole.' With all the lootin' going on there's no telling who'll end up with what these days."

She gave a weak grin. "Thank you so much, Allen. I really appreciate it. I'll take her home just as soon as I finish my business here."

He stopped smiling. Giving her chalky face a quick perusal, he asked, "What's wrong?" Then he caught her arm as she sank down. "Are you sick?"

Warm bile rushed into her mouth. She bent and vomited.

He tried to help by pulling her cloak back. His brow knit when he saw the gun. "You all right now?" he asked as she stood and wiped her mouth.

"Yes," she shakily replied.

"How long you been sick? There was typhoid in the camps last fall, but I ain't heard of any this winter," he said with a frown. "Reckon you ate something bad?"

"Yes, it's probably something I ate. I feel better now," she said. "Don't let me keep you. I'll be fine." She had to free Jim Loring before it was too late. She had no idea how soon they would take him away.

He fell into step beside her. "With all the lawmen gone, this is no place for a lone woman. I see you have a gun. Still, don't go anywhere alone unless you have to. I'll stick around and make sure you get home safe," he offered. When, wide-eyed, she objected, he brushed the protest aside with a wave of his big hand. "Need to send a telegraph?" he guessed.

"No," she searched for an excuse, "I…I need to see if there's an answer to the one I sent yesterday." He opened the door and followed her inside. *How could she make him go away*? While she pushed back her hood, her eyes darted about for any sign of Drew.

Allen studied her face. " Nelda, what's going on?"

"Why, nothing…"

He pulled her aside. "You're shaking like a leaf. What's wrong?"

She studied him a moment and then drew a deep breath. "They brought in Jim Loring yesterday. They mean to hang him."

Allen looked grave. "I knew they were after him but I thought Jim was hid out in the Nation." .

"He may have been, but they captured him."

He chewed his jaw. "It galled Bo mighty bad when Jim got away from the army a while back."

Nelda went on, "Opal said they pistol-whipped him. Drew says he'll hang. He says Papa and Jim are part of some group plotting against the Confederacy."

Allen's eyes narrowed. "What are you up to?"

"I'm not up to anything—"

Abruptly she stopped. Opal Loring, wrapped in the tattered shawl and still wearing the brogans, sat on a bench. She was weeping silently. Large tears made rivulets down the seamed cheek. When Opal espied them she sprang up.

"Allen, they've took Jim to Little Rock to hang him. You got to stop 'em!"

He took Opal's arm and drew her farther away from an opened office door. He put a finger to his lips and shushed her as he looked warily about. No one was in sight.

"How long have they been gone and how many soldiers?"

"They hain't been gone long—just a few minutes. They was six of 'em counting Drew Morrison and his brother, that lieutenant who tried to arrest Jim awhile back." She looked up with a flicker of hope lighting the gray eyes. "But I seen how afeared that lieutenant was of you—that night at the party when you helped Jim get away. I know you kin stop him!"

Nelda shot Allen a look. So he had once helped Jim escape!

His brow furrowed. "Opal, go home. Get a pack of food ready and a blanket. And do you have a gun in case Jim needs it?"

"I do." Opal was already hurrying away.

While putting the hood up, Nelda edged toward the door. "I think I'll take Lily on home and feed her. I can come back later and check on the telegram," she stammered, "Poor Lily looks half-starved."

Allen frowned. He grasped her arm and pulled her out the door. "I saw something in your eyes just now... you got no intention of going home."

"There are six of them, Allen! I can't just sit here while you face them alone!"

"*Damn it, woman!*" As a soldier passed by Allen lowered his voice. He expelled a deep breath. "Don't be a fool."

"But they're determined to incriminate Papa. Drew already said he needed shooting. No, Allen. I can help—"

"You'd do more harm than good. I'd be having to look out for you instead of doing what needs doing."

Argument died on her tongue. Of course he was right. She recalled the altercation with Jess and meekly dropped her head.

He propelled her toward the street. "Take the mare and hide her before she gets stole' again. I'll see to it that your pappy ain't shot in his cell." He stood near as she mounted. "Don't try to follow, Nelda. It wouldn't faze some of them men to shoot a lady. Besides, I'll have help. I won't be facing them alone."

"Are you sure?"

"Yes."

She looked down into his solemn face. "You'll be careful?"

He grinned. "I was born careful." He patted Lily's neck. "You go straight home and stay there."

Leaning forward, she touched his shoulder. "Thank you, Allen—for everything."

With a puckered brow, she rode home slowly. She supposed Allen Matthers had saved her life again.

CHAPTER 5

"Allen!" She threw open the door. He filled the dark doorway. She let out a relieved breath. "Thank Goodness!" She motioned him inside and quickly shut the door. "All day I've been imagining you with a bullet in your head."

"No, I'm fine except for being froze half to death."

"Why! You're soaking wet!" She drew him into the kitchen.

"Fell off my horse into the creek."

She knew he was lying. "Sure you did. Those scrapes and bruises on your face and knuckles... I suppose your horse stepped on you." She pointed to the stove. "Here, stand by the stove. The fire's already banked but I'll stir it up and get a blaze going in no time."

He shivered and held out his hands to the still-warm firebox. She opened the damper, raked back ashes, and poked in a small pine knot and a handful of kindling. She blew on the coals and a tiny flame leaped and licked hungrily at the pine and soon spread to the oak sticks. She closed the firebox door and pulled a half-filled coffee pot onto one round stove eye.

"Hungry?"

When he nodded, she split open cold biscuits and then inserted pieces of fried ham left over from supper. He nodded his thanks as he took the food. He stuffed a bite into his mouth and chewed ravenously while she got a mug for coffee.

"Coffee's not hot, yet," she observed.

"It'll be fine." He took the cup and drained it before lowering the cup. "A body never knows how good food and fire are until they've been without."

She refilled his cup and got one for herself. "Tell me quick, what happened?"

Before answering he grinned and looked at her hands. She had not realized her fingers were tapping impatiently on the mug in her hand. She smiled. "Patience is not one of my virtues."

"Jim got away. And Drew won't be bothering your pa."

"You killed him."

His eyes stilled. "No, but I let him know I would if anything happened to your pa." Then he chuckled. "I'll be damned if you ain't disappointed."

"I want him punished for what he did to Fred." Her voice was harsh. She drew a deep breath to steady the turmoil in her breast.

He gave her a quizzical look. Then he said, "I figure sooner or later we all pay for what we do. But Drew ain't all bad—just weak. He tends to follow Bo's lead. And that usually ain't in a good direction."

"I thought you liked Bo."

Allen snorted. "Far from it. I used to think he was just wild. But I've learned he's got a mean streak. I doubt those others would have fired your house without him egging it on."

"I suppose you're right. When he was just a kid, he was mean to animals and kept the house slaves crying half the time." She took a sip of coffee and eyed him over the cup rim. "I don't suppose you're going to give me any details—such as how you bested six men and set Jim free."

His eyes danced. "Aw, Nelda, I don't recollect the details."

She set down the cup. "Will you tell me this much—do you know if my papa is part of some group that Jim and Fred Reynolds belonged to?"

He sobered. "Some things you're better off not knowing."

She stared. "Men on both sides of this war are risking their lives for what they believe in. I have a feeling you're one of them."

He shrugged. "My pappy says that as far back as he can recollect, the Matthers have never fought in any war. We're a rowdy lot, but we pretty much fight for ourselves and no one else. I intend staying out of this ruckus as much as possible."

"But you risked your life to help Jim."

"He's a good neighbor. I figure I might need to borrow a plowshare or a mule off him someday. I can't do that if he's dead, now can I?"

"Ha!" she scoffed. "You don't fool me one bit. But you're right. I probably don't need to know." She bit her lip. "I just hope there's no proof against Papa that will get him hung."

Allen stepped out of a puddle on the floor. "Reckon I've dripped all over your clean floor."

"Don't worry about that. But you do need dry clothes. There's nothing of Papa's that's big enough."

"If you don't mind, I'll sleep here by the fire for a bit and hang mine to dry on this chair here by the stove."

"Certainly. I'll get you some blankets and a pillow." She brought them from the linen closet and some towels for him to dry on. Without a doubt Allen was brawny and daring, but just now, looking wet and weary, he seemed almost vulnerable. His usually bold eyes were soft in the lamplight.

"Much obliged." He smiled. "I'll be gone before you wake up, so I reckon I'll say good-bye. Take care of yourself, Nelda."

She sensed this was more than a casual farewell. "You're going away, aren't you?"

His eyes dropped to the coffee cup. "For a while." He looked up.

She stared into his blue eyes. "Allen Matthers, you take care of yourself."

He smiled. "You can count on it." She was halfway up the stairs when he called, "Good night, pretty lady."

She chuckled and kept climbing.

In the morning when she came back down the stairs, the sun had not fully risen, but Allen was gone. He had mopped up the floor with the towels and hung them on a chair to dry. The blankets were neatly folded and stacked in the seat. She smiled. It appeared he had not inherited the unkempt ways of his kin. While gathering up the blankets, she paused. His smell still clung—not an unpleasant odor, she decided. Then she shook her head. Obviously she was suffering from isolation.

She cooked a pot of oatmeal and ate a bowlful sweetened with honey. Louise had developed the habit of sleeping late so Nelda did the morning housework and then she went out into the sunny, frosty morning. A dazzling blanket of white lay over everything, hiding the deadness of winter. In spite of the biting air it was good to be in sunshine. The boarded up house was depressing. As she drew near the wild plum thicket down near the creek, Lily nickered. She fed the mare a bucket of corn while ruminating on a plan birthed in the deep of night as she lay in bed studying the dark ceiling and thinking about Papa. She was convinced he and Jim and Fred had been involved in some clandestine group—and probably Allen too—in spite of his denial. They had risked their lives to further the Union cause while she had sat quietly twiddling her thumbs. She must do something or go mad!

Cold days crawled by with no news forthcoming. Biting wind howled around the tall house and crept under doorways and seeped in through the boarded-up windows. Nelda grew frustrated with the idleness. There were rumors of an upcoming push, but like animals gone to den, the army appeared to have burrowed in for the winter. Colonel Churchill's regiment was camped along the river near the Spadra bluffs. Hardly a night passed without her being awakened by the hilarity of drunken soldiers returning late to camp. And all too often, in daylight, army wagons drove slowly past with tarp-covered bodies. Disease was rampant in the camp.

For the first time in memory there were no Christmas festivities in Clarksville. Women and children remained inside behind closed doors, dreaming of better times, wishing and praying for the safe return of husbands, fathers, sons, and brothers. In the past there had been parties all season long, presents galore, and delicious food in abundance.

Her sad eyes roved the blackened parlor. She sighed and shook her head while remembering the gala there last Christmas Eve. Now the mantel was bare of candles and greenery. No cozy fire roared in the dark cavernous fireplace. No feast was spread on a gleaming sideboard.

In spite of the depressing sight she was grateful to still have plenty to eat. Food in town was getting scarce. And who could afford twenty dollars for a sack of salt! For some reason Mama had always preserved enough to feed an army. In light of the revelations of her past, Nelda suspected she had once known hunger.

She picked up the candelabra and pulled the door shut. Their only celebration on this bleak evening would be extra candles to brighten the library. Nelda nursed a terrible cold. Both she and Louise had passed the day in the library in front of a small fire, quietly reading. It was almost dusk when Louise looked up from re-reading Phillip's last letter.

"I think we should read the Christmas story," she said.

"I don't want to, Mama."

"It would please Phillip to know we kept up the tradition."

Nelda rose, lit the candles, and got the worn black Bible from Phillip's desk. She handed it to Louise.

"No daughter, my head hurts. You read it."

She found the place, Papa's favorite account in the book of Luke. "And it came to pass in those days that there went out a decree from Caesar Augustus ... "

Nelda swallowed the lump in her throat. Every Christmas, in front of a cheery fire, Papa had read the account of the birth of the Christ child. Was he all right tonight in his lonely cell? Was he ever coming home again? And where was Allen on this cold night? *On earth peace and goodwill toward men.* The present circumstances seemed a mockery of the Christmas promise.

In February, just when it seemed spring might be on the way, a storm swept Clarksville with sleet, snow, and freezing rain. When the storm abated Nelda went to town. Although she hated the cold stares and suspicious eyes, she went often, loitering long in the aisles of the store on the pretext of buying some small item, a spool of thread or some yarn or a bit of lace. She sought information—anything to help the Union cause. If she learned anything of import, she would catch a steamer at Spadra and carry the word to Papa. He would know whom to contact.

She often saw Mary Beth. Each time the beautiful girl turned her back and, without speaking, hurried away. With the exception of Enos Hadley, who was always cordial, even the old gray beards seated near the stove in Emmitt's store barely greeted her. In spite of the snubbing, she considered the trips necessary. Snatches of conversation always reached her attentive ears—their vociferous strategy always winning the war for the Confederacy. But some day there would be worthwhile news.

Today as she made her way to town, army freight wagons waited near the courthouse and troops loitered nearby. She spoke to a soldier, and in the guise of a reporter, asked for information.

"Alls I know is we been ordered to hurry up and head north, 'cause the whole blamed Yankee army is headed this way." He pointed to a man dressed in rugged, well-worn civilian clothes. "But that-there is a scout name of Curry. He ain't telling us nothing, but he might palaver with you."

Nelda thanked him and made her way over to Mr. Curry. However, he proved to be taciturn. "Mr. Curry, do you know how strong the invading force is?"

"You'll have to ask Lieutenant Morrison any more questions, ma'am. I'm just a scout. I might get in dutch if you print something I say."

So Bo is back, she thought. Keeping hatred from her face, she smiled and thanked him. By evening the troops were gone and she had learned nothing except the rumor of an invasion.

Louise remained unwell. It was a week before Nelda returned to town. As she stepped through the door of the mercantile, the men paid her no heed. Gill Harris held every eye.

He practically shouted, "Army had to conscript to fill our quota!

Hardly a man left in the county except for you old geezers." As an afterthought he stammered, "And a few of us planters who had to stay behind to farm."

Enos Hadley snorted.

Then a man with blazing eyes spoke up, "So they took young'uns so the likes of you and your boys could sit home by the fire!"

He was a short, barrel-chested, bow-legged man. Nelda recognized him. He was Granny Tanner's son, Caleb. He was married to Viola, the prune-faced woman she had met at Granny Tanner's cabin.

Gill grew red-faced. "My boy Tucker joined up! With him gone and with three hundred acres of rich bottom land to work, me and George got our work cut out for us, riding herd on all those lazy darkies."

Nelda stepped to the shelves scanty of canned goods and pretended to study the label on a can of beans in the light coming through a dingy window. She kept her eye on the agitated men.

"I'm shore Elijah will feel real sorry fer you while he's dodging bullets, Gill." Caleb said no more but his sour expression spoke volumes.

Elijah! Nelda's breath caught. She could hardly wait until the old man went out the door. She hurried after him. "Mr. Tanner," she called, stepping around an ice-crusted puddle.

He quickly removed an old black hat. "Howdy, Miss Nelda."

"Oh, please, tell me I misunderstood! Elijah didn't get conscripted, did he?"

"Shore did."

"Oh, no!" she cried.

Caleb was near tears. "Him and a neighbor young'un, Dillon Matthers."

"Allen's brother?"

"Yep, the very same. When not enough men volunteered," Caleb's voice grew snide, "that oldest whelp of Morrison's stole our young'uns! Roped and tied them boys and drug 'em off at gunpoint."

"This is outrageous! Can't someone stop them?"

"You bet I'd have stopped 'em!" Caleb shot out. Then his shoulders sagged and his hot eyes cooled to sorrow. "But I was gone to Dover. By the time I got back they was long-gone. I trailed 'em. They was too far ahead—done gone past Lewisburg. Allen would have gone after 'em but he had took out to Newton County—went after them bushwhackers that got you a while back. They sneaked back and took them horses again."

"Did he find them?" she quickly asked.

"Yep. Killed a couple of 'em. The others got away but he got the stock back."

She fervently hoped Heavy was among the casualties!

"Anyways, by the time Allen got home Dillon was done back. He had managed to run off. Elijah tried but he got caught." Caleb's jaw tightened. "Morrison shot one boy fer trying to run. I still don't know if poor Vernon's gonna live er die. His ear is swole up big as a basket."

"You said Bo did the conscripting?"

"Yep. And he's the very one shot Vernon. He's a real maggot. Wish he'd died instead of his pa."

"Bo's pa? *Robert Morrison is dead?*"

"Yep, so I just heared. Died a few days ago. According to Emmitt he had something wrong with his heart."

She was shocked. For an instant she recalled better days and her heart saddened. Papa would be sorry to hear of it. Of course he had no idea how the Morrisons had behaved lately. Nelda's brow furrowed. *So much for Robert's political plans!* She wondered if Louise and Mary Beth now regretted their actions.

Caleb drew a deep breath. "I'm just hoping Elijah can run off before a fight comes off. Feller at Lewisburg told me the whole army is on the move."

"I interviewed some of the troops. The scout I spoke with wouldn't give me any information. One soldier said they had been ordered north. Poor Elijah might have been tied up in one of the wagons! Did the man at Lewisburg know where the army is going?"

"Heading up to Missouri, I reckon." He looked back toward the store and scowled.

She placed a comforting hand on his arm. "Maybe Elijah will escape. He's a very bright boy."

"Yes, he is. But I reckon they'd likely track him down and shoot him."

With a shudder she silently agreed.

"Well, good day to ye Miz Nelda. I got to get on home."

She turned away and then suddenly remembered. "Oh, Mr. Tanner, would you please tell your mother that her herbs did the trick. My mother's leg is fine."

He nodded. "Ma will be real pleased to hear that." He turned to go and then stopped and looked back. "Did your ma get word that her brother came through on his way to the army? Him and the fellers traveling with him stopped at Becky's for a bit."

"No! When was that?"

"If I recollect right, hit was just about the time you come to see Ma. He said he stopped by yer place but weren't nobody home. He thought you all had left the country."

She walked slowly home. She was upset about Elijah. He was such a fine young man. He and his young sister, Deborah, were her only cousins—that is unless Uncle Tap had a family. Mama would be devastated to know he had been so close and yet she had missed him. She stopped in her tracks. Had Uncle Tap come the day she was at Granny's, the day Mama refused to answer a knock on the door? She decided not to mention the possibility to Mama. It would upset her.

She wondered how Mary Beth and Tabbatha were handling Robert's death. How impossible it seemed that she and Mama were not there to give comfort. But of course the Morrison women had plenty of rebel friends, she recalled, and her heart hardened.

The army was on the move. The first week in March the telegraph brought word of the Yankee invasion of Arkansas and a gruesome battle at a little place in the northwestern part of the state known as Pea Ridge. If not for concern for Elijah and Uncle Ned, Nelda would have been overjoyed at the news of the disastrous defeat of the Confederates. The new major general—sent by President Davis to outrank both Generals

Ben McCulloch and Sterling Price of Missouri—had failed miserably and General McCulloch had been killed. Now the earlier victory of Wilson's Creek was forgotten. The southern army, bruised and bloody and minus many in its ranks, fled south.

Each day for a week she made the short walk to the courthouse to stand alongside pale and worried women viewing the names of the dead and wounded. As the lists trickled in over the telegraph wire, day after day, she also anxiously perused them. Attitudes toward her began to change. Today a few women nodded as she drew near. Only Tabbatha Morrison kept an averted face and a stiff back.

Nora Garrison gave a timid smile. "Hello, Miss Nelda."

She smiled and nodded. "Nora."

"I just hate the waiting," said Nora to no one in particular. Several women nodded.

Tall, thin Emmeline Hill spoke up, "After Wilson's Creek, when I stood here for hours waiting for those cursed lists, I swore I'd never do this again. But I just can't stay away." Her husband, John, was colonel of the 16th Arkansas, Ned's regiment.

Nora nodded. "I know what you mean. My son George was at Wilson's Creek, too, and I said the same thing."

Although many local men had fallen at Wilson's Creek, Nelda had had no personal stake then. Now, as John Gallaher tacked up the new list, she held her breath and quickly scanned the L's. She let out a relieved breath. No Lorings! Neither Elijah's nor Ned's name was posted. Then she quickly scanned the B's. Once again relief flooded. Since many Texas troops were in the fray, Mama feared for Uncle Tap. But there was no Tap Brooks listed either.

"Oh! God! No!" Nora Garrison grabbed her mouth and then moaned and crumpled into a heap. Women rushed to lift her. Tabbatha Morrison ordered someone to fetch a cup of water.

Nelda studied the list. George Garrison was dead. She felt a stab of sorrow. He had been a fine young man. How Nora would grieve! George was her pride and joy—and her sole buffer against a drunken, abusive husband. Nelda fled the tragic scene. As wet March wind stung her face, she shook her head. *Poor Nora! This wretched hateful war!*

March stayed frigid. But with April only a day away, the air turned mild. Nelda stepped onto the back porch and breathed deeply. A hint of perfume drifted from the white-blossomed locus growing near the barnyard. A blue jay flew low and perched on a limb and tilted its head to give her a saucy look. She laughed. The sound shocked her. How long had it been since she had laughed? And sometimes now, a day would pass without thought of Fred.

Tom hobbled around the edge of the house holding a shovel. "Garden all turned. Shore was hard with jest a ol' shovel," he quarreled. He was disgruntled about not being allowed to harness Lily to the plow. But Nelda was taking no more risks. A month earlier she had relented and let him use the mare to plow a large patch for corn and potatoes. With the approach of warm weather and more traffic on the road, she had ordered the mare left in hiding. The vegetable garden was not too large to work by hand.

Suddenly they both looked north. Shouts and cheers drifted from town. She stuck her head inside the front door.

"Mama, I'm going to town. I'll be back soon," she called.

As she pulled off an apron, she looked at Tom. "I'll be back to help you plant the peas. Why don't you rest until I get back?"

"Humph!"—he shuffled away, grumbling —"wouldn't be tired out if you'd let me use Lily 'stood of this-here ol' shovel."

She tossed the apron inside and smoothed her hair. The brown dress was a work dress but neat enough for a quick trip into town to see what was going on.

Down the dusty road, she hurried, with a quick glance at overcast skies. They needed rain but she hoped it held off until she and Tom got the early garden planted. Upon nearing the courthouse, she slowed. Her eyes widened. The telegraphed reports had said the Confederate army was encamped at Frog Bayou near Fort Smith. But a long line of Confederate troops snaked down Main Street, heading east. She eyed the Rebels with contempt. She hoped Union forces were right behind!

No. These soldiers appeared in good spirits, waving and calling to the crowd gathered on the roadside. Dust clouded from tramping feet and caisson and wagon wheels. Anxious-faced women called questions about husbands, sons, and brothers.

Abruptly her venom stilled. Perhaps somewhere in this melee marched Uncle Ned and Elijah and even Uncle Tap. She hated their cause. But she could not find it in her heart to hate them. They were just misguided. If only she or Papa had taken the time months ago to talk with Uncle Ned, perhaps he would not have joined…

With a wave of hand, she halted an older man with a scarred face. His long hair was pulled back and tied with a piece of leather.

"Sir, do you know Ned or Elijah Loring?"

He shook his head. "Can't say as I do, little lady."

"What about a Texas man named Tap Brooks?"

"Nope. But that-there is a Texas battery up yonder. You might ask them."

"Oh, thank you so much." She hurried forward to repeat the question.

"No, ma'am." The soldier marching just behind a caisson pointed to a man on horseback. "But Captain Good might know him."

Nelda lifted her skirts a bit and ran. "Captain Good, sir," she called.

The dark-haired slender man turned in the saddle and then rode to the edge of the road. He waited while she caught up.

She was breathless. "Do you know a soldier named Tap Brooks?"

He smiled broadly. "Why, yes, I do."

"He's my Uncle. Is he with these troops?"

The captain, with eyebrows drawn together in thought, rubbed his chin. "No," he said slowly. "Brook's regiment went east with the regular Confederate troops." He brightened. "But he was fine after the battle at Pea Ridge. I saw him just before the retreat."

"That is good news. Mama will be glad. I don't suppose you know Ned Loring or his son Elijah? Ned is with the 16th Arkansas."

"No, ma'am. But I think the 16th is back there somewhere. I hope you find them. If I ever see Brooks again, I'll tell him I saw you. What's your name, miss?"

"Nelda Horton. And would you please tell him his sister Louise sends her love."

"I'll do that."

She called her thanks as he rode on. Then she stepped back to let a carriage rumble past. A rotund white-haired gentleman riding inside nodded to her.

"Howdy, General Price!" yelled a grinning soldier. "How's the arm?"

The large man lifted an arm held in a white sling. "Mending very well, thank you," he called as the carriage pulled to a stop at the courthouse.

Captain Good and another officer rode back, dismounted, and shook hands with the general.

So that was Sterling Price, former governor of Missouri. He looked nothing like a general. Without uniform or insignia, he was dressed as a gentleman planter.

Nelda looked back down the road. The line of tramping men seemed endless. It was hard to imagine their ranks had been drastically depleted in the recent battle—the latest estimate over two thousand dead. Finally she spoke to a man who knew Ned. He claimed Ned had been wounded and transported to Little Rock in a wagon train along with hundreds more of the injured. The soldier had never met Elijah. He said the army was heading toward the White River now.

Dejected, she slowly walked home. Uncle Ned was a very strong man. Hopefully he would recover. And hopefully Elijah was unharmed.

Spring work soon prevented frequent trips to town. Tiny curls of pale pea leaves poked through the plowed ground. Along with hardy potato and cabbage and onion plants, they withstood a late frost. Then, as whippoorwills returned and the danger of frost was past, Nelda and Tom planted the cornfield and the tomatoes, okra, green beans, cucumbers, and squash.

She had done little gardening in her life—that chore had been done mostly by Tom. Now that he was getting feeble, he needed help. It surprised her how much she enjoyed the job. She much preferred it to housework. Covered in a work apron and kneeling, she pulled a sprig of grass and threw it, roots up, into the balk. She smiled, enjoying cheery wren and cardinal calls while she breathed deep of honeysuckle growing on the back fence. As she rocked back on heels and dusted her gloved hands, she eyed feathery green tomato plants standing at attention down the straight row. Already she envisioned large, red, ripe delicious fruit weighing down the tender stems. She glanced at Tom coming down the balk. He gathered the wilting weeds and grass and put them into a basket.

"You need a new hat," she said while reaching to pull more grass. "That one is more holes than straw."

"Reckon I do. Della weren't no hand at hat-making. My Rose was." Although it had been years since her death, his face saddened.

"Well, I'll see if Emmitt has one left at the store."

He gave a toothless grin. "Thank you, missy." He lifted the basket again and drew abreast. "You is mighty good at growing things. This gwan'a be the best garden ever."

She chuckled. "Tom, you wouldn't flatter a girl, now would you?"

"Old Tom don't know—what does flatter mean?"

"Flattery means to say something nice to someone even if it's not true."

He drew up stiff, a scarecrow with wounded dignity. "Tom don't lie."

"Don't go sticking your jaw out at me. I was only teasing."

He took the basket to the fence and dumped it. When he returned he still grumbled. "Hain't nebber lied to Marse Phillip ner Miz Louise. Ain't gwan'a lie to you."

"Tom, of course I know you're honest. I'd trust you with my life, so quit sulking."

Although he still bore the trace of displeasure, his wrinkled face was no longer a thundercloud. She had to admit the garden did look well. The weather had been perfect. If that held true the harvest would be good. Unfortunately, weeds and grass also flourished. She spent countless hours pulling weeds and hoeing.

In May torrential rains drove her indoors. With furrowed brow, she watched through rivers washing down the library windows while the garden became a lake and the red tubular blossoms on a buckeye bush growing near the back fence hung down like tired, wet hands. After three days the downpour finally ceased. It would be days before the garden could be worked again.

Of necessity Nelda suffered through a huge pile of neglected ironing. Mama insisted on wrinkle-free sheets, starched doilies, and freshly-pressed yards of petticoats. It seemed ridiculous. No one came. They went nowhere. Yet Nelda did the chore without complaint. There was little enough comfort in Mama's life these days. She suffered terribly from the headaches.

When the ironing was done and put away, the ground was dry enough for hoeing the rows of corn, and at the same time the early beans were ready to pick. As other vegetables ripened, Nelda and Tom worked from dawn until dusk. Although Louise helped snap beans and hull peas, headaches often forced her to bed before the chore was half done. Nelda tried to keep the thought at bay, but she feared some morning to find her dead in bed.

One morning in early June, Nelda prepared to pickle beets. The small red globes were washed and ready to boil before she remembered there was no vinegar on hand. It was doubtful there would be any at the store. The shelves were almost bare. Since Emmitt kept the vinegar kegs in the back room, there might be some left. If there were any spices left, she intended to purchase them also.

The sun was bright and the sky cloudless. Passing wagons stirred the dust that settled in a fine powder on her dark blue dress. The few ladies out tending to errands carried parasols or wore wide-brimmed bonnets. Although Louise had always scolded, Nelda rarely bothered with them. She loved the sun. By summer's end, to Louise's chagrin, she was always brown.

The store was unusually crowded with men when Nelda arrived. Some had returned when enlistments expired; others, it was whispered, had deserted. She browsed the near-empty shelves while discretely listening. She wondered why a knot of angry men had gathered around Gill Harris.

"I don't care, Gill! Tain't right!" exclaimed Enos Hadley. "No gol-dern general has the right to tell me I can't go nowhere without yer say-so!"

Diminutive Gill, with thumbs hooked in pockets, puffed up like a fat toad. He rocked on his heels. "Well, Enos, it don't much matter what you think. That's the way it is. I'm the provost marshal now"—Gill's close set eyes grew hard—"and if I catch you travelin' without a pass, you'll be in deep trouble."

With burly arms crossed over an expansive chest, Red Matthers sat on a barrel. "Harris, how did you get to be such big pumpkins?"

Gill cleared his throat. "General Hindman is Ma's third cousin."

Red gave a slow, belittling grin.

Gill stiffened. "Matthers, you be watching your step! I aim to enforce the regulations about selling whiskey, too."

Red's eyebrows rose. "Do tell. Well, if I run onto any whiskey peddlers, I'll shore warn 'em."

As laughter erupted, Gill's naturally florid face darkened. Nelda grinned. Now she knew where Allen got his dry wit.

"Provost marshal! Bah! In this here war fer freedom, we've done traded one tyrant fer another!" Hot-eyed, Enos stomped from the store.

Nelda sobered. He was right. Gill Harris endowed with power was as palatable as a toothache. It was a shame the provost position was an appointment. Even among hotheaded Rebels, he could never have won an election. The conversation once again drew her attention.

"My boy Tucker said it was a sight to behold." Gill laughed. "Them Yankees was begging for mercy but they never got it. Reckon that will give that Yankee General Curtis a thought or two about tucking tail and heading back to Missouri."

Emmitt straightened from leaning on the counter. "You're wrong, Gill. That mess at Searcy hurt us—hacking prisoners to death won't do a thing but stir up hatred. Curtis will be determined to get even. If he takes any more live prisoners after this, I'll be surprised." He picked up a cloth and wiped the counter as he went on. "After Van Dorn took off to Tennessee, I thought Hindman was the right man for the job—now I'm not so sure. Burning our own crops and now these new regulations—"

Gill interrupted, "If he hadn't burned that cotton, Curtis would have taken it and shipped it north. Would that suit you?"

Emmitt slowly shook his head. "No, I reckon not."

Red stood. "Don't matter who burned it—Yankee or Confederate—them farmers' hard work went up in smoke. I don't hold with that—not by a long shot." He leveled a stare at Gill. "I'll drop 'ery man in his tracks who comes after my crops. And if that-there Morrison mutt ever goes up the mountain again to conscript my boy Dillon, he'll not be comin' back down."

Gill shrugged. "If you want to get hung, that's your business." Then he turned to Emmitt. "I almost fergot—I'm supposed to ask folks to write some letters. I want you to write one"—he looked around and pointed—"and you too, Thompson. The letters don't have to be to real people . . . just so you mention that a bunch of Texas troops with cannons passed through here, headin' to Little Rock to join up with Price. The general wants some letters to the make-believe Texicans too. That mail pouch is going to accidental-like get captured by Curtis. He'll think twice before attacking Little Rock if it's full of fresh troops with lots of cannons." Gill rocked back on his heels again. "Whether you like him or not, that cousin of Ma's is one smart feller."

Nelda, heart pounding, stepped back against the shelf. Would General Curtis fall for such a trick? He might. It was a shrewd plan unless his intelligence sources warned him otherwise. Red strode from the store and Nelda started to follow.

"I've got my eye on you, too, Nelda Horton!" Gill scowled at her as she passed the counter. "Apple doesn't fall far from the tree… I reckon I know where your loyalties lie."

You're right, she thought bitterly. *The apple doesn't fall far from the tree. Your sons are despicable bullies!* But there was no use antagonizing the little tyrant. Without answering, she left the store and hurried to catch up with Red.

"Mr. Matthers," she called.

He stopped and turned and a smile split his big face. "Well, howdy, Miss Nelda! How are you?"

"I'm fine. Mr. Matthers, do you know how to get in touch with Allen?" When his eyes began to twinkle, she supposed he presumed that she was—like a dozen other women—besotted with his big son.

"Ain't heared from him lately, but I might get him word. What you need?"

"Tell him I have an important message for him."

Red sobered. "I'll sure try to get him word."

"Thank you so much." She started down the sidewalk.

Red called after, "If yo're ever in our neck of the woods again, drop in."

She turned and smiled. "If I'm ever in your neck of the woods again, I will. And next time I'll have two guns handy!"

His laughter boomed. "Allen's right about you—yo're full of spice. That bushwhacking Jess Holder had better watch out."

She strode home deep in thought. It would be a shame if Hindman duped General Curtis. By all accounts the Rebel army was vulnerable just now. Curtis could take the city with little effort. That just might end the war! At least in Arkansas…

She stopped to let a wagon pass. Lost in thought she did not acknowledge when the man tipped his hat. Curtis was supposed to be less than fifty miles from Little Rock. If Allen did not come within the week, she would go herself! Tom would have to care for Mama.

He would howl and so would Mama, but this was crucial information. Someone must warn General Curtis! Pulling skirts back from the dusty road, she started home again.

The beets lay on the table. She had forgotten the vinegar. That was the least of her worries. She wondered if Red could find Allen.

Three days later, in the June twilight, he appeared on the back steps. He could move quietly for such a big man. Nelda was in the hallway but had not heard a thing until he softly spoke. A broad-brimmed hat shaded his face. He removed it and glanced cautiously behind before entering. A whippoorwill called in the purple dusk.

"Allen, it's good of you to come."

"Sorry I took so long. What's up?"

She drew a deep breath. "Come into the library. I don't want Mama to hear us. She's upstairs."

He followed her into the dim room full of heavy furniture and tall windows encased in dark green drapes. In spite of the scent of roses wafting through open windows, the mustiness of old books lingered. When she pointed to a tall-backed leather chair, he sat down. His solid frame sank, easy and comfortable, as he propped the hat on one knee. She perched nervously on the edge of her chair.

"I heard you had another run-in with the bushwhackers. Caleb said you killed two of them. I hope Heavy was one of the casualties?"

He let out a deep breath. "Sorry to say, he wasn't—nor Jess either. Heavy wasn't there when I jumped 'em. But I gave the rest of 'em a good dusting. Wounded Jess. I don't figure he'll show his face around here for a while." He flicked some dust from his hat. "But I don't reckon that's why you sent for me."

For a minute she searched for words. "If a person needed to get an important message to General Curtis, would you have any idea how to go about it?"

His brows lifted with curiosity. "I take it you're that person. What's the message?"

She hesitated. "I have to ask something first." She studied his intent face. "Allen, I've long suspected you're in that Peace Society, or at least actively pro-Union. I need to be certain. You can trust me. I'd never give you away."

He stared into the empty fireplace and then back at her. "I can't tell you anything." When hurt showed on her face, he hastened to add. "Nelda, folks are getting tortured. No one knows how strong they'd be."

"That road runs both directions. If I give you information, you'll hold my fate in your hands. How well would you endure torture?"

He was quiet for a long while. "I'll tell you this much, we're both fighting for what we believe in."

She eyed him curiously. "Most folks around here are avid Confederates. I'm not because of Papa and his political leanings. But what about you?"

He gave a wry grin. "Well, my pa sure ain't political." He leaned forward. "I reckon there's more Irish than just red hair that got passed down to me. Ma says I'm a regular Fenian, a throwback to one of her grandpappies from way back yonder, name of Allen O'Connell. He fought for King James at the Battle of Boyne. She used to tell me stories about him. Got me all fired up until I was ready to go whup the tar out of that Englisher, William."

Nelda chuckled. "Just like me and Papa's stories of my Great Grandpa Horton. He was from Massachusetts and fought under Putnam at Breed's Hill. I was ready to *whup the tar* out of General Gage."

"How is your pa?"

"I have no idea. We haven't heard in weeks." She let out a deep breath. "From what I'm hearing it looks as though Rector won't win the election. Everyone thinks Flanagan will. Maybe he'll release Papa."

"I hope so. I admire your pa. I admire any man willin' to fight for what he believes in."

"You still haven't told me what influenced your politics," she said.

She noticed how strong his neck was, how it filled the collar of the butternut shirt.

He chewed his jaw a moment before slowly saying, "I reckon you could say Jim Loring influenced me."

"*Jim Loring*?"

He nodded. "When I was just a kid, Pa was laid up for a while with a deep ax cut in his leg. Jim helped me make the crop that year"— Allen grinned—"and he helped me make some fine liquor." He grew serious. "When he found out I couldn't read, he taught me. My primer was William Blackstone's *Commentaries on the Law of England*."

Nelda smiled. "Odd choice for a Fenian."

"Reckon so." Allen chuckled. "But that's what Jim used. His grandpa had been a lawyer up in Indiana. His pa was studying on it, too, until he got into some kind of trouble and had to leave town one step ahead of the law. The old man sent him here to a friend living at Dover."

"So that's how a Loring ended up married to Granny Tanner's daughter," said Nelda. "I wondered about that." She shook her head. "Isn't it odd how our lives are constantly changed because of other people's choices." She went on, "Because James Loring's pa got into trouble with the law, you read Blackstone and became a proponent of the Union."

For a moment Allen's brows knit. He cleared his throat. "I got to say, it was good reading. As a rule I ain't high on the English, but Blackstone was smart." His blue eyes twinkled. "I ain't so sure he wasn't Irish. He knew the government and the law ought to be servants of the people instead of the other way around." He went on, "You might not think it, but I've done a lot of reading about governments and such."

"I know you're a thinker."

He fidgeted with the hat. "Well, I can't stay long."

She quickly told of the letter-writing plot and then asked, "Do you think you can warn Curtis?"

He shook his head. "You're too late. Curtis is long-gone—gone way too far to turn back now."

"How do you know?"

He gave her a steady look. "I know."

Her shoulders drooped. "I should have tried to go myself!"

"Don't you ever do anything so foolish!" His voice was harsh. "You've got no idea how awful things are out there." He pointed out the window. "I just came from the White River. I've seen the leavings of both armies—houses burned, crops destroyed. Why a man's life ain't worth a damn! And a lone woman . . . !" He groaned. "Promise me you won't ever try such a stunt!"

She was taken aback by the vehemence. "No. I won't promise any such thing."

His eyes grew angry. "I never took you for a fool."

"I'm not. Neither am I prone to making stupid promises."

He stood. "Then I reckon it's time for me to go."

She quickly rose. "Oh, Allen, don't be angry." She put a hand on his arm. "Please try to understand. I sit here day after day while Papa is languishing in jail. I've given this a lot of thought. You know as well as I do that both sides are using women spies. I think Mama is dying, and when she passes, I intend to offer my services."

"That's a dangerous fool notion."

"I suppose everything you're involved in is nice and safe and rational. I suppose you think I should just sit and wait and see how it all turns out." Her spine stiffened. "Well, I'm not cut from that bolt of cloth, Allen Matthers. If a noise scares me, I don't sit in a corner quaking. I go after it."

His stance softened. He grinned. "Don't I know it! And according to ol' Jess you bite pretty hard, too." He sobered. "I don't reckon there's any way I can talk you out of this?"

She shook her head.

"Well, at least"—he took her chin in his big fingers and tilted it—"send for me before you take off half-cocked."

Her breath caught making her voice sound unnatural to her own ears. "How would I get in touch with you?"

He thought for a moment. "Get word to Opal Loring. One of her boys can get word to Pa. I'll check in occasionally." He grinned, exposing even white teeth. "Maybe you and me can work together at spying—travel through enemy territory as man and wife or some such."

When her face blazed he chuckled and placed a friendly kiss on her forehead. Long after he had gone, she still felt his lips. She must be starved for friendship. Would he laugh if he knew the teasing peck had moved her?

Chapter 6

In the summer of 1862 the Union Army held the ground gained by victories at Fort Henry on the Tennessee River and at Fort Donelson on the Cumberland and a bloody victory at Shiloh. The almost bloodless capture of Corinth, however, was now considered barren. The wily Confederates, permitted to escape Corinth almost unscathed, were still wreaking havoc. Early in June when Memphis fell to the Union, Nelda was elated. But in Arkansas—to her disappointment—there had been no recent bold moves by union forces to retake what the rebels had stolen.

Today, however, she had worries of a different nature. She hurriedly packed with care, only one small valise. She must make a trip to Little Rock and as quickly as possible. It smote her conscience to leave, especially after all of Mama's protests. But Papa might be dying! Mama was unable to go, although she insisted on trying. Nelda had already wasted precious hours trying to convince her that she was too frail. And she had wasted time begging Gill for a pass. Now her frown deepened. Gill Harris—*the little worm*—was drunk with power and delighted in any opportunity to deny a pass. She would take the first boat, pass or no pass. Ever since Mr. Danley's letter had arrived, she had been terrified that Papa might die. Except for Mr. Danley's ministrations, he was probably getting no medical attention!

When Tom learned of the plan, he objected as strongly as had Louise. And he grumbled even more vociferously when he was told to climb aboard on Lily in order to bring the mare home from the boat dock.

"T'aint right, missy. Decent females ain't gw'in nowhere alone these days. You gwan'a get yourself into trouble, just as sure as the good Lord done rose on Easter Sunday!"

Nelda adjusted her long blue skirt and pulled a little on the blue ribbon to loosen the wide-brimmed hat tied under her chin, regretting that she had promised to wear it even to appease Mama. "Hurry up. And be careful of the satchel. I'm taking Papa some muscadine wine. Uncle Ned's old granny says it's good for the heart." She expelled a deep breath. "Right now, Tom. Climb up here behind me. The steamer leaves in less than an hour, and I'm taking a round about way through the woods so fewer folks will see us."

He shoved the battered hat low on his forehead, put a foot into the stirrup, and swung up with Nelda lending a helping hand. His lips were a thin line.

"You always was the headstrongdest creature what ever was," he muttered.

"Yes, I am, so stop your arguing. You know I won't change my mind."

He remained silent all the while she guided the mare between the leafy trees along the creek bank. But his lips stuck out in a pout.

Nelda jerked when the trill of a wren erupted close by. She had not realized how tense she was. She weaved Lily around berry briars and dense thickets. Here the musty smell of the creek bottom was overpowered by the sweet odor of tiny white blossoms peppering a tangle of honeysuckle.

"I'd take Papa a honeysuckle bouquet, but it would be so wilted the flowers would fall off before I got there."

"You be the one wiltin,'" Tom prophesied. "Probably won't nebber even get there."

"That very well could be. But I have to try. Papa needs me."

She angled a course through the trees, heading toward the river and the Spadra Landing. Finally, up ahead she spied smoke coming from a steamer's stack. Her heart suddenly pumped and her mouth went dry. How she needed that pass! She pulled Lily to a standstill.

"Just stay put, Tom. I don't want you having to climb up again." And holding aside her skirt and lifting her leg over the front of the pommel, she jumped down. When he slid forward into the saddle, she handed him the reins. Then she untied the satchel and held it in her clammy hands. "I want you to wait here until after the boat leaves—wait a few minutes to make sure I got on. Then go home and hide Lily."

"You ain't got a lick o' sense. Serve you right whatever happens." His wrinkled face was a mask of disapproval as he sat high on the mare's back. Before Nelda had gone ten paces, he relented. "You be kerful, missy," he called in a loud whisper. "The good Lord watch obber you."

She smiled a quivery smile and waved. Holding her skirts back from the briars, she headed for the road. It would appear to anyone at the landing that she had walked from home.

The steamer was moored to the dock. A pot-bellied man wearing a black brimmed cap, a black vest, and a long-sleeved shirt with sleeve garters stood near the gangplank consulting a large pocket watch. Just as Nelda rounded the bend, he called to a workman to raise the gangplank and unmoor the boat.

"Wait! Please wait!" she shouted, trying to keep from tripping on the long skirt as she ran. She was uncertain if he heard her over the boat whistle that suddenly split the air.

He raised a hand to halt the workman. "Hold up. We've got a passenger."

Two butternut clad soldiers sitting on upturned kegs near the dock paid no attention as she rushed past. They were engrossed in the playing cards fanned out like turkey tails and studied through squinted eyes and tobacco smoke.

The boatman stuck out a helping hand as she scrambled aboard. "You're a bit late, ma'am. We almost left without you." His friendly smile eased her apprehension. Relief was short-lived, however, when he spoke again. "I'll need to see your pass."

Her face blanched. "Oh, I forgot to get one. I've been in such a rush because … you see … " she stammered out the lie. "I just got word that my father is very ill. He's in Little Rock and I must—"

"I'm sorry, miss." The blue eyes in the weathered face were sympathetic. "No one travels without a pass."

"But surely in cases of emergency—"

He glanced toward the soldiers who had stopped their game to listen. "No exceptions, ma'am. Orders of the Provost Marshal." He chewed his jaw for a moment. "I'll tell you what—if you'll hurry, I'll hold the boat another half hour. If you're not here by then, though, I'll have to shove off."

She let out a deep breath and her shoulders sagged. "Thank you, sir. But you should just go on." There was no way on earth Gill Harris would give her a pass. "I'll catch the next boat."

"Whatever you say, miss. I really am sorry. I hope your father is better by the time you arrive."

She started off the boat as the man turned away; but she paused when he spoke low, barely audible. "I think I'll stop today at Pittsburgh landing. Might even get off the boat for a bit and stretch my legs."

"Thank you," she whispered. She left the boat and tried not to appear in a rush, trudging back the way she had come. Before she was out of sight the soldiers were once again lost in the card game.

Rounding the bend, she began to run while holding to her hat with one hand and clutching the valise in the other. Pittsburgh Landing was just downriver, a place near where Cabin Creek entered the river. She doubted there would be soldiers there. If she hurried, she just might catch the boat after all!

Her breath came in ragged pants. "Hurry, Tom, scoot back! I have to catch the boat downriver."

"Why you gotta do dat? De' boat was just here!"

"Yes, but so were some soldiers. They might tell the provost marshal," she panted as she swung a leg over the front of the pommel. "If there are no soldiers about, I think that captain—I guess he was the captain—will let me aboard at the Pittsburgh Landing."

"Plain as the nose on your face, the good Lord don't want you gw'in—He done sent them soldiers to stop you," Tom argued.

"Hang on!" Nelda kicked Lily's flank and urged the mare as fast as she dared through the trees and over the uneven ground along the river. "We'll gain some time along here," she said, while angling the horse away from the river. "We'll cut across country and catch the river when it bends back this way."

Constantly avoiding obstacles—fallen logs, deep gullies, and marshy ground—she finally turned the mare toward the river. Her heart pounded much faster than Lily's hooves. She must catch that boat! She kicked the mare in the flanks and the horse leaped across a small tributary winding its way toward the river.

Tom clutched the saddle with a groan. "Slow down! This hoss gwan'a break a leg!"

She ignored him and urged Lily forward.

The boat was moored and waiting when they finally arrived. But she frowned. A man stood on the bank. It was Harlow, the unsavory fellow who had been offended at the party when she would not dance with him. He carried a large crate filled with squawking chickens.

"Well, Harlow," called the captain, letting down the gangplank, "I didn't think there was a chicken left in the state."

"Between the foraging Confed'rit army and the danged thieving bushwhackers, there ain't many," agreed Harlow as he struggled aboard, hauling the crate.

"You should get a good price for them."

"Figure to trade these here fer salt. Salt's gettin' scarce as hen's teeth." He grinned showing broken stained teeth. "That's where I'll turn a real profit."

"Salt is scarce everywhere," acknowledged the captain.

"Yep. But I figure the thought of chicken and dumplings will probably fetch some out of hiding."

"Harlow, you'd sell lemonade at your own mother's funeral."

"Now that's a right good idea. I'll keep it in mind if Ma ever dies. Here's my damn pass. Had to walk to Clarksville to get the damned thing."

Nelda sprang down.

"Tom, go straight home and hide Lily. Take good care of Mama for me. I'll be back soon."

"You be kerful," he admonished for the hundredth time.

"You, too."

Harlow stared with tilted head and a hateful look as she stepped aboard. Immediately, the boat got underway.

"Welcome aboard." The captain beamed. He lowered his voice so Harlow would not hear. "I love giving those dang provost marshals the slip. When a man,"—he tipped his cap—"or a woman is required to have a pass to travel in this country, things have gone too far. Yes sirree, too far!" He frowned. "I'll have to let you off before we land at Little Rock. They're checking folks coming and going." He patted her arm. "But don't worry, I'll get you as close as I can so you won't have far to walk."

"God bless you, sir."

"Ballinger is the name. Have a seat, miss. You look out of breath." He pointed to a chair. "I hope you won't be too uncomfortable. We're not well set up for passengers. But it's nice to have a lady onboard," he said with a smile. "We mostly haul freight and cattle."

Even as he spoke she could hear squealing hogs and bleating sheep while a pungent, unpleasant odor drifted on the breeze. When he strolled away, she sank gratefully down into a chair sitting in the shade of the pilothouse. Harlow was busy getting his chicken coop situated and talking to workmen moving some barrels. She untied the hat and let the cool breeze coming off the river fan her hot face. She pleated the hat ribbon through her fingers and gave a wry smile. It was a constant argument—Mama insisting she wear a hat or bonnet. Poor Mama. She really was failing. It would be hard to keep that from Papa, but she intended to try. He had enough worries.

She drew a deep breath and turned to watch the bank sliding past. Green willows bent low over the lazy water where tall rushes grew in an inlet off from the main stream. A fish jumped in the inlet and left an ever-widening circle. Nelda smiled. Any fisherman would surely have whooped with delight at the size of the bass that had jumped at the long-tailed mayfly.

Her mind drifted to happier days. The last time she had traveled to Little Rock had been on a much nicer steamboat—just over a year ago in May, also a lovely day with birdsong and sunshine. It was the day the state had voted to secede from the Union. How tragic that decision! After the terrible losses at Wilson's Creek and Pea Ridge and the atrocities all across the state by lawless bushwhackers, she wondered, if given the choice, would the delegates do it again? She sighed. "*Yes, they probably would,*" she whispered. At least in Clarksville, the Rebels seemed more fanatical than ever.

With hands clasped behind his back and a rotund belly protruding, the captain wandered back down the deck. He smiled and deferentially tipped his cap. "Are you faring all right, ma'am?"

She smiled. "Yes, thank you."

"Good, good." He squinted upriver. "In just a bit we'll be at the Dardanelle landing. Sometimes we take on passengers… sometimes even be a soldier or two. Last week there was a provost marshal checking passes." He pointed to a door. "There's a room over there with a bench inside."

Nelda nodded. "I'll try to be inconspicuous."

"Good idea." He grinned and headed on.

She enjoyed the idle time. How long had it been since she had simply sat in the sun doing nothing? Without success she attempted to put away worry, and yet she enjoyed the scenery. Squirrels frolicking in the oaks along the bank hardly gave the boat a glance. A doe flagged her white tail and bounded away, taking along two white-spotted fawns.

Then Nelda's eyes sought the wide paddle wheel churning the water. Each turn brought her closer to Papa. If only she could avoid the provost marshals!

When the boat whistled, announcing the approach to the Dardanelle landing, she went inside a room filled with barrels and wooden boxes and a bench against one wall where she supposed passengers sat in inclement weather. She chewed her lip and stood on tiptoe to look out the porthole.

She was relieved that Harlow remained outside. She had gotten a whiff of him that smelled worse than the dank hold.

When the boat was underway again, the captain said there would be no more stops until the steamer reached Lewisburg. Nelda began to relax. She sat down, and leaned her head back against the rough wall behind the bench. Hopefully Tom had made it home. And hopefully Mama was all right. Nelda could hardly believe she would soon see Papa. She refused to think of a worse possibility! She sighed and closed her eyes. She was a good sailor. The motion of the boat never made her sick. Instead it rocked her to sleep like a cradle.

The shrill whistle woke her. There was an answering whistle from a vessel going upstream. She sat up and smoothed her hair. Her mouth was as dry as powder. She must have slept with her jaws hanging open. There was a water barrel on deck. By the low slant of sun, she knew they would soon reach Lewisburg, the stopping place for the night. Just as soon as Harlow left the boat, she would venture out for a drink and a trip to the privy. After the long nap, she doubted she would sleep much. But she was ready for the meat and bread tucked into a package in her valise. She would love a comfortable bed and a good meal at the Markham Inn where she and Papa had always stayed when passing through Lewisburg. But prudence dictated she stay onboard for the night to avoid the local provost marshal.

Captain Ballinger heartily approved her plan, and even fetched her a blanket and a pillow. He assured that no one would bother her. Nonetheless he advised locking the door with the rusty sliding bolt.

Lewisburg still appeared a thriving town with fine homes and numerous businesses spread out on rolling hills leading down to the river. Nelda peeked from the porthole to see soldiers in Confederate gray mingling with stevedores at the dock where a large boat lay anchored.

It resembled the *Quapaw*, but she could not be certain, for the lettering was not visible from where she stood. The cargo appeared to be supplies for the army. At least the soldiers were busy loading boxes and barrels onto large wagons. She watched until, finally, the wagons pulled away. And she watched as daylight faded and lamplight dotted the waterfront and twinkled like fireflies on the stair-step hills.

With a sigh, she turned from the porthole and sought the bench. As anticipated, she slept but little on the hard bed. Mosquitoes were a constant torment. Worse yet, the dark night brought haunting visions of Fred's murder and fear for Papa. Even the gentle current sweeping past the boat seemed to whisper danger. But she must have dozed, for she jumped when the captain knocked on the door. Opening heavy eyelids, she noticed a sliver of gray dawn on the horizon through the porthole.

"Ma'am, we'll be leaving soon. I took the liberty to bring you a bit of breakfast."

She quickly sat up. While rearranging disheveled hair, she slid back the bolt and opened the door. "Thank you, so much." She reached for the plate of steaming grits and a heavy mug. "Coffee! It smells wonderful!" She breathed deeply. "Around Clarksville coffee beans are getting—to quote your friend Harlow—as scarce as hen's teeth."

Captain Ballinger snorted. "That cross-eyed Harlow is no friend of mine. A bigger scoundrel never lived." Then his eyes twinkled. "But he's right about one thing. With the right things to trade, it's amazing what will come out of hiding."

She chuckled. "I can only imagine what this coffee cost you!"

He grinned and then quickly sobered. "I think it would be best if you stay inside until we shove off. There was a provost marshal nosing around town." He took the bold-faced watch from his vest pocket and checked the time. "I'd better get busy. We'll be getting underway soon." He glanced up. "If nothing unforeseen happens, we'll be in Little Rock by late afternoon. I'll let you off as close to town as I dare."

"I appreciate everything you've done."

"Glad to help, ma'am." He raised a hand in parting.

"Thank you," she called again. Before closing the door, she noticed Harlow across the deck standing in shadow. She blew on the hot liquid and took a sip. Then she glanced out the porthole and saw him looking after the captain. She wondered if he had overheard.

Nelda spent the long warm day watching acres of green cotton push up almost to the river. Occasionally slaves, with ragged hats shading dark faces, stopped hoeing long enough to watch the boat glide past. The creaky old steamer was incapable of much speed, but heading downstream helped. She, however, felt they were standing still and willed them onward on wings. But the creaking boat had no wings. By mid-afternoon, tall clouds piled up in the west and soon obscured the sun. She winced as a clap of thunder echoed off the log walls. She quickly went inside. The portholes let in scant air and what little there was had grown heavy and sultry.

The door pushed open. Harlow entered. Head tilted, his weasel eyes searched the dimness until they found her standing near a porthole staring at the darkening sky.

"Reckon you won't mind sharing the dry with me." His thin lips smiled, but the smile did not reach his eyes.

She minded very much. But she merely nodded as she pulled a handkerchief from her pocket, and pretending to cough, covered her nose. With steel resolve, she stifled a gag. She put her face near the porthole and watched the trees along the bank shiver in the whipping wind. She shuddered when a cottonmouth lying on a low limb slithered into the water.

Harlow sat down on the bench and stared. Under his scrutiny, she felt her skin crawl. If eyes were windows to the soul, Harlow's was small and mean.

"These is dangerous times for a lone female."

As thunder rumbled, the room suddenly grew darker. She nodded at her valise.

"I brought protection."

His cunning eyes narrowed.

"I'm very proficient with a handgun. My Papa taught me."

When she drew out the pistol and left it lying on top of the valise, his eyes tapered even more and he grew silent.

The storm proved to be short-lived. Nelda breathed a relieved sign when Harlow exited the cabin. Little Rock was only a few miles away. Her thoughts spun faster than the paddle wheel. *How was Papa? If only the old boat would go faster!*

Captain Ballinger edged near the steep bank and helped her descend the gangplank. "This is the best I can do to get you close to the road. Sorry about all the brush." He frowned. "I don't like putting you off all alone, especially this close to dark. I'm glad you told me you have a pistol. Keep it handy."

She glanced about but Harlow was not in sight. "Do you think Mr. Harlow would turn us in to the provost marshal?"

The captain's eyes twinkled. "Can't figure out how, but Harlow's chickens got out of the crate." He nodded to the other side of the pilot-house. "He's as busy as a hog on ice, trying to gather them up again."

She joined him in a chuckle and put out her hand.

The captain took it and gave it a squeeze. He nodded toward a hill. "There's a road just over that rise. It's not much over a mile on into town."

"Thank you, so much for all you've done for me."

He turned her gratitude aside with a shake of the head. "Not sure I did you any favors by bringing you here, miss. Country is full of unsavory characters. I'll be heading back to Fort Smith day after tomorrow. If you want to go back home, I'll pick you up at this same spot early that morning. You take care of yourself."

"I'll be careful," she assured. "Goodbye." She carried the valise in one hand, and with the other, hitched her skirts out of the grass and weeds.

"Hope your pa gets better," he called. With furrowed brow, he watched her out of sight.

Nelda looked back. As the smokestack disappeared from view, a shiver traced her spine. *"Don't be such a goose!"* she scolded herself aloud. Nonetheless, she unlatched the satchel to keep the pistol handy. Taking a deep breath, she squared her shoulders.

Trees and brush hugged the swampy riverbank. Again and again, as she fought her way through underbrush, briars snagged her clothing. She would be a sorry sight by the time she reached town.

Finally, after topping the hill, she was relieved to see a well-traveled wagon road with no other travelers in sight. Brush thinned, making her way easier through the sparse scrubby pin oaks. Upon reaching the road, she disentangled a strip of blackberry briar from her skirt. A few fat ripe berries clung amid the small hard green ones. She plucked a ripe one, winced, and put a finger into her mouth to stop the prick of a thorn. The tart berry was hardly worth the pain. As she stared at puffy coral clouds hugging the sun just above the horizon, she realized she would have to hurry or dark would overtake. Mama always insisted that a lady must never appear to hurry; but Nelda held up her skirt and ran.

It was not long until a freight wagon rolled into view. The freighter was a friendly old gentleman, and Nelda gratefully accepted a ride. Long before the first dwelling came into view, she had a plan. She would go to the boarding house where Papa had stayed. Perhaps Mrs. Ellis would know where he was being held. If not, she would go to the Gazette office and ask Mr. Danley. Now that she was sitting still, she realized how very tired she was. And her left heel was burning from a blister. Her shiny high-topped shoes were not meant for running.

The boarding house was a three-story buff-colored house with a wide wrap-around porch. Mrs. Ellis stood at the door, drying her hands on an apron. The white hair, drawn up and piled high, and the thin aristocratic nose gave her a patrician air.

Scandalized, she raised arched brows. "Upon my word! You didn't travel all the way from Clarksville unescorted!"

She fancies herself royalty, thought Nelda, *but the worn shoes and threadbare dress give her away.*

"It was necessary. My mother is too ill to travel. There was no one else." She added, "My father is sick. Do you know where he's being held?"

Mrs. Ellis shrugged. Her mouth thinned. "If they haven't moved him, he's just up the road in the old gray building across the street from the livery." She glanced around to make sure no one was listening. "His boarding here brought suspicion on me." She scrutinized Nelda through wary eyes. "These days one never knows whom to trust."

Nelda stiffened. "I'll find somewhere else to stay. I imagine there are places where my money is welcome." She watched the struggle play across Mrs. Ellis's face.

"No, no. I'll have the girl take your satchel up to a room."

She wanted to storm away in a huff. But just now it seemed wiser to ignore the insult.

"I'll keep the satchel for now. I brought some things for Papa. I'll be back as soon as I've seen him."

Nelda hurried through the twilight, lugging the satchel. Her breath came in quick pants. She hurried but her feet seemed weighted with lead.

Since her last visit the city had undergone a drastic metamorphosis. Dingy storefronts were locked and vacant. Little Rock merchants had suffered the same fate as Clarksville's. The men she passed were seated on chairs and benches in the evening shade, crippled men, broken men, men who were missing hands and arms and legs, some with eyes as vacant as the store fronts. Some spoke and she returned the greeting. In answer to her question, one left off whittling on a stick to point at a building down the street. The young man had brown hair and eyes and looked no older than Elijah—eighteen years at the most. Both legs were gone below the knee. She tried to keep pity from her eyes and voice as she thanked him and rushed onward.

The long squat building he had indicated was not a jail. It more resembled a warehouse. A scrawny bearded man answered the door after the third knock. He rubbed his jaw and screwed up his face. "I dunno . . . I got no orders about visitors—"

"Please, sir! Please let me see him. I've come a very long way, and I'm so worried about him. I had word that he's ill."

"Well, I reckon it won't do no harm. Your pa is a nice man. He's been right puny, but I think he's on the mend."

Her heart soared at the good news.

Suddenly he looked dubious. "Ain't got a weapon, have ye?"

"There's a gun in there." She handed over the satchel. "But please give me the bottle of wine. It's for Papa."

He took the bag. "This pistol's bigger than you are. Hope you don't hurt yerself with it." He brought forth the wine and unconsciously licked his lips. "Foller me."

Then he shuffled down a dim hall toward a closed door. Taking a key from a hook alongside the door, he opened it. "Visitor fer ya."

Small windows let in just enough light for Nelda to see Phillip lying on a bed. The ticking-covered mattress was bare of sheets but partially draped with a worn blanket. He quickly sat up.

"Nelda!"

He stood as she rushed to embrace him. His ribs were pitifully thin.

"Oh! Papa! Thank God you're alive." She drew back to stare. He had always been a distinguished man, clean-shaven, and impeccably dressed, the empty sleeve of a crisp white shirt neatly folded and penned at the shoulder. Now he looked old and stooped and his clothes were dirty. Why had she not thought to bring him more!

Her eyes grew teary. "How long have you been ill?"

"A couple of weeks. But I'll be fine now that you're here. How is your mother?"

She was unable to speak past the tears in her throat. His face drained of color. "Is Louise—"

"She's fine," lied Nelda.

"Daughter, daughter." He drew back and stared hard. He frowned.

"Your face bespeaks trials and tribulations. What are you keeping from me? The truth now."

"Oh, Papa, it's nothing more than being worried sick about you. Ever since Mr. Danley's letter came, I've been scared to death."

"I was pretty bad there for a few days—high fever. C.C. brought medicine and poured it down me himself. Slowly but surely, I'm recuperating."

"God bless him!" breathed Nelda. "Oh, I brought some muscadine wine."

He smiled and took the bottle. "This will fix me up. No wine on earth tastes better." He sat the bottle on the table unopened. "How did you travel? And who came with you?"

"I came by boat." She rushed on, hoping he would forget she had not answered the rest of the question.

He pointed to a chair drawn up to a scarred writing desk. Except for the cot, it was the only furniture in the room. "Sit down. I can't tell you how wonderful it is to see you."

"Are they feeding you, Papa?"

He gave a rueful grin and sat down on the rumpled bed. "It's not your mother's good cooking—but I imagine I'm dining as well as the soldiers. No one here is feasting on the fatted calf these days. When C. C. is in town he brings food … or anything else I need." Absentmindedly, he straightened the sleeve penned over the stub of his right arm. It was a habit of years. Nelda had seen the gesture all her life.

"I can't believe I forgot to bring you more clothes—"

"I have a change right over there." He pointed to a bundle in the corner. "C.C. brought them. They let me bathe occasionally. When they do, I wash these and hang them to dry." He changed the subject, "What's the situation in Clarksville?"

"Shortages of just about everything; and prices have soared on what little is left."

"I suppose some are going hungry," he said with a sigh. "Poor misguided people! They had no idea what war would be like." He shook his head.

Nelda wondered if he would be as sympathetic if he knew the truth. Then, on second thought, she knew he would. Papa was a saint.

"Mama and I have plenty in the cellar."

"I'm sure I don't have to tell you to be generous with our neighbors. Oh, I know you don't have enough to feed the whole town, but make certain Robert's family has plenty. Never forget—in spite of our political differences—the Morrisons are good friends."

It took all of her will power to keep from blurting out the truth. But it would wound him deeply so she pressed her lips together.

"Yes, Papa."

"Ned told me that he and Elijah helped you butcher the—"

"How is he? Are they still here?" she quickly asked.

"No. They've both gone. Ned was wounded in the Pea Ridge battle, but he was finally able to march. His shoulder is weak. He said he doubted he could aim a rifle ..." Phillip's voice trailed off. "I'm not sure where they sent Elijah." For a moment silence reigned.

"Oh, Papa! This awful war! Men shooting each other. Killing and maiming. The crippled soldiers—they're so pitiful."

"Yes, they are." He was grim. "And on both sides many a good man has died. It was tragic about Fred. He was a fine man—a good and loyal friend." He drew a deep breath. "Such passion on both sides."

"So you did get my telegram about Fred."

His brows knit. "No," he said slowly, "I heard about it from another source."

When he said no more, she looked at her hands clasped in her lap. Then she drew a deep breath and leaned forward. She lowered her voice. "I want to help. I've been listening for any information that might be helpful to General Curtis."

Phillip grew stern; but she rushed on, "I tried getting word to him when General Hindman had citizens write letters to nonexistent people, exaggerating troop and weapon strength and saying fresh troops had arrived from Texas. But I was too late—"

"No!" He cut her short. "I won't have you taking such risks! Don't you realize, your sex is no protection?"

"I'm well aware of the barbarity of the Confederates, Papa!"

"The Confederates aren't the only ones. Unfortunately war breeds barbarism. It's being reported that in New Orleans General Butler and his Union troops are brutalizing women—even ladies of the best families—treating them like prostitutes and jailing them for no reason. I shudder to think what the rebels might do in retaliation."

"But Papa"—she leaned closer— "I want to do something to stop the killing—bring the war to a quicker end. At least in Arkansas," she pleaded.

He stood and began pacing the room. "No." He violently shook his head. "No." He wheeled and returned to her. "It's too dangerous. Curtis has spies and scouts enough without you."

He walked over and took her hand. His skin felt paper thin and hot.

"Daughter, I love the Union. You know that. And I've risked much for it. But I won't risk you!" He wagged his head again. "You've already put yourself in harms way by coming here." His gray eyes pierced her. "I want you on the next boat headed home. I have a feeling Louise needs you more than I do."

She nodded and squeezed his hand. "I'll leave just as soon as I know you're well enough," she agreed. "Is there any news, any hope for your release?"

"Over fear of an invasion, Rector ordered the state government moved to Hot Springs." He pursed his lips. "With the governor on the run, my case has sort of slipped through the cracks. But that may be a blessing." He smiled. "Where there's life, there's hope."

"Yes, I suppose so." She swallowed a lump in her throat.

He pulled a gold watch from his pants pocket and flipped open the case. To Nelda the watch was as much a part of him as his hand or his foot. She had never seen him without it.

"I'm surprised they let you keep your watch."

With a thumb, he caressed the engraved initials on the case. "I was pleasantly surprised myself. The officer took everything else in my pockets but when I told him my wife gave this to me on our twenty-fifth anniversary, he let me keep it." He gave a slight grin. "Besides, I doubt his initials were the same as mine."

She did not argue when he insisted she leave. Shadows in the room had lengthened, and she had no wish to be abroad after dark.

"I'll be back in the morning. And I'll bring you a good hot breakfast."

He smiled. "Just bring yourself. That will be better than food."

Mrs. Ellis ushered Nelda inside into a spacious hall with high ceilings. Off to the right was an airy parlor where two men sat on stuffed chairs in the last patch of fading sunlight coming through tall windows. The room was immaculate; but the furniture and drapes had—like Mrs. Ellis—become faded and worn.

"How was your father?" she asked. Before Nelda had a chance to answer, she was busy giving orders to a wispy slave girl with a thin face and huge eyes.

"Fairby, I told you to shut those drapes each evening when the sun shines in. It's hot as blazes in the parlor!" She turned back to Nelda.

"I'd prefer if you ate in your room. The fewer people who know you're here the better. I'll have your supper sent up." Mrs. Ellis pointed to the valise. "Fairby, take her to the west room."

Nelda's jaws tightened, but she was too tired to entertain thoughts of going elsewhere. Instead she followed the young black woman up the stairs as a man came limping down, using a twisted stick for a cane.

Fairby nodded. "How you today, Mr. Yarbrough?" When he had gone out the front door, she lowered her voice and talked over her shoulder. "House used to be full of payin' boarders. Now they's only a handful of crippled soldiers."

"Doesn't the army pay their board?" asked Nelda.

Fairby hooted. "Army don't even pay the soldiers!"

The room on the top floor had pink drapes and colorful braided rugs on clean but scarred hardwood floors. A white counterpane covered a four-poster mahogany bed. The room was stifling. Large windows facing west had trapped the heat of the sun, which was now a mere crimson glow on the dusky horizon.

Fairby blew a disgusted breath. "Mr. Yarbrough won't leave his door open to let no breeze come down the hall. Keep it locked tight." She pulled the heavy drapes back farther. "It cool off now the sun's gone down. But you best keep them drapes closed if you light a candle. Skeeters and black gnats flock to the light and then stays to chew on you."

Nelda was already dotted with mosquito bites. And in the last few minutes, she had become keenly aware that chiggers had infested the berry briars she waded through. Now they feasted on the tender skin of her ankles and waist. It was all she could do to keep from clawing in front of Fairby.

"Cloy be up soon with the tub and some hot water for yore bath. I'll bring yore supper."

"Thank you."

As soon as Fairby left the room, Nelda lifted her skirt and peeled down her stockings and had a good scratch. It did no good. Even though she had almost scratched the red welts bloody, they itched worse than ever. And when she finally stepped into the tub of warm soapy water prepared by the black girl, Cloy, she cringed from the sting. But nothing could disturb her relief that Papa was not dead! He was far from well. But now she had hopes that he would survive. She stretched, savoring the warm suds and thought how good it would feel to have a real bed tonight.

She was ravenous and enjoyed the meal of beans and cornbread. But her sleep was restless. The insect bites kept her clawing. And worry kept her equally agitated.

The next morning, after a breakfast of buttered grits eaten in her room, she asked Fairby to make Phillip a hot meal of meat and eggs.

"Laws-a-mercy! I ain't seen a chicken or a egg since kingdom come! But I'll send what I got." It was nothing more than cornbread smeared with molasses but it would be filling.

As Nelda made her way into town, it was a perfect morning, pleasantly cool and perfumed by the scent of red roses clinging to trellis and fences along the way, the foliage still moist and glistening from yesterday's shower. Many houses she passed had overgrown yards and a vacant, neglected air. She supposed the occupants had fled. She wondered if they would ever return.

Phillip looked better. Although his cheeks were still hollow and pallid, his eyes were brighter and he was in a good mood. He ate the cornbread with good appetite.

"I haven't tasted molasses in a while. How is Mrs. Ellis?"

"She seems in good health. But she's certainly nervous over having me as a guest."

He grimaced. "Don't be offended, daughter. Arkansas has become a hotbed of suspicion and guilt by association."

The morning passed all too quickly. Phillip, after consulting the watch, insisted she leave in time to book passage for the next day. She hated leaving him so soon.

"I'll be back later this afternoon." She kissed his sallow cheek and left reluctantly.

It was windy near the river where men scurried about loading the boats moored at the dock. Nelda found Captain Ballinger busily directing two stevedores, muscled shirtless black men, about the placement of wooden crates. His eyes brightened when he saw her. He quickly agreed to stop for her the next morning at the same spot where she had disembarked.

As she made her way to the Gazette office, she fervently hoped Mr. Danley was there. She wanted to speak to him more candidly about Papa's prospects for release.

She stepped inside out of the bright sun, blinking to adjust her eyes. Then she batted back tears as the smell of the printer's ink and paper filled her nostrils. How she had missed it!

A stooped man in an ink-covered apron worked at a tall-legged press, his fingers ink blotched. Across the room Mr. Danley perched on the edge of a cluttered desk. He was talking to a short, bearded man in a well-tailored suit. The discussion was heated. Neither man seemed aware of her arrival. She shoved aside a stack of papers and sat down on a bench to wait.

"I know you've been handed a tough job, General; but this"—Danley waved a small piece of paper in the air—"this edict is a bit drastic, don't you think?"

Nelda eyed the officer. Her heart began to pound. This must be the new commander of Arkansas' Confederate troops! General Thomas Hindman!

From what she had heard, he was working miracles in Arkansas for the destitute Confederacy. But his appearance was not impressive. Although he was handsome— with a dark, thick beard and dark hair springing from a slightly receding hairline above a strong brow—he was barely over five feet tall and had the small frame of a youth.

The general bristled, reminding Nelda of a pint-sized bulldog Papa had once owned. "No. I do not think any such thing, sir." He had a strong drawl.

Nelda recalled he was originally from Mississippi before moving to Arkansas and becoming a congressman.

He went on in high dudgeon, "No price is too costly to rid us of the plague threatening our liberty!"

Danely, hands braced on the desk, remained unflappable as he replied to the general's outburst. "Considering the straits the state is in, perhaps your conscriptions and tariffs and marshal law are necessary; but asking citizens to burn their own crops, kill their own cattle, poison their own wells to stop the Yankee advance—they'll never do it, General."

"Then the army will," avowed Hindman in clipped tones. "General Curtis must not have carte blanche to feed his troops!" Then the general took a deep breath and used a more conciliatory approach. "No, Mr. Danley, it's not asking too much. I'm asking even more. I'm calling on all males between ten and eighty, who aren't of conscription age, to form companies. They're to arm, equip, and ration themselves." He stared at Danley's raised eyebrows. "Oh, they'll receive the value of subsistence and forage furnished, as well as soldier's pay for the time actually served." Unflinching, he returned Danley's skeptical stare. "We'll obtain the funds to pay them—and our army too. Please print my demands in tomorrow's paper, sir." He wheeled and left the room.

"In a pig's eye, you will," muttered Danley as he reached for a cigar and crammed it into his mouth. He struck a match on the bottom of his shoe. Squinting through puffs of smoke, he saw Nelda. He quickly removed the cigar and stood, using the cane propped nearby.

"Why, Miss Nelda! What a pleasant surprise. It's been far too long since your last visit. Let's see … was it the Secession Convention?"

"Yes, it was. It's good to see you, too." She took the hand he offered. "Although I wish the circumstances were happier. Thank you for sending word about Papa. I was so relieved to find—thanks to you—that he's better."

Danley grunted. "Wish I could really help by getting him released. I didn't get by to see him this morning. How is he?"

"Some better. Very weak though."

He patted her shoulder. "He'll be better now that you're here."

"I do so appreciate all you've done for him. We've been worried sick. Until your letter, we hadn't heard a word in weeks."

"I'm afraid that's my fault," he admitted. "Phillip depends on me to mail letters and I confess, I haven't been diligent about that lately." He pointed to a stack of letters lying on the desk. "Travel in your direction has been sporadic. As you can well imagine, things have been hectic around here. Until recently everyone was expecting Yankee cavalry to come charging up the road at any second."

"I heard the Union forces have pulled back."

"Yes, at least for the time being." He gestured toward the door. "In spite of that, our new commander is in a snit. Can't say as I blame him." He shrugged. "Word is that Curtis is heading for Helena, the general's hometown."

His lips turned down as he sighed and put the cigar back into his mouth. "But you're not here about military matters. I'm sure Phillip was overjoyed to see you. Not a day passes without him fretting about you and your mother."

"Mr. Danley, what do you think are Papa's chances of getting released?"

He expelled a deep breath. "Honestly, I have no idea. Under ordinary circumstances, he'd be a free man by now. But with the political situation now, anything can happen. There's just no way of knowing what the governor might do."

He retrieved a hat from a rack on the wall. "I'm just on my way to see Phillip now. Want to come along?"

"First, I'd like to buy a few things for him. Do you know if there's any good tonic left in town?"

"I doubt it. The army used up every ounce of medicine for doctoring the wounded after Pea Ridge."

As they left the office she slowed her steps to match his limping gate. She knew he had been wounded in the Mexican War. It was the same battle where Papa had lost an arm.

"How is the war going?" she asked. "Since the telegraph is often down, we get so little news in Clarksville."

He shrugged. "Sort of depends on whom you believe. There was a big battle a while back near Richmond at a place called Seven Pines. Both sides claimed victory. As far as I can tell, nothing much was accomplished—except getting about ten thousand men killed or wounded." He shook his head and went on, "Only good I can see is Robert Lee has replaced Joe Johnston as commanding general. Both your father and I knew Lee in Mexico. He's a fine gentleman with plenty of grit and savvy. Unless I miss my guess, he'll be a great commander."

"That's good news," she said. But she fervently hoped Mr. Danley was mistaken.

Phillip gave a huge smile when he saw Danley arrive along with Nelda.

"Well, today is a wonderful day—two of my favorite people coming to visit at the same time!"

But after a few minutes of conversation, Danley backed from the room.

"I'll leave you two alone. Miss Nelda, stop back by the office later."

The next hours flew. She cherished each word, each look. For the most part, she stayed silent and let him talk of inconsequential things.

"Daughter," he said with a sad shake of the head, "progress will be the great casualty of this war. Especially here. We were finally fixing these deplorable roads and planning to build the railroad beyond Little Rock. Why, there's no telling what the next decade would have produced. I read about a fellow in Wisconsin who patented a railway braking system operated by electromagnets—brakes that use electric current from a battery! Amazing, isn't it?"

He went on, "That started me thinking about improving my printing press. I'm jotting down a few ideas on a design that would take less manpower and less work. What a wonderful age of discovery we're living in... if only the war hadn't brought everything to a screeching halt." He lowered his voice. "I'm also keeping a detailed diary. It keeps me from boredom." He gave a wan smile. "Who knows—when this is over, I might write a book."

With an undercurrent of sadness, they laughed and joked and reminisced until the sun had crept low enough to cast long shadows. Finally he took the watch from his pocket. Taking her hand, he placed it into her palm and closed her fist.

"I want you to have this."

She recoiled in horror. She could not express how his fate seemed implicitly tied to the watch.

"Oh, no, Papa. Please keep it."

He drew a deep breath and took back the watch. "I'm ready for whatever Providence wills," he tried to reassure. "I'm at peace."

She eyed the dingy room. "At peace in here? Knowing they might hang you."

He looked quizzical. "Of course. The Apostle Paul said he had learned to be content no matter what. If I die—as Paul also said—*'to be absent from the body is to be present with the Lord. And that will be gain for me—'"*

"Don't say that, Papa. I can't bear it."

He held her, patting her back. Finally, she pushed away and wiped her eyes. She had never seen him cry. Now his eyes were wet. His usually straight shoulders had slumped lower.

"Go now, daughter, and God bless you." His hand lingered a moment longer on her head.

She fought sobs rising in her throat. She kissed him, and then with her head down, she walked quickly from the room. As she stepped into the street, she looked back. *Would she ever see him again?*

Slowly, she retraced her steps to the Gazette office. She would ask Mr. Danley if Papa had any friends who would care for him when Mr. Danley was out of town.

She had just rounded the corner on Main Street when her eyes widened.

Harlow stood on the sidewalk pointing a long skinny finger. "There she is! Just like I told ya!" He practically danced with glee. "That's her!" Then his beady eyes narrowed. "She's traveling without no pass. She's up to no good I tell ya."

The tall man alongside him stared. Nelda wanted to run. Her instincts said to flee. Her mind, on the other hand, instantly cautioned that would be the worst course of action. Instead, head high, she approached with a haughty glare for Harlow.

"Marshal, what is this riffraff caterwauling about? Can't a decent Southern woman walk down the streets of Little Rock without being accosted!?"

The marshal reddened. "Well, ma'am ..." he stammered, "This fellow has leveled some serious charges. He says you arrived on the boat with him and that you're traveling without a pass."

She rolled her eyes. "Let me guess—did he also mention collecting a reward?"

The marshal's eyes slid sideways to Harlow.

She snorted. "I figured as much! Captain Ballinger warned me about him. He said Mr. Harlow will do anything for a profit."

"Be that as it may, ma'am, I'll have to see your pass."

She drew a deep breath. She lacked the beauty and feminine wiles that Mary Beth would have used to charm the marshal. But perhaps an appeal to chivalry would serve. The white-haired marshal had the look of a gentleman.

"Mr. Harlow is right. I don't have pass," she said.

Harlow rocked back on the balls of his feet and grinned.

"I learned that my father, who is here in town, was very ill, and I had to catch the next boat." She hurried on hoping the marshal would assume her father was a sick soldier. "There wasn't time to get a pass. Mr. C.C. Danley—I assume you know the editor of the Gazette—wrote that he feared Papa was dying." She hoped the name would have influence. "I'm no criminal." She lowered her head and let her lip tremble. "I'm just a very worried daughter who loves her father deeply." Then she faced the marshal. "Now that I know Papa will live, I can face anything. If you must, go ahead and arrest me."

He cleared his throat and shuffled his feet. "I don't think that will be necessary—"

"Aw! Don't get took in by that-there story!" cried Harlow. "She's a weasel!"

Nelda drew up tall. "A weasel!" she sputtered. "Of all the despicable…" She faced the marshal. "Sir, Mr. Danley will vouch for my story!"

The marshal eyed Harlow with disgust. "Someone around here is a varmint all right. And it ain't the lady." He put on his hat and then tipped it. "Sorry to have bothered you, ma'am."

He put a hand on Harlow's shoulder and propelled him forward. "I'd better not hear another word about you bothering the lady! I'd throw you in jail, but I don't want to stink up the place."

She watched them walk away. Her legs began to tremble. That had been a close shave. She must be more careful! Taking a deep breath, she started forward.

"Well, that was smoother than Pappy's whiskey."

She jumped and whirled. In the shadows of the alley, Allen leaned with a shoulder against the red brick wall. He pushed away and tilted back his hat. "Thought I was going to have to rush in and save you, but you handled that fine. Didn't even have to use your teeth." He grinned. His teeth gleamed in the sun-browned face. His clothes were rumpled as if they had been slept in and his face had two day's growth of sandy-colored beard.

She hurried toward him. "Allen! What on earth are you doing here?"

He sobered. "Following you. When I stopped by your place, Tom said you had stowed away on a boat without a pass. Thought you might be in trouble, so I got on the next boat. I've been waiting around here—figured you'd get in touch with your pa's boss."

She was both touched and surprised. "Why, thank you, Allen." Then her eyes narrowed. "You didn't think I'd come on a spying mission, did you?"

He took her arm and jerked her aside. He quickly looked all around. "Hell, woman! You tryin' to get us both hung!"

"No one is within hearing," she insisted.

"Well, lower you voice anyway. I don't aim to get my neck stretched." He looked at her. "Yes, the thought did cross my mind, especially since the Union isn't faring too well these days."

Her shoulders sagged and she sighed. "From some things General Hindman said this morning, I was afraid of that."

Allen blinked. *"You've been talking to Hindman!"*

"He was in the newspaper office—"

Allen's blue eyes grew stormy. "Damn it, woman, I gave you credit for having more sense! Don't you know if they suspect you even a smidgen, you'll be locked up right alongside your pa!"

Her own eyes snapped. "I'm well aware of that. I didn't take any risks."

He quirked an eyebrow. "Why do I have a hard time believing that?"

"General Hindman never even saw me, Allen. I was sitting on a bench in the corner waiting to speak to Mr. Danley."

He weighed her words. "All right," he said, growing matter-of-fact. "What did the general say?"

"He's urging citizens to burn their crops, poison their wells—do whatever it takes to hinder Curtis."

Allen snorted.

"When Mr. Danley told him it would never happen, he got mad."

"Yeah, he's a radical son-of-a-gun. Fiery temper, too."

Now she was surprised. "You know General Hindman?"

"Not on a first name basis," he quipped and then changed the subject. "You've seen your pa?"

"Yes." She bit her lip. "He looks awful, Allen. He's ragged and dirty. I don't think they feed him enough. Do you know any way to get him out of there?"

"Right now I'm more interested in getting you out of here. That marshal might change his mind any minute."

"I've already made arrangements to leave in the morning on the same boat I came down on with Captain Ballinger."

"Good. Ballinger is a good sort." Allen glanced into the street at a group of passing soldiers. "I'd better make myself scarce. I got no desire to get conscripted."

She nodded. "I'm staying at Mrs. Ellis' boarding house. The captain is picking me up a short way out of town. The marshal might give me a pass but there's no need to risk being told no." She suddenly asked, "By the way, do you have a pass?"

"Yep."

"Where did you get it?"

"Gill Harris."

Her eyes widened. "Gill Harris gave you a pass? He didn't act as if he liked the Matthers family very much."

"He don't."

She pursed her lips. "I know better than to waste my breath asking *you* for details."

He chuckled. Then he tipped the sweat-stained hat and melted into the deepening shadows of the alley.

Long after he had disappeared she stared down the alley. Why had Allen come?

In the morning mists rising from the river, Nelda strained to listen. The only sound was lapping water. She feared she had missed the boat! Now what? She chewed her jaw in indecision. Suddenly her head shot up like a frightened doe. She peered toward the sound of a paddle wheel. Before showing herself, she must be certain it was Captain Ballinger. Two boats had already passed going upriver in the fog. As the old freight boat lumbered into sight, she heaved a relieved breath, picked up the valise, stepped to the bank, and began waving a handkerchief.

Captain Ballinger waved back and soon the boat nosed toward the bank. Her smile widened. Allen leaned on the rail smoking a cigar. The tip glowed red, but the smoke was lost in the mists.

"Good morning, Miss Nelda," the captain heartily greeted as she scrambled aboard. "Good to see you, safe and sound and ready to go home. I couldn't help worrying about you."

"That was kind of you. As you can see, I'm fine." She slapped at a mosquito on her neck. "Except for being chewed to death."

The captain laughed. "My hide is so tough, they don't even bite me." He spent a few minutes chatting with them before finally saying, "If you'll both excuse me, I have work to do."

Allen pointed to the hat hanging down her back by its ribbon. "If you'd put on your bonnet it might keep off mosquitoes."

She leaned comfortably against the rail and watched the brush covered bank slide past. "I don't like blinders. I like to see what's going on around me."

He squinted against the smoke of his cigar. "Never thought about it before, but I reckon those wide brims would cut down on a body's vision."

"They do," she said. "All in all, women's fashions are stupid—hoops and heels and mountains of skirts to wash and iron and mend." She cut her eyes sideways. "Men are more practical. I envy you."

"Don't," he said. "We're the ones who start wars and then have to fight 'em—at least so far I've not seen a woman on a battlefield."

Her eyebrows rose. "I didn't know you'd been in battle. I thought you were keeping out of the fight."

"Figure of speech," he said. "I only meant woman seem to be less inclined to violence."

She grimaced. "Don't elevate the female sex above what we deserve. Plenty of women have egged on this war. I heard them." She turned toward him. "I was at the State Capitol the day poor Isaac Murphy voted against secession. The women were incensed."

He leaned with both arms on the rail and looked down at his boots. "I reckon it just sets better to think of women as gentle."

She smiled. "Allen Matthers, I'm beginning to suspect—under all that tough exterior—beats the heart of a romantic."

He snorted. "I'm no Galahad," he denied, once again surprising her with his knowledge of literature.

Allen was more than he seemed—certainly not just an illiterate mountain man.

"Still and all," he said, "I reckon there's good and bad in all of us. It just appears lately the bad is winning out."

"Yes," she agreed bitterly. "I used to think people were mostly good. But I've gotten my eyes opened. Now there are very few people on earth I trust." She met his eyes. "And you're one of them."

He gave an odd look. Then he quickly dropped his eyes and toyed with the cigar. After taking another puff, he flipped it into the swift water.

"I mean it, Allen. And I do thank you for all you've done for me."

He pushed away from the rail. "Can't say as I've done anything for you without selfish motives. Like you said—don't elevate me beyond what I deserve." Without preamble he walked away.

Growing perplexed, her eyes followed him.

Chapter 7

All summer Nelda had worked preserving food from the garden. Constantly busy, she found the days had flown on swift wings. The harvest was abundant. Both cellar and pantry were full to overflowing.

War news was sparse, full of rumors of Confederate victories in the east. But in mid-September many mouths in Clarksville turned down over news that Robert E. Lee had failed to work his magic in an invasion of Maryland against Union General McClellan. At Sharpsburg the two-day battle netted twenty-three thousand casualties. Lee had finally ordered the battered Army of Northern Virginia to withdraw across the Potomac. Nelda was appalled at the loss of life. Nonetheless, she was overjoyed that Lee had left Maryland un-victorious.

In October the gray beards gathered at the store—everyone a seasoned general in his own estimation—did more than frown over the news of Van Dorn's defeat in Tennessee. All heads nodded in agreement with Emmitt's assessment.

"You'd think they would have learned something about Van Dorn at Pea Ridge. What did they expect... letting him outrank Old Pap! Why if they'd have let Sterling Price boss things instead of Van Dorn that mix-up at Corinth would have turned out different!"

"Well, there ain't no limit to worse." Enos Hadley shook his head sadly and rolled around a cud of tobacco and spit between his fingers into a tin can. He wiped his mouth and said, "Price had better get his walking soldiers and Marmaduke's critter company busy guarding the rivers. If the Yankees get control of them, hit'll be like a octopus wrapping it's long testicles around us. Hit'll squeeze us to death."

Emmitt's face purpled as he glanced at a lady customer who had suddenly ducked behind her handkerchief with a choking cough. Nelda turned away, her shoulders shaking, and thought about how hard Papa would have laughed.

As the days shortened and the air grew crisp, she joined Tom in the cornfield to pull long dried ears from brown stalks. Her eyes often lifted beyond the field to woods swathed in color; coral maples as brilliant as a torch and crimsoned sassafras intermingled with hickories and persimmons gold enough to rival the sun. The sky, a shimmering blue, held southbound geese, their clarion calls echoing across the valley. Soon the corncrib was bulging. They piled the extra in a corner of the barn, and then cut and shocked the stalks. Lily would not want for fodder.

The weather was flawless, the evenings nippy, the days cloudless and warm. Nonetheless, she grew morose, her thoughts again retuning to Fred. He had been dead a year. It seemed an eternity! She wondered if the Indian wife had ever learned what befell him.

And she faced constant concern for Louise who was now practically an invalid and rarely left her room. Along with housework and outside chores, Nelda now climbed the stairs three times a day to serve meals. Louise had daily grown more childish, unaware or uncaring of the extra weight this placed on her daughter's overburdened shoulders.

"Close that window before you go!" Louise arranged the lace bed jacket tighter around thin shoulders. "This room is like ice. Have Tom lay a fire."

Nelda turned and set down the chamber pot in order to close the window. "Mama, Tom hasn't been able to climb the stairs for months. He can barely get around on flat ground. Besides, it's a lovely fall evening. We shouldn't need a fire for weeks yet."

"If your blood were as thin as mine, young lady, you'd have a blaze going soon enough!"

The petulant voice was sandpaper on Nelda's tired nerves. "I'll get a quilt. We don't have wood to waste. There's not a lot left from last year, and

I have no idea who will cut for us this year. Tom can't, and I would make a pitiful hand at it." It was one of the worries that kept her awake nights.

"Ask Robert to have one of his slaves cut it."

Nelda turned to stare. It was the first time Mama's mind had slipped.

"Or wait until Phillip comes," Louise added, "He'll be home any day now, and he will attend to it."

She fled before Mama could see the horrified expression. She stopped in the hall and looked back. Her world tilted. Mama was the only support she had. Now even that was gone! She went outside and stood in the backyard until a full yellow moon rose over the barn. Even when the breeze grew chill and damp, she had no desire to return inside. The once cozy house was a dismal prison. She thought of Papa and wept.

The next day a commotion drew Nelda to the window. Under a golden leafed hickory tree, Sirius, the old black and tan hound, stood straddle-legged, barking at scores of ragged men tramping past the house. Although they did not march like soldiers, they moved in a unified group. Some wore threadbare uniforms. However, there was not a visible weapon in the crowd.

"Oh, that noise!" Louise rose slightly from the pillow, moaned, and grabbed her head. Lately even the rooster's crow caused her torture. "Make that fool dog stop!"

Nelda hurried down the stairs and out into the autumn sunshine. She would lock Sirius inside the barn until the men had passed. When she reached for his collar, the old hound pulled back and continued barking.

"Appears he's got us treed," called a soldier.

Nelda looked up and smiled at the grinning, lanky man who had stopped to lean on the white picket fence while filling a pipe with tobacco. "It appears you're right," she said as Sirius kept barking. She took a few steps and then looked back. "You men are with the army?"

"Yep."

"But you have no weapons?"

"Four thousand of us and nary a gun. Sorry mess, ain't it? But General Hindman has a promise from old Granny Holms that he'll send us some. We're supposed to hold up here till they come. Then we'll join up with the others again," he said as a cloud of smoke wreathed his head.

Nelda knew the new commander of the Confederate Department of the Trans-Mississippi was not popular. The men considered Major General Holms both infirm and inept and hence the nickname Granny.

Just then a wagon rolled slowly past and the man scowled. "That is iffen there's any of us alive by the time Granny gets them guns together." He backed away, nodding at the wagon. "Smallpox. I done had it, but most of these boys ain't. You got a doctor in this here town?"

"No. They left with the army months ago."

"Well, they must be with the regulars. Ain't none of 'em with us."

She eyed another passing ambulance with troubled eyes. "Those infected men could spread disease to the town."

"Naw. We're gonna steer clear of town. Our orders said after we had crossed the river to head out of town and camp at a place on Horsehead Creek."

Nelda nodded. "Jim Wilson's farm, I imagine. It has wide fields near the creek. Before the war the county militia always drilled there."

"Pretty country around here. Never seed such bright colored timber."

Nelda glanced where he pointed beyond the pasture. The trees and bushes spreading the low hills were brilliant.

"Don't have color like that where I come from in the flat lands down south." He knocked tobacco from the pipe, put it into his pocket, and pushed away from the fence. "Reckon I better step lively and catch up."

She hurried to get information. "Some of my relatives are with General Hindman. Where are his regulars now?"

"Last I heared, they had a lively mix-up with the Yankees and got drove out of Fayetteville again. Hindman is over on the Mulberry River right now lickin' his wounds."

So, thought Nelda, *the Federals are back in Fayetteville*. Since Curtis was now entrenched at Helena, the Fayetteville troops must be under a different commander. She wondered how long it would be before they pushed south to Ft. Smith and ultimately on to Little Rock. She tugged Sirius toward the barn. He seemed to have lost interest in the troops, but she was taking no chances.

Smallpox had indeed infiltrated the ranks of the unarmed men sent to Clarksville. The Confederate dead continued to fill graves in the oak-bordered cemetery. The infected were quarantined in a log house north of town. Nelda heard that an army doctor had finally arrived to treat the sick and to vaccinate the well. One blustery day in late November, in spite of never having had the disease or the vaccine herself, she went to the makeshift hospital. For two days Louise had been holding her head and writhing in pain. If the physician would not come, Nelda hoped at least to get some laudanum.

Wind whipped dead leaves from the path and occasionally puffed grit into her eyes. She guided Lily along the road past fields which had lain fallow while the farmers fought for Hindman. The pistol made a reassuring bulge under the cape as she strained to hear every noise over the clip-clop of Lily's hooves. She arrived without mishap, the only fellow travelers, a few scampering bright-eyed squirrels and two young boys astride a scrawny mule.

A soldier guarded the lane leading to the log hospital. Unlike the men who had marched past her house a few weeks earlier, this man was in uniform and he held a rifle. He stepped forward.

"I can't let you pass, ma'am. This area is quarantined for smallpox."

"I know, but I need to speak to the physician. My mother is very ill."

He shifted, turning aside a bit from the cold wind whipping into his face. "I'm very sorry. The doctor left a few days ago. The disease seems to have abated here, and he rejoined the main army at Fort Smith."

Nelda groaned. "I don't suppose he left behind any medication for pain?"

He shook his head. "I'm sorry," he repeated.

She glanced in the direction of Fort Smith. "Would you know if the army has any laudanum?"

"I doubt it." He gave a sympathetic shake of the head. "But unfortunately, even if they do—with a big battle in the offing, it's unlikely a civilian would get any."

For a moment Louise's suffering was forgotten. Nelda pretended alarm. "The Yankees aren't invading again are they?"

He hesitated and then shrugged. "All I know is that orders came last night for all the troops here to hurry up to Fort Smith."

She drew in a scared-sounding breath. "Oh, no! I hope there's not another awful battle. My uncle is with the 16th Arkansas. And I have a young cousin with the troops, too." Her eyes widened. "Do you think the Yankees might come this far?"

"Oh, I wouldn't worry about that," he said, soothingly. "General Hindman has amassed almost the entire army at the fort. From the report I heard we have a much larger force than the Yankees, and the element of surprise is on our side. They don't even know he's marching to meet them."

She pretended to relax. "That is good news. Thank you so much for the reassurance." She turned the mare. "I have to get back to my mother."

Instead of heading home, however, she went east and then turned north toward Jim Loring's farm. The roads remained deserted. In haste, she cantered Lily, and then, after leaving the main road, urged her into a gallop.

The Loring cabin sat on the backside of a wide field, stripped of everything now save the stubs of cornstalks. The farm was neat, with good fences and a few outbuildings. But the lack of prosperity was evident in their simplicity.

A young boy sprinted across the field, running toward the cabin. Nelda suspected he had been guarding the trail. She slowed and approached with caution. She wondered how the large family managed to fit inside the small house. A curtain fluttered when she climbed down and tied Lily to the hitching rail near the porch. Before she knocked the door opened.

Opal Loring stepped onto the porch. While quickly shutting the door behind, she pulled a ragged cape around her shoulders. Winter sun emphasized the washboard wrinkles in shrunken cheeks where jaw teeth were missing.

"Mrs. Loring, I hate to disturb you, but Allen Matthers told me if I ever needed to get word to him to come here. He said one of your boys could take a message to Mr. Matthers."

Opal's eyes narrowed. "Hit's mighty dangerous fer a young'un to be out and about theses days ..."

Nelda hurried to explain. "I wouldn't ask if it weren't very important. I have vital news to pass on about the war."

Opal remained a sphinx.

Nelda threw caution to the wind. "Mrs. Loring, I've just found out that General Hindman has gathered all his troops at Fort Smith."

"Everybody has knowed that fer weeks," Opal scoffed.

Nelda nodded. "Yes, but he's about to make a surprise march against the Union forces. Perhaps if their commander knows in time he can avert disaster."

To Nelda's surprise, the front door opened. Jim Loring stood in the doorway. His eagle eyes were narrowed.

"How do you know this?"

She quickly related the details.

Jim nodded. "I just came from that direction. General Blunt is moving south. Hindman might take him by surprise." Jim chewed his lip. "Opal, I better ride. Pack me a mite of food."

Opal's shoulders drooped. "But Jim, ya just got here! And you ought not to travel in daylight." In spite of the protest, with a resigned look, she entered the cabin.

Jim faced Nelda. "I'll try to get through, but I have to go careful. I'm a wanted man."

"Perhaps you could get word to Allen ..."

"Naw," he said. "No time. I got no idea where he is. Besides, I ain't real sure but what Red and some of them boys of his has rebel leanings."

Nelda drew a deep breath. "Well, good luck." She stepped off the porch and mounted. "I have to get home. My mama is suffering with terrible headaches. I wish I could go see your granny and ask if she has anything to stop pain."

"Wait a minute," he said. He stepped into the cabin and returned with a small leather pouch. "Here's some dried plants and roots. Ain't sure just what kind. The Injuns give 'em to me when I was wounded. I chewed 'em. Give me mighty strange dreams, but they stopped the pain."

"Thank you so much!" She gratefully clasped the pouch.

"What do you hear from your pa?" he asked.

"Not a word in months. I'm hopeful since Mr. Flanagan got elected governor that Papa will be released.

"I hope so," said Jim, "but don't get your hopes up."

"Mr. Loring … " Nelda stopped. Now was not the time to ask questions. "Thank you for all you're doing. Please be careful."

He smiled. For just a moment his hard eyes twinkled. "I intend to. I'm sort of fond of my hide."

Nelda smiled and waved as she rode away.

The Indian herbs did calm Louise. Although she remained weak and had some pain-filled days, the teas seemed to lessen the agony. She slept more and Nelda was overjoyed that the thrashing and moaning had stopped.

Now she risked leaving the house more often. Tom needed help gathering dead snags to use for firewood. Neither he nor Nelda had the strength to fell and chop trees. It distressed her how slowly the woodpile grew and then how quickly it disappeared as the weather grew colder.

One day, as they unloaded the meager load near the back door, the Hadley boy stepped through the front gate. He pulled a cap off tousled dark hair. His squared jaw now had a hint of beard.

"I saw you out gatherin' wood. I have a bucksaw. I can get you up a good pile."

Nelda eyed the skinny, shivering boy. "You're David Hadley, aren't you, the one who delivers telegrams." When he flushed she supposed he was recalling his last trip here. He had smirked over Phillip's arrest.

"Aren't many telegrams these days." His eyes grew wary. "I don't charge much for wood cuttin,' providing your money ain't Confederate script."

She nodded. "I have a little coin left. Come inside where it's warm, and we'll talk business."

"I'd rather talk here." He stood with hands shoved into ragged pockets, looking through narrowed, suspicious eyes as if she were a dishonest horse trader.

Nelda shrugged. "Suit yourself."

His hunched shoulders shivered, and for an instant, fear overshadowed his eyes. He stammered, "I ... I'm just in a hurry to get home. Grandpa is expecting me."

She felt a rush of pity. He must need the money badly to practically come begging. "I'll need several loads," she said. "What's your price per rick?"

With a poker face he quoted a fair price. When Nelda nodded, his face lit.

That afternoon rumors swirled in Emmitt's store. Tom Sorrels said there were thousands of troops camped nearby, and they had just come from a great victory against the Yankees. Gill Harris growled at him to keep his fool mouth shut until he knew what he was talking about. Nelda took comfort in Gill's surliness. Perhaps it was no victory after all.

"Marmaduke is camped over on Wire Road," put in Emmitt. "A couple of his officers were just in here. But the way they tell it Hindman had no business sending them to fight with no ammunition and no food. They said if they hadn't sneaked off in the dead of night with rags on the wagon wheels they'd have all been captured."

Nelda heaved a relieved breath. Jim must have gotten through! At least the Union commander had prevailed. Then her lips drew down. What about Elijah and Uncle Ned?

Emmitt went on, "Hindman ought to go to Virginia and take lessons from Lee. General Lee doesn't win battles by sneakin' away. The Yankees won't be forgetting Fredericksburg in a hurry."

Gill's lip curled. "Emmitt, since you're so damned smart, they ought to put you in charge."

Emmitt left off wiping the counter to give him a hard look. "I figure I couldn't do any worse."

When Nelda arrived home, she was surprised to find Louise alert and sitting up in bed, eyes bright and a hint of color in her shrunken cheeks. Nelda beamed. Maybe Mama was improving! Then—as she recalled the old saying that just before death, a person often rallied—her smile faded.

"I called and called but you didn't answer," Louise scolded. "Where have you been?"

"I went to the store to hear the latest news." Nelda went on, "There are Confederate troops camped over on Wire Road."

Louise sat straight up. "I want you to go see if Tap is with them. I want to see him once more before I die."

Nelda's eyes widened. Did Mama have a premonition?

"Mama, don't you recall—Uncle Tap was sent out of state along with the regular Confederate troops."

She dreaded Mama's death but it was more heartbreaking to watch her mind slip away.

The days ran together in boring monotony. The only visitor at the house was young David Hadley bringing loads of wood on a sled pulled by a bony white mule. Nelda invited him inside to warm by the fire, but he declined.

Christmas passed almost unnoticed. Louise had a terrible day. Nelda spent the day at her bedside. Although the roaring fire in the bedroom fireplace devoured wood as fast as a hungry wolf ate a rabbit, she kept logs blazing. She could not stand to see Louise shiver and pull at the covers.

Late in the afternoon Tom came to the back door with an armload of wood.

"Just put it in the kitchen wood box, Tom. I'll carry it upstairs."

He dipped his gray head. "How's Miz Louise this evenin'?"

"She seems a bit better. She's asleep just now."

"Glad to hear it. Miz Louise been good to me." As Tom dumped the wood into the box, Nelda followed him into the kitchen. Wind moaned at the eaves and rattled the opened shutters.

"Tom, sit down a minute. I need to talk to you."

His eyes widened. "No, missy." He looked offended. "Tom don't sit in the house!"

"Well you certainly may if you want to. I'm too tired to stand."

She dropped into a chair. He remained stiff and erect.

"That's sort of what I want to talk to you about." She hesitated. "Did you know that on the first day of January, Mr. Lincoln is freeing all the slaves in the rebel states?"

"The Emancipation Proclamation." He nodded the grizzled head. "I knows all about it. All the colored folks is talking about it. Some of the young ones is even gwan'a join up with the Yankee army."

Nelda was surprised at his knowledge. She had mistakenly thought Tom stayed isolated. He must go visiting after dark. She drew a paper from the apron pocket. "The South won't honor the proclamation, but I found this in Papa's records. It's your freedom papers. In case anything ever happens to me, you should keep these. You know how Papa insisted you go free, even though Mama had different ideas."

"Miz Louise is quality. She knows a lady got to have colored folks to do the fetchin' and totin.'" But Tom reached a bony hand to take the paper. "I seen this here paper years ago. Marse Phillip give it to me, but I tol him to keep it." Tom eyed the paper with regret. "I can't read it no how."

"Tom, it says you're free. You can take this paper and go anywhere you like."

He grinned. "I likes the barn fine. Ain't many colored folks got a real feather tick on the bed like Old Tom."

Nelda smiled. "I'm certainly glad to have you. However, if you ever decide to go, it's your choice."

The next day was Sunday. But with no services to attend, Nelda lost track of the days. It was almost noon, with the laundry well underway, before she realized she was breaking the Sabbath. Pale sun was a respite from recent days of downpour. Since the laundry had piled up, perhaps the proverbial ox was in the ditch, she reassured herself and kept on with the chore.

In such frigid weather she refused to stand outdoors over a wash pot. A good scrubbing in the kitchen had to suffice. As water dripped from her wet hands back into the washtub, she sighed and plunged them back into the suds and scrubbed the dress back and forth and back and forth.

She scowled at her cracked, red hands. Had they ever been soft and pretty? After drying them, she rubbed her tired back. To ease the crimp between her shoulders, she stood straight and walked to the narrow window and looked out. The yard was dead and overgrown. Yellowed brittle grass waved in the pasture. Bare winter woods stood beyond. Thick clouds roiled making the day as gray as a Rebel uniform. She felt more barren than the winter landscape. It was a new year—1863. Dread washed over her. What lay ahead? She wondered how much longer Mama would survive. And lately old Tom was so weak she doubted he would see another spring. How would she manage without any help? Along with nursing Mama, there were more chores now than she could do. And in the spring there would be the garden to plant and afterwards the harvest again.

With a heavy heart, she turned to the tubs. The rinse water was soapy, but she was too tired to change it. She rinsed a dress as much as possible, wrung it out, and after piling it on top of some wet sheets, she carried the full basket outside. Cold wind whipped her mercilessly each time she hurried outside to hang the heavy wet laundry. Clouds were piling up again and the sky had grown dark. It was probably useless to hang the laundry. But she despised wet clothing draped all over the house!

Suddenly, she whirled. Loud cries arose from the direction of the courthouse. Tales of recent atrocities flashed through her mind. Gangs were combing the county. Along Piney Creek, houses had been looted and torched. Women had been ravaged and tortured to learn hiding places of valuables.

But this was no cry of terror. It was the ferocious Rebel yell. Hindman's force must have arrived! A rumor had sped through town the day before that the entire army was on the run. Enos Hadley and a few old graybeards with muskets had even gathered on the courthouse lawn, ready to repel the Yankee invaders who chased after.

She hauled the full basket back into the house and changed into her good cape.

"Mama, I'll be right back," she called up the stairs and then hurried away before Louise had a chance to object.

The road was a muddy mess. Her boots, soon caked in red clay, made a sucking sound with each step and almost pulled from her feet. Even before reaching the Methodist Church, she heard fifes and drums. It was a rollicking tune, one she did not know. Hundreds of marching feet kept time. She drew the cape close and hurried ahead.

The army did not appear to be fleeing. But they were a ragged, pitiful looking group. In spite of being scarecrows, they stepped lively. Each passing regiment tried to outdo the other by giving the blood-curdling Rebel yell. Chills traced Nelda's spine. She could only imagine how intimidating the cry would be in battle! Hoping for a better view, she weaved through the crowd. Women waved white handkerchiefs. Excited children ran alongside the marching men. Happy cries of recognition rang out as familiar faces passed. Although Nelda tiptoed, she saw neither Ned nor Elijah. Before her arrival many regiments had tramped down Main Street and disappeared across the covered bridge. Perhaps they had already passed.

As the last troops departed, a group of civilians gathered around the newspaper office. She went to join them. A dart of sadness pierced her upon seeing the boarded up windows where she had once spent so many happy hours. A paper was tacked to the front door. She pushed forward to see the notice signed by General Hindman. The civilian population was ordered to act as pickets and report any enemy movement to the local provost marshal. Gill Harris stood nearby, his narrow chest pushed out.

"Yep, folks. If you see anything—anything a'tall—get word to me as fast as you can, and I'll pass it along to Cousin Tom... He pretended chagrin. "Excuse me. I meant to say the general." He espied Nelda and his mouth turned down. "No telling what those Yankees will try now that the army's been ordered to Little Rock."

Enos Hadley spoke up through his long flowing beard. "Gill, are you saying, the army ain't running away?"

"Of course they're not! Cousin Tom simply got ordered to Little Rock."

"If the Yankees ain't right behind him, why did he put up notices fer us to be pickets?"

Gill's nose flared. "Enos, go find a rocking chair and sit in the sun. Leave this business to folks who know what we're doing."

Enos snorted as Gill walked away. "I seen that strutting bantam a few minutes ago when he met *Cousin Tom*. The general had no idee who he was. When Gill made his acquaintance and said they was kin, Hindman's nose wrinkled like he had smelled a polecat."

Another old man laughed. "I reckon that's exactly what he did smell."

Enos shook his head. "Don't know what the South is coming to—Hindman giving orders to old men and younguns to guard his back. Most as bad in my book as Lincoln and his Emasculation Proclamation."

Nelda was too preoccupied to smile. Deep in thought, she retraced her steps home. When Union troops did arrive—and they were sure to, some day soon—what would happen? Would the gray-beards and the women and children resist? She could picture Enos Hadley and his grandson, David, with old squirrel guns cocked and primed. It would be a futile attempt, but since so many had lost loved ones in battle, there was deep hatred in the breast of Clarksville for all that was Union

Upon arriving home, she glanced up, dejected. The sky looked heavy, pregnant with snow. It was doubtful the clothes would dry at all. Even though she hated clothes dripping on the floor, it would be better to hang them inside.

She had just sat down a heavy basket full of the wet clothes in the kitchen when she heard a wagon approaching. It stopped at the front gate. She picked up the pistol lying close by on a chair. It was never far out of reach. After hurrying down the hall, she peeked through the window and then drew in a sharp breath. *Soldiers!* Undoubtedly they were foraging. The wagon already held heaps of provender. Desperate, she wondered what to hide first.

A knock echoed. If she did not answer they would kick in the door. She hid the pistol under her apron, and with a deep breath, opened the door. Her eyes grew hot.

Drew Morrison stood on the porch. He looked down the hall and then stepped inside. "Army is pulling out, and we need food."

Nelda eyed him with a stormy glare. He turned back and ordered two soldiers inside. He led the soldiers into the kitchen and soon feet tramped on the cellar stairs. Before long the men returned with arms loaded. Crocks of cabbage, jars of fruits, jams and jellies, and then winter squash and large pumpkins followed the strings of dried beans, peppers, and braids of onions into the wagon. The soldiers rifled smoke house and barn before finally mounting and riding away.

"We left you a few things," said Drew.

She cut him with blazing eyes. "Only because your wagon is too full already."

He shrugged and mounted his horse. "I could have taken it all. Get uppity and I'll come back and get what I left."

He could come back. How could she stop him? He had the protection and the power of the army. She could not fight them all. It was only by the grace of God that Tom had warned her to hide most of the smoked meat. It was stowed away in barrels hidden under hay in the barn.

She entered the pantry and frowned at what little remained. The cellar had been depleted of almost everything, but there were the packets of garden seed on the top shelf of the pantry along with two large sacks of dried beans and peas sitting in the corner that Drew had missed. Although most of the chickens had disappeared, there were a few hens left. They would start laying again when the weather warmed. The cabbage and turnips remained buried in straw and dirt where Tom had hilled them last fall. It would not be sumptuous fare, but it would feed them for a long while—if she could keep the foraging army from finding it! She must find a good hiding place.

She jerked when Louise rang the bell.

"What is going on down there?" the weak querulous voice drifted down.

"Coming, Mama," she called tiredly. Mama claimed that troubles came in threes. Lately it had come in droves. Nelda wondered, *"What next?"*

It came even sooner than she had anticipated.

A week later she had still not found a good hiding place. She was ruminating on the dilemma as she entered the kitchen and glanced across the field toward the woods. She froze. A pillar of black smoke roiled in the east. It was a backdrop for riders galloping across the field. There were at least a dozen hard-bitten men, most dressed in ragged coats and slouch hats. Some led packhorses. Behind them fast-moving wagons careened across the field.

Bushwhackers! Nelda went stiff from fear.

"Tom!" she screamed.

The raiders would be upon them in seconds. She ran for the pistol. When she burst through the library door, she was astonished to find Louise, trembling and white-faced, fumbling on the desk for the pistol. As Nelda grabbed it, shots exploded in the yard.

"Mama, stay here," she yelled and ran for the window. Her breath caught in her throat and her knees threatened to buckle.

Tom lay sprawled face down on the frozen ground. Men swarmed the barn. Some had already opened the smokehouse door. Others chased squawking chickens across the barnyard. Smoke soon poured from the barn roof. Three men headed toward the house.

Nelda opened the window and leveled the pistol. The tall man was dressed in a Confederate uniform coat. She aimed the gun at the gold buttons on his chest. Her hand shook. She paused. As Papa had taught, she held her breath and squeezed the trigger. He pitched back, still holding a chicken. The hen squawked and flapped, and in a dash, escaped through the back fence. She fired again and another man grabbed his side. With his long coat flapping, he fired and ran toward the back gate and a plunging horse. She ducked as his shot hit the back wall. Again she fired, but missed. With her next shot, the man jerked and almost toppled from the prancing horse.

She dodged just as glass exploded from the window. As more shots riddled the house she hunkered down, staying well below the window. Pistol ready, her eye trained on the back door. But no one entered. Finally she risked a quick peek.

"Thank goodness! Mama they've ridden . . . " She turned from the window. "Mama!" she cried and ran to the crumpled heap lying on the floor. "Are you shot!?" Frantic, she turned Louise over. There was no blood, no wound. But Louise's eyes were open, staring into nothingness.

Nelda dropped alongside, taking the limp head into her lap. With a low moan, she rocked her back and forth, stroking her hair.

"Mama, you'll never have another awful headache," she whispered, stroking her brow. "Poor Papa! This will kill him."

She was never sure how long she sat and held Louise. Finally her cold limbs began to ache as the fire burned low. She arranged Louise's arms across her chest and then stood and walked to the shattered window. She had killed a man—in reality probably three. No matter that they deserved it. It was still an awful thing and her palms grew sweaty and her stomach heaved thinking of it. Her knees trembled as she opened the door and leaned on the door jam.

It was snowing. Small flakes swirled down on the smoldering heap that had been the barn. The chicken house was still standing and so was the empty smokehouse, but the corncrib had burned.

Someone must have heard the shots. There had been so many. But no one came. Should she go for help—but to whom? There was no one left in town but old men and women. *And Gill Harris*. Her lip curled. She would not go to him for anything!

She drew on her cloak and closed the door behind her. Clinching her teeth, she walked straight to Tom. He lay sprawled, one thin arm flung out, alongside the marauder. Blood wet his hair and puddled on the ground under his head.

"I will not get sick. I will not get sick," she muttered, fighting waves of nausea. Papa always said the best way to do a bad job was to do it quick and get it over with. And this was the worst job she had ever faced.

Avoiding looking at the faithful black man, she turned her back and grasped his feet, one in each hand, and gave a hard pull. He was frail. He was easier to pull than she had feared. She dragged him to the chicken house, refusing to think about the trail his bumping, bloody head was making on the ground.

This is cold as a tomb, she thought, shivering. *The bodies will be fine here until I get holes dug. I can't leave them outside. There are too many hungry dogs roaming about*.

Although she was certain he was dead, she dreaded touching the bushwhacker. He was tall with broad chest and shoulders straining at the seams of the dirty gray coat. She should search his pockets. She could not make herself touch him—at least not yet. She stood for a moment and through the swirling snow watched the trail of black smoke still penciling the eastern sky. It was the kind of smoke made by a burning house. Someone else had lost barn or house—or both.

It took a long while to drag the body. She could pull only a few inches before stopping to pant. If it were not unchristian, she would leave him to the animals. But it did not seem right.

Finally, when both men were inside the chicken house, she shut the door and stood in the cold, dreading to reenter the house. It would be a lonely wake. If Mama had died two years ago, the house would not have held all the mourners. Now with Papa jailed and Mama and Tom dead, she was alone, truly alone. She bent her head but her eyes stayed dry. She mentally scolded herself when she realized she was also grieving over the loss of all the smoked meat that had been hidden in the barn and the corn that had burned in the corncrib.

There was no casket. She wrapped Louise's body in the best white counterpane, and pulling and tugging, laid her on the sofa in the parlor. In spite of the horrible blackened walls and smoke stained fabric, it seemed the only fitting place, this room—Mama's pride. In the gloom of twilight, Nelda pretended it was as it had been. She could see it in her mind's eye as she lit a candle and placed it on the mantle.

She turned. No! Nothing was as it had been. She dropped to her knees beside the sofa and laid her head against the stiff cold woman lying there.

"Oh, Mama," she moaned. "I loved you. I wish I had told you. I wish I had tried harder to understand you." Tears wet her clasped hands as she tried to pray.

A loud rapping on the door startled her. She grabbed the gun and hurried down the hall. She sucked in a breath. Mary Beth and Tabbatha Morrison stood on the porch! The women wore soot-covered dresses and no wraps. The black earbobs dangling in Tabbatha's ears were the only remnants of former grandeur.

Nelda opened the door, just a crack. "What do you want?" she asked.

Mary Beth held tresses of loose, tousled hair from blowing in her face. On her hand was a bloody bandage. "They… they burned us out," she stammered. "Our house is gone—even the barns."

Hard faced, Nelda simply stared.

"Surely you'll let us in?"

"Go to your rebel friends."

Mother and daughter exchanged quick glances.

"But you're our oldest friends," said Mary Beth hesitantly.

"So no one else would take you in? I suppose your brothers made too many enemies, conscripting and foraging," guessed Nelda. "Well, Drew took my food. And Bo didn't endear himself to me when he set this house on fire."

Shock washed both faces. "B … Bo?" stuttered Mary Beth.

"I don't believe it," insisted Tabbatha. "Let me speak to Louise."

"No."

Her eyes batted. "Surely in the name of Christian charity—"

"Mother is dead. And you'll find no Christian charity here."

She slammed the door. Then she leaned against it. The Lord might strike her dead. And Papa would be sorely disappointed. And yet she did not call after them. Her eyes glittered. Let them suffer. They had turned their backs on her and Mama. Now they were reaping what they sowed.

Sometime during the night, the snow stopped. Nelda slept none at all. The next morning two inches of white coated the frozen ground where she stood digging, her only implement a mattock found leaning against the garden fence. She wore a woolen dress, heavy stockings, and work boots.

Raising the mattock high, she brought it down hard and grimaced when it bounced without making a dent. The ground was frozen solid. She made a few more ineffective swings and stopped to blow out a breath. Her frown deepened. She would never be able to dig a grave.

She bit her lip and looked toward the far side of the field. There were some over-hangs, little caves down in the bluff along the creek. She supposed she could bury Mama in one of them and pile stones at the opening. It seemed barbaric. But she could think of nothing else.

With squared shoulders, she refused to dwell on the horror of the task. It must be done—so she would do it.

In the cold she trudged through the woods toward the small valley where the mare was penned. Upon topping a rise she stopped. The mare nickered and came trotting. Although the tack had burned along with the barn, she had found a frayed rope hanging on the chicken house wall. She slipped it around Lily's neck and then patted her side, worrying over the thinness of the mare.

Before returning home she went to the bluffs and found a small overhang with a crevice sufficiently deep enough to be a grave. Then she led Lily across the white pasture, past what had been the barn and on past the ruined smokehouse and through the gate.

She glanced toward a charred door, the outside entrance to the cellar. It stood open. She doubted there was anything left. But the marauders had not found the salt hidden in the chicken house. And there were still cabbages and turnips in the hill. If she rationed carefully and if no more raiders came, she would not starve—at least not for a while. But she must find a better hiding place for the food in the pantry, just as soon as the bodies were buried.

She shook her head and mentally scolded, *Mama's not even in the ground! How can I be thinking of food!*

The house was dark and cold and empty. Nelda stopped at the parlor door and steeled herself before going inside. Without looking at Louise—certain she would break down if she did—she grabbed the corners of the counterpane and half-dragged, half-carried Louise's body outside. Lily, tied short to the fence, snorted and sidestepped. After a mighty struggle Nelda finally hefted the body onto her skittish back. With grim determined steps, she led the mare to the bluffs.

There were no flowers, no grieving friends, no pastor to pray, no comfort whatsoever to soften the harsh reality of the ragged, cold grave. Nelda fought hysteria over stuffing prim, proud Mama into a hole—like hilling a head of cabbage for the winter. She gritted her teeth and did it anyway.

After an hour of hard work, rocks covered the opening. Not wanting to leave even a crack, she felt along the icy ridge for more loose rocks and filled even the tiny holes.

There was only one more overhang large enough for a body. She would put Tom in it. Her jaws hardened. She would simply drag the marauder away. The varmints would take care of him. She returned to the house and got Tom's body and placed it in the crevice. This time she had to go farther to find enough rocks.

In late afternoon snow began to fall again, a gentle white curtain. She trudged behind Lily and the marauder's stiff body dragging behind, making uneven tracks in the snow. After going far into the woods, she untied the body, looped the rope on her arm and looked down. She squared her jaw and searched his pockets. They held only a plug of tobacco, a pocketknife, and some money, although not much. His ill-gotten gains from previous raids must have been hidden or already squandered. Someone, somewhere, might love him. But she felt no pity.

"Well," she said aloud, "you shouldn't have turned to crime."

She was not content to return home until she had checked the caves one more time and piled more rocks at the opening. Finally satisfied that she had done the best job possible, she turned away. In the dusk, snow gave the pasture a luminous glow and cedars and pines were iced with white. Skeletons of bare trees stood black against the horizon.

"Come on," she urged Lily. Stumbling along behind the horse, she was too frozen and weary to climb the bank. She searched for a less steep incline and finally reached the top. It had been the longest two days of her life, and the strangest. She glanced back to where Mama and Tom now lay, side-by-side, in shallow caves. The rocks she had just placed were already snow-covered. .

She bit her trembling lip. "I hate not doing better by you, Mama. And you too, Tom," she whispered. "You were a faithful friend."

CHAPTER 8

A week crawled by. Nelda could hardly drag out of bed. Sometimes, when she first awakened, for a few blissful moments, she forgot. But the respite quickly faded. And necessity forced her to leave the house in search of a hiding place for the food.

Frozen ground crunched beneath her feet but the sky was clear and blue. It was abominably cold with the thermometer hovering near zero. Her breath made clouds around her face as she started across the pasture. She cut through the woods to climb the steep hill beyond. At the top she stopped to stare in disbelief at the ruins. Where the stately Morrison house had once dominated the skyline, now only four blackened chimneys rose stark and naked from a heap of smoldering debris. Barns, stables, and outbuildings were rubble. At the end of the long graceful drive, a heap of blackened bricks now shouldered the massive chimneys and spilled onto a lawn covered with dead grass. Tall, brittle ironweed edged the walkways and flowerbeds; and across the fence, yellow sage and tiny pines dotted pastures where purebred horses once frolicked.

With a moan she sank onto a rock and stared. She was shocked at the personal sense of loss. And yet the loss was great. Here had once lived friends. Here she had passed delightful, carefree hours. Here she had danced with Fred…

A step echoed. In one swift motion she grabbed a rock, stood, and whirled. A gray mule topped the rise, brayed, and rushed forward. With a nervous laugh, she lowered the rock. It was only old Jepner, a mule ridden by the Morrison's slaves.

"Hello, Jepner." She dropped the rock and rubbed his muzzle as he nuzzled her hand. "I don't have a treat for you. Poor old fellow." She ran her hand down his side. "You're skin and bones. I guess even the bushwhackers didn't want you. But I do. Yes, I do. I have plenty of use for you. Let's go search the ruins and see if we can find anything useful."

Then her eyes widened with surprise when someone stepped from the shadows of a nearby oak tree.

"Della! What in the world—"

Nelda caught the young woman just as she collapsed and eased her onto the ground. Della, who had always been handsome, was drawn and thin and her dark skin was sickly gray. Tattered rags barely covered her emaciated frame.

"Are you ill?" Nelda unconsciously stepped back and wiped her hands on her cloak.

"Just mighty weak and hungry."

"Let's get you home. Can you climb up on the mule?"

Della nodded weakly. "I just come from the house. Where's my pappy? I seen the barn burnt up."

"I'll tell you everything after we get you home and warming by the fire."

Jepner meekly accepted the burden and walked placidly alongside Nelda as they made slow progress across the pasture. He remained near the back door when she helped Della into the kitchen and into a chair drawn near the stove. She brushed ashes from atop buried coals and pushed kindling near the faint glow before turning to face Della.

"Your pa is dead."

With a pained expression, she took the news in silence.

"It was quick. He didn't suffer. Marauders shot him."

Her face crumpled.

Nelda turned away to give her a moment alone with her grief. She set the coffeepot to heat while she got a cup and some cornbread left from supper. There were no beans left from her meager supper, but the bread would hopefully assuage Della's hunger.

The sad news did not affect her appetite. She ate ravenously while

Nelda studied the pretty face. Della's skin was still flawless, but now her cheeks were hollow, the cheekbones sticking out sharply. Nonetheless she was still a beauty.

"Where have you been?" Nelda finally asked.

She hung her head. "I reckon you're right put out at me for runnin' off like I done ... " She looked up, her eyes defiant. "I was mad at Miz Louise. Gideon run off. He wouldn't take no more beatin's. If he stayed, he woulda killed one of them Harris.' But he wouldn't let me go with him, so I follered."

"Where is Gideon?"

Della's large dark eyes were suddenly full of pride. "He's a soldier, missy, in the Second Arkansas Colored. They at Helena now with lots of white soldiers. I was there, too, but Gideon made me leave. He was scared I'd get the fever. Lots of colored folks are livin' there down close to the river. But there's not much to eat and folks is gettin' sick and dying like flies. He told me to come home. He said you wouldn't be too mad at me for running off?" She had made it a question; but she hurried on. "He says it won't be long before they run all the rebel trash away from here, anyway. Then we're goin' north to live." She bit her lip as she realized that might not be news to Nelda's liking. "But I'll work hard for you 'til Gideon comes for me."

Nelda felt weary. How often she had heard the sentiment—it won't be long! Well, it had been long, day after dreary day of pain and suffering, as the war dragged on and on.

"Go to bed. We'll talk tomorrow. Your things are still in your room."

Della sagged with relief. "The good Lord bless you, missy."

Nelda was surprised by the benediction. To say the least Della had never been religious.

"Where is Miz Louise?"

"She's dead."

Della gasped. "Shot her, too?"

"No. She died the same day as your pa, but she wasn't shot. I think it was the headaches that killed her. Now, go lie down."

Della said no more as she went into the small room below the staircase and shut the door.

Nelda sighed. It would be good to have Della's help. Along with the other countless chores, there would soon be the garden to plant and tend. But now there would be one more mouth to feed. It would be months before the harvest. The cornmeal was almost gone. She had found some corn in the chicken house, but not much. There were, thankfully, still plenty of dried beans. And soon there would be wild greens to gather, poke, dandelion, and dock. But she must hide what little food there was!

However, for the next week, there was no time to search out a hiding place. Della was ill. Although Nelda hovered at her bedside, bathing her scorched body with cool water, the fever raged. She feared each ragged breath would be Della's last. She brewed tea from the last of Jim Loring's herbs and forced the liquid between the woman's parched lips. On the third day, exhausted and emotionally spent, Nelda awakened from a fitful doze in a chair drawn near the bed. Della lay still. Too still.

With a trembling hand, she reached out. She dreaded touching the smooth black forehead. She dreaded more sorrow—another body to bury. Most of all, she dreaded being alone.

Della's eyes flew open. "Missy," she rasped, "you look awful."

Near hysteria, Nelda laughed.

"Get yourself to the bed," ordered Della, in a weak voice. "I be fine." She reached a frail hand to squeeze Nelda's arm. "Thank you for lookin' after me. Even after I run off, you been good to me. You a good Christian, missy."

"Don't give credit where credit isn't due," she said and immediately thought of Allen and the day he had cautioned her in the same way. She wondered where he was. She would like to see him again.

Her wish was soon granted. He arrived a few days later. She smiled as she opened the back door and he quickly stepped inside. His blue eyes were bright in the morning light.

"I heard you'd had trouble. I see the barn burned. Are you all right?"

She nodded and then succinctly told of the attack.

"Damned bushwhackers! Tom was a fine old man."

"Mama died, too."

"Your ma was killed too," he echoed in disbelief.

"No. She died during the attack. I think from the shock as much as anything."

He swore. And when she told of Drew foraging, he swore again.

"Do you have any food left?"

"Enough to get by for a while—unless Drew comes back again."

His frown deepened. "We hid our food in a cave near the house. You got any place like that nearby where no one's likely to find it?"

She nodded. "There's a bluff not far away—"

"Naw," he said, shaking his head. "Too likely to get wet in a blowing rain. You need someplace dry... like a cellar or a cave."

"I'll try to find some place," she said wearily.

"When you do, be mighty careful coming and going. Make sure no one is watching. I'll be gone for a while but I'll check on you when I get back. I hate leaving you all alone—"

She cut him off. "Della came back. She's here with me. She was very sick but she's better now."

"Good," he said and put a hand on the doorknob. "I was worried about you being alone."

"Surely you have time for a cup of coffee," she suggested.

"Wish I did. But I don't. Take care of yourself."

He's always hurrying away, she thought with regret. And then, frowning, she chewed her jaw and wondered what he was doing.

She took his advice and hid the food at the Morrison's. Since the place was a heap of rubble, no one was likely to pilfer. In the burned out cellar, she and Della placed the food into a wooden barrel and covered it over with gunnysacks.

"I wonder what happened to Miz Tabbatha and Missy Mary Beth," mused Della.

Nelda's face grew cold. "I wouldn't know. After the raid, when they came banging on my door begging for help, I sent them packing. I haven't seen them since."

Della was shocked. "Law, missy, don't you know the golden rule—do unto others? Besides that—you ought to be careful. We all reaps what we sow."

Nelda's eyes glinted. "That's exactly what I thought, Della. They reaped what they sowed."

Della's eyes followed Nelda's rigid back up the steep stairs and her brows drew together in a worried frown.

Nelda stopped near the cellar in the mild sunshine. "Della, go on home. This nice weather has me thinking that we should get some seed into the ground soon. I'm going to see if David Hadley will plow the cornfield and garden. Of course it's way too early to plant corn, but we can plant a few things in the garden."

"You sure you don't need me to come along?"

"No, it's too far. You're still weak. Go home and rest. I won't be long."

David and Enos lived in a shack alongside Spadra Creek. David was in the yard when she arrived. His eyes grew large with surprise.

"Howdy, ma'am. Grandpa's not here. He's at the store."

She smiled. "Is Enos ever not there?"

David grinned. "Mr. Emmitt has threatened to charge him rent."

She laughed. "Well, you're the one I wanted to see, anyway."

They soon made the agreement. When the weather allowed, he would use his harness and plow and turn her ground for the loan of Jepner. His own mule had died during the winter. She wondered if bony Jepner would be strong enough to pull a plow. If not she would have to take the mare from hiding. A crop was imperative.

As she walked home wind stung her cheeks and tugged at the long cape. But it felt good to be outdoors in the sunshine. The road was knee-deep in muck so she walked on the grassy bank.

She had not gone far when a group of soldiers appeared in the distance. Lately the roads had been full of them. Four soldiers were mounted; the fifth drove a wagon. In spite of the six-mule hitch, the wagon made poor progress. She stopped to watch the wheels suck through the mud.

Suddenly she recognized Tyler Callaway, one of Mary Beth's ardent admirers. Nelda, herself, had danced with him on numerous occasions. His golden-brown eyes had always twinkled with good-humor.

He soon spied her and urged his mount forward. Tall, medium framed, with muscled legs, he sat the horse as if born to it. Light-brown wavy hair fell past the Confederate uniform collar. Always handsome, now he was striking in the tailored uniform.

With a big smile, he reined in and removed the hat. "Miss Nelda. How nice to see you. How are you?"

"Surviving."

"How are your folks?"

"Mama is dead."

"I am truly sorry!" Then he quickly asked, "How are the Morrisons?"

She hid a frown and related information, some of which David Hadley had just shared. "When their house was burned by bushwhackers, they migrated to Texas. The same bunch of marauders attacked my place and killed our hired man."

His jaw hardened. "Damned bushwhackers—begging your pardon, ma'am. They'll pay when we catch them. That's why we're here. General Holms ordered us to rid the country around here of the scoundrels. Don't worry. We'll get them." He glanced in the direction of the Morrison's. "I had so looked forward … " He let the thought die.

Nelda chewed her lip for a moment. Tyler might be a good source of information. She hastened to ask, "Would you gentlemen like a cup of coffee?"

"Real coffee?"

She smiled. "Yes, real coffee. The marauders didn't find my beans."

"I'd love some! But we have to report and unload this corn."

"Corn?"

"A wagon load. Most of it is going on upriver to the Territory—that is if the boats can slip past the Union patrols. The Yankees don't want us feeding the Indians. They're trying to toll them into the Union camp."

"I understand the people at the fort are starving, too," she said.

He nodded. "It's bad there. Hopefully there'll be enough to go around. With eight boats, surely some of them will get through."

She was glad to get that information so easily. "Is there a strong force of Yankees patrolling the river?"

"Enough to stir the pot. We've had several skirmishes lately. A few men killed on both sides."

"Are there enough soldiers to keep them from taking the boats?"

"Most of Brook's regiment is here. But we're divided between the river and chasing bushwhackers. It's a lot of territory to cover."

Nelda grew quiet. She would have to tread carefully and not seem to pry. "Well, if you can, drop by anytime."

"There's nothing I'd like better. But it all depends on how long we're here. We'll likely head out soon chasing the bushwhackers.

"You take care, Miss Nelda." Touching his hat, he kicked the horse's flanks and caught up with the wagons.

She walked on, thinking about the boats, and more importantly the corn being used to toll the Indians into the rebel camp. She must get word to Allen. He had said the Loring boys would still get word to him when necessary.

Abruptly she turned and hurried home. After a quick explanation to Della, she set out again, this time in the opposite direction.

The trip to the Loring farm made Nelda aware of how weak she had grown. She had to stop often to get her breath. It made her wonder how the soldiers could fight on empty stomachs. Although she dreaded facing Opal, she hoped she was home.

Opal peeped from the window and then opened the door. "What do ya want?" There was no friendliness in the question.

Nelda rushed to say, "Mrs. Loring, I need to get a message to Allen Matthers. He said your boys—"

"My boys ain't going nowhere." Spots of color highlighted the shrunken cheeks. "I'll thank ya not to come here no more. We've done had all the trouble we need."

"I'm sorry—"

Opal shut the door. Nelda sucked in a breath. She left the yard in a quandary. How would she get word to Allen? The entire long walk back to town, the question plagued. As the sun abruptly disappeared behind a thick cloudbank and wind swayed the pines, she shivered and wished she had worn heavier clothing.

After raking mud from her boots she entered the store. Although there was no food and very few supplies left, Emmitt kept the doors open. She thought it more a means of learning news than of selling merchandise.

Her spirits lifted. Tom Sorrels was seated near the stove. His obese girth hung off both sides of a straight-backed chair. Tom was a loud-mouthed know-it-all, but he lived on Little Piney near the Matthers and he could take the message.

"Hello, Mr. Sorrels. Are you going home soon?"

Before answering, he swallowed a cracker and wiped his mouth.

Nelda's mouth watered. She had eaten only a small bowl of beans for breakfast and a tiny sliver of bread made of corn ground in the coffee mill. She was not the only one eyeing the cracker greedily. Enos, seated nearby, licked his lips.

"Yep. I was just leavin.'" Tom's eyes narrowed. "Why?"

She had thought of a good excuse for sending for Allen, an excuse that would not arouse suspicion. "I have a message for Allen Matthers. I'm planning a party for the soldiers. I want him to play the fiddle."

Just then she saw Gill Harris near the back of the room. He strode forward, and then stopped and crossed his arms. Suspicion overspread his face.

"Most folks don't have enough to eat and you're throwing a party?"

She wanted to tell him to mind his own business. But since he was the provost marshal, he would be quick to point out that everything was his business. Resisting the sharp retort, she said, "It's not a supper, Gill. Just a friendly get-together. Don't you think the soldiers would enjoy some good music?"

He grimaced. "Just which side are these soldiers on?"

"Tyler Callaway just arrived. He's a friend of mine and of Allen's."

Tom stood. "I'll give Red yer message. Won't do no good, though. Allen ain't been home in a coon's age. You want I should send Caleb Tanner? He kin fiddle most as good."

Gill's beady eyes were on her. She hesitated. "Why, yes, that'll be fine."

"I misdoubt Caleb will come." Tom stuffed another cracker into this mouth and talked around it. "He hates travelin' in the cold. Makes his bones ache."

Nelda hastened to say, "It's not necessary to get Mr. Tanner out in this weather. If Allen isn't home, I'll just cancel the party."

She hurried away before Gill could ask more questions. She must not cast suspicion on Allen! She wanted no more loyal men martyred.

She arrived home cold, tired, and cross. Her eyes widened as she spied Tyler Callaway and two more soldiers lounging on the porch.

Della came out the door and hurried down the walk. "Missy, I was getting' worried about you!" She crossed the yard and took the mule's bridle.

"I'm fine."

Della spoke low. "That rebel trash has been here a hour. I figured you'd want a fire goin' in the library?"

"Yes. Thank you, Della."

She removed her gloves and started up the sidewalk.

"Good evening."

The soldiers all stood. Tyler made an elegant bow and then introduced his companions.

She nodded to the men. "I'm so sorry I wasn't here when you arrived. I heard there was coal oil for sale at Roseville. But it was only a rumor," she lied. "Please come inside." She opened the door and led the way into the library. "Please take a seat. If you'll excuse me, I'll have Della start the coffee and then I need to freshen up. My skirt is almost as muddy as the roads."

It took an effort to climb the stairs. She was light-headed from hunger and the bed looked inviting to her aching body, but she quickly washed up. After changing into a clean dress, she hurriedly fixed her hair and joined them in the library. Her eyes flashed as she spied Tyler Callaway seated in Phillip's favorite chair. The other men sat nearby with booted legs stuck out toward a roaring fire.

"I think there were at least a hundred of them—" Tyler stopped and quickly stood as she entered the room.

The others also rose.

"No, no, keep your seats."

Della arrived carrying a tray. As she passed out steaming mugs of coffee, Tyler inhaled deeply.

"Haven't smelled anything so good in months!" He took a sip and beamed. "This certainly beats that parched corn we've been swilling."

Nelda smiled. "Please go on with what you were saying Mr. Callaway."

He grinned. "I fear you caught me exaggerating our latest heroics."

The lanky man in the far chair shook his head. "No exaggeration to it, Tyler. There were a hundred of those bas..."—he grew red to the roots of his blond hair and swallowed—"umm, men," he stammered.

The other soldier spoke. "Yes, and there were only thirty of us. They rode at us with guns blazing. We're mighty lucky it was only our horses that got killed."

"Did you kill any of the Yankees?" she asked. She tried to sound concerned and sympathetic as she sat down near Tyler. When his hand rested on the worn fabric of the chair arm, she noticed only the left one was frayed... Of course Papa had no right arm to fray the other. For just a moment, she squeezed her eyes tight to keep from crying.

"Four at least. Maybe more. When they rode off, some of them were bleeding."

She sat up straight. "Where was this skirmish?"

"Last week at Ozark. The Federals are, of course, trying to gain control of the river. So far, they don't have many troops in this area; but small patrols are causing us a lot of grief. And there may be more Federal troops soon. As a matter of fact, I just learned that General Marmaduke and his troops are on the way here to take up our command. We're all ordered to Fort Smith. General Holms fears an attack is imminent. If we lose the fort, the Indian Nation is lost. We must prevent that at all costs."

He tossed down the last of the coffee and stood.

"We have to go, but thank you for your hospitality. It has been a special treat."

"You're very welcome. Come anytime. I get no news here, and I welcome the company."

She escorted them down the hall. *Soon there would be a much larger Confederate force at Fort Smith!* She wondered if the advancing Union troops were aware of that. Well, she had sent word to Allen. Hopefully he would arrive soon!

"And there was already fighting as near as Ozark," she mused. It would come to Clarksville. Spadra was the best river crossing for miles around and certain to be a contested prize. She would try to keep informed of the number of Confederate troops guarding it and pass that information along.

It was a week before Allen came. She was in the backyard getting firewood. During the night the temperature had again plummeted. Fog swirled the fields and yard. She could hardly see the clothesline.

"*Arkansas*," she grumbled. *"From one minute to the next, you never know if you'll need a coat or a fan."*

More by intuition than sound, she turned. He stood not five feet away. She wondered how he had gotten so close without her hearing.

"Allen!" Her voice was joyful. "I'm glad you came but I fear you're too late." She hurriedly related the information. "I suppose it's too late to stop the boats?" she asked.

"Yes. But we knew about them. Some of them got through, but two others turned back without unloading. As a matter of fact they're docked at Spadra right now." He paused. "Reckon I'm glad some of them got through. Women and children at Fort Smith are starving. And I don't want to see anyone starve—red or white.

"Let's go inside," he said.

His face was grave. She took a step back. Intuition kept her silent. She dreaded more bad news.

He stepped inside and removed a wide-brimmed hat and followed her into the library.

There was pity in his eyes. "Nelda, sit down."

She dropped into Phillip's high-backed chair, suddenly overwhelmed by a dark foreboding. Allen's broad face was drawn and tentative. Never before had she seen him apprehensive.

Nervously, he cleared his throat. "I have some bad news. I sure hate to—"

"Go ahead and tell me."

She steeled herself for disaster, but she was not prepared when he pulled something from his pocket. Her hand flew to her mouth. A cry escaped her. It was Papa's watch! Her stricken eyes stared and then lifted to his face. Pain pressed her chest. She could hardly breathe.

"I'm mighty sorry," he said softly and then stared at the hat in his hand.

The watch ticked, loud in the silence. As a child, she thought the day ended only when Papa wound it. A sob caught in her throat. He was never coming home! She swallowed. Her chest suddenly hurt so badly, it felt as if her heart were being torn in two.

Finally she managed to ask, "What happened?"

He let out a deep breath. "It might have been lung fever."

She pressed quivering lips tightly together. Then she spoke. "At least he'll not have to mourn Mama."

She let out a deep breath. "I wake each day wondering what awful thing will happen next. Mama always said trouble came in threes."

He hesitated, looking at her with compassion. "I'm afraid there is more bad news. I'd not tell you, but I reckon you'll hear it anyway."

"I doubt I can feel worse," she said. "Go ahead."

"A few weeks ago Jim Loring got hung for spying. Someone saw him giving information to the Yankees."

For a long moment she stared at the wall. Then she groaned and closed her eyes and covered them with her hands.

"It's my fault," she uttered while shaking her head.

"*Your fault*?"

"When I got word of Hindman's march, I went to the Loring cabin, hoping their boy could get word to you. Jim was there. He took the message instead."

She looked up with horrified eyes. "Oh, Allen! They might have hung you!"

His jaw worked. "At least I don't have a passel of hungry kids to leave behind."

"Poor Opal. What will she do now?"

"She'll make out somehow." He touched her shoulder. "You will too. You've both got grit." He glanced out the window at the gray sky. "I hate to leave so quick, but I have a long ride ahead of me.

She followed him into the hall. "Allen, are you telling the truth?" She went on, "I mean it's just such a coincidence. Both Papa and Jim were arrested at the same time, for the same thing, and they die at the same time. Did they hang Papa, too?"

Allen flushed. "Damn it, woman." He shook his head. "You're too smart for your own good." He drew a deep breath. "It was several weeks ago. They found some papers in his room, some things he was writing. Seditious things, they claimed."

He took her into his arms and held her while she cried. Finally she pulled back.

"I know you don't think so now," he said, "but you will be all right. The hurt of this will fade in time. Is Della still here?"

"Yes."

"Good. At a time like this, I don't want you being alone." Then he stepped outside and was gone.

In a daze of grief, she returned to the library. She sank into a chair and stared at the watch. Papa's death was bad enough, but to know how he died! She could hardly bear it. Her eyes traced the room. Papa's library! It held so many precious memories of him. It was inconceivable that he would never sit here again.

Somehow, life went drearily on. As Della grew stronger, Nelda had less physical burdens, but depression made her weary.

"Missy, you need to get hold of yourself," scolded Della, "stop wallowin' in misery. Your papa would be plum ashamed."

Nelda took a deep breath. Della was right. She had been too idle. She had no patriotic zeal now. She felt no zeal about anything. She simply existed—breathed in, breathed out, put one foot in front of the other. The only thing that set her heart pumping was the thought of revenge. Yes, revenge was an incentive. Perhaps she could yet repay the rebels for all they had taken from her!

That afternoon she made her way to town. A few geese flew overhead, high and swift. Along the way, she spoke to each soldier who called a friendly greeting, but her eyes narrowed in contempt.

"Rebel scum!" she muttered.

If the regiment had previously gone to Fort Smith, they had returned. There were hundreds of the ragged gaunt skeletons marching from the direction of the Spadra Crossing. Many had no shoes and no guns. Why did they keep on—even after all the defeats? She watched a group limp by and grudgingly admitted the rebels were stouthearted.

More than two hundred tattered cavalry on gaunt horses were gathered in the pale March sunshine near the courthouse. They appeared to be waiting for the two officers who were conversing on the courthouse steps. Both men—John Hill and Hall McConnell—were well known to her. Before becoming a colonel in the 16th Arkansas, John had been the county sheriff. And Hall, now a major, had been a prominent businessman. Both had been good friends of Papa. She approached them to glean information.

"Hello, Gentlemen."

They swept off hats. She noticed much more gray now in John's long drooping mustache.

Hall, his handsome, broad face ill at ease, spoke first, "Miss Nelda, how are you?"

"All right, I suppose."

"I was very sorry to hear of Phillip's death." He glanced nervously at John.

Nelda thanked him but her lips thinned. She had been a fool to think these men would tell her anything. Of course they would know that Papa had been hanged as a spy!

"Good day." She began to hurry past.

John's voice briefly stopped her. "Nelda, I feel mighty bad about the bushwhackers hitting your place. I wish my men had been here that day to stop them. We've killed several of the varmints... of course I can't be certain they're the same ones. Slowly but surely we are thinning them out."

"Thank you," she said. But resentment burned in her breast. These men had been good and dear friends. Now they would barely meet her eyes. They ought to feel shame.

She entered the courthouse. Just inside the doorway were more officers in conference.

"Well, William, they don't call you Old Tige for nothing!" Laughter followed the comment. The man who spoke was tall, dark-haired and handsome. "Yes, it's a bold plan, but I think a good one."

"Ma'am, can I help you with something?" When the young lieutenant spoke, the officers glanced her way, and then dropping their voices, walked on down the hall and exited through a side door.

She smiled her friendliest. "Yes, thank you, perhaps you can. I saw all the troops and was wondering if my uncle might be with them. Tap Brooks? He's with a Texas regiment.

The soldier returned the sunny smile. "You might be in luck. There are two Texas regiments camped just outside of town. One of the gentlemen who just left is their officer. Wait here, and I'll go ask him how you can find out."

He returned shortly. "Ma'am, General Cabell sends his compliments. He didn't recall the name but he just now sent a man to check the roster. If you can return this afternoon, I should have the information. But Colonel Brooks is wondering if you might be one of his own relations. He asked if you would wait here for just a moment so he can speak to you."

"I'd be honored." Nelda's mind whirled. "By the way, who was the tall dark-haired gentleman?"

The lieutenant's grin broadened. "General Marmaduke, ma'am. All the ladies notice him."

She did not want the lieutenant to become suspicious of her questions. "If the long-haired general fights as well as he looks, the Yankees haven't a chance."

He laughed. "With your permission, I'll tell him you said so."

"Goodness gracious, don't do that! I'd be mortified if I ever saw him again." Nonetheless she figured the remark would be related to the general. She now tried a coquettish imitation of Mary Beth. "Upon my word, judging by all those men, we do have the handsomest officers in the world. Who are they?"

"Generals Marmaduke and Cabell and Colonels Brooks and Carroll, ma'am. Fine officers, every one."

"Gracious! And to think I saw them all! My friends will never believe me." Then she suddenly pretended horror. "Oh! Is there about to be a battle here?"

"No, ma'am. Don't you worry. The army will soon be gone—except for Colonel Hill's men. They'll be around to guard things here."

She let out a relieved breath. Then she laid a hand on the lieutenant's arm. "Are the rest going to some great battle?"

He grew chagrined. "Ma'am, it would be best if you didn't mention seeing the generals or the colonels to anyone—at least not for a few days. We've been warned about Yankee spies in this area." He stiffened and suddenly looked at her with more scrutiny.

She grew wide-eyed. "Certainly, Lieutenant. I won't say a word! At least not for a few days—even though it will almost kill me not to tell my friends. They'll be green with envy. How long should I wait?"

"A few days should be fine."

"A few days it is." She smiled.

The lieutenant relaxed. The colonel soon joined her. He was about forty, but worry had etched premature lines deep in his face. His accent was strong Virginia. He bowed over her gloved hand. To her regret, it did not take long to ascertain that in all likelihood they were not related. It might have proven a valuable connection in the future. After a few words of pleasant conversation—in which she made certain to mention her other Confederate relatives—Colonel Brooks took his leave.

She stood a moment, biting her lip, looking down at the scarred wood floor and wondering what to do. Something important was happening. But she must be careful. The lieutenant was already on his guard.

"Thank you so much, Lieutenant," she said with a smile. "I'll be back this afternoon to see if you have any news of my uncle."

He nodded. "I hope we find him." As she walked away down the long hall, he called after. "Ma'am, don't forget what I said."

She turned. "Rest assured, Lieutenant, I want the Yankees to get what they deserve, and I'll do my part to see that they do!"

In hopes of eavesdropping, she chose the same door the generals had exited. They stood outside in a tight group. A stiff wind stirred the leafless oak above them. Nearby a brave flock of robins pulled worms from ground softened by warming weather.

Suddenly, Nelda sucked in a breath. Every head was turned toward Allen Matthers. Every ear was intent on what he was saying. Dazed, she drew back into the courthouse and let the door close softly.

Allen talking to Rebel officers! Why?

Her heart skipped a beat and then pounded as she considered the possibilities.

Allen a Rebel?

No! Surely he was playing a duel role to glean information, just as she was doing.

Why, look how he had helped the Union cause—*or had he*?

Her mind reeled. *Had he simply been using her?*

He had used the excuse that it was too late to warn Curtis when she had passed on information. And he had followed her to Little Rock because he thought she was spying.

"Don't give more credit than I deserve—selfish motives." The words haunted.

She felt faint. Then her eyes widened and she covered her mouth.

What about Papa's death?

She groaned aloud and groped for the arm of a nearby bench in the hallway and sank down. She recalled the tender kiss.

The Judas!

Tears rimmed her eyes, but her mouth drew into a tight line. She had been a fool. A total, complete fool!

And yet perhaps she was wrong. Perhaps he was merely gathering information, pretending to be one of them. Perhaps …

She hurried homeward, not caring that mud from a passing wagon splattered onto her gray skirt. Her thoughts were a whirlwind. She could scarcely think. Although her mind said one thing, her heart protested loudly.

She looked toward town. "Nelda, you're a fool!" she muttered. "He is a rebel, a rebel scout!"

Overwhelmed by a murderous rage, she suddenly longed to put a bullet right between his handsome, laughing, blue eyes. All this time they had been laughing at her—making a fool of her! In spite of the anger suddenly lacing her veins, her heart squeezed. Then she clamped her jaws until they hurt. How much dangerous information had she already given him? At that moment her thoughts were too harried to recall.

Well, it wouldn't happen again! She would trust no one. Not ever again. And she would beat Allen at his own game. *She would use him!*

The troops soon left. Although Nelda went to town every day for a week, there was no news. Today upon arriving at the store, she knew something unusual was afoot. A lathered horse was tied at the rail and a large group of graybeards were congregated inside.

"Shot right off his horse! Dead before he hit the ground."

A universal groan arose from the bystanders.

She tried to recall where she had once before seen the man who spoke. He was of military age but not in uniform. He had keen gray eyes and the hard-bitten look of a scout. Yes! The week before he had been standing near Allen and the officers under the oak tree.

Suddenly her breath caught and her heart squeezed in her chest. *Who had been shot off his horse? Who was dead?* She wanted to grab the scout's dirty shirt and demand the answer. Instead she held her breath and waited.

He shook his head. "It looked like easy pickin's. There was only about forty of 'em and more than two hundred of us. They scattered like scared chickens when we come at 'em. Hall was leading the charge. One of them blue-bellies got off a lucky shot as he was running backwards. I seen it all. Like I said poor ol' Hall never knowed what hit him." While words of regret and muttered curses arose, the thin, ragged man stopped to wipe his face. "We killed some of 'em. Wish we'd killed 'em all, but they took out through the brush like their pants was a'fire. That White River country is mighty rugged."

"Hit is fer a fact. You done the best you could," was Enos Hadley's comment as others nodded in sympathy. "Hall made us all proud—plum extinguished hisself."

Nelda quickly left the store. She paused outside in the pale sunshine, waiting for her unsteady heart to slow. She was furious—furious at herself. How dare she react so! *So what if Allen was still alive and breathing somewhere in the world. He was still a reprobate! A treacherous vile traitor! It would serve him right to fall bleeding in the dirt!* She left without returning inside.

So Hall McConnell was dead. He had once been a close friend of Papa's. She supposed, in spite of being a rebel, he had been a good man.

When she arrived at home, Della, her face pinched in a worried frown, met her at the door. There was a tremor in her voice.

"The cabbage and the turnips is all gone, and so is the potatoes. There's only enough beans for tonight. I hope them seeds we planted comes up."

"I'll go to the cellar first thing in the morning to get more beans."

Della nodded and gathered all the laundry and headed outdoors to the wash pot boiling in the back yard. Nelda's eyes followed her. Della had certainly changed. No longer sullen and resentful, she seemed more contented when busy. In idle moments distress colored her eyes. Nelda suspected she would wake some morning to find her gone back to Helena to rejoin the handsome Gideon.

Nelda left early the next morning. She always made the trip before people were likely to be abroad. She walked quickly, looking around often through the mists hovering the creek and hanging low in the fields and pastures. Tall dead grass still peppered the fields where new green was quickly encroaching. She crossed the partially plowed cornfield. Dew wet her dress tail but the ground was almost dry enough to plow. She hoped the rain held off so David Hadley could resume plowing. Before crossing the Morrison's yard, she paused in a thicket, listening and looking. Nothing stirred. Then, almost running, she darted to the cellar and descended the steps before lighting the stub of candle in her pocket.

Holding the flickering light, she stood in the dank cellar and stared with fearful eyes at the limp bean sack that she had just lifted from a wooden keg. Beans trickled through a hole where the sagging sack had been riddled. There was only a small lump at the bottom—the last of the dried beans. An empty sack lay nearby. It had held the last of the peas before she and Della had planted them. It would be weeks before the garden would provide anything but greens. *Could a person survive on greens?* She was not sure. She had already searched every imaginable venue for food. No one in town was willing to part with what little they had, no matter what the enticement. She had gone to the Spadra dock each time a boat arrived, hoping to find some smuggled goods for sale. On Captain Ballinger's last run, there had been a speculator who traded a small sack of cornmeal for an exorbitant price. But it made barely enough bread for three meals. The kindly captain had given her a few potatoes with the promise of more on his next trip.

Just then a rat darted from behind the barrel and scurried across her foot. She gasped and shrank against the damp cellar wall, cringing with revulsion as it fled into the early dawn. Her heart pounding in her throat, she shuddered. *How could anyone eat such a vile thing!* She wasn't that hungry… not yet! But as she glanced at the bean sack, her heart sank. She would pray; but God would not hear her. She had not forgiven. She had not forgiven Drew. She had not forgiven the entire Rebel cause. And she would not forgive Allen. Not ever! In the darkest recesses of her mind lurked an unacknowledged but persistent bitterness. God could have prevented all of this!

With the drooping sack in hand, she climbed the steps and stared at the blackened ruins of the Morrison mansion and the massive charred oaks nearby. For a moment she envisioned things as they used to be—the stately house; long tables covered with white linen cloths and laden with a sumptuous feast; throngs of happy people—*Papa, Mama, Fred.* Her shoulders drooped as she slowly made her way down the hill. Before entering the house, she stopped and took a deep breath. How would they survive?

That evening at supper Della set the last dabble of beans in the center of the table. The women stared at the pitiful supper.

"Too bad we don't even have a baby to boil and eat," Nelda said in an attempt at humor; but her eyes were fearful.

"Missy! Don't talk so!" protested Della with startled eyes. "The Lord's listenin'!"

"Then perhaps you should ask *Him* where the next meal is coming from," she snapped. "Besides don't get in a snit. I was only referring to the Bible story—"

"I know. The one where them wicked women ate that chile; but I don't like such talk!"

Della had put a hand to her stomach. Nelda stared at the slight paunch.

"Oh dear God, Della! You're not—"

"Coming in September." She smiled shyly. "I figured you had enough worries so I never told you."

Why, she's actually pleased, thought Nelda, incredulous, *even though we're starving—she's pleased! How could anyone want to bring a child into this world!*

Her legs buckled. She dropped into a chair and laid her head on the table. *Two hungry women. And now a child!*

"Don't take on so, missy. The Lord takes care of his own. We all belong to Him—and so does this child."

She sat up. "Della, when did you get religion?"

"In Helena. Me and Gideon both saw the light. Brother Sam was a fine preacher man. We had service right out in the open, down by the river—just like in the Good Book. He baptized us and married us, all on the same day." Her eyes shone. "It was a fine wedding. You never heard the like of music and singin'! We didn't have much food but the Lord multiplied it, and no one went hungry." She looked at the beans. "I figure if we pray over this here mess of beans, He'll stretch it too, till more comes. Brother Sam says everything works out for the good."

Nelda grimaced. *Nothing in her life had worked out 'for the good.'* Nevertheless, out of reverence, she bowed her head.

"You pray, Della. I'm too tired."

That evening, in early dusk, Allen rode into the yard. Nelda glanced from the window and saw the sorrel bearing his big rider. Her fists clenched. Then she drew a deep breath and sternly reminded herself that she had a role to play. With sheer grit, she pasted on a smile and opened the door.

"Why, Allen," she said, "it's still light out. Aren't you afraid the Rebels might see you?" In spite of her best intentions, a hint of sarcasm crept in.

He didn't seem to notice.

"I think it's safe. Haven't seen any hereabouts lately." He smiled. "Besides, I've been worried about you. Couldn't seem to get you off my mind. And since the Irish are known for having second sight, I figured I'd better come see if you were all right." After a quick scrutiny of her face, he grew grim. "What's wrong, Nelda?"

She turned away and rubbed her arms.

"Nothing—nothing at all. Nothing except war and poverty and hunger and the people I love dying. Other than that everything is simply wonderful." She turned back. "And you?" she asked. "How are you?"

His eyebrows knit.

"Better than you, I'd say."

With big hands, warm and gentle, he took her shoulders and led her to a chair. His touch was loathsome now. She recalled it had not always been so, and her jaw hardened. She resisted the urge to pull away and slap him.

"Sit down," he ordered. "You look worn to a frazzle." Then he mumbled to himself, "And from the looks of you, you're not eating much."

"Why, Mr. Allen!" Della beamed as she stepped through the kitchen door into the hall. "Thought I heared your big ol' voice."

"Howdy, Della. I thought you'd left these parts—heard you took off with that good-lookin' buck Gideon," he teased.

She grinned. "Sure did. But he sent me back from ..." she stammered, becoming suddenly wary after taking in the quick shake of Nelda's head, "he ... he sent me back until he can come get me"—she laid a hand on her middle—"and the baby."

"Congratulations." Allen smiled. "I always liked Gideon."

"He thinks a heap of you, too." Her eyes sparkled. "All of us coloreds do. I recollect how you used to sneak down to his shanty and fiddle up a storm, just like it was a regular party."

He laughed. "As I recall, there was no sneaking. But we did have some good times. Gideon plays a mean French Harp."

Della's brow furrowed. *"Mean?"*

"That just means he plays good," Allen explained. Then abruptly he started toward the door. "I'll be back shortly."

Della's brows rose. "Where he off to in such a rush?"

Barely an hour had passed before he returned. This time the sorrel's back was loaded with food—sacks full of smoked meat and corn meal and even a small jar of honey. While he unloaded the sacks onto the kitchen table, Della voiced praise to the Lord over each new treasure.

"You should have told me you were going hungry," he scolded. "There was no need for it."

"The army didn't leave much after Drew's last foraging expedition," Nelda replied bitterly. "I'm surprised you found a thing."

She knew where the food had come from. The Confederate Army! And before that from some civilian's smoke house and cellar.

He studied her a long moment. "I know where to look."

She bit her lip. He must not become suspicious.

"How can we ever repay you?" She tried to sound sweet and grateful. She did not feel sweet. And yet, in spite of her anger, she was grateful. Her mouth watered. It had been months since she had witnessed so much bounty. It was all she could do to keep her hands off the jar of honey. And she doubted the ham that Della was already slicing would get done before they devoured it.

He gave a rakish grin. "I can think of several ways—"

Della giggled. Blood surged into Nelda's face. She turned away to keep from betraying herself.

"*He has motives all right*," she silently seethed, "*just not the ones Della imagines!*"

She managed to keep a stiff smile and make a few comments while he laughed and joked. Occasionally he shot her a puzzled glance. She would have to be careful. Allen was cunning. He was already suspicious. Her nerves were screaming by the time he took his leave.

"Well ladies, it's been good visiting, but I have to go. Might not be back for a while. Step outside with me for a minute," he added with a keen look at Nelda.

He shut the door behind them. A cool evening breeze caressed her tense face and lifted tendrils straggling from the heavy knot. In spite of herself, she cringed when he reached to tilt her chin. His calloused fingers were gentle on her skin.

"Nelda, you're as nervous as a whore in church. What's going on?"

She turned away and stared up at the breeze-stirred leaves trembling in the walnuts. "I'm feeling pretty desperate these days . . . Della to feed and now a baby." She braced herself and faced him. "The food you brought will help for a while. But you and I both know, this war is far from over."

His eyes were serious. "Brace up. Weak animals in the pack get took down."

"You're right," she acknowledged. "I'm just tired. And here I am doing nothing useful for our cause." She stared into his eyes. "You would tell me if there was any campaign afoot that I could help with?"

"Of course I would," he said. But his eyes dropped.

April arrived as gentle as a baby's breath, soft and warm and sweet. In the tall newly leafed oaks in the yard, thrush, cardinal, and wren sang in joyful chorus. Nelda supposed she should be joyful. Although both she and Della were skin and bones, they had survived the winter. But she felt no joy. Physically she was fine; and yet it seemed as if some dark, dreadful disease ate into her bones and robbed her of peace. Her sleep was troubled, her dreams dark and foreboding and often peopled by Allen Matthers. Even when she was awake, he was never far from her brooding thoughts.

She was glad about one thing. With the coming of spring the fighting had commenced in earnest and the results were not favorable to the rebels in Arkansas. Clarksville groaned when General William Cabell led an unsuccessful raid to retake Fayetteville. And when General Marmaduke led an equally unsuccessful raid into Missouri, they became more despondent. It had been hoped that with the coming of Marmaduke's army the Missouri Rebels would rise and throw off the Yankee yoke. The rebels did not rise, and although the handsome Marmaduke was credited a victory, he had barely escaped with his army—so rumor said—by the skin of his teeth.

The next month, news for the Confederacy was better. In May, Lee won a great victory at Chancellorsville, and Clarksville rejoiced. They were, however, deeply saddened at the news that the valiant Stonewall Jackson had been killed. And, a dire threat loomed near. A Yankee general named Grant was besieging Vicksburg. If Vicksburg fell, the Mississippi was lost with Arkansas almost certain to follow.

While Clarksville mourned, Nelda worked in the garden, and with anticipation, waited for news of the surrender. In spite of tales of unparalleled suffering, she felt little sympathy for the besieged city. Having to eat rats might make the rebels appreciate the previous bounty of a united federal government. Then she drew a deep breath when she thought of her own food problems.

The next afternoon David stood on the steps swiping his sweaty forehead with a ragged sleeve. "The cornfield is all plowed and ready to plant. If it's all right, I'll be taking the mule home so's I can get started on our field."

"That'll be fine, David. You've done an excellent job—as good as any man." She smiled at him. Although he did not actually smile, his eyes were pleased. He had not been hostile lately, not since she had agreed to the loan of the mule. He had even begun to talk a bit each evening before returning home after a long day of plowing.

I won't need him long. No need to plow much. We hardly got enough seed corn to sow half an acre. No need for me to plant more than I can care for anyway. Grandpa don't do anything but sit at the store jawing."

"How much tillable land do you have?"

"About five acres—rich bottom land down by the creek."

"I'll share—but all the seed I have is field corn."

The seed had come dear. It had taken every bottle of Phillip's brandy to entice the overseer at Arbaugh's plantation to part with it. Much to her regret, there was no sweet corn seed to be had at any price.

His face grew sullen. "We don't need charity."

"You can pay me by giving me a portion of your crops."

"How much?" he asked guardedly.

"Would a tenth be fair?"

He chewed his jaw. "I reckon so. But that might not be much if the crop is no good."

"That's the risk I take," she said and put out her hand.

He eyed it a moment and then shook it firmly.

"Would you like a drink of water?"

"Yes'um. That would be refreshing."

He thanked her and then drained the crystal glass and handed it back. "That's a right pretty glass," he observed. "We only have a tin cup we share at home." Embarrassed by having revealed his poverty, he flushed and looked away.

She quickly changed the subject. "Is the telegraph working again?"

He shook his head. "Not the last I heard. But I sure wish they could keep the lines up. I liked that job." He glanced at the sun midway down the afternoon sky. "I best get on home. There's still plenty of daylight left to plow by."

She went to the cabinet, took out a pail filled with white kernels, dipped a large portion into a tin can, and gave it to David. With a curt nod, he took it and hurried away. She returned to the kitchen and picked up the pail.

It's a good thing, she thought, *that this is going into the ground today. Otherwise we might be too tempted to eat it.*

Lifting a handful of the grains, she let it sift slowly through her hand. For an idle moment she recalled how as a child she had loved following Tom across the fields as he dropped the kernels into the long plowed furrows. Ever patient, he had answered all her questions: *What makes the corn seed all shriveled? Why do you have to cover it with dirt? How does the seed know to send up a shoot?* And he had answered the additional questions that his answers had generated. She missed the kind old man.

"Della, get your hat. We have a cornfield to plant."

For the first time in months, Nelda felt a tinge of pleasure. Surprised, she concluded it was the rigorous exercise in spring sunshine and the satisfaction of covering the small, equally spaced, white grains with clean-smelling dirt in anticipation of a bountiful crop. The kitchen garden that she and Della had planted was doing nicely. If the weather was good and nothing untoward happened, they would soon have plenty to eat.

She rose from stooping for a moment and placed a hand to her tired back and looked at the field. It fell away toward the east and then lay slightly downhill where it ended at a thick fringe of trees. When he was a young man, Tom—with a love for growing things—had cleared and planted it. Now the rows were not as straight as his had been. But David had done a good job for one so young. She had watched from the window while he struggled with the errant mule and an equally errant plow.

Unless I miss my guess, she thought, *someday his grandpa will be well provided for by that hard-working young man.* Abruptly, her mouth drew into a straight line. *Unlike me—who'll have no one!*

After grabbing another handful of seed, she stooped again and did not look up.

Chapter 9

In June a rebel sky refused life-giving moisture. The vegetable garden that had sprouted with promise now sent out spindly shoots producing little. And as summer grew hot and dry and a cicada chorus filled the sultry afternoons, Nelda watched with anxious eyes while young corn withered and yellowed. If there were no crops—in spite of Della's protestations otherwise—she knew they would starve. Already the few cattle left in the valley were tottering skeletons stretched over with fly-bitten hides. Even the Rebel army would have no food for Allen to purloin.

Tyler stopped by to say the troops were leaving. But Nelda had been unable to discover the Confederate Armies' destination. The only pleasure she derived these days came with word of Grant's victories. She gloated when Port Gibson, Jackson, and Champion's Hill were taken.

With heat and hunger came lethargy that gripped even the industrious Della. More and more both women retired to the shady side of the house to sit listless on the long porch, attempting to fan away heat and mosquitoes. After the sun dipped low, Della often slipped away. Nelda never pried. She presumed Della visited friends. One evening she did not return.

Although the windows were open, the air was sultry. Nelda closed her bedroom door and quickly blew out the candle. There was no need for light. Every square inch was as familiar to her as her face in the mirror. Since the cradle it had been her sanctuary. The comforting intimacy wrapped around her like a hug. Tears sprang to her eyes.

No! She stiffened a trembling chin. *As Allen said— the weak are doomed.*

She pushed back the white curtains. From the trellis below the sweetness of roses drifted upward. Neither moon nor star softened the darkness. She stood for a long while, trying to keep her mind as empty as the night. At least for tonight, she did not want to think—to feel, to remember. A rumble of distant thunder rode the hot breeze suddenly stirring the curtains. To the west, flickers of light dashed the sky. It was going to rain. But it had come too late to save most of the corn.

A dark shape quickly crossed the yard below. Nelda turned from the window. She must unlock the door for Della.

By the time she descended the stairs, Della was pounding on the door.

"Missy!" she gasped, almost falling inside. "There's gonna be an attack! We got to get word to Gideon."

"An attack? Where?"

"Helena! The whole Rebel army is headin' there!"

"Are you sure?"

"I hearded it all while I was visiting Leona—"

"Gill Harris' slave?"

Della shook her head. Her words rushed out in a torrent. "Mr. Tucker Harris came home tonight. He told his pa they're marching on Helena. Oh, missy! He said most of the Union soldiers was sent across the river to Vicksburg. He said with no trouble a'tall they can whip the few Yankees left! Mr. Tucker said there was a passel of runaway slaves at Helena. He bragged how they was gonna teach 'em a lesson." Della caught imploringly at Nelda's arm. "If they find Gideon in the army, they'll kill him!"

Della was right. And Gideon would not be the only one. Confederate president Jefferson Davis had ordered that any colored soldier in uniform be given no quarter. Even after surrendering, they were being shot or hanged.

"Shhhh," she shushed and cocked her head to listen. There was no sound now but she thought something had stirred. On silent feet she slipped toward the door and looked out. Nothing appeared in the dark shadows. She returned to the hallway, and taking Della by the shoulder, she led her into the kitchen and closed the door.

"Sit down, Della, and let me think."

Wringing her hands, she paid no heed. "I got to warn Gideon!"

"Hush, I said! Let me think."

Della pressed her lips together but a moan escaped them.

"Della, what else did Tucker say? Calm down and think. I need every detail. It's important."

For a split second Della's eyes shone huge in a bright bolt of lightning. The storm was closer. Each night, in spite of the heat, Nelda bolted the downstairs windows. Now she opened one to let the wind in. When the coolness whipped into the stifling room and toppled a vase, she lowered it a bit. She turned back to Della.

"Now, start from the moment you arrived and tell me every detail."

Della drew a breath. A sob caught in her throat like a child admonished to hush crying. At first her words were trembling and halting.

"It was too hot to sit in Leona's cabin so we walked down to the creek. We had just gone a little ways when Gabriel came runnin'—he's Leona's boy. He said someone had come unexpected and Leona was to come up to the big house and get some vittals together." She went on, "I went along to he'p Leona. She was in the kitchen and sent me to the well for water. Mr. Tucker and his pappy came walkin' up from the barn and was there 'fore I knowed it. He was telling his pappy that…" she paused and spoke slowly and deliberately, "that most all the Yankees had gone to Vicksburg and Helena was easy pickin's. He said they was only about four thousand of 'em left, and they outnumber 'em two to one. He said he had been assigned to James Fagan's command and that Fagan was a general now. That made Mr. Harris happy."

Nelda could well imagine that it would make Gill happy. Even when Fagan was a colonel in far-off Virginia, Gill was forever bragging that they had been classmates over at Pleasant Grove. Knowing both men, Nelda doubted that a fine man like Mr. Fagan would reciprocate the delight of acquaintance.

Della went on, "Mr. Tucker saw me. Then he said what all I tol' you about the slaves." Della rocked back and forth and moaned. "Oh, lordy! He'll kill Gideon!"

Nelda grabbed her shoulder and shook it. "Stop it!" It was the first time she had ever been harsh with Della. When Della stared up, her dark eyes were wide like a startled doe.

"We're not going to let that happen. Now, did Tucker say anything else—anything about when they were leaving, about when the attack would be?"

Thunder boomed, rattling the window. Della jumped. The next lightning flash lit the room as bright as day and a torrent of rain came crashing down. Nelda hurried to shut the window. The room had cooled so suddenly that there were chill bumps on her arms. She rubbed them and turned back to see, in the brilliant flashes of light, Della's brow furrowed in thought.

"No," she said slowly, "All he said was the Yankees would pretty quick see some real fireworks and some real independence."

Independence Day! The fourth of July! Just like the Rebels to pick that day thought Nelda with disgust. The holiday was only a short time away. The authorities at Helena must be warned! If Della was right, soon the entire Rebel Army would be moving against the skeleton force at Helena, a river port vital to the Union cause. And with them came certain death to any black soldier in uniform. She would have to move quickly. She had made up her mind to take the warning herself. She had learned her lesson. She trusted no one.

"Della, pack my small black valise with a change of clothes and get Mama's gray one out of the closet and put your things in it. In the morning I'll ask David Hadley to care for the animals while we're gone. We'll go to the dock early. I'm pretty sure there will be some boats along since this rain will raise the water."

After lighting a candle, she headed for the library. The Rebels were likely to let a genteel lady and her slave through the lines if she had documents from General Hindman—*that is, if the sentries had never seen the authentic signature.* Taking a sheet of parchment from Phillip's desk, she proceeded to dip a pen into ink. She wondered why she had not thought to forge a pass for her trip to Little Rock.

She stopped for a minute to listen to the pouring rain. When it lessened she would go dig up the moneybox. Biting her jaw, she wondered how much cash she should take.

When she knocked, David answered the door. "Miss, Nelda." He hesitated and then stepped back. "Come in and sit a while."

Good manners required the invitation. She recognized his reason for hesitation was shame of the poor dwelling.

"No, thank you, David. I have a favor to ask. I have to go away for a while. Papa left some unfinished business." She kept her destination vague—just in case Gill questioned him. "Would you take care of my animals, Sirius and the horse and mule? There will soon be enough feed corn for the stock. They can make do on grass for now. And I'll leave some money to buy anything you need for Sirius. He doesn't eat much."

"I'll be glad to, ma'am. You don't have to give me no money. I can kill enough rabbits to feed the dog." He smiled. "I always wanted a dog. But Grandpa never let me have one."

"Oh," she said, "then perhaps he wouldn't want you taking this on?"

"Stay right here," he said excitedly. "I'll go ask him!"

He soon returned with a beaming face. "He said it would be fine. I'll take real good care of them."

"I know you will," she said and gave him some coins in spite of his protest. "You'll have to keep Lily hidden or someone will steal her. I suggest you keep her where she is now in the woods behind my house."

He nodded.

She said, "You may bring Sirius and the mule over here." He grinned when she added, "No one in his right mind would steal Jepner." She turned away. Then she turned back. "David, if for some reason I don't return, you may have them all. Lily is a fine mare. If you ever have to sell her, please make sure it's to someone who will be good to her."

His eyes widened. "I sure will, Miss Nelda."

She should hurry, but she found herself lagging, taking in each detail of the town as she passed through. In spite of all that had happened, it was home and full of many happy memories. She stopped by the newspaper office and peeped between the boards covering the windows. Through sudden tears, she saw the heavy press, unmolested but covered with cobwebs. *Would good times ever come again?*

Della was ready and waiting anxiously when she returned. They left the house with valises in hand. Nelda looked back. She shivered with premonition. It would be a long time before she saw the beloved house again.

The downpour of the night before had left the ground steaming. A misty shroud enfolded the river, almost obscuring the moored boats being lapped by a stout current. There were two vessels at the dock. One was the Chippawa but it was going upriver to Fort Smith. The other, a much smaller vessel with the words Lottie Ann scrawled on its side, already had steam roiling from the stack. When Nelda called to a thickset, black-haired man on deck, he strode down the gangplank.

"Is this your boat, sir?"

"It is. Bull Smith at your service."

Something about the way he said it made her doubt Smith was his real name. His face was flushed, and in spite of the early hour, whiskey was strong on his breath.

"My girl and I need passage as far as you can take us downriver." She held up the document. "I have travel documents and gold coin."

From the sudden glint in his steely eyes, she doubted the documents would even be given a glance. And she was right. He stepped aside and waved them aboard.

"Will there be other passengers?" she asked, feeling a bit leery of the odd looking apparition who had appeared on deck. He was stooped and thin. Abnormally long twig-like arms hung to his knees and ended with ham-like hands, completely out of proportion with the rest of his body. A scraggly brown beard outlined a pitted face once white. Now each pockmark was blackened with soot. He exuded some dark force, evil and repugnant.

"Nope. It'll just be me and Obadiah. He's my crew." Bull grinned. "Obadiah looks scary but he's harmless." He nodded toward a roof held up with poles. "There's a shed over there. It's not much but you can get in out of the sun and the wet."

After he had walked away, Della protested, "I don' like that man. Matter of fact, I don' like neither one of 'em!"

"We have no choice," snapped Nelda. But she knew Della was right. It had been foolhardy. Especially since no one else even knew they were on the boat. It was too late now. As it was, they would be hard pressed to arrive in time to give the warning. "Perhaps we can get another boat downriver," she conceded.

By the time a red sun had begun to burn away the mists they were underway. The wooded bank glided by and water churned from the small paddlewheel.

Della had never been on a boat. She hugged the shed post until finally a wave of nausea forced her to the side rail.

"Ohhhh!" she moaned. "We're gonna hit a stump and get drowned!"

"Calm down. From the looks of it, this boat has been up and down rivers for years."

Della still looked dubious but, after losing her breakfast, she stayed at the rail and stared anxiously ahead as if she now wished they were going faster. She chaffed at the delay when the boat made a quick stop at Dardanelle. And at noon she complained loudly when they stopped again at Lewisburg.

Lewisburg spread out, pleasant and inviting, on green hills in the sun. Bordering the river were false-fronted businesses and a fine house shaded by magnolias and a stately white inn. Nelda wondered if Ruben and Berilla Markham still ran the inn. Probably not. More than likely, Mr. Markham, along with every other able-bodied man, was in the army. Nothing in Arkansas was as it had once been.

She saw Bull Smith enter a dusty building with tall black letters that read saloon. Unfortunately they would be captive to Mr. Smith's schedule. She had made inquiries at the other boats. All were headed upriver. From one loquacious sailor, she made discrete inquiries about the port nearest Helena. Since the Arkansas entered the Mississippi far south of Helena it would mean traveling the Union held Mississippi or riding miles overland. He informed her that nothing but a canoe could slip past the Yankee patrols. He suggested she go overland.

She ruminated on the information while they ate in the shade of a tall magnolia. She had packed a large basket of cornbread and meat. Della only picked at her food, but Nelda was ravenous. She leaned back against the tree and closed her eyes. Bull Smith struck her as a man who would take risks—with the right inducement.

They returned to the dock long before the boat was finally underway. Later that morning, she managed a private word with Bull. To avoid the whiskey breath she kept her distance.

"I desperately need to reach Helena. The Yankees are holding my papa prisoner. He's very ill. I have special permission to pass through the Union lines." She was astonished at how effortlessly she could lie. They rolled off her tongue as easily as proverbial water off a duck's back. She knew Pastor Wheeling would be stricken. "I know you probably go nowhere near Helena—but you seem a bold man, not averse to taking risks if there was a profit."

He raised a brow. "Depends on how much. I got no political proclivities—Union or Rebel—doesn't mean a damn to me. But I still pride my hide quite highly."

"Say fifty dollars in gold."

"Make it a hundred and I'll take you to the gate."

She chewed her lip. "All right," she slowly agreed. It was almost all she had. It made her wonder if his sharp eyes could see right through the skirt to the hidden pocket on her petticoat.

A wide grin split his face, showing straight teeth framed by the curly black beard. He looked more pirate than businessman.

"I want to see it now," he said.

"All right, but you only get forty now and the rest when you drop me off." She turned away. "I'll be right back."

He grinned knowingly. "Got that gold hid away good, have you?"

When she returned from stepping out of sight behind the pilothouse, he took each twenty-dollar coin and bit it. Satisfied, he handed three back but slowly, begrudgingly.

"We'll have to travel careful. It'll take the better part of a week. And it's risky. Rebel gunboats on this river and Yankee gunboats on the Mississippi and they're all on the lookout for spies and smugglers. Little Rock is as far as I usually go. Not sure what kind of defenses we'll find on downriver. Of course when we get to the Mississippi, we'll likely get stopped by Union patrols. Your papers might get us through."

She nodded. "I certainly hope so."

"I know the water around Helena. I've run it for years. Was a pilot on a big boat before ... before the war."

Nelda wondered what prompted the hesitation. Perhaps she would be happier not knowing. She wouldn't be surprised to learn that Mr. Smith had gotten drunk and sunk the big ship. She had seen him nipping at a flask all day. But he was the only means of reaching Helena in time. At that it would be a close call. The fourth was less than a week and a half away.

He added, "I'll have Obadiah put a tarp around the shed and fix a couple of pallets. You and the girl may as well make yourselves at home. We'll travel as far as we can each day. Nights, we'll have to sleep on the boat."

"Yes. I want to get there as soon as possible." Her eyes narrowed. "But what about food?"

"I have enough onboard. For an extra ten dollars, Obadiah will add a few more beans to the pot."

The thought of eating what the grotesque little man prepared was repugnant. But Nelda had no choice. She handed over another coin. The glitter in Bull's eyes outshone the gold piece.

Each day a baking sun beat down, making even short stops almost unbearable. Time seemed to crawl. As the paddlewheel cut the water, slowly, methodically, she stood at the rails and watched the wake fanning out behind the boat like the tail of a strutting turkey. A hot wind chopped the water into white-topped waves. She fretted over the slow speed and wondered where the Rebel troops were now. When Bull had stopped briefly at Little Rock, she had seen lots of wagons and infantry as well as scores of cavalry. Since this river emptied into the Mississippi far south of Helena, they would have to double back a long way. And if the army took a faster overland route, she would be too late. In spite of her pleading, Bull refused to travel at night. He said there were too many treacherous obstacles lurking in dark waters.

Each evening in purple dusk he nosed the boat toward heavily wooded banks where Obadiah lashed it fast. When the engine stilled, mosquitoes descended in droves. Like squaws, the women huddled under blankets while Obadiah dished up a concoction of cornmeal gruel dotted with minuscule dabs of tough stringy meat. For two days Della refused to eat until Nelda reminded her the baby would suffer. She, herself, could barely choke it down.

Each night it was long past midnight before a reprieve from the heat allowed sleep. There was no reprieve, however, from the bloodthirsty mosquitoes. The pallets of canvas and sacks barely softened the hard planks of the deck. In spite of the torment, Nelda eventually grew so weary that she slept. Della, lying nearby, thrashed about in her sleep. Nelda's own sleep was fitful, often filled with dreams of bountiful feasts—Ma's succulent roast pork along with tender orange-fleshed sweet potatoes slathered in butter; crisp golden-brown fried chicken served alongside white mountains of mashed potatoes awash with cream gravy. One night the vision of a steaming apple pie seemed so real, she woke with mouth watering. She groaned and curled into a tight ball. *If only she had tasted it before awakening!*

She must have drifted off again. A nearby footfall startled her awake. Unsure if it was just another troubled dream, she pried open heavy eyelids. Then her eyes widened. In dim gray dawn, a dark shape loomed directly above. With a gasp, she rolled away, at the same time grabbing for the pistol hidden under the sacks used as her pillow. A swift kick shoved the pistol out of reach, and Bull scooped it up.

"Now, there's no need for that. I got no intention of hurting you ... if you're smart, that is."

Della rose onto an elbow and blinked.

In yellow shafts of rising sun Nelda saw the leer on Obadiah's face as he hovered nearby with a ghastly smirk. Like the coward in a pack of wolves, he hunkered back and yet anticipated a share of the kill.

Bull held out his hand. "Give me the money and you can go on your way."

Nelda sat up, angry now. "Go on my way!" Her gaze took in the wilderness on the dark shoreline. "Surely you're not intending to put us off here—in the middle of no where. You said you'd take us right to Helena."

He gave a quick derisive laugh. "You're too old to believe everything you hear."

Her eyes narrowed. "You won't get away with this."

He gave a belly laugh and Obadiah joined in with a shrill cackle.

"Who's gonna stop me?" He gestured to Della. "You or your darkie bitch?" He shook his head. "I don't think so. Now give me the money, or I'll take it. And I won't be none too gentle about it."

"You'll pay for this," she threatened. Nonetheless, she turned away and removed the money from the hidden pocket.

When she handed it over, he shook his head. "Naw, give me the petticoat. I figure you left a coin or two."

Nelda's teeth gritted. That is exactly what she had done. Now Bull would have it all. All except for one coin hidden in Della's skirts—a ten dollar gold piece. As she hedged, his dark eyes flashed with impatience.

"All right!" She stood and angrily removed the garment.

He took the white petticoat, hunted until he found the pocket hidden in a flounce, removed the two coins, and slipped them into his trouser pocket along with the rest.

She jerked back the slip.

"I'll take whatever that is you're wearing on that chain around your neck," he said.

She grasped the chain. "No!"

He gave it a jerk. The gold chain did not break. But she knew he would have it. She pulled out the watch and lifted the chain over her head.

"It has my father's initials engraved on the case. No one is likely to buy it."

She flinched as he grabbed it. As he caressed it silent rage boiled in her veins.

"I could use a new timepiece. Obadiah, wasn't I telling you just the other day that I needed a new timepiece?"

"For a fact, Bull. You sure did."

"Let me see those valises," he said and rummaged each thoroughly, even cutting the lining to make sure nothing was hidden. "Nothing here but their duds and such," he complained and stuffed them back and tossed them to Nelda. "Now get off." He nodded toward the narrow gangplank already lowered into place and leading to the tree-lined shore.

As she studied the wilderness, dread abruptly replaced anger.

"Exactly where are we?"

He pointed. "Arkansas Post is downriver a ways. If you plan on going to Helena, you'll have to head northeast. You'll run across a road sooner or later."

"At least leave us some food."

"Obadiah, toss 'em that little sack of meal."

"And give us some matches so we can make a fire."

Bull scowled but complied by reaching into his pocket and pulling forth a few large-headed lucifer matches. "Barely have enough left to light my pipe," he grumbled.

Nelda took the matches and the grits and gathered up her travel case. She left her unfashionable narrow hoops lying where she had removed them the night before. Travel on foot through rough country would be hard enough without them. She looked at the pistol.

"I don't guess you'd let me have it. You could unload it and toss the shot pouch a little way off so I couldn't get to it until after you've gone."

Without bothering to answer, he gave an ugly stare.

"I didn't think so," she said. "Come on, Della."

Della grabbed her valise and hurried right behind. They had barely touched foot on land when Obadiah pulled in the gangplank and Bull nosed the boat into the stream.

"Praise the Lord and good riddance!" said Della.

Nelda turned to stare. "I'll declare, Della, I thought you'd be weeping and wringing your hands."

"Humph! I'd rather wade ticks and chiggers and moccasins than be with them two snakes. I 'spected we'd wake up some morning with our throats slit. I knowed they was wicked the first time I laid eyes on 'em."

Nelda let out a deep breath. "I did too. I'm disgusted with myself. I ignored my better judgment and got us into a real mess." Fear sent prickles down her spine. It was desolate here.

"Well, at least we're still alive. The good Lord is looking out for us." Della took the white cloth sack of cornmeal from her. "Let me help tote that. What you reckon is the shortest way to Helena?"

Della's calm was tonic. It fought back the wave of panic threatening to suffocate Nelda as she eyed the tangled underbrush and shadowy woods.

"We'll follow the river, at least until we come to a road." She got a better grip on her valise and started forward up the shallow bank. "More than likely we're miles from a settlement. Bull would have planned that—just as he planned leaving at first light on the remote chance that we might find help. Now he'll have a full day of travel to distance himself."

Della was already walking.

The land was flat but covered with briars that caught at clothing and tender skin. Long stretches of swampy ground and intersecting streams wet boots and forced them away from the riverbed. Gnats buzzed and mosquitoes rose in clouds from the marshy grass and tormented them. Oppressive heat bore down from a cloudless sky and lay as heavy as a quilt, smothering and wetting them with sweat. They did not stop to eat until the relentless sun was almost overhead.

"I don't know about you, Della, but if I don't eat something soon, I'm going to drop. That looks like a creek flowing into the river just ahead. The water should be cleaner than the river."

"I'll fetch some to boil the mush." Della stopped short. "Missy, we got nothing to boil water in!"

Nelda sank down on a nearby rock in the shade of a spindly black oak tree. "Let me rest a minute and think." It was a few minutes before she spoke. "We'll make a fire on one of these rocks and get it hot enough to bake a hoecake. I'll try to find something to fetch water in."

Without a word, Della began gathering sticks. But her eyes were wide with worry.

Nelda stooped, opened both valises, and began to rummage. With a disappointed sigh, she rocked back on her heels.

"There isn't a thing in here to hold water, so we'll have to make do." She stood and began to search the ground. Finally she espied a small flat rock with an indention in the center. "Here's our dipper, mixing bowl, and skillet." After picking it up, she tilted it for a better look. "Complete with decoration—the fossil of some unfortunate clam."

It was an hour before the wet meal had baked into the semblance of a hoecake. The women devoured the crumbling mess and washed it down with water from the creek.

"Cornmeal ain't much account without a tad of salt," observed Della.

"No, but it will strengthen us. It looks as if we still have a long way to go—"

Her head shot up with ears cocked. "Maybe we don't have such a long walk after all." She picked a crumb of hoecake from her lap, popped it into her mouth, stood up, and grabbed the valise.

Della began to smile. "A cow bawling, sure as you're born! And that critter sounded close."

"There might be a farm just through those trees," said Nelda.

"Lord Jesus, let us find a horse!" With a groan, Della stood with a hand to her belly. "Even a raw-bone mule would look good about now."

There was no farm, no sign of human habitation. Nelda decided to follow her instincts. When the river curved away, she walked straight, stopping often to listen. Before long, she was rewarded by the sight of acres of plowed ground lying in long furrows, thick and green with cotton. In the distance rose a tall white house surrounded by outbuildings. The place looked prosperous, at least from a distance.

"Plantation!" Della was delighted. "Bound to be horses... maybe even a wagon."

"For all the good that will do us. We have no money except that ten dollars hidden in your skirt. That will hardly buy a meal these days, let alone a horse." Talking more to herself, she added, "Of course gold is more valuable than Confederate script."

"Don't you worry, missy. Where there's cotton, there's bound to be coloreds. We help each other. We'll get us a ride." Her face screwed up in thought. "I ought to go down to the shacks by myself and ask a few questions."

Nelda saw the wisdom in that. "All right. I'll wait here."

She sat down on the ground in a shady spot and watched while Della skirted the fields and the pasture beyond where a few cattle fed. Soon she disappeared from sight behind the big house.

It would be wonderful, thought Nelda, *to find hospitable people*. With a sigh, she leaned her head against the hickory tree and closed her eyes. It was doubtful there were hospitable folk left in Arkansas... and for good reason. Fresh resentment for Bull and Obadiah washed over her. She hoped they hit a snag and drowned!

The gnawing in her stomach felt as if she had eaten nothing. A rustling in the grass made her eyes fly open. A squirrel scampered up a nearby hickory, causing a blue jay to scold and flutter.

"*Contention everywhere,*" she muttered and closed her eyes again.

She awakened when Della shook her shoulder. "Missy, here's food."

Even before her eyes opened, Nelda smelled the heavenly odor of roasted corn. Della held out an ear still attached to the shuck and dripping in butter.

"This here is Jonathan. He's gonna help us." Della smiled at a slender gray haired black man who stood a short way off, straw hat in hand. She lowered her voice. "They still got lots of food here—being back off the road, ain't no soldiers found 'em yet."

Nelda's hand shook as she grabbed the corn. *Never had anything tasted sweeter!* She gobbled it without bothering to wipe the butter from her chin until the entire ear was eaten. As she sucked the sweetness from the cob, it flashed across her mind how scandalized Mama would be.

"Where you all headed?" Jonathan asked.

"Helena—and we must get there quickly."

"You all don't wanna go there, missy! That a awful place. I was there a while back with Massa. Them soldiers calls it, 'hell in Arkansas.' Folks is dying like flies at first frost."

"I'm sure you're right, Jonathan, but that is where we must go. Can you help us?"

He scratched his nappy head. "Massa gone up river...We got a old buggy—don't use it no mo'e. I reckon the wheels still turns." He grinned. "Old mule in the pasture. He blind in one eye, but he pull—if you don't go fast."

Inwardly Nelda groaned. "That would be wonderful." She hesitated. "I can't pay. But I promise to bring them back if I possibly can."

With a frown, he studied on that. "I don't 'magine anyone gwan'a miss that buggy and Massa done give me old Hermes. He ain't no good fer nothing, 'cept fer young'uns to play with."

They followed him to the barn and sat in the shade while he disappeared into a shed. Children peeped at them from behind bright calico skirts of mothers who were equally curious. One young woman brought a bucket of water. First Nelda and then Della drank thirstily from the metal dipper.

"Get on back to work," scolded Jonathan as he arrived with a decrepit set of harness. "Massa come home and catch you lollygagging, he'll sell you south." The women drifted away, but the children lingered. "Hey, you picaninnies! Get on out of here!

"Act like they ain't never seed a white lady," he grumbled.

He went to the pasture and returned leading a mule that was more gray than brown. He led it into the barn. After a bit he returned with both mule and buggy. Sun filtered through the ragged top of the buggy and lay in bars across the cracked black leather seat cushion where horsehair stuffing poked from the rents.

"It still sort of rickety," he apologized. "But I tighten and greased them wheels and dusted the seat off best I could." He eyed the mule and shook his head. "Old Hermes—he mighty poor."

"He'll do," said Nelda while patting the bony animal. She hoped he didn't die in the traces going up the first hill!

"Well, Hermes," she muttered, "winged feet, you have not. But hopefully you have heart."

She turned to Jonathan. "I do appreciate all you've done. You have no idea how important this is."

"Miss Della done tol' me. It all about freedom fer black folks."

"Yes," she stammered, "yes, it is." She didn't say what she was thinking. It was about besting Allen Matthers and the whole nest of rebel vipers! "Jonathan, what is the quickest route to Helena?"

"It's a right fur piece from here. But Massa knows a way to cut across. Save miles from goin' by the main roads." He outlined a series of landmarks and roads and turns and Nelda hoped she remembered them all. "You all gwan'a have to sleep on the ground. Ain't no houses along most of de trail. Ain't no place to buy food neither." He glanced nervously toward the house. "You all wait right here. I'll pack you up some vittals and try to find a old quilt or two for you."

Nelda supposed Jonathan was taking a risk. Likely no one would miss the blind mule and dilapidated buggy. Food was another story.

He soon returned with a bulging gunnysack. After it was loaded, they wasted no time hurrying away. She drove while Della pawed through the sack.

"Oh, my! Fried ham and biscuits and cornpone and a whole sack of boiled eggs! Even a jar of plum jelly!" Eyes sparkling, she looked up. "Enough here to last a good while—if we're careful."

As the aroma of fried ham wafted from the sack, Nelda shifted the reins to her left hand. "Give me some ham, Della. And get some for yourself, too. We'll worry about rationing later. For now I intend to stuff myself!"

The next week was a nightmare of rutted roads, heat, mosquitoes, and jolting. Nelda arose from the hard ground each morning stiff from aches and pains. She avoided dwellings, knowing the less contact, the less likelihood of trouble. Thanks to Jonathan's kind offerings, they did not go hungry. And his advice was proving invaluable. There had been no provost marshals, few travelers, and no sign of either army. However, Helena was much further than she had imagined.

On the level ground Hermes plodded along at a snail's pace. There were no hills on the flat delta, but he balked at the slightest incline. Nelda was often forced to climb down and tug the recalcitrant animal forward as Della walked close by.

Although Della never complained—except to fret over the lack of progress—she frequently held her belly and grimaced. Nelda kept a watchful eye on her drawn face and fervently hoped the baby did not come early.

One morning Della reached into the sack and then looked up with a frown. "Food's almost gone. We got just enough for today." She looked east. "How much further, you reckon?"

"From what that old man said yesterday, I think we'll be there by nightfall." She pointed to an odd ridge of steep hills in the distance that edged the delta. "He said Helena is just over there."

That afternoon, as a blazing red sun sank lower, farms became numerous and travelers became more frequent on the road. Filled with anticipation, Della leaned forward on the frayed seat. In spite of a steep hill, Hermes picked up his pace. Nelda wondered if the hot breeze carried the scent of army mules.

Near sundown a young sentry dressed in Yankee blue halted them. Nelda's heart beat fast as she pulled Hermes to a stop.

"I need to speak to your commanding officer—actually to the senior commander in Helena."

He chewed his jaw and his dark eyes were uncertain. "I can't just let you go sashaying through camp. No offense, ma'am, but we've had trouble with female spies. Do you have any papers?"

"Please, just take me to an officer. I have information of an imminent attack."

His eyes grew large. "Yes, ma'am!" He turned to another private who lolled nearby. "Thompson, take over here. I'll be back as quick as I can." He glanced down the road. "And Thompson, keep a sharp lookout. Trouble's coming." He mounted a bay horse. "Right this way, ma'am."

Della leaned forward. "Where the Second Arkansas Colored camped?"

"I'm not sure… some colored troops may have gone to Vicksburg."

Nelda slapped the reins and without hesitation Hermes complied. Dust roiled from the buggy wheels.

Della held her stomach. "I never thought he might not be here," she said, her lips quivering.

"We'll know soon enough." Nelda's own stomach fluttered. What if the commander did not believe her? What if he thought she was a Rebel spy? She had no proof. Before she could agonize more, the soldier halted to explain their errand to another sentry. Soon they were allowed to proceed.

The road paralleled the wide sluggish Mississippi. Sun glinted off the muddy water gently lapping the grassy banks. As the buggy passed, a crane rose on flapping wings, but desultory, it soon lit again. A boat midstream had three smokestacks like fingers pointing skyward and an overcoat of armor.

"That's an odd-looking boat," she called.

The soldier replied, "Gunboat. U.S.S. Tyler. She'll give them Rebs hell if they try anything around here."

Nelda surmised the rebels would not have an easy time against the fortifications. Fort Curtis was bordered by rifle pits and cannons aimed toward the steep hills that ringed Helena.

A terrible odor suddenly drifted on the breeze. Holding a hand to cover her nose, she shuddered and wished Hermes would go faster. The stench was unbearable. Then her eyes widened in disbelief. Hundreds of dilapidated tents and hovels hugged the torpid river. They housed masses of black humanity, hundreds of men, women, and children who stood or sat in the shade, idle and dejected. Dead, hopeless eyes stared as the buggy rolled past. Della occasionally raised her hand to wave. One woman stood near the road holding a child on her skinny hip. Two more clung to her dirty skirt. She did not bother to shoo the flies lighting on herself and the child.

"Hell in Arkansas," whispered Nelda. *No wonder Gideon made Della leave! It's a wonder any of them are still alive,* she thought. *And they came here seeking freedom!* She wondered how so many had made their way here. And she wondered what the Union Army was going to do about it.

Finally the misery passed from sight, and she ventured a deep breath. It was stale but bearable.

Soon they came to a busy wharf where stevedores unloaded boxes and barrels and soldiers in nearby wagons received the cargo. Della craned her neck.

"I don't see no colored troops. Lordy! I hope Gideon's not done sent to Vicksburg!"

"He might be better off—" Nelda stopped. The big man coming down the gangplank with his shirt open to the waist and balancing a barrel on one shoulder had red hair just the color of… She sucked in a breath. *It was him! It was Allen! Right in the middle of Helena!*

She pulled the reins. "What in the world is he doing?" she muttered. Then her heart raced. *Spying of course. Checking out the fortifications before the attack. Perhaps even sabotaging… Well, he wouldn't get away with it!*

Allen looked up. He froze. Shock washed his face. Then he shot a quick, beseeching look.

For a moment she weakened. Then she remembered Papa and her jaw clenched. "Soldier! Arrest that man! He's a Confederate spy!"

Della turned horrified eyes. "Missy, what you—"

The soldier hesitated, looking from her to where she pointed. "Are you sure… ?"

"Positive!"

Allen's eyes darted. Soldiers and stevedores hung back, reluctant to brace the giant. The sentry licked his lips and rode slowly forward.

"Sir, I'll have to—"

Allen heaved the barrel. Like pins in a game of lawn bowling, men toppled backwards. He dove into the water and disappeared. As if by magic, rifles appeared. All along the bank men ran and shouted, searching the water.

Nelda held her breath. The current washed on undisturbed. Surely no one could swim underwater for so long! She shivered and sat back in the seat. She felt numb.

"There he is!" cried a stevedore. "Way down yonder climbing out on the bank!"

Men ran. Shots rang out. Her heart leaped into her throat. On shaking legs, she stood, holding to the side of the buggy. She couldn't see a thing!

Della cried, "They're gonna kill him!"

It seemed hours, but was only seconds before the crowd parted just enough for her to see Allen, minus both shirt and shoes, claw his way up the bank. Then he slumped and fell, face forward.

Nelda sat down hard.

Della's eyes were hot with anger. "They killed him. They killed Mr. Allen ... and him so good to us!"

"Shut up!" she barked. Nonetheless she quaked. *What had she done?*

Finally the crowd surged forward. A stalwart figure came on, hands tied in front and prodded with a rifle. Even to herself, Nelda would not admit feeling relief.

Blood trickled down from a deep gash on his brow and ran into the beard of a few days' growth. His brown face had paled but his blue eyes were as bright as ever.

"Well, Nelda, I'd ask what you're doing here, but—."

Her eyes narrowed. "I know what you're doing. Spying for the Rebels. I've known about you for ages."

He gave a lazy grin. "Seems the fox got out-foxed."

"You Judas!" she hissed.

His eyebrows rose. He looked at his bound wrists and then at her. "Who's the Judas?"

"Take him to the guard house," ordered the soldier. "I'll go report to General Prentiss." He climbed back onto his horse. "Let's go, ma'am."

In spite of being ordered to move, Allen stayed still and watched as she drove away.

Della's jaw jutted. "That was a wicked thing you done."

"He's a spy!" Nelda was defensive. "Besides, he only helped us because he was hoping to get information for the Rebels."

"You're wrong, missy. I see how he always looks at you—the same as Gideon looks at me."

Nelda opened her mouth and then shut it.

They drove past a forest of tents. Scores of blue-clad men were busy with numerous tasks. The soldier stopped at a large, gray, two-story house flanked by an army of tents and overshadowed by a battery on the hill just beyond. The grounds already resembled a battlefield, the grass trampled by soldier's feet and stumps the only evidence of once massive trees. It appeared as if every tree in town had been cut down for fuel.

The soldier asked Nelda to wait with the sentry as he hurried up wide steps to disappear inside. He quickly returned.

"The Major General is here and will see you."

Nelda handed the reins to Della and stepped down. She brushed dust from navy blue sleeves and skirt and quickly smoothed back sweat-dampened hair before following the private into the cool interior. An orderly ushered her into a large drawing room, which had been converted into an office. Major General Benjamin Prentiss, seated behind a desk strewn with papers, quickly stood, and with a wave of the hand, offered a tall velvet chair.

"Won't you please be seated?"

The general, a slender man—whom Nelda guessed to be about forty—had intelligent eyes, a tall brow, and a thick neatly trimmed dark beard.

"Thank you." She sat but remained nervously perched on the edge of the seat.

He sat down. "I understand you have information of an attack?"

"I do." Succinctly, she related the information and how she had come by it as his keen gaze probed, dissected, and weighed each word. "The Rebel officer said you now had no more than four thousand troops and would be outnumbered two to one," she concluded.

"And you also discovered a spy in our midst?"

"A spy—or a scout or something." She told how she had seen Allen conversing with Rebel officers.

Abruptly, he stood and strode to the door. "Perkins, please summon the major. I believe he's in his office."

Upon the major's prompt arrival, General Prentiss introduced Nelda and then quickly related the Rebel plan.

"It was bound to happen. But I just wish so many of the men weren't ill. And I wish we had half the troops we sent to Vicksburg," worried the major.

"Well, we don't, so we'll make do." Prentiss paced to the window and pulled back the drapes. "Double the sentries, have all troops up and ready for action by 2:30 each morning, and block all roads by felling trees." He stared out the window at the steep hills and frowned. "Thank God for those thicketed ravines—they're almost impregnable for caissons and wagons. And the gunboat will be invaluable—" He turned. "Major there is a Rebel spy in the guardhouse. Bring him to me. I want to question him."

"He won't tell you anything," said Nelda. "He's very stubborn."

"We'll see," he said. "Miss Horton, you've done us a great service. May I offer you lodging?"

"Yes, thank you, sir. My maid and I are weary. We've been sleeping on the ground for days." She stood. "Her husband is in the Second Arkansas Colored. Are they still here?"

"Yes—yes, they are. What's his name?"

"Gideon... Mr. Harris was his owner. But I'm not sure if that's the last name he goes by now."

"Perkins, please take the ladies to the Bradford house. Tell Mrs. Bradford to assure their every comfort. And then see if you can locate this Gideon."

As she stood, her knees trembled. The last of her strength drained away, but she bit her lip and willed weak legs to carry her down the hall and out onto the porch. Stopping for a moment, she leaned against a tall white column and looked toward tents with supper fires dotting the sultry twilight. Then her eyes strayed toward the distant thick-walled log guardhouse.

Had she done right? Was he really the blackguard she supposed? What if—

"Sir, I need to speak to the general again for just one moment."

"Certainly." Perkins held the door as she returned inside.

The general pinned her with quizzical eyes. "Yes?"

"General, do you suppose I could see the prisoner?"

He gave a perplexed stare.

"It's personal sir, and nothing to do with the war, I assure you."

"Very well, but Perkins will have to stay with you."

She nodded.

"Perkins, please escort Miss Horton to the guardhouse."

Allen sat in the shadows on a cot, bent forward and holding his hands between his knees. He stood as soon as the door creaked open.

"I never expected this pleasure, Nelda. How are you?"

She ignored the question. She wished Perkins a thousand miles away, but he stayed alert, watching her every move.

"I've been a stupid fool," she said bitterly. "I suppose you had a good laugh over duping me. All that talk about King James should have tipped me off. You see President Lincoln as a modern day William, don't you?"

He was matter-of-fact. "He had no right to march his army down here. We're free men—free to conduct our affairs as we legislate ourselves. Even English law says a man's home is his castle. Even the king can't enter uninvited."

"That's a warped comparison," she scoffed. "King James raised an army to defend what he thought was right, just like Lincoln did."

"Well, I'm Irish. You know what they say—he quoted a well known Charleston newspaper article— 'The people of the South belong to the brave, impulsive, hospitable, and generous Celtic race; the people of the North to the cold, phlegmatic Teutonic race.'"

He shrugged and then crossed his arms. "I just couldn't side with northern folks against my own kind. But I don't figure you came to jaw about ancient history or heritage."

She flushed. "No. No, I didn't." Her chin went up. "I want to know one thing. Please do me the honor of telling the truth."

He gave a lazy grin. "I don't have any reason to lie. If you'll recall, I never did lie to you, Nelda, not once."

"Did you have anything to do with Papa's death?"

The smile faded. He grew deadly serious. "God as my witness—no.

I even tried to get his release. But I didn't have that kind of sway. I admired your pa. We didn't agree on politics but he was a fine man. And a brave one. I figure that's where you get your spunk."

She whirled. "I'm ready to go, Mr. Perkins."

Allen chuckled. He began to whistle and then to sing.

She waited impatiently for Perkins to unlock the door. Her jaw stayed stiff as the singing softened.

"There is a fair maid in this town,
Who sorely has my heart beguiled.
Her rosy cheeks and ruby lips,
I trow she has my heart enthralled,"

The door opened and she stepped out. Allen kept singing, raising his voice to follow her into the night.

But since it fell into my lot that
I must go and she must not
So fill to me the parting glass
Good night and joy be to you all."

She glanced back. The guardhouse was a lonely dark lump in the night sky. No matter what he said, he was probably lying! And yet her heart ached.

Chapter 10

Mrs. Bradford's large house was nearby, just beyond a long row of tents. A servant opened the door and ushered Nelda into the dining room. After studying her crumpled state, Mrs. Bradford's eyebrows rose, but she invited her to join the dinner party. Nelda wanted to be alone. And good manners dictated she wash the layers of grime from her body before sitting at the elegant table graced with damask cloth and fine china and a bevy of Union officers already seated. The portly hostess was greatly vexed, however, when just then, upon receiving a summons from General Prentiss, they all left with haste.

"Would it be too much trouble to send a tray to my room for my maid and me?" asked Nelda.

Mrs. Bradford looked relieved. "Certainly not. No trouble at all."

A servant girl led the way to a small but neat room on the ground floor with an adjoining room for Della. Soon a laden tray arrived. The beefsteak was tough and stringy but it was nonetheless meat, and there was a small biscuit actually made of flour. Nelda expected to savor every bite. Oddly, it became tasteless as Della pinned her with accusing eyes.

Della hardly seemed to notice the feast. She paced the room and kept staring out the window into the darkness filled with the heavy scent of roses and a chorus of katydids.

Finally she spoke. "I hope Gideon don't get mad at me for comin' with you. He was awful worried about the baby and all this sickness."

"More than likely he'll be so glad to see you, he'll forgive anything."

Della's dark eyes softened. "Be mighty good to see him, too." She strained forward, over the windowsill. "That's him coming! Yonder across the yard!" She whirled. "You go on to bed. I'll be back directly."

Nelda gave a wry smile. "I won't wait up for you."

In spite of the substantial meal and the hot bath in a large tub, Nelda couldn't relax. Allen thought *her* a Judas ...

She was still awake in the wee hours of the morning when a bugler blew reveille. Gooseflesh peppered her arm. Sometime after that she drifted off. But accusing blue eyes haunted her sleep.

Mrs. Bradford's servant awakened her with a cup of steaming coffee and a biscuit on a tray, and she had her freshly washed and ironed clothes draped over her arm. Abruptly, Nelda got up and began to dress. Her fingers were clumsy and her eyes felt full of sand. She had never felt so drained... so empty. After breakfast she would go see the general.

Just then Della returned. Her face was tear-streaked and ashen.

"Gideon says we got to hurry and get on out of here before the Rebels come. He got us some food. He's waiting outside."

"Why, Della, I had supposed we'd just wait here until after the battle—"

"Gideon says what if the Rebels win? He says we'd be in big trouble if they find us here. They're bound to know we brought the warning. If we leave real quick, we'll be gone before they get here."

Nelda glanced out the window. There was sense in what Gideon said. But was it wise to leave the protection of the fort? Out there somewhere was the entire Rebel Army and she had no idea where.

"I'm not even sure if the general will allow us to leave."

"Gideon's done talked to his commander and he done talked to the general, and they all said maybe we best get on home."

"Then I suppose it's all settled."

Della cut her eyes sideways. "I told Gideon about Mr. Allen—and about how good he was to us. Gideon says he's a good man no matter whose side he on."

"That's a matter of opinion. Gideon is entitled to his. Mine is entirely different."

Della looked as if she would say more but changed her mind. "I be waiting on you outside."

"I'll thank Mrs. Bradford for the hospitality and be right out."

As Nelda left the house, Gideon stood at the end of the walk holding the mule's reins. Broad-shouldered but slim, he stood tall with head high in the neat blue uniform of a Union private. Della clutched his muscled arm and big tears ran down her cheeks. Upon Nelda's approach, his grim face broke into a brief smile.

They're a handsome couple, thought Nelda, *their child will be beautiful—if it survives. Della looks terrible today.*

"It's good to see you again, Gideon."

"Miz Nelda." He tipped his head. "It was mighty good of you to come with Della. I won't ever be forgetting that. But you need to get on away from here before the fight commences." He peeled Della from his arm. "Go on with you now—get into the buggy." He helped her up.

Just as Nelda climbed up and took the reins, the general's aid arrived.

"The general sent this pass to get you through our lines. He said to show it to anyone who bothered you."

Along with the pass was a note from the general, once again expressing his thanks. Included was a crude map, sketched by his own hand, of a route he considered less likely to host the invading army.

"Be sure to thank General Prentiss for me."

Perkins nodded.

"Mr. Perkins, did the General learn anything from the prisoner?"

Perkins chuckled. "Maybe a few new salty words... that's about all."

"What is going to happen to him—to the prisoner?"

Perkins shrugged. "Nothing right now. We're too busy. After the ruckus, I figure he'll hang."

Della gasped.

Gideon frowned at Perkins and then changed the subject. "This here ol' mule is about played out."

"I know you asked for a horse but every spare animal has been sent to Vicksburg." Perkins turned to Nelda. "I wish you Godspeed, ma'am." Looking harried, he rushed away.

"Well," said Nelda. "Take care of yourself, Gideon."

He nodded. "Lord bless you, Miz Nelda. I'll be praying—praying for the both of you."

His mournful eyes stayed glued on Della as she leaned far out of the buggy to get the final view. Nelda glanced back. He stood dejected with hand raised.

On the outskirts of Helena, she presented the pass to the third sentry. And for the third time, she guided the reluctant mule off the road and around a mound of felled trees blocking the way. The Rebels would have the devil's own time getting a battery through here, she thought with satisfaction. If the attack was planned for Independence Day—tomorrow—the army was already near. With apprehension, she glanced at the steep hill ahead. A blood-red sun bathed the battery facing west. In ominous premonition she envisioned the cannon belching fire and smoke and death. *Only four thousand men.* She hoped it was enough! She looked back. Why should she feel guilty? He was the traitor!

Although Nelda's every nerve screamed for hurry, they made slow progress on the back roads advised by the general. A half dozen times—at the sound of approaching riders—she guided Hermes from the road and waited with bated breath, hidden in the brush, as patrols passed. Thus far it had been squads of less than twenty. Each time she stopped not a breath of air stirred, but gnats and mosquitoes swarmed in pestering clouds; she could already feel chiggers feasting on her ankles.

Then she had barely gotten concealed when horse hooves stirred the dust. *Hundreds of them!* With a hand on Hermes' nose to keep him from braying, she hid in the thick brush feeling naked and exposed. Only a few feet separated her from what appeared to be the entire Rebel Cavalry!

On and on they came. *So many!* Ragged men but armed and determined. She watched through dust-covered leaves, trembling at the fate of Helena.

Finally they passed. Only the dust remained.

"Must have been a million of 'em," whispered Della. *"Oh Lord Jesus… what's our poor soldiers gonna do!"*

"General Prentiss has good fortifications. And there's the gunboat too." She spoke more positively than she felt as she guided the mule back onto the road and headed west.

By noon she was wet with sweat and exasperated enough to shoot Hermes. In spite of the buggy whip, he balked at almost every step and upon arriving at a stagnant creek with steep banks, he utterly refused to cross, no matter how hard she plied the whip.

"May as well put it down. He ain't gonna go," observed Della wearily.

Nelda's jaw hardened. "He'll go if I have to drag him!" She jumped down. Grabbing the halter, she grunted and pulled with both hands. "Whip him, Della. No! Not just a tap. Hit him hard!" In the tirade, she failed to hear the hooves.

"Trouble, ma'am?"

She spun around. Two Rebel cavalrymen sat across the creek. A third man was dressed in civilian clothes. About thirty years old and lean, he had the look of a man who lived on a horse. He looked vaguely familiar.

"Mules are contrary, ain't' they?" he called. "Fellows, ride on over there and give the lady a hand."

The soldiers did as bidden. Heart pounding, Nelda relinquished the bridle and climbed back into the buggy. Meek and compliant, Hermes willingly started forward, pulling the buggy effortlessly into the shallow water, across the potholes, and up the far bank.

The man grinned. "Mules are smart, too. They know when the jig is up." He pulled a tobacco pouch and a pipe from his pocket and packed it while he talked. "I'd rather have one than a horse for rough country." He struck a match on the leg of his trousers. "Of course, it appears that one has seen better days—" He stopped puffing to squint through the smoke. "Why, I've seen you before… " He lowered the pipe.

She licked dry lips. "I seriously doubt—"

"I never forget a face. Clarksville. The newspaper lady—asking all the nosey questions right before Pea Ridge." His eyes narrowed. "I heard they hung your pa for treason. And what might you be doing way over here close to Yankee territory? And right before a battle." He pointed the pipe stem. "Phillips, keep hold of that mule. Let's escort the lady back up the trail to the general and see what he says. I figure he'll be downright curious."

"But, Curry, we got orders to hurry—"

"Oh, all right. Go on. I'll handle this." With that he got down and came toward the buggy. Nelda's eyes widened as he took the buggy whip from the sprocket. "Give me your wrists," he said. "I got no desire to search you and I got no desire to get back shot." He cut a length of whip and lashed her wrists together and did the same to Della. "Now just sit there and behave yourselves, and if you're innocent of wrongdoing, nothing will happen to you." Then he mounted his horse and, leading a compliant Hermes, turned the buggy and crossed the creek.

Della's eyes were huge. "Reckon they'll hang us?"

"Of course not! They certainly won't hang a woman with child."

"We should have stayed with Gideon! I told him so!" she moaned.

"Hush up. You'll just make yourself sick."

"I'm done sick. My back feels tore in two and I been fighting cramps in my belly all day." She turned scared eyes to Nelda. "Lord help me—I think I'm gonna lose this child." Big tears spilled onto her drawn cheeks.

"Oh Della..." Nelda sat back and closed her eyes.

In an instant they flew open. Curry had stopped. Soon other riders joined them, cavalrymen in uniform.

The captain's eyes widened. "What the—"

"She could be a Union spy. Where's Fagan?"

"Up ahead. Thought you were with him."

"Naw, he sent me over to palaver with General Price."

"Fagan is in a hurry to meet up with Holmes. I doubt he'll want to mess with this now."

Curry glanced back at the buggy. "I figure she knows what's going on inside the fort. I'm pretty sure she just came from there. I cut across buggy tracks early this morning made by those worn out wobbly wheels."

"Then bring her along. The generals will likely want to question her."

Curry nodded. "This mule is done in. I need a horse."

The captain turned. "Gibson, give him your mount. You can ride double until we catch up with the rest."

The private relinquished the black mare, but not without grumbling, to which the captain and Curry paid no heed. Hermes, released from the harness, at first ran off into the woods but then astonished Nelda by trailing along behind, until finally, he fell far behind and she saw him no more. Curry, leading the black mare, kept up a fast pace while Nelda kept a concerned eye on Della.

"Sir, I implore you to slow down. My maid is ill and all of this jostling is making her worse."

He didn't look back. "Can't be helped. I'm not stopping until we get there."

"And where might that be?"

He looked back with a cynical smile. "You're not stupid. I figure you know where this army is headed and why… and I figure since you're from Clarksville, you know General Fagan and he knows you. I heard he lived there for a while."

She did know James Fagan but he had not been a general then, just a young man whose widowed mother had married Samuel Adams who eventually became governor of the state. James Fagan was, so far as she knew, a good and a fair man. She looked down at her chaffing, bound wrists and hoped he was also merciful! But surely she would think of some way out of this mess…

Every bone and muscle ached. Nelda was weary beyond words. She could only imagine how miserable poor Della must be, slumped on the tattered cushion of the jolting carriage. Except for an occasional groan, she appeared dead. Curry had no mercy. He even denied her delicate request for a much needed stop.

"I really need to stop."

"Lady, I don't care if you can't hold it. I ain't stopping."

The sun, low on the horizon, washed rose and coral across the sky. Just when it seemed the horrific journey would never end, Curry pulled rein.

"I see you drew sentry duty, Omer."

A chuckle echoed from up high in a nearby tree.

"Howdy, Curry." The tall, lank soldier slid to the ground and spit a stream of tobacco juice between his fingers. He wiped them on his pants and grinned. "This old elm ain't no sycamore but I never figured that Zacchaeus stunt would fool you anyhow. You got eyes like a Injun."

"Fagan here already?"

Omer nodded. "Yep, he's up at the house. Things are hopping. Looks like we'll see some fireworks in the morning."

"Could be."

"Brought your woman along, did ya?"

"You know damned well I didn't. Phillips and Taylor made it here at least three hours ago and told you all about it."

Omer chuckled again and held out a plug of tobacco as a peace offering.

Curry glanced around. "Lady, you can go over in them bushes now. But hurry up."

"We'll need our hands un-tied."

He stroked his short beard.

"All right," he said and cut the leather with a pocketknife. "You go first and I'll hold a gun on her till you get back. And don't think I won't use it."

Before leaving the carriage, Nelda roused Della. Her legs were full of pins and needles. She could hardly stand. In a stumbling run, she tried to hurry. If she delayed, Curry seemed capable of shooting Della.

When both women had returned, Curry turned off the main road onto a trail that wound alongside a creek. Through leafy gum and elms in the distance beyond a wide field rose a tall weathered house with crumbling, rock chimneys. The yard was overgrown and the bare windows had a haunting vacant look; nonetheless numerous horses were in evidence and even a carriage sat near an overgrown rosebush, which encroached onto the narrow front porch.

Curry, walking behind, ushered them inside. The room was dim, with only one small lamp holding twilight at bay. Somewhere in the house, a cricket chirped.

"Curry, glad you made it back. I hear you found—" The man bending near the lamp and studying a map glanced up. With brows knit, he stood straight. "Miss Horton?" he asked surprised.

"Mr. Fagan," she acknowledged.

He was ten years older than when she had last seen him. His hairline receded but he had remained slender and the black beard thick and curly.

"Good gawd, Curry, un-tie her hands."

Curry flushed. He pulled out the pocketknife. "She might have a derringer hid in her clothes."

The general turned. "On your word of honor, do you have a gun?"

"No. But if I did I wouldn't tell you."

He grinned. "Fair enough."

He motioned her to a chair, and after Curry cut Della's bonds, she sat down nearby.

"What are you doing here?"

Lying was useless. She raised her chin. "I warned them about you."

"Spunky, ain't she?" said Curry.

Omer stepped through the open door. "Begging your pardon, General, but this dispatch just come." He handed a paper to Fagan who quickly scanned it and then sat down at the small desk and wrote a return message.

"Give this to the rider. Tell him to take it back immediately and tell the general I'm expecting my man back from the fort soon."

"Yes, sir."

The general crossed his legs, leaned back, and faced her. "So you were at the fort?"

"I was. And if you're smart you'll stop the attack. You haven't got a chance. They have cannons and gunboats and thousands of soldiers."

"We have spies, too. And we're aware—"

"One less than before," she said snidely and instantly wished she had not spoken.

His brow wrinkled. "One less?"

"Allen Matthers won't be coming this evening."

He crossed his arms and stared. All congeniality disappeared.

She felt a dart of fear.

"Is he dead?"

"No."

"A prisoner, then."

She did not answer.

He swung back to the table and took up the map. "Curry, lock them in an upstairs bedroom and post a guard. I'll deal with them later. General Holmes has ordered the attack for first light."

There were no beds in the empty room. A private brought holey blankets for pallets. A sultry breeze stirred tattered curtains at open windows where a shaft of lightning suddenly brightened the twilight.

"There's no way you can climb out the window, so don't even try. There's a guard out there in the yard with a rifle, and he won't be opposed to using it."

Nelda nodded tiredly.

Soon Della's deep breathing filled the darkness where Nelda lay awake. Every bone ached from weariness; her mind would not slow down. In spite of the stifling room, fear became a cold bed partner. Would the Confederates hang her or would she languish in a Rebel prison? She had heard tales ... perhaps a quick rope was preferable.

She did not regret coming to Helena. The warning might prevent a

Rebel victory. And yet her own heart became traitor when envisioning Allen on the docks, as bold as a swash-buckling pirate, his laughing blue eyes reflecting the shimmering river. They had filled with astonishment upon seeing her and then darkened with stunned disbelief when she sounded the alarm. She winced in the darkness.

Her eyes were still open when the first distant shots pierced the night. She guessed it was about three o'clock—far too early to begin a battle, she thought. But the noise was unmistakable. Shells exploded and rifles spit venom.

She arose and pulled on dusty boots and made her way to the window, expecting to see flashes of rifle fire. Instead a thick fog shrouded the yard. Lanterns on the porch cast an eerie glow on the soldier just below with rifle in the crook of his arm and head cocked toward the clamor.

Abruptly a loud shell exploded. Nelda jumped as the window shook.

"What—" Della jerked up.

"The battle," answered Nelda.

"Lord, help 'em," she whispered. "But it's too dark out to even see," Della protested. "How they gonna know where to shoot?"

"I suppose they just aim in the general direction."

"Lord, help my Gideon!" With a hand on her swollen middle, she lay back and curled into a tight ball as her lips kept moving in silent prayer.

Morning finally arrived. In yellow bands of rising sun, fog drifted away in wisps. Nelda remained at the window but could see nothing but towers of billowing smoke rising beyond the trees. As cannon fire grew fever pitched, the sound was deafening. Again and again the house shook.

Della rolled over. "Missy, what's gonna happen to us?"

"As soon as the battle is over, I'm sure they'll let you go."

"What about you?"

"I have no idea. Probably something awful."

"Don't say that. You're forgettin' the promises in the Good Book. The Lord takes ker—"

Eyes blazing, Nelda whirled. "Don't talk to me about the Lord! Where has He been for the last two years! So far as I can tell, He deserted me!"

Della shook her head. "You wrong, missy." She drew a deep breath and expelled it slowly. "I been wantin' to tell you somethin' for a long time. Reckon now's as good a time as any—even if it make you mad. You ain't no real Christian. Your pappy was a God-fearing man, but all you got is hand-me-down religion. Bible says a Christian got Jesus in his heart. But you just full of hate. Jesus done prayed for the folks who was killin' Him—I misdoubt you even prays for your friends."

A chill traced Nelda's spine. *You'll find no Christian charity here*... The thought haunted. On Judgment Day she supposed Tabbatha and Mary Beth would testify against her. She turned away and kept her back stiff.

The door flew open. "You ladies are needed below. They're bringing in the wounded and the surgeon needs all the help he can get."

"Della is in no shape—"

"No, I want to help." She began pulling on shoes. "I'd want someone to help my Gideon if he was wounded."

Nelda had read stories. And she had heard Papa's tales of war. But she was ill-prepared for the sight of mangled flesh and pleading fear-filled eyes. Bloody stumps remained where arms and legs had been. Some limbs clung by the merest hint of sinew and tendon. The table, which the day before had held General Fagan's maps, now held a man with a huge dark blotch on his chest. Nearby on cots more than two-dozen men groaned and tossed in agony.

A middle-aged man with premature gray hair and deep wrinkles nodded to Della. He pointed a blood-covered hand to a basin of water and then toward a man lying on a cot. "Girl, get a rag and wash as much filth from that wound as you can. I'll get to him in a minute."

"You," he addressed Nelda, "get over here and hold this lamp so I can see."

While the doctor probed a deep wound, she held the lamp with one hand and covered her mouth and nose with the other. And yet with each breath the foul stench of warm blood, urine, and feces crept through. The wounded soldier kept his teeth tightly clenched. But he screamed as the doctor finally drew forth a large metal fragment and tossed it onto the floor. Then mercifully the man lost consciousness.

"Move him over there," the doctor barked.

Two men who were carrying in more wounded stepped forward and grabbed the unconscious man by legs and shoulders.

The doctor looked around. "Put that man on the table." As he washed blood from his hands he glanced at Nelda. "You eventually get used to the smell," he said. "But never the sight," he added in a murmur. "What's your name?"

"Nelda Horton."

"Well, Miss Horton, for today your name is nurse."

She nodded. Her stomach roiled and her eyes filled with dread. "Is there no laudanum?" she whispered.

"We've been out of that luxury for ages." His eyes were sympathetic. "In spite of that, we manage to save some of them."

He approached a cot. "This leg will have to come off, son."

The boy on the cot turned his face to the wall and his shoulders shook. Then the doctor tied his arms to the cot and gave him a stick to bite down on. When the saw bit into his flesh, Nelda held the boy's hand and swallowed hot bile rising in her throat. In spite of the stick he screamed and struggled to get away. She marveled at the surgeon's persistence. Clearly he was a compassionate man. His jaw was set and sweat rolled from his brow in a face reflecting agony to equal the boy's. How could he keep sawing?

The sun rose higher. The morning passed, but the nightmare continued. Nelda held arms and legs, slick with blood and still clothed in shirts and boots, while the doctor sawed into raw flesh. She knew she would hear the screams for the rest of her life.

The battle was a lost cause, or so Omer reported. And yet they fought on. She shook her head. Her eyes swept the room. All this suffering—and for what? Obviously these men thought their cause worth suffering for, worth dying for. They truly believed it!

"Nurse!" The doctor's voice was sharp. "This man needs a new bandage!"

The door opened and Omer stepped inside again. He and another dirty soldier hoisted a stretcher onto the table.

"Doc, I figure this 'un needs you more than any of 'em." He wiped at tears running down his leathery cheeks.

When the surgeon groaned, Nelda turned to look. The man on the stretcher had two stumps where hands had been. Blood soaked the hastily applied bandages.

"Both hands." Omer sniffed before adding, "Cannon ball got 'em both at once. And he's got a hole in his chest, too."

The dazed, mangled soldier stared at his bloody stumps.

Nelda gasped. It was Drew… Drew Morrison, or at least what was left of him. As if irresistibly drawn by a magnet, her eyes stared at shreds of mangled skin that had once been hands—hands that had taken so much from her. Hands that had torched her house, hands that had taken her food, hands that had killed Fred. She should feel overjoyed.

But revenge had turned to ashes. All she saw was Drew, the blond-haired boy who once could throw a ball better than any boy in the county.

When the doctor touched the bandage, Drew cried out.

"Hesh up, now," comforted Omer. "The Doc will fix you up."

Omer shook his head. "I reckon we're cursed, trying to down Old Glory on the Fourth of July. But in all my born days, I never seen braver men. Even with them cannons chewing 'em to pieces, they just kept on charging that hill. Even this boy never stopped till he got to the top."

Nelda's knees went weak and she sat down in General Fagan's chair. When she licked her lips, tears were salty on her tongue.

"Get over here! Quick!" barked the doctor. "Unroll the bandages while I hold pressure on this arm."

With dread, she complied. Her hands shook as the bandage unfurled.

"That's the best I can do for his wounds," said the doctor. "Give him a drink if he wants it. And wash the blood off his face. Coming," he answered a call and turned away to tend the next man.

When she touched Drew's face with the damp cloth, his pain-clouded eyes flew open. In confusion, he studied her. Then, through dry, gunpowder-caked lips, he rasped.

"Nelda?"

"Yes, it's me."

"Figured I was hallucinating." His teeth gritted. As she wiped his face, sweat rolled off his brow. "Figured you must be a tormenting spirit sent to pay me back for what I did. I'm sorry for all of that—"

She shushed him.

His breath came in quick, short pants. "I'm dying, Nelda. There isn't any use saying otherwise—besides, I'd rather be dead than like this." He glanced at the handless stubs. "But Ma and Mary Beth will take it hard." For the first time, tears overflowed his eyes. "Damn," he said, "can't even wipe my own eyes."

She wiped his cheeks and dipped the rag back into the basin.

In an attempt at levity he added, "Guess it's a good thing I'll be gone before I need to go to the privy." He groaned and his eyes closed, but quickly opened again. "I was always sorry I killed Fred. He was a good man."

Her hands stilled from wringing the cloth.

"And I sure am sorry about your house. Never had a worse beating than the one Allen gave me and Bo over that. Couldn't eat for a month—damn jaws wouldn't work."

Her eyes stilled.

He stopped to cough and then drew a wheezing breath. The spittle on his lips was red froth. "I swear I wasn't going to make trouble for your pa—not even before Allen threatened me!" He muttered, "Allen... I never liked that big son-of-a-bitch."

Suddenly his knees drew up. He writhed in agony.

She laid a hand on his shoulder.

"Pa!" He cried out. Then, wide open, his eyes glazed over.

Nelda bowed her head and stared at the rag in her hands. It was a minute before she spoke. Her voice quivered.

"Doctor, this one is gone."

He turned from probing a leg wound. "Can't say I'm sorry. Poor bastard would have had no life," he muttered. "Here, give me a hand. Hold that lamp over here so I can see what I'm doing. It's dark as a tomb in here since the sun went behind the clouds."

As a person in a nightmare who has no choice, she complied.

It was almost noon when Curry arrived. "Doc, we're whipped. Holmes gave the order to pull out. We need to load these fellows into wagons and get going quick."

The doctor shook his head. "A few of them can travel, but it would kill the rest. No, I'll stay here with the worst of them. We'll fly the yellow flag."

He bit out another crisp order for assistance.

"Coming," said Nelda wearily.

"No," said Curry. "I got orders to bring the lady along."

"Why?" she protested. "I'm no threat. And if I stay here I can help the doctor."

He shrugged. "General Fagan says, considering who your pa was, you might know things that would interest General Holmes."

"Well, I don't!"

"I'm just following orders." He jerked his head toward the door. "Come on."

She met Della's wide eyes. "What about my servant? She's unwell."

"She stays," he said. "I got no orders about her."

"Missy, I'll be all right," assured Della. "I'll send word to Gideon. He'll come for me." She squeezed Nelda's hand. "I'll be prayin' for you."

Nelda nodded, and with sinking heart, preceded an impatient Curry out the door. A hot breeze whipped dust into her face and ruffled the canvas on an army wagon waiting nearby. As if already tired from a journey, the mules stood with heads drooping. Dejected men, also with heads hung low, straggled past, rifles on slumped shoulders. They shuffled instead of marching. The defeated Confederate army was, she thought, a sorry sight. She could still hear desultory firing in the distance.

"You can ride beside Omer on the seat, or you can ride in the back. Either way, I aim to tie your hands," said Curry.

She cut him with snide eyes. "You really think I'm that dangerous." Her eyes darted to the wounded men being loaded in another wagon. "I could help nurse those men," she offered.

He seemed to read her thoughts and snorted. "You'd jump out the first chance you got and run off. Then I'd be in dutch." As he spoke he lashed her wrists together.

She winced, but not from the ropes. Her fingernails were crusted with dried blood—blood from dead men. More than ever before in her life, she longed for a bath and a deep, forgetful sleep.

"Omer, keep a sharp eye on her. She's shrewd."

Omer, already perched on the seat, spit a stream of tobacco juice and wiped his mouth with a gloved hand. "I don't relish being nursemaid to no tied-up female," he grumbled. Nonetheless, he reached a hand to help her onto the seat. "Can't see how abusing womenfolk will help win a war."

A spark of hope rose in her breast. Perhaps he could be persuaded to let her escape. She would do her best to win him over.

As mile after jolting mile passed under the high wheels, Omer remained taciturn—and she finally decided—intimidated by the female sex. She fell silent and watched the long line of wagons, caissons, and tramping men cross the flat, monotonous landscape.

Mid-afternoon thunderheads piled high in the west. The smell of rain rode the winds. As lightning forked the livid sky, a brilliant flash was followed by a deafening crash. She gripped the seat as the mules shied.

"Whoa, there!" scolded Omer. Raising his voice against the gale, he reached under the seat for a slicker. "Fixing to pour. You ought to get in back."

She scrambled inside just as the downpour shook the canvas. With hands tied, she had difficulty wending her way through the jumble of boxes, kegs, and barrels. After finally getting situated on an upturned keg, she looked up and groaned. Rain dripped through a small rip in the top. Once again, she hunted and found an uncomfortable perch. She would ask Omer to untie her but it would do no good. She stared at the dried blood caked on her dress. Perhaps Omer would give her water for washing.

She wondered what they would do to her. But mostly her thoughts were of Allen. He might, she realized, be dead. She had no idea how quickly General Prentiss would hang him. Without success, she tried to forget Drew's claims. So what if Allen had beaten him—everyone knew the Matthers loved a brawl. And even if he had threatened Drew regarding Papa, it may have been to keep her fooled. Her thoughts stayed as tumultuous as the storm.

Through the rain, the retreating army marched slowly on—she supposed toward Little Rock. Through the small puckered opening at the back, she watched rain pour down. It was only a thunderstorm and soon passed, but it slowed the weary army even more.

They did not halt until the storm had passed and darkness had fallen. Even with Omer's assistance, she was almost too stiff to alight.

"You can sit by the fire while I rustle up some grub. After supper I'll fix a place for you to sleep in the wagon."

"I'm very thirsty."

After lifting a wooden lid, he plunged a dipper into the barrel lashed to the wagon.

"Would you please untie me?"

He scratched a bearded chin. "All right. But I warn ya, don't try running off. We're miles from nowhere. And Curry can track a fish through water."

"I won't go anywhere." She rubbed her wrists and then thirstily drained the dipper. "May I have water to wash all this blood off?"

He shrugged. "I reckon so. We'll cross the White River before too long and I kin refill the barrels."

She washed her hands and face. After supper she would have a good wash—as much as possible without soap—and rinse her clothes. She would rather sleep in a wet chemise than a bloody one. She hoped Omer hurried with the meal. She could hardly wait to peel off the offensive clothing.

Just then Curry rode into camp. Omer glowered at the news, but Nelda hid a smile. Vicksburg had fallen. Little Rock was bound to follow! Surely, the war would not last much longer.

After taking a ravenous bite of rancid beef and sticky dough, she grimaced. Omer was not a good cook. Then she spied weevils in the open meal barrel and decided perhaps the fault was not all his.

"Here's a cup of corn-bran coffee," he offered. "Tastes awful, but it's black and hot."

She took the cup and sipped and then pursed her lips. She swatted a mosquito on her neck and leaned near the smoke. Steam rose from wet earth, and with the exception of scores of campfires, the night was pitch black. She could hear the horses cropping at the pickets and the distant murmur of conversation, but no one was camped close by. With the coming of darkness, her courage waned. Even though everything in life had soured, she suddenly had a desperate will to live. Of course God had every right to punish her. She had been as rebellious as the Israelites in the wilderness. She furtively wiped away tears before anyone saw them.

The next day the sun beat down with stifling intensity. Nelda stayed soaked in sweat and Omer became so rank, she scooted away from him as far as possible. His attitude towards her had changed. She wondered why. She was shocked when he broke the long silence.

"Curry said you warned the Yankees we was coming."

"I did. I'm a loyal American." Her jaw jutted. "And if I am responsible for the defeat of this army, I'm proud of it."

His mouth turned down. "Don't go patting yourself on the back too hard. Prentiss already had good fortifications. Oh, ain't no doubt your warning helped. But we got no one to blame but our own officers. From the start that battle was a royal mix-up. Holmes said to commence the attack at daylight from three directions. Fagan commenced at first light, but Price never joined in until sunrise. Then Walker never showed up to protect Marmaduke's left flank. Even so, the men fought like demons and purt' near turned the tide."

"Surely you'll give up now that you've been so soundly defeated both here and at Vicksburg."

He shot her a sour look and fell silent. She wished he would keep talking. It helped to pass the time.

"Omer, do you think they'll hang me?"

He looked over.

"They hung my father. And he was an honorable man, a veteran of the Mexican war. He lost an arm in that fight."

He looked at the reins gripped in gnarled hands. His eyes were granite. "I don't know what they'll do to you."

She sighed and gave up any notion of his help.

After another bone jarring day on the wagon seat and another unpalatable supper of beef and cornbread, she crawled into the back of the wagon to toss and turn and try to keep horrible thoughts at bay. Finally she fell asleep to visions of Allen's ghost, his blue eyes, angry and accusing.

She was jarred awake by a hand on her mouth. She struggled but a firm grip held her shoulder. She gasped. Then her eyes widened with shock.

Allen held a finger to her lips and then released her.

"Put your shoes on," he whispered.

Befuddled she sat up and blinked. Perhaps she was still dreaming, she thought, and rubbed her eyes.

In one hand he gripped a pistol. With the other he cautiously held the canvas back and peeked out. Nothing stirred except for a flicker from the small campfire. He motioned to her.

In a daze, she followed.

A loud click echoed. Allen froze. Then he turned around slowly.

Omer stood near the low blaze, holding a rifle. He hissed in astonishment, *"What the hell, you doing, Matthers?"*

"I don't aim to see her hang, Omer. She's just fighting for what she believes in, just like you and me."

"Yeah, and some of us died. And I figure she's partly to blame."

When Allen brought his own pistol level, Omer's eyes widened.

Allen spoke quietly but the words were harsh. "You can shoot, or you can holler and wake the camp. Either way you'll be dead. Why not just go with us peaceful and I'll turn you loose when we're far enough away."

Omer swallowed, indecision strong on his face. Then he lowered the rifle and Allen took it and motioned him forward.

Nelda stumbled along, following Allen's broad back through the darkness. Nearby a horse blew. Soon two animals appeared as dark blots tied to scrub timber. The night was hot, and yet she shivered. Her mind refused clear thought.

Allen tied Omer's hands and ordered him to mount. After Allen mounted he drew a longer rope from the saddlebag and knotted it. Omer's eyes grew large when he slipped the loop over his neck and pulled it snug.

"You might want to keep real quiet. If I have to run, I'll jerk you out of that saddle and I ain't slowing down." Allen held down his hand. "Nelda, get his reins and climb up behind me.

In a trance she took his calloused hand and climbed up. As they slipped away from the sleeping camp, Allen held the pistol drawn and ready; but no one stirred.

"You'll ride easier if you put your arms around me," he said speaking low.

"I'm riding fine," she snapped and he chuckled. In reality, even though she had tried, she was finding it impossible to avoid contact with his wide back. She barely gripped his shirt to keep from sliding off the rough-gated horse.

When they had ridden a ways, she asked, "How did you get away?"

His teeth flashed white in a grin. "There's a Yankee guard nursing a bad headache."

She was silent for a long while. "Why did you come for me?"

He didn't answer but Omer snorted. "If you ain't figured that out, you ain't near as bright as I had you pegged."

She glared. Of course Omer's conclusions were understandable. But he had no idea what was going on here. Allen played some deep game. She had not figured it out exactly, but he was not to be trusted—no matter how gallant he appeared. He would not fool her again!

They rode on in silence. After two hours of slow riding, cutting across country, avoiding roads, and going carefully in the dark, he halted. He reached over and lifted the rope from Omer's neck and then untied his hands.

"You can go now."

Omer slid off the horse. "Matthers, you're in big trouble. You'll never scout for Marmaduke again."

"Don't intend to."

It was too dark to see Omer's face clearly but she felt the venomous stare. She was surprised when Allen tossed him a bottle.

"This will make the walk more enjoyable."

"Well, much obliged," he said snidely.

With relief, she slid off Allen's horse and mounted Omer's. They rode away and left him scowling.

"Where are we going?"

"I'd take you home but word might get back there, and Gill would arrest you. Reckon I'll take you to Fayetteville."

"Fayetteville!" she marveled. *"Why?"*

"Closest Yankee post I know of without heading back to Helena. And I'm sure not going back there. Ever so often the Federals desert Fayetteville, but they come right back. All that country up in there is mostly pro-union. You'll be better off there than anywhere I know of."

"What do you intend doing?" she finally asked.

"Keep you alive for now. I'll figure out the rest later."

"I meant now that you can't work for the army, what will you do?"

He laughed. "No one will believe Omer. He's overly fond of whiskey. He'll be dead drunk for two days. When he does catch back up with the army, they'll think he got drunk and let you get away and then headed out to find you. But just in case, I'm taking a round about way to the river. It'll take longer; but better safe than sorry."

Her eyebrows rose. *Yes, Allen was a conniving man.*

The country was mostly uninhabited, although they passed an occasional farm, which he rode far around. When the sky began to pink, he halted at a small creek and stepped down to let the horses drink. Birds twittered and fluttered about in the sparse timber along the bank.

"We're not far from the White," he said. "I'll feel better when we get there. I aim to ride hard, but for now the horses need rest. Step down. There's a stash of food in the saddlebags, biscuits and jerky, compliments of the United States Army and Gideon." He flashed her a grin. "You ought to quit scowling, Nelda. As my ma says, you'd hate for your face to freeze like that."

If anything, her scowl deepened.

He removed bedrolls from behind the saddles and stretched them on the ground.

"We'll rest a while before pushing on. I figure to catch a boat north for a ways."

He handed over a canteen and a piece of jerky. Then he pointed to a bedroll.

"Better get all the rest you can. It'll be a long trip."

He lay down, propped a hat over his face, and was soon breathing deeply.

Although doubtful of sleep herself, she lay down. The sun was directly overhead when he touched her shoulder.

"We need to go," he said.

Stiff and groggy, she climbed onto the horse. It was a while before she noticed his apprehension as he kept looking back.

She turned in the saddle. "Is someone following us?"

"Yep," he said. "I saw him from that last rise. Still a ways back, but coming fast."

"Curry!" she said. "He's the one who captured me. Omer said he'd trail me if I ran off."

Allen frowned. "That complicates things a mite. We'll not shake Curry. He's a bloodhound."

"What are we going to do?"

"Sit right here till he catches us," he said.

"And then?"

"I'll figure that out when he gets here."

His smile surprised her. She was not surprised, however, when he checked the load in the pistol and then unsheathed the rifle. He rode into a patch of shade and calmly chewed a piece of jerky.

She stared down the road. Her nerves chaffed.

"Surely we should run! The river must be close. We might even find a steamer before he arrives."

The suggestion was useless. Allen would not budge.

She huffed an aggravated breath. "Then may I have the pistol?"

He chuckled. "You're just as apt to use it on me as on Curry."

They remained in plain sight. When Curry finally rode into view, Allen cocked his rifle, resting it on the saddle horn.

Curry stopped and then edged the big roan slowly forward. His rifle was unsheathed and cocked.

"Matthers, never expected you. I found Omer a long ways back passed out alongside the trail." He eyed Nelda. "See you found our spy." He sounded bold but his eyes were wary. "I'll take her now."

"Nope."

Curry stiffened. "I got orders."

"She stays with me."

Curry tightened his hold on the rifle. "What's she to you—she worth dying for?"

Ever so slightly Allen raised the rifle. "Good question, Curry. You ought to give it careful consideration."

He licked his lips. "Hell, she ain't nothing to me. Besides, you've saved my bacon more than once." He pulled on a rein, turning the horse. "The general will be plum sorry to hear she ran off and met with a fatal accident."

Allen nodded. "Thanks, Curry. I owe you."

"Naw, by my reckoning you're still a couple ahead."

Dust puffed from the roan's hooves as he cantered away.

Nelda slumped with relief. She was light-headed from holding her breath. She stared at Allen. Had he been willing to die for her? She shook her head to clear it.

If she weren't careful she would fall under his spell again. Curry was his friend. Of course he had known he wouldn't shoot him! *But why had he rescued her?*

Chapter 11

It was late afternoon before they reached the White River. Nelda nodded in the saddle, dreaming of a hot bath and a soft bed. The vision abruptly faded. The river was low and empty of traffic. Reeds stood in the stagnant water of a marshy inlet strong with the odor of decaying vegetation. She groaned when Allen said there would be no boats until rain raised the water. Except for an occasional cloudburst, July was typically a hot dry month in Arkansas. Now there was not a cloud in sight. She dreaded the long ride ahead.

"There's coffee and cornmeal in the saddlebags. If I can spear a fish, we'll have a regular feast. I figure there's carp feeding along the bank here." He climbed down and took a knife from his pocket. "Compliments of the Yankee guard. 'Course it wasn't his idea to give it to me," he said with a grin. "You ought to stretch a bit, but we won't camp here. Mosquitoes would eat us alive."

He hunted until he found a stiff reed and sharpened one end. "Green cattails are too limber but the dead ones dry hard as rock. This one ought to make a tolerable spear." Still wearing boots, he waded into the river.

"Hate wet boots," he said, "but they're better than getting snake bit or stepping on a sharp stob."

She sat on the bank, wishing for a breeze to cool her sweaty body. It would be interesting to see if he actually could spear a fish. She had heard of it, but never seen it done. Suddenly she sat up straight.

"Watch out!" she cried.

He had already seen the snake, a long dark streak, darting back and forth on top of the water. The snake raised its head and hissed like a cobra. A forked tongue flickered from the slit of a mouth.

Allen swung the reed. The blow cracked like a whip and the snake crumpled. He scooped it onto the reed and carried it out onto the bank. Its neck was broken, and yet it writhed and twisted. He pinned it to the ground with the sharp end of the stick, took out the knife, and cut off the blunt-nosed head.

"I see why you kept on the boots," she said with a shudder.

"I've heard cottonmouths are good eating," he said.

Her nose wrinkled. "They certainly don't smell appetizing," she said.

"Well, if you don't want snake for supper, you best get to praying for fish."

After tossing the carcass onto a nearby rock, he reentered the marshy bog.

"Yep, there's carp, feeding on the cattail roots." He waded closer and then stood, statue still, with spear raised.

A primitive savage, she thought, *muscled, bronzed, and capable.*

The reed plunged. Allen swore.

"Missed it! Bounced right off the scales. And it was a monster," he grumbled.

Maybe not so capable, she thought with a sly smile.

Again he waited. This time he held the reed at a slant. When a fish swam near, he struck hard.

"Got it!" he shouted, pinning the fish to the bottom. He reached down, caught it by mouth and gills, and tossed it onto the bank. "It's not too big. I'll try for another."

Nelda scrambled forward to place a boot on the flopping fish. She scooted it farther away from the water. In less than ten minutes, he had snagged two more and waded out.

"Why don't you gut 'em while I pour the water out of my boots," he said. He sounded serious, but his eyes twinkled as he sat down and tugged off a sloshing boot.

"I'm certainly not afraid of a fish, Allen Matthers."

He threw back his head and laughed. "Full of vinegar," he said. "Reckon that's what I like about you." He stamped back on the wet boots and picked up a fish and split it open. "Carp's not as good as the brownie I catch on Little Piney, but I figure you'll like them better than water moccasin. After I gut these, we'll ride on a ways, and hopefully find a stream to camp by."

They found a stream meandering through small trees and underbrush. Katydids sang a loud chorus, but Allen declared them far enough from the river to avoid the worst mosquitoes.

"We'll make camp here and get an early start tomorrow." He set about gathering snags of dead wood. Using dead grass and twigs as kindling, he struck a match and started a blaze. Then he placed a flat rock into the fire to heat. He soon returned from the stream with the coffeepot filled with water and set it on the fire.

"I'll mix some cornmeal cakes to bake on that hot rock," he said. "I'll have to roast the fish. I borrowed the pot from the army but never found a skillet handy."

Clearly accustomed to camp life, his movements were agile and unwasted. He gathered more wood for the fire and then chose green sticks from a persimmon tree. Near the fire, he drove one, a forked stick, into the ground and used it as a prop for the other stick that he had sharpened into a skewer. On it he laced the fish, scales intact. Upon seeing her grimace, he assured, "After it's roasted the hide and scales peel right of." He pulled the rock from the blaze and laid on the cornmeal patties.

A whiff of roasted fish set her mouth watering. It might not be as good as the brownie caught from Little Piney but it smelled wonderful.

"Will Gideon get into trouble?" she suddenly asked.

He shook his head. "No one saw him. He only slipped a gun through the window. I stole the horses and outfits myself."

"They hang horse thieves," she said.

"I didn't have a lot to lose," he shot back.

"Well, I see you're human after all." She was snide but her face had reddened.

He shot a quizzical look.

"Even though I had you arrested and almost killed, you forgave all and rescued me. I was beginning to think you were a saint."

"I'm no saint," he said. "Actually never had much use for 'em. Ma prays to them all the time. But I figure—like preacher Simon from the mountain says—a fellow ought to go right to the top, talk to the Lord himself."

She blinked in astonishment. *"You pray?"*

"On occasion," he said. "Only a fool thinks he can get along without God."

"Allen—" She started to speak and then stopped.

He turned from stoking the fire. "What?"

"I've thought for months that you had something to do with Papa's death. But during the battle at Helena, Drew was brought to the house where I was being held. Both of his hands had been blown off. He finally died."

"That's too bad," he said. "Drew wasn't a bad fellow."

"He told me you had threatened him and told him to have nothing to do with harming Papa. And he told me about the beatings you gave him and Bo."

"Wish I'd done more than beat Bo—that son-of-a-bitch," he muttered.

He rubbed his jaw. "Sounds as if maybe you don't hate me so much anymore?"

She stiffened. She would not be taken for a fool again.

"I haven't forgotten how you deceived me," she bit out.

He leaned forward and slowly turned the cornpone. Then he hunkered back on his heels and pinned her with a penetrating gaze.

"Nelda, if you ain't careful, you're well on the way to being a bitter, lonely woman."

She shot him a look of pure hate. "If you Rebels hadn't taken everyone I love, I would be neither bitter nor lonely. You have no idea what it's like to lose beloved parents, a home—everything you cherish."

"Reckon I do," he said, "at least the part about parents and home." He looked at the fire. "Pa is dead. And Ma went to Texas to live with her brother."

Her mouth fell open. It seemed impossible that big Red Matthers was dead. "How ... when?"

"Months back."

"But you never said a word—"

"I figured you had enough troubles without hearing mine."

"Was he ill?"

"Nope. Hale and hearty—until he made the mistake of not cooperating with a conscription officer. When he wouldn't tell where my brothers were, the fellow shot him. Ma described the killer. I've been looking for Bo ever since."

"Bo!" exclaimed Nelda. She slowly shook her head. "I don't guess I should be surprised," she added. "From what I've heard, there are lots of people who want Bo dead."

He quirked a brow. "Well, I'm one of them."

"Your poor ma!" she said with heartfelt sympathy. "I could tell your parents loved each other deeply."

He dropped his head and swallowed.

After that she sat quietly and watched him work. She was surprised at the grief she felt over the breakup of the Matthers family. Although she had resolved to hate Allen, the short time spent with his family had remained a pleasing memory. How sad that those happy times on the wide front porch were gone forever! She wondered where his brothers had gone. Under the circumstances, it was a question best left unasked.

When the meal was finished she declared it delicious.

Allen stretched and yawned. "It was filling," he admitted. "But I'd give a dollar for some of Ma's chess pie." He glanced over. "Can you cook?"

"Not one thing," she lied.

"I figured as much," he muttered and then began spreading the bedrolls several feet apart. He pondered for a moment. "Wish I had a tent for you."

"I've slept under the stars before."

"Not many stars tonight, but the moon is pretty," he observed. "Well, get some sleep. We'll be up at first light."

She lay down and gazed up. The moon was pretty. It rode low in the sky, just above the trees, casting silver light on the water. In the darkness, a whippoorwill called. Another soon answered the plaintive summons. She wondered if they were mates.

She gave a tiny smile imagining what Mama would say to her sleeping arrangements. Allen lay not ten feet away. She could hear him breathing. He was restless tonight. He had turned over several times. She jumped when he spoke.

"You know the first time I ever saw you?"

Her eyes widened.

"It was a dance in town. You were about sixteen. There was a big crowd. The girls were all laughing and flirting. All but you. You were standing behind your pa, writing notes, fast and furious, while he and some fellows talked politics."

He rose on an elbow to look her way. She saw him plainly in the moonlight.

"Right then I knew you were special, and I've admired you ever since."

He lay down and turned away. She lay still but sleep was long in coming.

A fire red sun topped the horizon as they followed the river north. By nine o'clock Nelda's blouse had glued to her with sweat, but the soreness of early morning had begun to abate. She hoped she would quickly get toughened to the saddle.

Allen avoided other travelers, leaving the road when anyone appeared in the distance. When contact was unavoidable, he was terse and unfriendly. Strangers seemed relieved when they rode on.

"We'll cross the river at Clarendon, take the river road north, and then head west. Better roads that way. We'll steer clear of towns. I reckon Curry will keep his word; but better safe than sorry." He went on, "And if the river rises, we'll catch a boat for a ways."

"The last boat ride I took was a disaster." She told of Bull Smith and the robbery. "I hated losing Papa's watch more than the gold."

"I'm acquainted with Bull," he said, his eyes flint. "His type gives pirates a bad name. He used to pilot a big boat on the Mississippi, but he stole some cargo. Later I heard he ran afoul of the law again in a shooting scrape and went to jail. I didn't know he was back on the river."

They crossed the river at Clarendon and then traveled fast, carefully avoiding towns. In the next three days, they left the road twice to avoid army patrols—one Union and one Confederate—and stayed shielded in the brush to let them pass. Nelda wondered aloud how often such patrols ran into each other.

"Too often," said Allen with a frown. "There's been a lot of blood let between the White and the Arkansas."

She was appalled at the devastation they passed. All along the river were burned farms and deserted plantations, homes with nothing standing but blackened chimneys.

"This was prosperous country once," he commented. "Curtis burned everything in his path on his way to Helena. And I reckon Hindman burned the rest to keep Curtis from getting it."

Each day he managed to kill enough small game to feed them. Although the rabbits and squirrels were often tough, Nelda was famished and ate them with pleasure. Each night they avoided dwellings and camped near a stream and refilled the canteens lashed to the saddle. Allen remained uncharacteristically quiet. But often, in the light of the campfire, she felt his eyes upon her. She had no idea what he was thinking. Of one thing she was certain—she would be glad when this journey was done!

She was becoming toughened to the saddle, and her face and hands had browned almost to copper. She imagined it would take weeks of glycerin and rosewater to soften them again. In early mornings she actually enjoyed being outdoors in the dawn's invigorating air filled with birdsong. By noon, with a hot sun beating down, she wilted and craved day's end.

On the fourth day they reached the wide Arkansas just above Lewisburg. With a sigh, Nelda stared at the water and felt at home. Then she sobered. She was not going home. She wondered sadly if she would ever see the tall white house again.

"Oh, how I'd love a bath and a bed at the Markham Inn," she said. "When Papa and I traveled, we always stopped there. The beds were clean and the food was excellent."

"Better than stringy rabbit and tough squirrel?" he asked.

Her eyebrows rose. "I haven't complained. Rabbit and squirrel is a feast compared to some meals I've had."

He shifted his weight in the saddle. "I hate that you went hungry," he said. "If I have my way, it won't ever happen again. I figure the army at Fayetteville gets supplied pretty regular from Saint Louis. I hope you'll stay there until this thing is over. As long as the war is on, Clarksville is no place to be. When they're traveling south, every army and every patrol heads right for the crossing at Spadra. You'll be a lot safer at Fayetteville."

"How long do you think it will last—the war?"

He slowly shook his head. "Honestly, I have no idea." He cocked his hat forward and squinted into the morning sun. "From what I saw and heard at Helena, it looks better for your cause than mine," he admitted. "I figure Holmes can pack his bags. I doubt Little Rock will be in Confederate hands come fall. But you never can tell," he said with a shrug. He kicked the horse in the flanks. "I know I'll feel better when I get you to Fayetteville. But first we'll make a stop at that inn. I'd like a bath and a bed myself."

It was late afternoon when Nelda caught sight of the hills of Lewisburg sloping down gently to the lapping river. A wave of nostalgia brought visions of happier days and trips here with Papa. Then she stiffened.

"That's Bull Smith's boat!" she cried. "There he is on deck now! Allen, give me the pistol!"

He grinned but his eyes were solemn. "Yeah, I see him. But I'm not letting you have a gun. I didn't bring you this far to see you hang for murder. That's a provost marshal standing over there. And there's at least a dozen soldiers at the rail of that other boat. Now, don't go getting in a huff. Bull is going nowhere in this low water. We'll come back later when there's not so many people about. Now where is this inn you've been telling me about with all the good food?"

She pointed up the hill and followed as he rode on. But her eyes stayed hostile and aimed at Bull Smith as he strode the deck of the Lottie Ann. Of course Allen was right but it irked to simply ride away. He had her money and Papa's watch. She intended to get back both of them.

They rode up the hill and between large magnolia trees. The two-story white inn was as gracious and inviting as she remembered, and the hosts, the Markhams, as congenial.

Mr. Markham had scarcely ordered the slave to stable the horses before his wife had seated them at a long oak table, polished to a shine, and placed steaming cups before them.

"Of course it's not coffee," she apologized and sat down. "But there's none to be had at any price."

Nelda blew on the drink to cool it before taking a sip. "I love sassafrass almost as much, anyway." Her brows lifted in surprise. "And this tastes like real sugar."

Mrs. Markham beamed. "I saved a small stash for extra special guests. You and your pa were two of our favorites. How is he?"

"He died several months ago," Nelda replied. "His health had been failing for quite some time."

Mrs. Markham's face fell. "Oh! I'm sorry to hear it. He was such a fine gentleman." She cut her eyes at Allen but left unasked the question uppermost in her mind. "So you're traveling upriver or down?"

Nelda smiled to herself before answering. "Upriver. I've been traveling on business for a while. When my maid was taken ill on the trip, I was left to my own devices. Mr. Matthers protected me from a dangerous confrontation."

Her curiosity somewhat satisfied, the matron relaxed. "Well, we're very pleased to have you both. Lately there are few travelers—no women and few men. Mostly military is all that passes through. I'm thankful that Ruben broke his arm awhile back or he'd be in the fighting too." She stood. "Well, I need to get out to the kitchen. Unless I stand over her, Sully burns the fish every time." She picked up the toddler clinging to her skirts and then called to a young boy playing in the hallway, "William, show Miss Nelda to the pink room upstairs."

She turned back. "Mr. Matthers, I have a fine room for you right here." She opened the door of a room just down the hall. "I'll send Sully with fresh water so you can wash up. Supper will be ready in a few minutes."

After supper Nelda leaned against the railing of the upstairs portico and stared at the river flowing past just a stone's throw from the Inn. It was a nice night, a reprieve from the heat. The moon was only a small curve of silver but the stars were vivid. Katydids overpowered all but the loudest bullfrogs; yet it was a peaceful sound, the typical music of an Arkansas night. She drew in a deep breath that mingled supper's fried fish with the musty smell of the river. Then she heard voices and caught a whiff of cigar smoke.

On the porch below Allen was conversing with Mr. Markham. Soon a door closed; and then she saw Allen stride across the yard and down the street, heading for the river. Her breath caught. Unless she was badly mistaken, he was heading for the docks and an altercation.

She slipped from the house and followed as fast as she dared.

The wharf was dark. A dim light came through the window of the pilothouse on the deck of the Lottie Ann. Bull sat inside. He stood, stretched, and picked up the lantern. He had just stepped through the door when he drew up short and stiffened.

"Well, howdy, Matthers. Haven't seen you in these parts for a while. What can I do for you?"

His eyes widened when he saw Allen's gun. He put a hand near his belt.

"Don't pull that derringer you got hid, for starters. Then you can give back a watch and the money you took from a young lady you picked up at Clarksville a while back. I'm sure you remember her."

Bull's lips rolled back in a predatory grin that was half snarl. "I don't return passage money. If she didn't like the price she should have taken another boat."

Allen stepped closer. "I'll have it now—*or you die.*"

Bull glowered. "Here's the damned watch—"

"Careful! Slow and keep you hands where I can see them."

Bull sat the lantern on a nearby cask and carefully removed the gold watch and chain from his vest pocket.

Nelda, watching from the shadows, swallowed nervously.

"Now the money."

Bull jerked his head toward the cabin. "It's in there. In a drawer in the desk."

"Show me. But I'll open the drawer. Never know where a gun might be hiding. Get the lantern."

As Bull reached for the lantern, there was a sudden noise on the far side of the pilothouse as Obadiah ducked from sight. Allen glanced away for a split second. It was enough for Bull to whirl, throw up his arm, and knock the gun from Allen's hand. Nelda watched, horrified, as it splashed into the river. Bull lashed out, plowing a big fist into Allen's chin.

Allen's head snapped back. He staggered but was brought up short by a barrel. This time, he dodged Bull's assault.

Nelda gasped. Allen was tall and powerful. But Bull was thicker, his massive chest like a bull's. His arms bulged with muscle as he made his hands into fists.

Hardly flinching, he took the uppercut Allen landed in his midsection. When Allen followed with another blow to the face, his head snapped. He licked blood flowing from a busted lip. But as Allen stepped near, he landed a hard blow to Allen's stomach, sending air whooshing. Then he landed two more quick blows.

As the fight moved out of sight, Nelda stepped aboard. With small regard for defense, each man took the blows and quickly returned them, smashing again and again at his opponent. Soon both were bloodied.

Allen sent a fist into the side of Bull's head, staggering him. The return blow rocked Allen back on his heels and overturned a barrel. He kicked the barrel out of the way and shook his head to clear it.

Bull landed an especially brutal punch. She watched, appalled, as blood splayed from Allen's nose and mouth. Allen shook his head and charged forward. With a vicious swing of solid fists, he knocked Bull to his knees. With another blow he knocked him to the floor and began kicking with violent swings. Then grabbing his shirt by the neck, he pounded the upturned face. Just as Bull brought a knife from his boot, Allen caught his arm in a powerful grip. He bent the arm backwards and over the barrel. When the bone snapped like a shot, Bull cried out in agony.

Movement near the pilothouse caught her eye. Something glinted. Her eyes widened in terror. Obadiah gripped a pistol—her pistol! It was cocked and leveled at Allen's chest!

"No!" she screamed. Just as she jumped, he pulled the trigger.

The blow spun her around. She slammed onto the deck. For a few seconds everything went black. Dimly, she heard a scream and a splash. She wondered who had screamed. It was high and shrill like a woman. Perhaps it was her. Perhaps she was sinking down, down, down into the river. But no, the deck was hard beneath her. In a spasm of pain, her fingernails clawed rough wood.

"Nelda!" Allen bent over her. He put a hand on her side and it came away bloody. "My gawd, girl, don't die on me." He took her face in his hands and shook it. "Wake up, you hear me! Wake up!"

She moaned.

He scooped her into his arms and began to run. When he stumbled, her eyes flickered open long enough to see Bull staring sightless at the sky. His throat gapped open and streamed blood like the hogs on butchering day.

Her eyelids fluttered. She was in a room with curtains. But it was not her room. Her eyes fell shut and she groaned. Pain, raw and throbbing, tore at her side, catching her breath and leaving her panting. A calloused hand smoothed her brow.

"I'll get help for you, girl. I promise."

When she opened her eyes, she was alone in the bedroom of the Inn. Then her lids fell shut.

It was hot here. Della's finger poked at her accusingly. Perhaps she was in hell. No. There was Mama, laughing and happy. She smiled and called out to her, but the smile faded when Mama turned disapproving eyes. As Mama stared her skin grew soot-covered and her flesh sagged from her bones, melted, and ran down like hot wax. Nelda tried to run but her feet were nothing but bloodied stumps. Her head thrashed. It was so hot. She licked dry lips and tried calling for water. Jet earbobs danced as Tabbatha threw back her head and laughed. "No! You'll get no charity here." Her nails clawed the door but Tabbatha refused to open.

"Miss Nelda, can you hear me? Try a sip of water."

She vaguely saw Mrs. Markham bending near. Coolness ran down her cheek and wet the pillow. A few merciful drops slid down her parched throat. She opened her mouth again and swallowed.

She croaked. "Allen?"

"He went to find a doctor. You've been unconscious for a long time."

Nelda was too tired to keep her eyes open. There must be a red-hot poker burning her side. She wished someone would remove it. Then she grew so cold her teeth began to chatter. But she was too weak to ask for more covers.

With a stabbing pain, she groaned and opened her eyes. A strange man stood over her, but it was Allen who held her shoulders. She screamed and then all went black. Sinking in and out of consciousness, dreams and reality intertwined. She was unsure if the voices were real.

"It missed her vital organs and went clear through—but a bullet can carry trash inside to fester. She's lost a lot of blood. I think her head is fine where she struck it but only time will tell. I'd like to stay and keep an eye on her, but you know I can't. As it is, General Marmaduke will have my hide for taking off without permission."

"Tell him I forced you at gunpoint."

The doctor washed and dried his hands. "I'll tell him I got abducted, Allen, but I won't tell him by whom. Besides everyone thinks the Yankees hung you."

"Thanks, Junius." Allen shook the surgeon's hand. "Sorry about being so high-handed. But I had to make sure you'd come."

Nelda did not know how much time had passed when she opened her eyes. The room was dark except for the small glow of a lamp sitting on the table. Allen sat with head bowed. His lips moved and she knew he was praying. Later she wakened again to find him slumped and asleep in a chair drawn near the bed. It was the first time she had noticed signs of age, tiny wrinkles around his eyes and a bit of gray lacing the three-day growth of beard. She closed her eyes and slept.

When she awakened, light flooded from the windows. The chair was empty. But as she glanced around, she saw him standing at the open window. He stayed back a ways peering from behind the sheer white curtain. Then she knew she was dreaming for she heard Bo Morrison's unmistakable shrill voice. But the sun was bright. It hurt her eyes. When she lifted a hand to shade them, Allen turned.

"You're awake!" He sounded relieved. "How do you feel?"

"I must be awake. My head throbs terribly—but only a speck more than my side does. I thought I heard Bo Morrison outside."

"You did. He just rode off with a couple of soldiers. They're foraging. I figure he cleaned out the Markham's pantry."

"You'll be going after him," she said, her voice a weak whisper.

"I reckon not."

"But you've looked for him for months. He'll get away—maybe kill some more innocent people."

"I'm not leaving you."

She was glad. She did not know why. Nevertheless, she was. "I don't know why you're staying."

With a smile he quoted Omer, "If you ain't figured that out, then you ain't near as bright as I had you pegged. Now I've got a question for *you*. Why did you jump in front of me? That bullet in your side ought to be in mine."

She lowered her eyes and pleated the sheet with trembling fingers. She could not tell him why. She didn't know herself.

His eyes grew probing and serious. "Nelda—" he began and then stopped short. "Now's not the time," he muttered to himself and walked over to pour her a glass of water. "The doc said you need to drink lots of water. Are you hungry?" He gently lifted her head and put the glass to her lips.

She shook her head and then eyed him over the glass as she drank. After he sat the glass down, he reached into his pocket and drew out a watch. He took her hand, placed the watch inside and closed her hand over it. Her eyes shone.

"Papa's watch!" she exclaimed weakly.

"Thought it might make you feel better," he said. "Bull got to feeling guilty and gave it back. And your gold too."

She looked up. "You killed him." She suddenly recalled hearing the scream. "And maybe Obediah, too?"

When he didn't answer, she asked, "Will you get into trouble?"

"No one is going to miss those two. Someone will find the boat downriver and figure bushwhackers did it or that justice was done."

As days passed, slowly she grew stronger and by the next week was able to sit for a short while in a chair. Allen left her alone, now, for longer stretches. He chopped wood for Mrs. Markham, helped with household chores, mucked out the barn, and entertained the children.

In the evenings, he delighted the family with music from a borrowed fiddle that had belonged to Berilla Markham's cousin. But he often checked on Nelda and saw to her every comfort.

She spent long hours in thought, mostly reflecting on the last few months. She had to admit, she had become a different person—and in all honesty, not a very nice one. Della's words still rankled. She had to own that Papa, and yes even Della, possessed an inner peace she lacked. But for some reason beyond her kin, God had spared her life again and again. Perhaps it was due to Papa's prayers and Della's. And yes, even Allen's. He was a rough one. And yet he seemed to possess a childlike faith—which she recalled Pastor Wheeling had said was necessary to salvation. She sighed. Thinking on such things made her head hurt.

Thinking about Allen and their relationship made her head hurt even worse. As much as possible she pushed it from her mind.

Two weeks later, he stepped into her room.

"Do you think you're strong enough to travel? Things are getting risky around here. There's reports of Union troops marching on Little Rock. If it falls or stands, there'll be lots of traffic on the river. And there might be fighting even here. I need to get you away; and I need to get on back." He left the thought unfinished.

"Get on back to helping General Marmaduke," she guessed.

He went on, "You won't have to sit up. I can fix a mattress in the wagon. Mrs. Markham has a spare she'll let us have. We'll take along the horses but I also paid Ruben for a wagon and a team of mules." He grinned. "Compliments of Bull Smith and his gold. He had a mite more in that cabin than what he took from you. Since he won't be needing it, I helped myself."

"Yes, I can travel," she asserted. And yet she wondered how. She was still too weak to brush her own hair. Sully did it for her each morning, and at bath time, sponged her off. She was too frail to get in and out of the tub. But Allen was right. They needed to get away from the river and the likelihood of traffic from both armies.

They left the next morning at daybreak. It was a cloudy morning and mists hugged the river and swirled the giant magnolias. The Markham family stood on the porch and saw them off with good wishes and regret. Lying in back of the wagon, Nelda pulled up the quilt and shivered. September could be hot in Arkansas. Today, however, held the first nip of fall.

She was surprised to find the road already crowded with travelers. Allen informed her they were refugees from Little Rock fleeing the Union advance. Although hundreds had left the city early in the war, now even the die-hards were leaving. Buggies and wagons loaded high with plunder vied with saddled horses and pack mules for a spot on the crowded road.

Solicitous of her condition, Allen drove slowly. We'll head north from here. Go up to the Buffalo and then west to Fayetteville. We'll take it slow. I figure to make around ten miles a day. We'll have to stop ever so often for a day to let you rest. We should get there in about three weeks. Anytime you need to stop, sing out."

When they turned north and away from the river, the traffic lessened. As the sun climbed higher, the fog melted and the air warmed. Pushing the quilt away, she dozed, jerked awake, and dozed again. Finally she awoke and lay thinking. What would she do in Fayetteville? She knew no one—not a single soul. What if the Federal authorities did not believe her? After all, she was arriving with a Rebel spy! Of course she would not mention that…

Allen was quiet. He also must have much on his mind. She lay on the mattress and with one arm shielded her eyes from the sun. Finally she broke the silence.

"Allen, why do you side with the rebels? I can tell you're a thinking man—and in spite of trying to hide it—you're self-educated and fairly well read. I just don't see how you can be a Confederate sympathizer."

He was silent for a while. "You seen oxen—cattle in a yoke?"

She blinked. "Yes."

"Well, folks wear yokes, too. You just don't see them as readily. Take governments and taxes for instance—there're yokes of a kind. Pa was fond of saying that he left Ireland to throw off the heavy yoke. A few years back in this country men fought a war over what kind of yoke they'd wear; government of the people, by the people, and for the people. I see it this way— we should still have the right to decide whose yoke we wear. And we choose not to wear Lincoln's."

She rose to an elbow, clutched her side, and turned toward him. Her voice was beseeching "But Allen, what about Gideon? What about the black man? Don't you see Lincoln wants to take the yoke off an entire race!"

He chewed his jaw. "Got to admit, that part has give me pause. I want no man in bondage. Although some are, I sure as hell ain't fighting to keep slavery. The way I figure it, each man is responsible for his own yoke. If he don't like it, he can fight to get it off… just like I'm doing now. Just like Gideon is doing. I don't fault him one whit. Matter of fact I admire him. But that don't mean I'll bow and scrape to a big federal government with a big yoke that's wanting to take the chains off one fellow and put 'em on another. I'm for keeping power close to home. That keeps the yoke as small as possible. My voice will carry a whole lot louder in this state than it does in Washington City."

"But, Allen," she argued, "that's what this nation is—individual voices with equal power! Why, your vote counts as much as anyone's in Maine or Massachusetts!"

"Then why didn't the vote to secede count? Each state should have the right to do as she sees fit. The South has always played second fiddle to the North. And a yoke whittled by some Maine politician doesn't fit my neck any better than an English yoke fits an Irishman."

Exasperated, she lay down. She wouldn't be able to argue any better than had Lincoln with Douglas. And popular opinion had given Douglas the victory! Some things, she supposed, were just irreconcilable matters of opinion.

He stopped the mules and faced her. He chewed his lip before saying, "I'm going a route I know—one I travel often. I have friends…" He cleared his throat. "They're good people, Nelda. And I wouldn't want to see them hurt."

"They're rebels," she guessed.

He nodded. "Most caught up in this thing through no wish of their own. They're just trying to keep body and soul together and survive."

"I won't turn them in, if that's what you're worried about."

"That's what I'm worried about." He frowned. "I wish we was on the same side," he said. "This way sure is awkward."

"To say the least," she muttered. "I think I'll sit up a while," she said.

He helped her onto the seat. But before many miles had passed she had to lie down again. She was shocked at how weak she felt. When he whoa-ed the mules at a small farmhouse, she jerked awake and groaned. Gratefully she took his hand and climbed down. Every bone ached and her side was a dull throb.

The elderly couple made them welcome, and the tiny woman soon had supper on the table.

"Ain't fancy," she apologized, "but—such-as-tis—there's plenty."

There was no meat except for the generous piece of fatback floating in the brown beans. The cornbread was thick and hot.

"We ain't had no butter since they took the cow. I reckon she got et. I can't see them soldiers a dirtying their hands to milk. Hit's a crying shame, too. She was a good milch cow."

"Union patrol or Rebel?" asked Allen.

"Union. They come sashaying through here last month. Drove her off ahead of 'em and two of my sheep. Hope they choke on the mutton," she grumbled. "Asa here has tried to see both sides of this here hullabaloo—and I had a open mind myself. I never held with one man owning another and made no bones about it. But they come in here all high and mighty and treated us like dirt. Knocked Asa backwards in the dirt. And told me to shut my filthy, lying mouth. Never even got to tell 'em my nephew got kilt at Prairie Grove fightin' Union. If that's how they aim to treat folks, they'll not get no sympathy from me when Joe Shelby gives 'em a dusting!"

They had no extra bed or bedroom. Nelda slept on the mattress that Allen brought from the wagon. He lay nearby on a bedroll that was only inches from the old couple's bed. She could hear their snoring and would have much preferred sleeping outside. But in late evening, when clouds had begun building in the west, Allen had insisted they find shelter. The hospitable couple had assumed she and Allen were man and wife, and he had not disabused them of the idea.

They were off early with a hearty goodbye from the man and woman who waved from the doorway.

"Watch out fer them patrols," she called. "They ain't got no mercy."

The road was rough, actually a rutted trail strewn with potholes. Allen drove slowly, and yet on occasion, when the wagon lurched, Nelda had to bite her lip and grip the seat to keep from groaning.

"You all right?" he asked as the wheel thudded and then bounced out of a hole.

"Didn't hurt much worse than Obadiah's bullet," she gasped, white-knuckled.

He grinned but looked concerned. "This trail is rougher than the River Road. But I figure we'll avoid more patrols this way—Union and Rebel. And we don't need to meet either."

"I guess you could say, we're between a rock and a hard place," she quipped. "If the Union finds you, we're sunk. And the Rebels, to say the least, aren't fond of me."

"Appears all we got is each other," he said and flashed a quick smile. "But, according to my lights, that's not so bad."

Her eyebrows rose. Their situation—according to her lights—was nothing to be lighthearted about. Actually, she was still confused by *their situation.* Of course any relationship between them was hopeless. She doubted any two people on earth had much less in common. Lately that did not seem to trouble him.

She asked him to stop and help her into the back of the wagon; then she closed her eyes. It seemed ages since she had felt strong. She wondered if she ever would again. Supposedly there were wounded soldiers who returned to battle right away, even officers who directed affairs soon after amputation. She envied their stamina. Perhaps she would feel better soon.

When the trail allowed, she slept, but was often jolted awake. That night they stopped at a roadhouse. Allen knew the proprietor who made them welcome. The dim smoky cabin was a far cry from the Markham Inn. Although it was late evening when they arrived, the long plank table was strewn with greasy breakfast dishes. The rough garbed man simply pushed them aside when a stringy-haired woman set bowls of watery bean soup in front of them.

"All we got," he apologized. "Need to get to the mill and get more corn ground, but foraging patrols have been thick as fleas lately. I figure there's no need to get corn ground if they're just gonna take it." He laughed and his ample belly shook. He sat down and propped his elbows on the table. Nelda wished he had remained farther downwind. She pushed the uneaten soup aside and listened.

"Hank rode through yesterday and said Marmaduke's cavalry had a big run-in with Yankee cavalry over near Brownsville. I figured you'd be right in the thick of that, Allen. What are you doing off the reservation?"

Allen ignored the question to quickly ask, "How did the skirmish turn out?"

"Well, Marmaduke held them for a while. But the next day Price ordered him to fall back about twelve miles from Little Rock. Plain as the nose on your face"—he shook his head—"there's no way Price can hold Little Rock much longer. Hank said folks were leaving town like rats from a sinking ship."

Allen nodded. "Yeah, the River Road was full. And every boat on the river." He glanced at Nelda slumped in the chair. "You got an empty bed, Kelly? The lady's been sick."

"I thought she looked peakid. No empty beds but she can bunk in with Stella's ma. Granny Holder is skinny and doesn't snore too loud."

Nelda's eyes widened. She had visions of unwashed old ladies, bedbugs, and filthy sheets.

Allen read her mind. "No use crowding up. There's a mattress in the wagon. If it's all right with you, I'll just pull the wagon into the barn to keep off the dew."

Kelly stood. "Sure. Help yourself." He stretched and yawned. Then he cut his eyes and gave a sly, knowing grin. "Reckon, you won't be needing a bed either."

"Nope," said Allen. "Granny can have her privacy."

Kelly haw-hawed loudly.

Nelda lay awake in the barn, thankful for the roof overhead where a soft rain drummed the shakes. Allen's deep, even breathing drifted from a hay-filled corner. She could not sleep. Perhaps she had slept too much that day, she thought and sought a more comfortable position. She heard scurrying and was thankful to be up off the floor. Mice probably held no dread for Allen, but she hated them. She finally slept but imagined tiny, bewhiskered creatures nibbling at her toes.

The next morning she was thankful the rain had stopped and they could travel. She had no desire for further acquaintance with Mr. Kelly or his vile soup. That day, they made several miles but at great taxing of her strength.

That evening they stopped at another dwelling, this one a sort of inn—although it too was nothing like the Markham establishment, Nelda observed as she stepped down, holding to Allen's hand. This was a big log house with wide front porch, a dogtrot, and a separate kitchen. A blousy-haired woman stepped through the door, wiping her hands on a long blue apron. She was middle-aged, full-busted, and pretty. She spied Allen and squealed. She flew down the steps, grabbed him, and gave him a big kiss squarely on the lips. Her own were an unnatural red. Although Nelda had never before seen a painted woman, she was sure these lips were rouged.

When the woman noticed her, she jammed hands on her hips and turned saucy eyes on Allen. "Allen Matthers! Did you take a wife?"

"I'd like to," he teased, "but she won't have me. Knows me too well." He took Nelda's arm and started for the porch. "Jewel, do you have any good whiskey left? I could sure use a dram."

"Saved some just for you, love."

She flounced ahead of them and opened the door. When her eyes met Nelda's, there was no friendliness in them.

While Allen had his drink, she talked. She ignored Nelda who sat wearily in one of the numerous cane-bottomed chairs in the large dim room.

"It's been bad around here since you left. Union patrols all over the place. They've taken everything they wanted and burned the rest. They found out Joe comes through here a lot, and they started torturing folks to get information. Shot old man Snider's kneecap off—and hung several others, Pat Inman, Cal Taylor, and Harvey Bogs. We heard that two of Slim Brown's boys were shot by a firing squad for deserting." She shook her head. "I've heard horrible tales. I will admit though," she said, "the Union soldiers who've come here have been nice to me. Of course, I've been nice to them, like you said, and kept my ears open—"

She paused seeing Allen's tiny shake of the head. Her eyes narrowed with understanding as she cut them at Nelda and gave a quick nod.

The little by-play had not escaped Nelda. *So this woman was Allen's cohort.* She took a sip of the water he had given her. *Well, he certainly had poor taste in comrades!*

She assumed Joe was Joe Shelby. She knew he and his men were often purported to be in this area.

Before long Jewel left and returned with a violin case. "Here it is. All safe and sound."

Allen's smile broadened as he reached for it with hungry hands. "Oh, I've missed this! Thanks, Jewel."

She waved her hand. "No trouble at all. Just see to it that you play me a tune before you go."

Nelda ate the supper of roast mutton in silence and climbed the stairs to the bedroom Jewel had indicated. When she glanced back down, Jewel had drawn her chair close and leaned her blonde head near to Allen. The smile on her crimsoned lips was broad and happy.

Before drifting off Nelda heard soft violin music. But the sound gave her no pleasure.

The next morning Nelda sat at the table when Allen came downstairs. His hair was disheveled and his suspenders hung down. When he saw her, he pulled them up and raked fingers through his hair.

"Never thought you'd be up yet," he said, reaching for the coffee pot. He took a sip, grimaced, and almost spit it out. He wiped his mouth with the back of his hand.

"Damned parched corn bran—ain't fit to drink. I'd as soon have hot water." He glanced at her. "You're up early."

"I spent my night sleeping," she said with an icy stare.

His grin started off tiny and hesitant. Then it broadened. He threw back his head and laughed. "Why, Nelda, it's amazing how many leaves fall out of the tree when the wind blows. That almost sounds like you're jealous."

She blinked. She had rather over-reacted and she wasn't sure why.

Jewel came in, arranging the puffed hair that ended in a bun on the back of her head. "What's so funny?"

Chagrined, Nelda noticed she had exited a downstairs bedroom.

"Aw, Nelda was just telling me what she dreamed last night. Seems she has quite an imagination."

Jewel poured a cup of brown liquid and studied her over the rim.

"I'm surprised you can sleep at all, honey. The way your poor bones stick out, it must be mighty uncomfortable laying down."

"It is," agreed Nelda acidly. "But my conscience is clear and that helps."

Allen stifled a laugh, choked, and coughed. "I had planned on leaving today," he ventured, "but we could stay till you're more rested."

"No, no. I'm more than ready to leave," she said and took a sip of the fake coffee. Allen was right. It was awful.

It was noon before Nelda was able to sit up. Even then she would have preferred lying down but the sun directly overhead was bothersome.

"Allen," she said. "I think I'll sit up a while."

He whoa-ed the mules and set the brake. "Good. I was beginning to wonder if you were still alive."

She climbed carefully over the seat. Then her breath caught. "Oh, my!" she exclaimed. Here the road shouldered a steep mountain. Below fell away a canyon of open land and far in the distance towered serrated peaks. These were not the overlapping blue ridges of home. These mountains rose individual, stark, and jagged; craggy with outcroppings of huge rock.

"Where are we?" she asked with awe.

"Some call them the Judea Mountains."

"I can see why," she said. "It's as imposing as the Holy Land. Papa had some drawings. That mountain over there reminds me of Massada. It was an almost impregnable fortress."

"I'd hate to have to get an army up there," he agreed. "There's a settlement farther on named Mt. Judea, but most folks just call it Mt. Judy. Trail gets rougher from here on down to the valley. The wheel brakes won't be enough. I'll have to use a drag to hold the wagon back. You sure you want to sit up?"

She nodded. "I want to look."

"All right but don't overdo. We still have a long way to go."

After that he was silent and busy with the mules and with keeping the wagon off their heels.

In late evening, ridges of fast-moving gray clouds parted like giant fingers to reveal a sunset of orange and coral splendor. Nelda watched enthralled until the beauty faded. By the time they had descended the last steep incline, even Allen looked tired. And Nelda trembled with fatigue. When he stopped before a small cabin, she could barely sit up.

A sweet-faced woman, holding a toddler on her hip, rushed from the cabin to greet them. She beamed at Allen.

"It's so good to see you! I was just thinking about you yesterday—wondering when you'd be back this way."

"Howdy, Ellen. He's growing like a weed," he said and tweaked the toddler's chin. He hugged the woman and then looked all around. "Things don't look too prosperous. What's happened?"

She sighed and moved the baby to the other hip. "Not long after John left for the army, a Union scout came by. I was so glad John had already gone!" She shooed away a fly and pushed damp curls off the baby's forehead. "They took everything—livestock, food, blankets—everything. They burned the barn and the cotton. A lieutenant ordered them to fire the house. I begged them not to. But he said I was rebellious scum and deserved no consideration. Before he rode off, he ordered a man to torch the cabin. But I took Johnny and stood in the doorway. Thank God, the soldier fired the smokehouse instead.

"We've been living hand to mouth ever since. John's folks share enough to keep us alive." Her green eyes filled with tears. "Allen, why don't they just let us be! Why did they have to come down here and ruin our lives? I just don't understand! This is supposed to be a free country. We didn't mess in their affairs. Why did they have to stick their noses in ours!" She caught her teeth in a trembling lip. "Little Johnny took his first steps without his pa here to watch. I wish every damn Yankee was dead," she finished with venom. Then she noticed Nelda and reddened.

"Who's this?"

"A good friend." He turned and took Nelda's arm. "She's been hurt and is still mighty weak. Thought if it wasn't too much bother we'd stay here a few days and let her rest up. I have food."

She waved a hand. "Of course you can stay as long as you want. Get her into the cabin. There's a spare bed in the back room. Johnny sleeps with me now anyway."

Nelda appreciated the respite from the jolting wagon. Day and night, she slept most of the time while Allen hunted and fished to put fresh meat on the table. Ellen was a good cook, and with the good nourishment, she gained strength. By the third day she felt strong enough to travel.

Ellen stood in the yard to see them off. "Johnny sure took a shine to you, Allen. And Miss Nelda, I enjoyed having a female around. I wish you'd stay longer," she urged again. "It's awful lonesome with John gone."

"I'd like to stay," said Allen, "but Nelda needs to get to her people." He did not add that *her people* were the Union Army.

She hugged Nelda. "Get well and strong." She waved as they drove away. "Take care of yourself," she called. She picked up the child and then waved again, looking forlorn and dejected.

"Poor thing. It appears there are villains on both sides in this war," Nelda observed sadly.

"Always are," he said and shook the reins. "Getup," he called to the mules.

All morning she sat up and feasted her eyes on the grandeur. She pointed to a particularly odd shaped mountain. Near the top jutted a huge rocky escarpment. As a child she had enjoyed identifying shapes made by clouds. Now she fancied the rock was the head of a giant lizard, its body the long strip of land sunning on top of the tall flat mountain.

When they reached the Little Buffalo River they turned west on the trail that fronted the river on level ground winding through giant hardwood trees. Across the river were bluffs of gray limestone. It was, Nelda thought, a beautiful land of rugged bluffs and deep green pools of swift water. She looked up at scrub cedar growing from the crevices on the cliff above them. "You have to admire those cedars. In spite of all obstacles—rock, wind, and little soil—they just keep growing, clinging to life."

He nodded. "I've known people like that…" He glanced at her. "Matter of fact, you're like that."

She hooted. "What? Scrubby and twisted?"

"No. Tough and determined. There's no backup in you. No matter what, you just keep on. And get tougher because of it."

Her brows rose. "That's not exactly flattering to my femininity," she said, "but thank you. I don't feel tough. As a matter of fact, I feel pretty weak and vulnerable."

He surprised her by taking her hand.

She tensed.

"You're not weak, Nelda, not in the ways that count. And you're woman enough that it's been pure hell for me these last weeks, laying close enough at night to hear you breathe." He kept his eyes on the trail ahead.

She disengaged her hand. It annoyed her that her heart beat like a kettledrum. She hoped he didn't notice.

"Someday, you won't be jerking your hand away," he prophesied. "I wish this damned war was over."

Just then they rounded a bend. A large buck stood in the stream. He threw up his head, wheeled, and bounded from the river. Nelda was relieved at the diversion, for Allen said no more. Her thoughts whirled but she grew silent.

Deer and bear were abundant here. He often shot squirrel and when he took time out to fish in the clear water, they feasted on brownie and perch.

Although the sun warmed the days, the nights grew chill. In order to spare her, he halted each evening long before sundown. Thus far they had found shelter every night, the last several nights with strangers to Allen. Everyone had given them shelter, but not as willingly as in days gone by. They were, however, more agreeable once they learned that Allen had brought foodstuffs.

At Jasper they bought a few more supplies, had a hot meal and a bath and spent the night at a wagon yard. Allen stopped by the blacksmith shop and had the mules' shoes checked and the axels greased. The blacksmith knew the latest news. Little Rock had fallen to the Federals the second week in September.

As they drove away, Allen was quiet and thoughtful. Nelda kept jubilation to herself. Although, she had to admit, she was not overly joyous. She had seen too much suffering, too much heartache in a people fighting for what they believed in—just as devoutly as she did in her cause—to feel jubilant. He interrupted her reverie.

"We'll backtrack a ways and ford the Little Buffalo. There's a steep mountain ahead," he explained, "but it'll save us a lot of time, heading over it. We'll pick up the Big Buffalo on the other side."

The mountain was steep and rugged. Nelda held tightly to the seat. There were a few cabins in sight.

"Doesn't Jess hail from around here?" she asked. "I hope we don't run into him or Heavy," she said with a shudder.

"Don't worry. I'm keeping the pistol handy, and Bull's shotgun, too. More than likely they're off somewhere making mischief. I'll run across them again some day.

"Trees have started turning," he noted, pointing to the oxblood-red gums. "It's rare but I've seen frost by the last week in September. And that's just a week away."

"I love autumn," she said, perched on the seat beside him. "No place on earth is prettier than the Ozarks in the fall."

As the day wore on, she realized that she was growing stronger. Even on the rough trail she had managed to spend most of the day on the wagon seat. With interest she studied the multicolored ledges of red, yellow, gray and brown sandstone and limestone jutting from the hill bordering the trail. In crevices where waterfalls occasionally coursed down the rocky slope, the ledges were rich with moss.

She had just decided to lie down when they approached a gap in the mountains. When Allen stopped the mule for a breather, her breath caught at the panorama spread out below. Blue hills cupped, converging in a deep valley where the wide, mist-shrouded river wound out of sight through the timber.

"It's beautiful," she breathed.

"No prettier sight anywhere," he agreed. He pointed across the rushing water. "Someday I'd love to build a cabin right over there."

She drew a deep, appreciative breath. "I doubt you'll ever grow tired of the view."

He turned and stared into her eyes. "I don't aim to enjoy it alone," he said meaningfully. "I intend to marry, raise a fam—"

She quickly pointed below. "Oh, look! That bear just caught a fish."

"You're just changing the subject. One of these days, I won't be letting you do that, either." He slapped the reins and started the mules forward.

For the next two nights, they made camp. In spite of the damp night air, she was comfortable. Allen built a big fire each night and kept it going. He said it was to discourage bears. She knew he worried about her catching a chill. The surgeon had warned of the danger of pneumonia.

On both nights, he drew the fiddle from the case and played beautiful music. The melodies he chose were sad and haunting. They suited her mood as she leaned against a tree, closed her eyes, and let the sadness wash over her. At times she found it hard to remember not being sad. But there had been happy days once. Surely they would come again.

She often found her eyes straying to Allen. Firelight flickered over a strong face, no longer young but not yet old. He was a handsome man and—she was beginning to believe—a good one. It was too bad they had so little in common. Someday he would make some fortunate mountain woman happy.

The next day they traversed a valley full of farms that had been prosperous before the war. Rolling hills were visible in the distance. Nelda appreciated the level ground and smoother road.

That night a woman gave them shelter in her cabin. She said her husband worked in the Boxley saltpeter mines nearby. That way, she explained, he had been able to avoid conscription. The Confederate Army needed saltpeter to make gunpowder.

They left early and were in Kingston by nightfall. The small town, like most in Arkansas, was depleted of men. Graybeards, women, and children were all Nelda saw as they drove down the crooked narrow street. At the mercantile, one old gentleman informed them that bushwhackers had been plentiful and deadly in the area. He warned them to keep a sharp eye out.

There was no inn, but they stayed in a house on Main Street with a nice woman and her three young children who were delighted with the fiddle music after supper. Nelda gathered from the woman's guarded comments that her soldier husband was Union. She was aware that many in this area had remained loyal and many of the men served in the Union Army.

Travel was easier now with few steep hills or wide rivers. The next night they spent on the outskirts of Huntsville with a farmer who had been wounded at Prairie Grove and discharged from the army. He was proudly Federal. After Nelda admitted to having a pass from General Prentiss from Helena, he talked openly.

"Price can run, and Shelby and Marmaduke can do all the raiding they're a mind to—but the Confederacy is doomed here and everywhere else. The Mississippi is now firmly in Union hands. And over in the Territory, General Blunt took Fort Gibson away from the Indian rebel troops. Then he ran the Rebs out of Honey Springs. That pretty much sews up that part of the country. Things back east are a disaster for Lee. When he lost so big at Gettysburg, he should have surrendered right then and saved a lot of lives."

"Gettysburg?" questioned Nelda.

The man looked at her as if she had two heads. "You haven't heard about Gettysburg!"

Allen interrupted. "She was ill then, and I didn't bother her with war news."

The man snorted. "Well, it'll be no bother to learn that last month—on the 4th of July, to be exact—Lee got whipped badly in Pennsylvania. Battle lasted two days and had over fifty thousand casualties. Most of the slaughter was Confederate troops. Lee pulled back into Virginia, or so I heard, and vows to keep on fighting."

Nelda looked at Allen. "Fifty thousand men," she echoed. She thought of the bloody mess at Helena and tried to multiply that in her mind. It was a gruesome picture, and one she never wanted to see. "How tragic," she whispered.

"You folks going far?" he asked while puffing on a pipe.

"Fayetteville," said Allen, but offered no more information to the curious man.

The next day, Allen was especially solemn, almost morose.

"You're certainly quiet today," she ventured.

The countryside was pretty here, picturesque with soft rolling hills.

"We'll be in Fayetteville tomorrow. I've been thinking how to handle that. Do you really have a pass from General Prentiss?"

She drew it from her pocket. "Yes. I kept it just in case. It's dated July but I doubt anyone will be too mindful of the date."

"Good," he said and fell silent again.

After a bit, she asked a question that had been on her mind for days.

"Allen, I can't tell you how sorry I am for all that befell your family. It's none of my business—and I'll certainly understand if you don't want to tell me—but I've been wondering about your brothers. I really like them."

He cleared his throat and stared at the reins in his hands. "Last I heard they were fine. Sort of scattered out, though. I reckon Dillon and Shawn are the only two not in the army. They're still in the mountains, sticking sort of close to home. The others joined up last fall."

"Confederate?"

He nodded. "All but Seamus." He shrugged. "He always was an independent cuss. If we went left he went right. He joined Federal. For all I know he might be around here."

Dark caught them a few miles out of Fayetteville. He turned in at a fine white house with a wide sloping lawn.

"This is a stage stop. We can probably get a good meal here and clean beds. The Taylors have rebel leanings, but I think you'll like them."

And she did. Mrs. Taylor was a motherly soul who hovered over the table until all her guests had eaten their fill of the plain but heartening meal of beef stew and cornbread. Then she whisked the plates away and brought bowls of apple cobbler sweetened with brown sugar and honey. Nelda had not eaten anything so good in two years.

Apparently the two other guests were known to Mrs. Taylor, and known to have rebel sympathies, for she laughed and said, "There are some advantages to having the Yankees nearby—we occasionally have flour and sugar."

The well-dressed woman across the table from Nelda spoke up, "I suppose there might be some advantage, as you say. But how I loathe them! Charles and I had to flee our plantation near Little Rock. Who knows what will happen to our home! We left everything with our overseer. Charles couldn't afford to be taken. Since he's been active in the Confederate government, they might hang him."

Her mousy husband kept opinion to himself and devoured his cobbler in silence.

Mrs. Lord was educated and refined. It made her vehemence all the more surprising. She blotted her lips on a napkin.

"Even before secession, Charles served in the legislature in Washington City. Heaven knows I don't subscribe to Mr. Darwin's theory of natural selection, but Mr. Lincoln makes me wonder! He's an ape-faced baboon. I found him a bore as well as ugly. Why, he hardly strings two sentences together without inserting some backwoods witticism."

Nelda was hard-pressed to keep her mouth shut. She greatly admired the president and his wit.

"It's tragic what he's done to our country. Why, I've heard even northern people are rioting in objection to his policies. It was a black day for America when he took the oath. If he has his way, we'll be the ones hoeing cotton and calling the Negroes, massa." She shook her head and the dangling earbobs sparkled in lamplight. "Ever since he issued that emancipation rot, our darkies have grown sullen and unruly. Charles won't go to the fields without his shotgun. And I keep my derringer handy all the time."

She took a sip of water and changed the subject.

"Mr. Matthers, what do you think of Mr. Darwin's theory about the origin of the species?"

He chewed and swallowed before answering. "Don't believe a word of it. I've hunted and fished all my life, and I've yet to see animal or fish that's half one thing and half another. If things are changing like he says, apes wouldn't still be having baby apes. Like Genesis says—things keep begetting after their own kind."

She raised a thoughtful brow. "And what does your wife say?" she asked with a smile for Nelda.

Allen gave a tiny grin. "The little missus can speak for herself."

Nelda shot him a murderous look.

Although she might not be as devout a Christian as Della, she certainly believed the Bible—God had done it all in six days of mornings and evenings as Genesis said. She recalled a similar conversation with Papa shortly after he had read Mr. Darwin's book.

She spooned a piece of cobbler but left it in the bowl and said, "It takes as much faith to believe Mr. Darwin as to believe in a six day creation. I know that people have embraced his theory as science. But, as Mr. Matthers said, there's no real evidence—not one thing."

Mrs. Lord nodded. Then she asked, "What about the Negro? Don't you think he might be a link between man and ape?"

Nelda thought of faithful Tom and Della and of noble Gideon. Her face hardened and she glared. Allen looked as if he had just tasted something rotten. He pushed back from the table and stood.

"I more inclined to think, if such a link exists, it's the fool who believes such rot."

"Upon my word," said Mrs. Lord, her lips pouting. "I meant no offence. I think it behooves us to consider all possibilities with an open mind."

"An open mind can mean an empty one," Allen said. "Wife, are you ready for bed?"

"Yes, darling," Nelda quipped and stood.

In the bedroom across the hall from Allen's, Nelda lay long, staring at the dark ceiling. Tomorrow they would be in Fayetteville. Tomorrow he would be gone. It made her uncomfortable to admit how completely he had managed to melt her animosity. Was she being foolish—a forlorn woman alone in the world? She bit her lip. She had not exaggerated when she said she felt weak and vulnerable. What would become of her now?

Unwittingly she had visions of a fine log home, high on a hillside overlooking the majestic Buffalo. Allen sat there, with fiddle tucked under chin. In the yard were stalwart young Matthers wrestling and playing. Then she scowled. Jewel, with her puffed-out hair and painted lips, had entered the picture.

Nelda groaned, turned onto her side, and drew into a tight ball. A sharp pain in her side made her quickly stretch out. The wound had healed—but like her heart—it was still troublesome and sore. She passed a restless night, due, she suspected, more to the heart than to the side.

Mr. Lord was at the breakfast table. Nelda was neither sorry nor surprised to learn that Mrs. Lord was a late riser. The breakfast of biscuits, flour gravy, and fried salt pork was more enjoyable because of it.

Nelda promised Mrs. Taylor she would stop in again someday. After Allen paid the bill, they drove away. It was a fair morning, sunny, with high clouds and a soft breeze. The land was gentle, rolling hills. Cattle grazed in a nearby field and sheep dotted the hillside.

She sighed. "It's peaceful here. This reminds me of the days before the war."

"Yep, until you look closer. See over there. Those are soldiers guarding that livestock."

She groaned. "So much for my idyllic moment!"

"Bushwhackers steal army cattle the same as any other. We'll be in Fayetteville in a bit," he commented. "I found out where the headquarters are. We'll go straight there. The commanding officer is a colonel named Harrison. He's out on scout a lot but Taylor thinks he's there now. I'll have to leave right away."

"I assume you might be known to some of the soldiers. Likely they've seen you before?" she asked.

"Likely," he admitted. "Anyway, since someone turned me in as a spy, I have to be mighty careful," he said with a grin.

She flushed. "You should just drop me off at the edge of town and not take the risk."

"I'm not leaving until I've seen you settled, safe and sound."

"I appreciate that," she said. Dropping her eyes, she stared at her hands clasped in her lap. "As a matter of fact, I've been wanting to tell you that I appreciate a lot of things about you. In retrospect I've come to realize just how much you've done for me. Ever since the house fire, over and over, you've stood between me and disaster—disaster from outlaws, from hunger, and from the army." She lifted her eyes to his face. "You're always there when I need you."

He kept his eyes on the road ahead. "As I recall you took a pretty big risk for me. Almost got yourself killed," he said. He cleared his throat. "I hate leaving you, but you'll make out fine."

"Yes, I'm sure I will," she agreed. Really, she was not at all sure. She dreaded each mile that took her closer to town and, ultimately, farther from him. How had things gotten so complicated? It had been far easier to hate him. She stopped short of admitting the antithesis. As she beheld the town on the placid hills ahead, she could not deny a sinking heart.

Fayetteville was a mixture of fine homes, red brick buildings, humble one-story dwellings, and burned rubble—relics of the sacking done the year before by the Confederate army fleeing south. Soldiers, mostly cavalry, loitered about, their horses hitched at the quaint public square surrounded by stores and shops and an old tavern.

Allen drove the mules up the main thoroughfare and stopped them at a modest white house. The colonel agreed to see them, and they followed his aid down the hall and into a sunny library. Colonel Harrison rose from behind the desk to shake Allen's hand and then offered them a seat.

"What can I do for you?"

He was in his early thirties, of medium build with deep-set eyes, high brow, and a friendly face. His dark beard was long and wiry but neatly groomed. Nelda judged by the bloodshot eyes and deep furrows between his brows that he was a harried man. Nonetheless, he was cordial to them.

"How may I assist you?"

Allen replied, "Sir, I'm a scout. And I've just come from Helena with a report from General Prentiss." The lie rolled easily off his tongue as he handed over the note that Prentiss had given Nelda. "He said to give this young woman any aid she might require. She did the Union a great service—at risk to her own life—by reporting the advance and battle plans of General Holmes and the rebels on the 4th of July. She was wounded and is still weak. As you probably know, Helena is full of disease. He thought Fayetteville would be a healthier climate, so he's sent her to you. He said he'll hold you personally responsible for her welfare."

"I see..." he squinted at the note and then looked at her. "Well, ma'am, it seems you are a very brave young woman." He faced Allen. "Tell General Prentiss that I will give Miss Horton every consideration." He smiled at her. "There is a genteel, elderly woman just down the road who will be delighted to have you as a boarder. I'll walk you over myself just as soon as I tend to this urgent dispatch on my desk. Mr.—sorry I didn't catch your name."

Allen stood. "Daring, sir."

Nelda's brows quirked. Daring, indeed! How like him to pun at such a time!

"Mr. Daring, would you care to accompany us?"

"No, thank you, sir. I'll leave her in your care. I need to start back."

"Then please tell General Prentiss I send my regards and congratulations on his recent victory."

"I'll do that." He shook Colonel Harrison's hand and turned to Nelda. "Miss Horton, would you see me to the door?"

With dread, she walked alongside him down the long hall and into the sunlight. She knew he must leave. And yet, temptation was strong to ask him to stay, at least for a few days. She stopped on the porch.

"Allen—"

He took hold of her chin and tilted her head. "Nelda, me love," he said, faking a thick brogue, "When an Irishman kisses a lass, she won't be forgettin' him."

He gathered her into his arms and kissed her. His lips were firm and lingering. She returned the kiss with equal fervor. Finally pulling back, he ran a gentle finger across her jaw and gave her a long, deep look.

He dropped the accent. "Pretty, lady, don't forget me."

Then he swung down the sidewalk, singing loudly.

"There is a fair maid in this town,
Who sorely has me heart beguiled.
Her rosy cheeks and ruby lips,
I trow she has me heart enthralled,
So fill to me the parting glass,
I drink good health to all that's here
And gently rise and softly call
Good night and joy be to you all."

She leaned against the white porch column and watched him leave. There were tears in her eyes, but a tiny grin played her lips. That Allen was a rascal!

She shook her head and whispered, "*No, Allen Matthers, I'll not be forgettin' you!*"